RETURN OF THE HERO

Jeffrey Peter Clarke

RETURN OF THE HERO

FICTION4ALL

Prologue

The city burned, abandoned by the gods. Angry flames clawed skyward from the citadel and lower town. Dark smoke spread above sombre ruination – rising as a vast and ravenous beast to gloat over its prey. It billowed through shattered walls. It cast baleful shadows over mid-morning countryside. White-haired Priam, their aged king, was slain, his head struck off by the blow of an enemy sword. Those people of Troy not killed or taken as slaves wandered defeated and dispossessed through the blood-defiled streets of their once proud city. The dogs whimpered mournfully at their heels as they drifted back and forth, hoping to glean from the destruction whatever the now departed enemy and fate had left them.

The conquerors had sailed with the rising sun, welcomed into the purifying realms of a bright sea, their vessels containing treasures from palace and shrine, and those women and children they thought it worth carrying away to captivity. It had been a disordered, an ill-disciplined conflict: many heroes had fallen broken and bleeding to cold earth. Many warriors had been stricken from the ranks of both sides before the ten years siege had ended. Even Achilles, champion and slayer of men, had perished, victim of an arrow shot by accursed Paris, son of Priam.

But the great leaders of the Achaean Greeks, the victors of this bloody contest, were with their men: Agamemnon, famed king of Mycenae and leader of the expedition, his brother, Menelaus, king of Sparta, the abduction of whose wife, Helen, had been the kindling of a war already destined to ignite. With them, too, was Nestor the elder, king of Pylos and wise council to others – and Odysseus, lord of Ithaca, the man whose wiles, whose conception of the wooden horse, had in the end resulted in the crushing of their enemy.

They sailed with pennants flying, each group of vessels under its own leader, each group in sight of the other. But with land now vanished below the horizon the gods proved fickle. Before night closed over their diminished fleet, sombre clouds billowed to sweep threatening low across the sky. Glimmers amidst the darkness became raging flares, the primordial growl of thunder grew louder and the raging beasts of the sea arose, threatening to devour them. Vessels heaved, shuddered and rolled, shrouded in hard-driven spray as sails tore asunder and timbers screeched agony. This was a storm raised to crush their puny hulls. A storm to hold wretched humanity in utter contempt. Many among their crews believed it was sent by Poseidon to avenge the sacking of Troy in spite of that god's earlier favouring of the Greeks. They cried out to Poseidon and to Zeus, their pitiful voices damned to the chaos of wind and a sea they dreaded was soon to possess them.

Long before sunrise the storm had passed, the sea had calmed and with morning light the fleet began to regroup. From each contingent there were losses, though none as great as had been feared. Throughout that fresher, sunlit day, with sail and hard-worked oarsman, the scattered ships re-joined their leaders and made good where possible the damage inflicted upon timber and rigging.

But there was one contingent missing, that of Ithaca, and though they scoured the horizons, Odysseus' vessels were nowhere to be seen.

Chapter 1 - Telemachus

Under tranquil skies they fought a bloodless contest. Sword clashed with sword and sword with shield. The air shivered with ringing bronze under the blaze of a late morning sun. Telemachus parried and lunged, swinging blade and countering with shield, entwined in whirlwind dance with his two contestants as five other men of the palace guard, also armed for combat, looked on in judgement.

The contest ceased. Gasping, laughing, clattering down weapon and shield to the dust, wiping sweat from their brows, each congratulated the other. The two men stooped to regain their breath and the third man swayed back, panting hard.

'You'll more than stand your ground with any man, young master!' declared an onlooker with fist raised.

'Aye with any two I'll wager,' agreed Thoas, captain of the men with whom Telemachus, prince of the royal house of Ithaca, trained in arms.

'Then we'll call it a day,' responded Telemachus, lifting off his ornate bronze helmet then stepping aside to pick up and sheathe his blade.

The men relaxed and spent time in discussing among themselves, with appropriate gestures, the death-dealing techniques of armed combat. Telemachus glanced at the high wooden enclosure surrounding them, at the hills rising beyond then at the door opposite, presently barred. Close by it arose a post from which was suspended the carcase of a pig, focus of their contest earlier in the day when the sun was newly risen. They approached this and wrenched from it those spears that had

9

found their target in its flesh only to disturb a shimmering mass of flies that burst away into the air. There, too, were those shafts that had passed close but either lay on the dusty ground beyond or stood impaled in the timbers of the compound.

'Has no one yet questioned our presence here?' Telemachus asked, gulping spring water from a leather flask.

'No one,' replied Thoas. 'We're off the beaten track and away from farmland. And if they did I'd tell 'em the truth of it, that a small number of us want to practise our fighting skills undisturbed – except that I'd not mention your being here with us, of course.'

'Of course,' breathed Telemachus, adding, 'then I'll make my way back as usual from a different direction to that of our men. Then we'll meet another day, soon.'

'Whenever it suits you, young master,' nodded Thoas. 'Your time's been well spent. Yes, well spent indeed and I'll not say that out of deference though I may boast many years of experience.'

As Telemachus strode away to unlatch the gate one of the men turned to Thoas, 'He handles sword and spear mighty well – mighty well, as a seasoned warrior should.'

'There's a grim determination in him; anyone can see that,' remarked a second man. 'I see it in his eyes, I see a born killer. He doesn't waste his energy – no, he calculates and when he meets his man in battle he'll judge that vital instant to strike. For a moment back then I feared he might forget this is only drill and really cut me down.'

'I'll say one thing, though,' added the first.

'Aye, and what's that?' asked Thoas.

'He's yet to face a man set on killing him.'

'True enough,' responded Thoas, eyeing the gate through which Telemachus had made his exit, 'and the way I see it that day may not be far off.'

***

At the centre of the megaron, the great shadow-laden hall where a king once held court, a fire glimmered in the circular stone hearth. Wood settled to breathe a sigh of memories. Smoke drifted, mingling with the fragrance arising from incense pots set about the room on small bronze stands. It swirled in phantom wisps past high windows where the sky had darkened then to vanish amidst soot-blackened beams.

Firebrands were mounted high at intervals along the walls where they added a mellow shimmer to the interior. Their light glinted from the grim tools of combat mounted in between; bronze swords, spears and double-headed axes long ago placed on display between heavy, figure-of-eight shields. Ranged beneath these at ground level ran a fresco of prancing, stark-eyed warriors in plumed helmets, shields protecting their sides. Their spears were poised high, ready to hurl. In the sanguine glow they shivered life as if about to career along the walls and strike down their enemy.

Gone were the breezily chattering, bare-breasted female courtesans in their gaudily flounced, flagstone-sweeping skirts, the importance of their kind much diminished since the days of Odysseus. Gone also the handful of younger men who waited dutifully to serve those pampered butterflies through largely uneventful days. Gone the mop-headed slave boys and with them the plainly attired, straggle-haired serving girls. Absent, too, was Phemios, aged bard whose tuneful lyre and wistful, mellow singing evoked memories of happier days in what had over recent years become a place of melancholy brooding. Shades of a glorious past hovered in dark corners and lingered amidst the columns where the light of the firebrands did not penetrate.

There were only two people within the great hall. Penelope, a slim, pale figure whose honey-pale hair spilled over the shoulders of a richly embroidered gown, sat upon patterned cushions placed there as a concession to material comfort. The throne she occupied was carved from pale limestone with a high scalloped back and, with wooden seats close by, was positioned between two of the russet-hued, downward tapering columns that supported roof beams high above. By her side stood young, dark-eyed Niobe, the slave girl of her choice. Lost in thought Penelope gazed at the whispering fire whilst the girl caressed her mistress' hair with an ornate, gold-inlaid comb of precious ebony. Niobe sang with soft and comforting words at her mistress' delicate ear.

The throne had once belonged to Odysseus, warrior-king of rugged Ithaca and the islands thereabout. Agamemnon had returned with Trojan loot to Mycenae, wealthiest of the Greek cities. On stepping ashore he had sent out messengers to announce their victory. He had entered the citadel to the sound of blaring horns, passing beneath the monumental gate set into massive walls and topped by rampant stone lions. A great triumph was his -

but Agamemnon had dismissed the prophesies of Priam's daughter, beautiful Cassandra, who had been abducted by him and brought to Mycenae. She had warned him of the fate he was soon to meet but, cursed by Apollo, her prophesies were forever to be dismissed as false.

Ten years had passed since the return of Agamemnon to Mycenae but still Penelope waited for her husband. Eyes lightly closed Penelope savoured the girl's attentions. The comb slipped with sensual touch through her hair. Niobe's other hand fell to her mistress' breast, teasing gently through the fabric of the gown. Penelope slipped an arm around the girl's waist, drawing her closer, feeling the heat of her lithe young body. Niobe's breath, a flame of passion, burned her cheek. Niobe's lips brushed her ear as fire-moths from the secret realms of night. Her lips parted but no words came as she peered into the girl's eyes.

Unwelcome sounds! The chatter of servants and slaves making ready the nightly feast echoed along the short corridor passing from the megaron to a flight of steps that gave access to one end of the dining hall. Before long her suitors would begin to arrive from Ithaca's taverns and lodgings, as always expecting food and drink. As always calling for her presence. More insistent of late, demanding an answer to their question: who among them would she accept as her husband? Which of them would gain the throne and possessions of Odysseus and achieve domination over Ithaca's island kingdom? Penelope had until now kept them at bay through the backing of her modest palace guard, through her willpower and her cunning. For a while longer her cares would be allayed by the beguiling touch of Niobe. Penelope closed her eyes once more and drifted into rare contentment.

The scuff of sandals on flagstones invaded her reverie. The girl's hand slipped away but the comb maintained its soothing glide. From the gloom of the corridor entrance to her left a figure in pale tunic approached with confident stride, short sword in gilded scabbard at his side. Clean-shaven, sharp-eyed, his fair, shoulder-brushing hair circled by a turquoise and gold band, he was slim and well-built as any well-bred youth of his age. His voice rang bold and clear through the hall. 'Mother, here you are and looking regal as ever!'

Penelope eased back the hand holding the comb. 'Niobe, you may leave us now.'

The girl stepped away but as she vanished into the gloom of the colonnade behind the throne she glanced over her shoulder at Telemachus, a mischievous grin touching her face. With his mother's attentive eye on him, Telemachus thought it better not to acknowledge Niobe's smile.

'Telemachus!' his mother demanded. 'Where have you been these last two days?

Penelope had for too long regarded her son as a vulnerable boy. Since holding him at her breast she had desired only to protect him, realizing later that in so doing she had risked making him more vulnerable still. These last few years much about him had changed. It encouraged but at the same time unsettled her deeply.

Grinning broadly, Telemachus leaned against a column. 'Oh, out and about the country as usual.'

'Well stay clear of those men once they start drinking. How many times have I warned you?'

'I long ago lost count,' Telemachus replied, 'but your fretting will help neither of us.' He moved to stand directly before her. 'There's something I have to tell you but before that, when d'you plan to end this farce with the shroud. Our situation is changing for the worse as you are well aware.'

'I well know that,' she sighed, pressing hands against her pale cheeks. 'And you surely appreciate why I spend the time I do at the loom. "This farce with the shroud," you choose to call it - I determined I would weave a shroud for Laertes, Odysseus' father, *your* grandfather. I have made it clear - I'll make no decision over marriage until the shroud is completed. It is an accepted part of -.'

'All your suitors must have guessed by now,' he interrupted, 'even those with the brains of a goat, that you have no intention of completing the thing!' He gazed about the hall then added, 'You began it over two years ago and you undo much of what you've woven during the day so you have to begin again next morning. It speaks only of desperation. As for Laertes – I encounter his men in the marketplace and they assure me he works his farm as a man should and so far has shown no sign of dying, though I understand his health has never been strong.'

'Well, dear,' she replied, her face wrinkling with a forced smile, 'the "thing" as you choose to call it has helped us keep those men at bay a while longer. Even *they* have some respect for our customs and that's all that matters at present. And –

and, Telemachus, you ought not to be spying on me.'

'I haven't been spying on you,' he responded. 'And as for customs - those men have tolerated what you're doing because it's suited them to fatten their stomachs at our expense for the best part of seven years. They're convinced my father's bones lie rotting in some foreign land and I can't argue with that since we have no idea whatsoever what became of him.'

'They cannot know his fate!' she snapped, then closed her eyes adding quietly, 'And nor can you, Telemachus. No - nor can you.'

'Mother, he sailed for Troy when you were a girl of seventeen. He's been absent for all the years I've lived! You and others describe him as a brave warrior but some say he took too many ill-considered risks and maybe one day the gods turned against him. We drift in an ocean of hearsay and I seek only a rock of truth.'

'Make of idle talk what you like,' she countered angrily, 'but he *will* return! I *know* he will! I feel his spirit amidst the shadows when I sit here alone. I offer prayers daily to the gods – to Athena, yes, and to Zeus himself. And the oracles - they say he will return to Ithaca. Before he set foot in Mycenae, Agamemnon sent word to say your father had departed Troy with his ships and their crews in good spirits. King Nestor reported it also.'

'Fine,' shrugged Telemachus, 'but both of them sailed straight home. No one can say what happened after that.'

'Perhaps not!' she responded, her knuckles clenched white, 'but there have been rumours over the years from travellers abroad who tell of his being seen. Don't you listen to what these people say?'

'Hardly ever! Rumours are like wild birds; they arrive from nowhere, they alight anywhere and everywhere and then they're gone. As for the oracles, they tell you only what you want to hear. Truth is no woman in any land of the Greeks ever held a king's authority. Other rulers no longer correspond with you and because of it I know far less than I ought of what happened after Troy. I should by now occupy the throne of Ithaca but you contrived to prevent it over the years and to my shame it suited me to accept this longer than I ought.'

'Yes,' she glared, twining and untwining her fingers, 'I contrived to prevent it! Whichever of those men took me in marriage would expect his own heir to gain your father's throne after him. They'd assume you would raise support from among our people and try to claim your inheritance by force. If I'd stood down before you reached manhood you'd have been dragged away in the night and I'd have seen no more of you – not even your ashes!'

She watched in charged silence as Telemachus strode around the hearth to gaze up at those hanging weapons untouched even in the days of his father. As a child he had employed their harmless wooden copies to engage in combat with others of his age but even then he would never accept defeat.

He returned to face her, saying, 'People ask why Thoas and our guards do nothing when those men enter the dining hall to live it up at the expense of our treasury – *my* inheritance. I know a good few of them by the sound of their belching in the evening and the sight of their vomit on our flagstones before the slaves clean it up. There were only a handful of them to begin with and they actually brought gifts until the likes of Antinous and Eurymachus came along and disowned the rules of hospitality, though I - I confess I did drink with them on occasion.'

'Yes and you were invited only so they could keep an eye on you. Thoas and his men ensure they stay away from me and away from our private chambers. And when your father returns he will see how I and those who remain close to us have kept his affairs in good order.'

'Really!' responded Telemachus. 'Have you seen an account of our stores recently? No, you leave such matters to poor Euryclea who has no wish to cause you further anxiety and therefore says nothing. I frequently go into the vaults to check things. Through the demands of others our gold and our silver are diminishing of late quicker than they can be replenished in spite of a healthy trade, as are our oils, our wines and much else. I find the palace guard are costing us more in silver for their loyalty than they ought and as for Thoas himself – I think it's more than the occasional gift of silver that's kept him on our side.'

'Just - just what do you mean by that?' she demanded with fist-clenching anger.

'Mother,' he replied, 'I've seen Thoas enter your chamber during the night and I've overheard remarks from our servants. Your liaison is no secret.

They also comment on that slave girl of yours who's often in your chamber until dawn.'

'Telemachus!' she snapped, rising abruptly to her feet. 'You've said enough and, yes, you *have* been spying on me! This – this is not easy.' Penelope fell back onto her cushions with a pitiful sigh then added, 'I have always done what I must to help preserve your life.'

'If any man, if Antinous, Eurymachus or any of them offer me challenge,' Telemachus declared, 'I'll gladly take him on.'

'Telemachus, no! Do not provoke any of them - especially Antinous! I recall seeing him slip an arm about your shoulder as if you were one of his own kin. That man would just as easily thrust a knife between your ribs and he'd still be smiling. He considers himself first in line to your father's throne regardless of what the rest may think. He's a true son of that upstart they call "The ox-eater," that awful man who imagined himself another Heracles. Your father put him down by force of arms when he rebelled and because of it he refused to go with the rest of our men to Troy. Nothing would give him greater pleasure than to have his only son take possession of our kingdom.'

'I know what Antinous and some of them are capable of,' responded Telemachus, calmly. 'As for his father - merchants who've had dealings with the so-called ox-eater say he's grown fat as an ox himself through idleness and a surfeit of wine.'

Penelope relaxed into her cushions. 'At least you show less interest in the wine flagon than you once did, if not the blatant come hither looks of our serving girls – especially Niobe. I note her expression whenever your name is mentioned. Oh, I ought not to blame you, dear - it's only natural at your age.'

Telemachus rose from the seat. 'Yes and as you're well aware I train hard with Thoas and those men closest to him - and I do mean hard! I insist he treats me as he would any freeborn man expected to defend what's left of our kingdom and believe me I will.'

She gazed at him anew and saw before her a young warrior, a flame that might illuminate her life as his father once had. 'I hear comments over how fit and strong you appear. I overheard someone compare you with Apollo who slew the arrogant and unjust with his arrows.'

'Then I'll concentrate more on my target practice,' he grinned. 'And have no worries over my working with Thoas; we *never* refer to your affairs or those of the palace.'

'How very thoughtful of you, dear,' she mused.

Telemachus stepped closer, saying, 'Now I must tell you: Three days ago I spotted a stranger loitering close by. I took him to be a merchant so I went over to question him in case he wished to trade with us. His name was Mentes. He claimed he was a captain of the Taphians and so I -.'

'The Taphians!' cut in Penelope. 'They're little better than pirates!' She drew her breath then added, 'Well - they do on occasion supply our workshops with copper and tin - probably stolen from other traders.'

From the direction of the dining hall came shouting, thudding benches and a surge of raucous laughter. Penelope glanced uneasily aside.

Telemachus ignored the disturbance then continued, 'Pirate or no, the Taphian recognised me because he'd had dealings with the old man before he sailed off to Troy and seemed to think highly of him. He'd been trading along the coast of Africa for many years and was unaware until arriving on Ithaca that my father had disappeared. He'd overheard your suitors' conversations in the taverns when their tongues were loosened with wine and realised what was going on. I offered him wine and gifts but he declined these because he was pressed to quit our shores that morning. He offered advice I consider worth following.'

'Advice from a Taphian?' she responded. 'Need I call for strong wine before you go on?'

'No, mother; perhaps later. He suggested I summon a council of our citizens to demand your suitors return to their estates so we can be free of them. I understand such things were done in my father's day: it may work now.'

'A council of our citizens!' she exclaimed, rising once more from the throne. 'You imagine our problems can so easily be solved? There's been no such assembly called since the victory over Troy was announced because it would be unacceptable for me, a mere woman, to do so. Councils meant something in your father's day but I doubt they would now. And how much notice d'you imagine those thirty and more suitors and their hangers-on, yes, over a hundred all told, will take of farmers, craftsmen and traders even if they were outnumbered ten to one? Many among them once subject to your father's rule have since become independent men of wealth. They look upon our citizens, our artisans and our farmers much as they do their own peasants.'

'Men of wealth you say,' responded Telemachus. 'Well I'm informed a number of their menials were spotted making off with some of our livestock only three days ago. Did you know of this?'

'Yes,' she sighed, 'I – I was informed of the thefts. They're hoping Thoas' men will ride out on patrol and leave the palace unguarded.'

'Thoas' men will remain here whatever happens outside the city wall,' Telemachus assured her. 'Thefts or no - I have seen to that.'

There was further commotion from the dining hall. Penelope glanced aside, saying, 'If they thought our people might take up arms against them they'd summon help from beyond Ithaca. We'd need the gods themselves on our side as well as the palace guard but the gods have taken precious little notice these past years. If it wasn't for the oracles I don't know what I'd –.'

'Never mind the oracles!' he cut in. 'Tomorrow morning I'll have our slaves go out with rams' horns. I'll have our free men gather in the marketplace before the suitors arrive. It may still help matters if we're seen to retain the backing of our citizens.'

She was considering his words when Medon, a wiry, kilted, shaven-headed elderly male of North African aspect entered the hall. Though a slave of Odysseus' house the suitors had requisitioned him to act as their messenger. They had forced him with threats of humiliation, often violence, to carry a twisted wooden cane intended to mock the gilded staff traditionally carried by palace heralds.

'My Lady,' he announced, pausing to bow at a respectful distance, 'food and wine are prepared and those men are demanding your presence.'

'I'll do so when I'm ready,' she replied tersely, adding under her breath, 'Before their manners are dissolved by a surfeit of wine.' As Medon left, she placed a hand on Telemachus' cheek. 'For my sake, for the sake of your father's house do not give those men cause to act against us - against you.'

'Our people will lose whatever faith they still have in the House of Odysseus if I continue to do nothing,' responded Telemachus, lifting her hand away.

Penelope clasped her hands together and gazed into his eyes. 'Then do as you please, my darling. I will sacrifice again to Athena. I will beg the gods to protect you if only they will listen. Now I must go and face those men again.'

Her gown sweeping behind, his mother stepped away in the direction taken earlier by Niobe.

Her routine was well established. She would ascend to her chamber and prepare herself for confrontation before treading the narrow, windowless passage and dark steps down to the dining hall; steps once used by Odysseus and his queen to access the hall directly from their private rooms. There she would unbolt and pull inward the heavy wooden door. There she would stand to face her suitors at the base of the low steps beneath the colonnade supporting the gallery above. She would gaze across the dining hall in dignified silence. She would listen to their comments and their demands then inform them in as clear and calm a manner as she was able, 'I hear what you ask but I cannot yet make my decision.'

There would be murmuring and crass remarks but if wine had already loosened their tongues to expose their truer, baser selves she would turn away without speaking, bolt the door and retreat to her room. The palace contained a number of such passages, some never used, dim and forbidding, a world apart, their purpose long forgotten. As a boy Telemachus had found adventure in exploring with a firebrand to discover the secrets he imagined they must contain, often alone because he had no brother or sister with whom to share his adventures.

He was aware of the babble and the odour of food drifting in from the dining hall. When the noise subsided he listened for his mother's voice but if she spoke too softly it would not carry back to the megaron. He stepped up to the throne and, for the first time since those playful days of childhood, he sat where his father had sat amidst the colourful opulence and lively company of his courtiers.

Smoke from the hearth arose in spectral coils. A brooding stillness pervaded the great hall. In that twilight void he gazed across columns and shadowed walls.

His attention fixed upon the man-killing weapons placed there long before the days of his father. The glow of firebrands shimmered upon polished metal and it seemed the painted figures below quivered with hidden energy. The air stirred and in his mind the warriors gathered with spears raised high. There Telemachus gave voice to his thoughts, 'For too long others have defiled my house. Whether he lives or not, my father's kingdom will never be theirs. As Zeus stands large above our world, I will not let that happen!'

Chapter 2 - Confrontation

The sun had vanished below Ithaca town's gaunt walls of polygonal masonry when two figures entered the dusty marketplace. They had passed through the outer gate where the dispossessed and the lame huddled, bird's claw hands held quivering as desiccated boughs in a breeze of cold indifference to grasp any morsel a passer-by might offer. Their competition for scraps of food were the yapping mongrels who often fared better.

Euryclea, in her loosely belted, grey woollen gown and cowl, had lived longer than most people could hope to live in those harsh days yet the undiminished sharpness of her wits expressed itself in the lively brown eyes that peered from beneath her cowl. Born of a palace concubine and raised at the royal court of Assur in distant Assyria, she was hardly into her teens when seized by Hittite raiders and taken to serve at the palace within the daunting walls of their bleak mountain capital. She was later bought as a slave by an Ithacan noble, one of a delegation sent to negotiate a trade agreement with the Hittite king. The Ithacan had paid with an exchange of gifts to the value of twenty oxen not only because of her beauty but also for her many skills the Hittite court seemed less inclined to utilise. On being taken to Ithaca the girl had been given the Greek name she would thereafter cherish.

Because Euryclea soon learned to speak, read and write Greek, and because she was already fluent in the disparate languages of the Assyrians and the Hittites, she had assisted greatly in the task of translating tablets relating to trade and other affairs between Ithaca and those nations to the east. And though often sharing the bed of the nobleman, as one of her status was obliged to do, she had never borne a child. Laertes, once having taken power at Ithaca, adopted and treated her with kindness so when he later offered her freedom and gifts to ensure an independent status, Euryclea had asked to remain and serve at the royal house. She had also served as nursemaid to the infant Odysseus, then in turn to his son, Telemachus, to whom she imparted the gift of literacy. Granted supervision of palace accounts and records, she had taken a slave of her own, Leucon, to relieve her of more mundane tasks.

Telemachus had for some time been consulting with her over the palace accounts but this she had kept to herself because it was what he wished. She had always considered the boy more worthy of respect in his adolescent years than had the palace courtiers. She, too, had voiced her concerns over his safety should any of the suitors succeed in gaining his mother's hand. Never did Euryclea begrudge the fact that Telemachus took little more notice of her warnings than he did of his mother's or of other people's. Euryclea recognised in him a truly free spirit. She had once sent her trusted Leucon to follow in secret and watch from a hidden vantage point as Telemachus trained in arms to acquire the skills of a warrior in that secluded valley well beyond the city wall. It was one of many secrets she held close because she cared for him as the son she never had.

At Euryclea's side in the sultry air of that late afternoon was the equally aged Mentor. Swaying along in pale gown and leather sandals, his uncertain step was steadied by a gnarled walking stick that evidenced the fragility of his limbs. To this once sprightly man, now sparse-haired, watery-eyed and all but toothless, Odysseus had entrusted the care of his wife and new-born child before departing with his ships to join the fleet of Agamemnon. Mentor, one time ambassador for Laertes' court, literate and fluent in several languages, had also helped in the tutoring of Telemachus. He had explained the ways of the court and the hazards of an uncertain world beyond their island kingdom. He had fired the boy's imagination when telling of the part played by grandfather Laertes in the voyage of the hero Jason and his Argonauts on their perilous quest for the Golden Fleece. Mentor was these days excused all but the lightest duties because of his advanced years.

Unlike Euryclea he knew nothing of Telemachus' training in the brutal art of combat.

Most of the traders and foreign merchants who daily bartered in the marketplace had by now departed. Observing Odysseus' son on the palace steps, Euryclea and Mentor hesitated to watch him as he raised his spear high before a milling throng of Ithaca's male citizens, artisans, farmers and traders. This was a far larger gathering than any they had witnessed since the time when Odysseus had summoned to arms men of fighting age to accompany him on the voyage to Troy. Here were present, in Mentor's estimation, well over three hundred. He also noted several men of the palace guard positioned with spear and shield at a discrete distance from the crowd.

Euryclea and Mentor were unable to make out Telemachus' words because of the distance and the cackle of geese at a nearby feeding trough. And the passage of so many years had, of course, gnawed away the sharpness of their senses. As Telemachus addressed his people, a herald's staff was handed around so that any man possessing it was empowered to speak out and be heard. As the pair looked on it appeared the citizens were with Telemachus almost to a man. When the crowd began to disperse in animated conversation, Euryclea and Mentor moved closer. As space opened up before them they were spotted by Telemachus who stepped smartly over to address them. 'They are on the side of my father's - of my house,' he smiled. 'This evening I will address my mother's suitors and demand they no longer take advantage of us.'

'Very commendable, young sir,' replied Mentor, 'but they'll take little notice. Matters have gone too far, yes, further than ever they should have.'

'Much further,' agreed Euryclea. 'Your father, bless his memory, would have driven them out like the Furies - scavenging mongrels that they are.'

'He would,' growled Mentor, 'and most likely he'd have skewered a few of 'em up the arse with keen bronze while he was at it. You should keep an armed guard in full view when you talk to those buggers.'

'They'd see that as a threat,' replied Telemachus. 'I'll try to reason with them but I'll keep Thoas' men out of sight though close enough. Doing this may not achieve as much as I'd like but it may open the way to further action.' He glanced at those citizens still grouped in conversation by the inner gate then asked, 'But Mentor, be honest with me; d'you think it's possible after all this time my father still lives?'

'Sadly, young master, I do not. When news arrived of Agamemnon's return to Mycenae everyone expected your father's ships would sail into our harbour with pennants flying, yes, and brimming with Trojan spoils. Alas, too many years have passed. Much as I regret to say it, Lady Penelope must soon face the truth and choose a man she regards as the best of the bunch – though I doubt there's a best to be had among the lot of 'em. No woman should occupy a king's throne and they'd most certainly conspire against you if they thought you might take your father's place. The suitors see you as the only one with potential to defy their plans, those of your mother's age especially. They have more serious intentions than the younger upstarts who want no more than the pleasures of the dining hall. You may have the support of our citizens but I fear you may eventually have to flee Ithaca and that sorry day may not be far in coming.'

'I disagree about our king,' said Euryclea. 'I believe there is a good chance Odysseus lives. So many rumours have persisted throughout these sad years. Oh, we all know the worth of rumours but I say this; they cannot all arise from nothing.'

'But that is so often the case is it not?' Mentor sighed. 'These rumours are usually empty hearsay - gossip feeding upon gossip, though I'd give whatever is left of my life for his safe return. And this Mentes, this Taphian captain your mother informed us you were talking to the other day; we never saw him although one or both of us is always here in the morning. I'd better watch out in case someone confuses his name with mine. Dear me, that will never do.'

'Maybe he was one of the gods in disguise,' quipped Telemachus. 'If so I should take his advice all the more seriously.'

'Perhaps he was,' said Euryclea with an affectionate squeeze of Telemachus' arm. 'Your mother always maintained Athena watches over you and for that I also offer sacrifice to the goddess. Each day I go to her shrine and beg her to stand by you in times of danger – more so now than ever.'

Telemachus gazed into her bright old eyes, saying, 'I could ask no more of you.'

***

The skies were darkening over Ithaca when the suitors began to cross the square before the palace in their robed finery, each with one or more slave or attendant following close behind. When Odysseus failed to return from Troy there had been no suitors but after a year or so had passed they began to appear. Few for a time but as younger men reached maturity they added their numbers to the burden Odysseus' house seemed fated to bear. Antinous was among the first to arrive that evening, looking aggressively about, as were his closest rivals, Leiocritius and Eurymachus, also hoping for Penelope's hand.

The dining hall could be accessed at several places. The main doors stood at the rear of the palace, directly opposite the steps leading up to the megaron corridor. To reach the main doors the suitors were obliged to tread a narrow, unlit passage between the palace and its outer defensive wall. This passage also gave access to the dining area via a smaller doorway halfway along, intended originally for servant or slave. A number of the suitors would proceed past this modest portal to reach the main entrance because they saw it as validation of their perceived standing, whereas others opted to use the lesser entrance. When needing to take the air or to relieve themselves in the night they tended to exit via this side door as it was closer to the market square and gate giving access to Ithaca town and the countryside.

Antinous and a handful of other suitors had once tried to enter the main portal of the palace proper and pass through the megaron where the throne of Odysseus stood, intending to continue to the short corridor accessing the dining hall. Penelope, backed by her palace guard, had from that day insisted they must not. She could not bear the thought of them standing close, perhaps reaching with covetous hands to defile her husband's throne with their touch. These few had so far not challenged her prohibition but it was a minor concession in view of the benefits they enjoyed each night and for the greater prize that some among them awaited.

Once they had appropriated the dining hall, baskets of barley bread and plates of grilled fish were placed upon the tables whilst honey flavoured wine in flagons decorated with swirling marine motifs stood close at hand. Mutton, pig and poultry sizzled on spits above cracking fires positioned on metal grates and tripods set up by the walls. Smoke coiled through hazed air on spiralling ascent to the small windows above. A muster of ribald gluttony, the suitors and their retinue fell upon the food with fingers and knives. Some had brought dogs to which they would toss the occasional scrap. Goblets of precious metal were waved aloft to demand instant charge and recharge by scurrying, mop-haired boys; offspring in the main of those female slaves who, in subdued conversation, were busily attending to fire and food.

The chamber where these unwelcome guests sprawled was better lit than the megaron where walls were rendered in pale plaster. The least obstructed wall, that on the longer side of the room where stood the smaller doorway, bore clusters of burning firebrands. Much of the wall facing this bore the gallery accessed from outside the building by a wooden staircase. In the shadows beneath this gallery lay the fourth, less conspicuous door from which Penelope was expected to emerge.

On the gallery lounged a bevy of gaudy females; the bejewelled, red-lipped courtesans of the palace. Their nipples and pale cheeks were brazenly rouged, their elaborately coiled and banded hair entwined in silver wire strung with baubles but hanging loose at each side to sway down in long wisps over their cheeks to naked breasts left exposed by the short-sleeved bodice of their long dresses. For most of these young women the arrival of the men offered promise of carnal diversions after an idle day in the sparse court of elderly nobles, juvenile slaves and a woman who largely ignored their presence. Wagging patterned parchment fans they gossiped, cooed and fluttered bright eyes, one to the other and at the men below who, until sufficient wine has passed their lips, displayed only modest interest. When signalled from below a girl would leave the gallery to join her male partner outside the dining hall in the intimacy of darkness. Penelope's initial disapproval over their consorting with her suitors had achieved little. She had of late accepted how the presence of the women each evening had been a factor in preventing the men from pressing her too hard over the succession - until now.

There also would be aged, white-bearded, pale-robed Phemios, the strumming of his lyre eventually overwhelmed by clamour. The suitors regarded Phemios' presence as bestowing a semblance of respectability upon their gathering.

One of the starving and dispossessed of Ithaca town now and then crept into the hall via the side passage in desperate hope of obtaining food scraps and leftovers though they risked derision, assault by man or dog, even violent eviction with nothing to show for their pains. But one had succeeded in establishing a regular presence. Mop-haired, bird's nest-bearded, ragged and round-faced bulbous-nosed Iros had staked a claim on the stone floor beneath a gallery column a short way from where Phemios sat. His presence was tolerated in part because of his garbled efforts to sing to the bard's strumming but more so because his canine antics prompted ribald laughter. His occasional, inevitably disastrous attempts at acrobatics, encouraged also by the women from the gallery above, resulted in liberal offerings of wine that would sooner or later have him collapse senseless, after which one of the suitors might roll the foul, semi-conscious buffoon, under his bench to serve as a footrest.

Darkness lay across the city when Telemachus strode from the great hall into the unlit stone corridor where, a few steps along, the doorway opened onto a short flight of wooden steps giving access to that end of the dining hall opposite the principal entrance. He did not move into full view of those below but stood back in shadow a while to watch and to listen from beneath the stone lintel.

His gaze lifted to the far end of the chamber where high on the wall to the right of the main doors was boldly displayed the dust-laden reminder of Ithaca's long absent king, the great bow of Odysseus. By it hung his finely engraved, gold-embellished leather quiver of bronze-tipped arrows. It was claimed no man could successfully employ the bow except for Odysseus himself. Penelope insisted bow and quiver had been placed there before his departure as a token of her husband's power and his promised return. At them she would often gaze for comfort when first entering to face her suitors.

Several among the suitors had proposed removing these mementoes to eradicate such a blatant reminder of Odysseus. Antinous and others regarded these artefacts a prize in waiting and insisted they must be left in place. Until lately Telemachus had thought of them as little more than ornamental relics. Now he looked anew upon these warrior's arms and their presence stirred him.

Old Phemios began to sing; his theme the heroic exploits of those who had sailed against

Troy. Telemachus moved forward onto the uppermost step and halted to lean against the wall. A few heads turned but his presence was hardly to be welcomed and so there was no further acknowledgement. Except that the hard, pale-eyed gaze of fair-haired Antinous, seated close below Odysseus' arms, was fixed upon him somewhat longer from the far end of the room.

Telemachus was about to speak when from the entrance below the gallery to his left a figure appeared earlier than he had expected. She wore a copper-belted, dark blue woollen robe with gilded edges, the fabric of its cowl pulled across to partly conceal the lower part her face; an act of modesty lost upon the majority of the men she was to address. Several of them voiced a greeting but she offered no response as the hall became quieter. Apart from her customary glance at the wall displaying her husband's bow she was not inclined to survey the room and so was unaware of her son's presence. She turned to the bard who continued slowly, softly to strum his lyre but had suspended his words. 'Phemios, you play and you sing well, but far too often about those fallen in battle. Will you not recite words to tell of those heroes who returned in triumph and those yet to find their way home?'

Telemachus wondered why, on this particular occasion, his mother had decided to address Phemios and so extend her appearance. And while the gist of Penelope's request was hardly lost on the audience a small number, thinking themselves out of earshot and still unaware of Telemachus standing close above, uttered lewd comments concerning her physical attributes and their sexual intentions, words reinforced by digging elbows and churlish leering. Iros the fool, also hearing what was said, blew Penelope a spluttering kiss.

Phemios had ceased playing but was about to resume when Telemachus spoke. 'No, our bard must continue as he was! The dead heroes he sings of set a fine example to all here!'

His mother turned in surprise as did a number of the suitors, one of whom shouted across, 'Watch out, lads – we're for it now!'

'Telemachus, how dare you, how -!' Penelope began as sniggering arose among the suitors.

'Mother, leave us!' Telemachus ordered.

Penelope glanced at him open-mouthed, confused. Faces twisted from side to side with broadening grins, elbows nudged, laughter rippled to the far end of the room. Pushing his goblet aside, stabbing his knife into the bench, Antinous stared hard at Telemachus, a grim smile twisting his stubbled face. The boys and girls serving food and drink distanced themselves from the tables.

'I'm glad you find this amusing!' declared Telemachus, folding his arms then addressing Penelope once more. 'Mother - if you please!'

Angered and embarrassed but aware she must accede by custom to her son's authority, Penelope backed into the passage then with a final, anxious glance at him the door thumped shut and she was gone. Apart from the crack and hiss of cooking fires and the brief whimpering of a dog, there was silence as Telemachus declared, 'Now hear me! For too many years you have fed and entertained yourselves at our expense. I wish this now to end.'

'Can't see why,' remarked one man, letting out a long belch. 'It's a damned good arrangement if you ask me.'

Several raised their goblets and voiced agreement. Iros, eyes bulging, wiggled fingers either side of his head and thrust out a discoloured tongue between gappy, misshapen teeth.

Telemachus was unmoved by their response and the burst of laughter that followed.

'Too long!' he repeated. 'Too long because my mother always insisted my father the king would return.'

'No chance!' interjected one of the suitors. 'He's long ago dead and gone!'

'Gobbled up by little fishes,' declared another grinning face.

'All the more reason why we stay,' remarked a third, waving his goblet from side to side.

'I think not!' responded Telemachus. 'On behalf of myself and the citizens of Ithaca I ask, with the greatest respect, naturally, that you entertain yourselves and your retainers elsewhere at your own expense. I ask that you no longer harass my mother with demands for marriage. She will make a decision as and when it suits her and needs no help from any of you.'

'So mother's precious boy is taking charge is he,' taunted grizzled, bushy-eyed Eurymachus. He glanced from side to side as others smirked then added, gruffly, 'Well it's a real man needed on the throne of Ithaca! I saw you with that rabble outside earlier this afternoon. D'you think we'll be pushed around by peasants who tread the fields with pigs and goats or foul their hands with potters clay?'

A dark-bearded suitor close by the man who had just spoken, one Leiocritius, swung around with arm outstretched. 'Well, young lord and master,' he scowled sarcastically, stabbing his knife into a piece of meat whilst the grotesquely leering Iros mimicked his actions, 'does that mean you've had word of our long lost king? Did some wandering stranger bring news to fire up this sudden, this, oh so truly admirable urge to assert your noble self?'

The suitors were openly amused by Leiocritius' manner, one rising part way up from his seat to pass wind loudly from his rear as Telemachus replied, 'Whoever I speak to is no concern of yours.'

'Well take my advice,' sneered Leiocritius, 'busy yourself with those things you're good at – chasing game and fucking the country girls. As far as we're concerned the fate of Odysseus' house will be as the gods wish it, as was the fate of the man himself!'

'Then the gods may surprise you,' responded Telemachus. 'They may determine the fate of Odysseus' house to be in *my* hands because that is exactly what I intend! I trust I have made myself clear!'

There were cries of, 'Ooooh!' followed by laughter and thumping goblets as the suitors looked from one to the other. Some raised their arms in mock defence whilst a few, banging their goblets ever harder on the tables, demanded more wine from timorous slaves. Iros bent to expose his pallid backside but one of the suitors booted it hard enough to send him sprawling with a yelp. Others glanced up at the wide-eyed female courtesans who peered down none too discreetly from the gallery above. One man, Amphinomus, in considering there ought to be more respect shown to the son of their one-time king, glanced up at Telemachus to raise outspread hands, showing his disapproval of the rest.

Knife wagging Eurymachus sneered at him and again addressed Telemachus. 'So you think you might rule here as Odysseus' successor – well, pretty boy, before long you may need to prove it so until then you'd better keep the food and wine coming. It's not only Ithaca that matters, it's the other islands and that means our estates.'

'The only thing he'll prove,' called one, 'is how quick he can piss 'imself!'

At the far end of the hall Antinous rose from his seat with hard-fixed expression. Chatter abated as he spoke in words ominously calm and measured. 'Blame us all you like, boy, but get your mother to make up her mind and forget this time-wasting nonsense with Laertes' winding sheet. Until then things stay as they are - so if you know what's good for you, you'll stay out of our affairs.'

Telemachus remained calm, his gaze matching that of Antinous.

'That's it, dear prince!' exclaimed another, waving his goblet from side to side. 'We're not going anywhere until you have your mother do what she has to do – and while she's still worth jumping into bed with! Now if you'd care to run along,' he added, eyeing one of the sultry females on the gallery, 'there's men's work to be done!'

Eurymachus turned to Leiocritius. Both grinned in agreement. When they looked around, still grinning, Telemachus was gone.

***

The sea beyond lay at peace. Waves lapped amidst the rocks under the benign sky of a warm night caressed by the mildest of breezes. Out on dark water the lanterns of small fishing boats nodded as fireflies in the night. The darkness held a silence interrupted now and again by the chirp of crickets and the sporadic barking of distant dogs. Seated on a rock a few paces from the water, Telemachus was content to taste air free from the odours of the town, of burning wood and cooking vegetables, of pigs, goats and the foul excrement of dogs. He looked up at the bright stars and newly risen full moon. In their serene disregard of human folly he found a welcome consolation all too rare in this world.

He mulled over the encounter earlier that evening with his mother's suitors. Would their deep-rooted feelings against him germinate? Would they throw up shoots of hatred ready to ripen as a dark plot against his life? It seemed now he might have presented them with sufficient reason.

Telemachus pondered over options that, apart from his fleeing Ithaca, must only involve bloodshed. There were three among his mother's suitors who presented the greatest threat: Antinous, Leiocritius and Eurymachus. Any one of them he would confront man to man but they were never alone. They would move quickly against him with their companions before he could rally the citizens to defend Ithaca. And although the citizens had responded to his earlier summons, would they risk their lives for someone who had yet to shine as a leader of men? Where would it end?

41

The breeze whispered to the waters and with a sigh Telemachus spoke softly into the night. 'If the gods ever lend an ear to man it must surely be at a time and in a place such as this. Athena hear me now and give me your guidance.'

Deep in contemplation Telemachus became aware of close approaching footsteps. He half rose, a hand falling to his sword as a figure emerged spectre-like from the darkness. His apprehension was short-lived, his blade only half drawn from its scabbard as the gnarled stick and unsteady gait of the man revealed his identity moments before the face was recognised.

'Mentor, how did you -? What are you doing here so late at night? Surely you've not walked all this way alone.'

'I have, young master and I am alone,' came the reply in a voice sounding clear and unsullied by age. 'I watched you pass through the city gate and set off alone. I knew you would wish to think over the encounter you had with those men in the dining hall.'

'So you heard what was said. I didn't see you there.'

'No, I stood unnoticed beneath the gallery and left by the door used by Lady Penelope.'

Telemachus recalled momentarily that his mother usually bolted shut the door in question from the inside but then he decided she must have colluded with the old man. Grasping his stick, Mentor eased himself slowly down onto a flat rock before looking up with a moonlit smile. 'I thought you gave an excellent account of yourself, yes, and under the most trying of circumstances.'

'Then you'll know,' responded Telemachus, 'that all I gained there was derision. They'll realise I intend to oppose them. They'll also be aware I have little means of doing so other than to call upon our palace guard, or what's left of them.'

'And if you summoned our able-bodied citizens to arms the suitors would know of it straight away and bring over more men from the islands than you could muster here on Ithaca.

'You're right, Mentor. We'd end up treading blood on our own doorstep.'

'Alas, young sir, those men dress in the finery of nobles yet few of them can boast true nobility and few of them have cast a spear in true combat though they spend enough time at the hunt.'

At this last observation, Telemachus drew breath and looked up again at the sky, saying, 'Yes, and I regret much of my own time was spent that way.'

'Since their fathers also failed to return with Odysseus from Troy,' continued Mentor, 'Ithaca and the islands hereabout have lived with growing unease. So far we've had no real violence at home, yet of late we hear rumours of troubles beyond our shores.'

'It might be to our advantage if trouble did threaten from abroad,' said Telemachus. 'It would oblige those men to make better use of themselves if the lands they now claim as theirs were endangered. As things are I have to decide what I'm to do next. I can no longer continue to do nothing.'

For some time neither spoke, then: 'Young sir, I have a suggestion; one I offer you after much consideration. One involving less personal risk if you care to hear it.'

'Mentor,' smiled Telemachus, noting the glint in the old man's eye as he placed a hand on his bony shoulder, 'I know how highly others value your advice. Say what you have in mind.'

'As well you know, your mother and many on Ithaca believe your father is alive and hope in their hearts he will one day return to rid us of the burden we bear. Even those who are not so convinced of his existence truly wish it were so because in his day these were happier lands.' Mentor paused for a while before continuing. 'What I say is this: you will gain nothing here other than to heighten the tension with those men by your very presence. As for your confrontation with them and their refusal to do as you asked - that, I say, has opened a new opportunity for you.'

'And here I am thinking it had just closed one,' muttered Telemachus.

'No,' Mentor continued, 'I say it was no bad decision and I have reflected at length upon the situation. I believe there is much to be gained by your leaving Ithaca.'

'Running away is not an option, my friend. That will not secure my father's throne.'

'No it will not, young master, and running away is the last thing I would expect a son of Odysseus to do but things can no longer go on as they are. Consider the possibility your father still lives and is in good health. Set out and seek advice on this matter from those who were most closely associated with him. Go first to King Nestor at Pylos then on to Menelaus in Sparta. Doing so will create uncertainty amongst the suitors and knowing them as we both do, a measure of disagreement. Some will press harder for your mother's hand: first and foremost will be Antinous. Others knowing the purpose of your journey, his closest rivals perhaps, will think it best to await your return and their dissent will keep the likes of Antinous in order. It will also prevent their conniving against you personally but above all it may throw light on a situation we all wish to see clarified – does your father - does our one-time king, still live?'

Telemachus stared hard at him. 'Mentor, you assured me the other day you believed he was dead. Why this change of heart?'

'I spoke too hastily, young master, yes I did. Looking at the situation afresh I am convinced what I propose is a chance worth taking. Even if your search comes to nothing it will allow you time to plan a course of action. You will gain much experience during what will be no small an adventure – and possibly some useful allies.'

Telemachus gazed once more across the dark waters where lanterns swayed as bright stars. Those innocent lights casting their glow in the night seemed utterly remote from the troubles that beset the House of Odysseus.

'Maybe you're right,' he said at last, 'but I would be leaving my mother alone and I'd need to find a boat with a crew I could trust.'

'Thoas would ensure Lady Penelope came to no personal harm,' responded Mentor. 'He keeps her suitors out of the palace proper and has done so these past years.'

'Thoas,' mused Telemachus. 'Yes, I dare say he'd protect her as long as she didn't stray too far from the great hall.'

'As for the boat, young sir, my good friend Noemon the Cretan runs several trading vessels from our port. His is a large, extended family – more a Cretan colony. His crews consist entirely of free men and all are his own kin to a greater or lesser degree. And while trust may be an uncertain commodity elsewhere, you will find it in full measure with Noemon and with all of his men.'

'I'm well acquainted with Noemon although he deals mainly with Euryclea, and I know he served my father well.'

'That is so, they were close friends. Noemon added one of his vessels and her crew to your father's fleet. He himself would have gone to Troy but your father insisted he remained here to carry on trading for the good of Ithaca. Every man of his would have Odysseus with us again and though some were in their tender years when he departed they would spare no effort to further your enterprise. You are a true son of your father and I believe that should you go about this the right way then you will succeed in discovering his fate. You are young, strong and fit to face the world so whatever the outcome I'm certain you will return to Ithaca more than able to deal with her problems.'

Mentor's words illuminated Telemachus' thoughts as though the gods themselves had spoken - yet still there was doubt. 'Hmm, I may return wiser and stronger but that will not defeat our adversaries.'

'No, not in itself; but if you were to return incognito you would have an opportunity to see how the land lay and best of all, young sir, you would possess the advantage of surprise.'

Telemachus looked him in the eye, saying, 'Mentor, you're livening my hopes as no one else has. I've spent too much time on Ithaca for my own good – I realised that some time ago. Yes, I may have little to lose by such a journey and as you say, much to gain.'

'Fine, young sir, then I also suggest you allocate the necessary goods for your enterprise from the palace stores whilst I negotiate with Noemon. Euryclea knows where everything is as I believe you yourself do. She keeps a close eye on the scribes and she is a party to my thoughts.'

'Mentor, would I be right in thinking you've had this idea on your mind for some time?'

'Yes, young master, I confess I have - for the good of yourself and for the house of Odysseus that I have served these many years.'

'When will you speak to Noemon? I take it he'll come to see you first.'

'I'll be meeting with him after sunrise tomorrow. I'm quite sure he will have a vessel ready the following day. In fact I know he will – and with a crew of sixteen men.'

'The following day!' laughed Telemachus. '*And* with a crew of sixteen!'

Yes, young sir, sixteen men you'd find most capable with spear and sword should the situation arise. And being Cretans they are, of course, the very finest archers on land and sea.'

'This journey you propose seems already planned through and through. I won't ask quite how you managed it but - but I'm persuaded. Your words have opened a new portal and I see light shining beyond it. I'll air the thought to those overstuffed fools tonight if they're sober enough to listen.'

'Young sir,' pressed Mentor, 'do not have them believe you are going to make this voyage. Let them find out when it is too late in case they try to prevent it – or worse.'

'Very well, I'll put it to them as no more than a fanciful thought and not one of serious intent. It would help to find out in advance what their reactions might be when it really does happen. The more ridicule they dispense the more reassured I'll be. And I'll speak with Euryclea in the morning.'

Telemachus would have helped the old man to his feet but he managed this alone. They walked slowly together in moonlit silence up the steep track toward the town. Where the barely visible path divided, Mentor wished him a good night then carried on with swaying, stick-prodding gait into darkness. Telemachus stood alone to consider what had passed between them but was struck by something that had receded entirely from his thoughts. How could Mentor, so old and infirm, have possibly made his way unaided to the cove. 'I'll go after him,' he breathed. 'He surely cannot walk this far and back without help.'

Calling his name, Telemachus hurried along the path taken by the old man. Ahead to his left, silhouetted vaguely against the stars, arose the walls and citadel of Ithaca town – but Mentor was not to be seen. Telemachus was staring into darkness when something above caught his attention. A white owl circled against the night sky then vanished into darkness.

***

Telemachus entered the square alone to find a number of the suitors, some with goblet in hand, had spilled out from the dining hall, to breathe the night air or to relieve themselves. Adult male slaves stood by in subdued silence, lighted firebrands raised, while subservient juveniles hovered with wine flagons clutched to their chests. The revellers' shouts and intoxicated laughter echoed about the walls. With them was Antinous who, nudged by one of his companions, turned to see Telemachus approach. A smile twisted the lips of another man who, pissing against a column, switched his head around to call out, 'His lordship's heading this way! Ahhh - may the gods preserve us!'

With their thin veneer of breeding eroded by a surfeit of wine, most were leering, commenting, eyeing him with contempt. Telemachus sensed real danger but although apprehension stirred within he was determined not to show it. Antinous stepped casually forward to meet him, the smile returning fully as he reached out to shake Telemachus by the hand. 'Take no notice of them,' he offered calmly, 'it's only drink talk.' Telemachus ignored the man's gesture. Antinous' expression hardened. He drew back the hand, saying, 'Very well, let's see if we can't put an end to this pointless discord. Stay and drink with us the way you once did. Do that and we can sort matters out peaceably while there's still time.'

'If you mean persuade my mother to accept a man in marriage against her will then the answer is, no. Maybe I'll keep her weaving shrouds up there until there's one for each of you.'

Derisive comments burst from those who overheard his words. Antinous shrugged mock disappointment then stepped aside, bowing with exaggerated courtesy and a low sweep of his arm to gesture Telemachus by. A ripple of mocking laughter - then an ominous silence. Right hand ready to fall upon his sword hilt, eyes fixed ahead, Telemachus pushed defiantly by, aware of threatening gaze and angry murmur. On reaching the short flight of steps before the palace entrance he was obliged to step over the stupefied Iros who lay sprawled in his own vomit. At the top he halted between the squat columns and bronze-banded wooden doors that stood open beneath the great stone lintel. There he glimpsed a number of Thoas' guards waiting discreetly inside with swords drawn.

'By Zeus we're in for another speech!' wailed one of the suitors as Telemachus turned to face them, though now the tension had eased a little. They took scant notice when one of their number staggered away several paces, arm outstretched for support against a stone column where, bent forward, he noisily spewed up his food and drink.

Telemachus glanced over their heads at the man then smiled, 'How nobly you conduct your evenings and how glad I am you find my presence so entertaining.' Subdued murmuring resumed as he added, 'What would you do if I was no longer around to keep you in such good spirits?'

'Planning to bugger off are you?' sneered Leiocritius. 'And how soon might that be?'

'Oh, it was no more than a passing thought someone had,' responded Telemachus with broadening smile. 'They suggested I sail off to Pylos then ride overland to Sparta to find out if anyone knew what had happened to my father. I'd need to think hard on it though, wouldn't I?'

'I'll wager 'is old lady is trying to get rid of 'im!' a man called out.

'No,' growled Eurymachus to those closest. 'It could be more than that. If he left Ithaca he might call on armed help from the mainland.' He spat then said, 'We'll need to keep an eye on 'im – maybe when the pretty boy's out hunting. Accidents do 'appen.'

'I'll wager it's only his mouth,' remarked someone with an alcoholic slur. 'He's never sailed beyond Ithaca and the islands. He'd end up lost at sea like his witless father.'

'Maybe someone told mother's boy he's the new fucking Heracles!' scoffed Leiocritius. 'Someone hand 'im a lion's skin an' a fucking great club!'

'Wait, wait, wait!' exclaimed Antinous, stepping part way up to where Telemachus stood. There he raised his goblet high to address his companions. 'As our young lord made clear a while back, this situation really has gone on too long.' Swinging about to face Telemachus he declared, 'Why not give serious thought to this notion? If I were to organise a crew and one of my own vessels we could make it happen. The sooner you discover the truth, the sooner we get to settle our affairs here.'

'Yes, why not accept it?' asked one. 'It's the best offer you'll get tonight unless one of your slave girls opens her legs.'

'On one of *your* boats,' grinned Telemachus as Antinous stepped back to re-join the rest, 'and with *your* men as crew? Antinous - there must be other ways of getting myself drowned! Forget it; maybe I'll stay where I am.'

Antinous gulped from his goblet then exclaimed, 'No, do it mighty lord! Go ahead and sail away! It's your life to play around with!' Gone was the smile and in its place an ominously hard gaze as he added under his breath, 'At least for now.'

Telemachus sensed renewed antagonism. Wine emboldened Leiocritius, followed close by one of his sullen-faced men, strode forward and staring up at him, looked as if to draw sword or dagger. Telemachus, a hand slipping to his sword hilt, breathed, 'Come on my friend, make your move.'

With his intended victim positioned between columns and doors, Leiocritius would need to take three or four bounding paces directly upward, by which time Telemachus' blade would be poised to strike. His sword was part drawn as the snarling Leiocritius, dagger pulled from within his robe, started to the lower step, his murderous eyes, reflecting red from the firebrands, fixed upon Telemachus. Antinous moved suddenly forward, one arm thrust out to block Leiocritius, causing the man to growl then spin aside and turn vehement anger at Antinous. For several heartbeats it looked as if the two suitors might set upon each other until their followers intervened.

Telemachus let his own blade slip back into its scabbard. He eyed the suitors coldly, saying, 'If and when I'm convinced my father no longer lives then maybe I'll have my mother choose who she wishes to marry – though I doubt she'd find any among you worth the trouble. But take my word on it – that man will *never* occupy my father's place on the throne of Ithaca!' He did not await further comment or insult but spun about to enter the vestibule, nodding to Thoas and his handful of men as he passed by.

Antinous pushed his way through the rest, dismissing his followers, intending to enter the dining hall alone via the narrow passage leading to the servants' door. An older member of the suitors tottered after him, the portly, balding, wide-eyed Eudorus; one who harboured no illusions over his chances of winning Penelope's favour but was content to play his part in consuming the wealth of Odysseus' house. In near darkness he sidled unsteadily up to Antinous, eyes darting from side to side as he rasped close to the taller man's ear. 'Listen to me, Antinous - if that damned boy did set off to Pylos, if he came back convinced of Odysseus death, then she might agree to marry. If so it could make the situation difficult – difficult for you is what I mean. You've strong competition, particularly from our friend Leiocritus. He's a man of considerably more wealth than most – maybe even more than you, and he's just as much right to claim the throne of Ithaca.'

Antinous turned to face him but not too closely. He detested Eudorus' breath, a waft of rotten meat, and considered the man himself little more than a harmless fool.

'I wasn't spying, you understand,' Eudorus continued, 'no, I would never do that, but I overheard Leiocritius in the tavern earlier today. He talked of, er – he talked of bribing Laertes with much silver - gold, maybe, if he'd agree to ship Odysseus' wife – no, I mean, er, his widow, back to her father's dwelling in Sparta together with the value of her original dowry. It is something our customs would allow is it not.'

'Oh, suggested Laertes could send her back, did he,' breathed Antinous. 'And what makes him think the old man would agree to that?'

'Because it's said Laertes himself doubts that Odysseus still lives though he cares much over the woman's welfare and regrets her present situation. But, listen, should Laertes agree, and he may well do so out of fear for her safety, it will give Leiocritius the right by custom to remove her. And if her only son has left Ithaca – well it, er, it leaves matters somewhat unclear for yourself does it not?'

'Why are you telling me this?' queried Antinous, easing further away to avoid the other man's fetid exhalations. 'Before long it'll be my balls slapping the woman's arse and I'll have no man contest it with me. If that skulking twerp of hers hasn't fled Ithaca by then, I'll give him a different length and that'll be one of sharpened bronze.'

'I'm telling you,' spluttered the indignant, Eudorus, eyes bulging so wide that Antinous wondered if they might spring from their sockets, 'b-because Leiocritius insulted me in the tavern this morning. Yes, in front of others - in front of our damned menials. He called me a – a -.'

'Never mind what he called you,' cut in Antinous, hard-eyeing Eudorus. 'We keep this to ourselves – d'you understand?

'Y-yes, yes; strictly to ourselves, of course.'

'To ourselves,' growled Antinous, 'and let the rest of 'em think whatever they like.'

'But what of her captain of the guard,' pressed Eudorus, 'yes, what about him?'

'Thoas,' replied Antinous, calmly, 'is kept happy in the oh-so-faithful Penelope's bed - or so I'm informed by one of her palace women. True or not, his term of service could well end in his own blood – if he's still hanging around by then, which I suspect may not be the case.'

'But - but,' insisted Eudorus, tottering behind as Antinous turned to go, 'but the boy might return with evidence that Odysseus lives. Where would that leave matters - where I ask you?'

'Well it's a case of "if." That is *if* Telemachus ever has the guts to go, which I doubt, and *if* he gets back with any news at all. And if by some oversight of the gods Odysseus himself returned, he'd never reach his precious throne alive. That, my friend, none of us could afford – including you.' Part turning to step away, Antinous added, 'But I doubt we'd have cause to worry; the sea can be mightily dangerous at times.'

Antinous strode on to leave the other man with his thoughts. Hearing voices, Eudorus looked around to see firebrands clustering at the entrance to the passage. The other suitors were making their way back to the dining hall.

Chapter 3 - The Voyage to Pylos

Euryclea was busy spinning wool at her age-warped wooden table with rough pottery oil lamps spaced as a miniature constellation of lights to illuminate her work. This modest chamber was her temple of memories. When as now steeped beneath layers of silence it opened a portal to her innermost thoughts. It had been her private chamber since her earliest days at the House of Odysseus. It contained all the comforts she desired including her simple wooden bed. She could have chosen a better room long ago; one with a larger window, one more spacious and appointed with those luxuries enjoyed by other residents of the palace, but here resided the spirits of a past she had no wish to abandon. Soon she would end her task, extinguish all but one of the lamps and retire to her bed.

Much preoccupied in thought, she was unaware of any sound from beyond until Telemachus, clearing his throat, part eased aside the leather curtain that obscured the entrance to her sanctum.

'Young master,' she smiled, setting aside her work. 'Please come in. What brings you to visit me so far into the night?'

The flames of her lamps wavered in the draught as he entered. Shadows, billowing forms, swayed over plain, white-plastered walls. Telemachus stepped across to a cushioned stone bench and sat close by the side of her table. 'Euryclea,' he said in a low voice, 'I'm sorry to impose upon your privacy but I wish to confide in you. May I do that?'

'I tended you as I tended your dear father, from birth to adolescence,' she replied. 'I know you at least as well as your own mother does - bless her. I hope I would be one of first to share your confidence over anything you wish to impart.'

The small flames reflected brightly in her eyes but there was another more subtle light, an inner glow that arose from deep within. His mother had often claimed it was her divine soul shining through.

'Euryclea, there's a task ahead for me; it's one that has only lately become clear. I must find out as best I can what happened to my father and I won't do it by hanging about the islands. I realise now that by doing nothing I, my mother, all of us perhaps, face a great deal of trouble. The mood of the suitors has changed for the worse since I confronted them. Some are more offensive with their remarks and more threatening in their behaviour. I must leave Ithaca for a time. I will sail to Pylos: there I'll speak with King Nestor then I will ride on to Sparta. I'm assured Nestor and Menelaus are still alive. A boat and crew will be prepared for me and -.'

'Sail to Pylos!' interrupted Euryclea. Light from the little lamps danced in eyes that expressed deep concern. 'A boat and crew! And where will you find a crew you can trust? If any of them are in the pay of those men who descend upon us each evening then you'd be better off if you tried swimming to Pylos.'

'Not so - I discussed this with Mentor last night. He came to speak with me at a small cove along from the harbour after our fishermen had set out. His words were like a shaft of morning sunlight. Earlier today I went down to the harbour, to the waterside village from where his kinsman,

Noemon, sails. I needed to find out exactly what has been arranged. Noemon will supply the crew - sixteen good men, all close to him and all of them well known to Mentor.'

'Mentor - with you last night?' she responded with disbelieving stare. 'I don't understand. He went to his home a short while after sunset. I saw him from my window. I watched him going along the path leading to his house. He was walking with much difficulty as he so often does toward the end of the day. I would not have thought him capable of making his way to any cove and back.'

'Well then,' responded Telemachus, 'he must have spotted me on my way there, perked up and set out again. I'd hardly confuse Mentor for someone else even on the darkest night.'

'No, you hardly would,' she responded, then added quietly, 'Of course, how could you.'

'Euryclea,' he smiled, 'd'you suggest I may have encountered an apparition? The old man seemed real when I laid my hand on his shoulder.'

Euryclea considered his question before replying. 'Young master, you saw and heard what you saw and heard – of course you did. But I ask myself, might not the goddess herself have contrived this visit. I believe Athena has helped preserve your mother this far and each day I pray she will guide and care for you.'

'Are you suggesting she called by to see me in the dead of night disguised as poor old Mentor? Now why should Athena want to look like him when she could have appeared as herself? Then I would really have been impressed. But I - I did realise after he departed that he might need my company on his way home so I chased after him. He was nowhere in sight but then it was dark and I was distracted by an owl circling above.'

'You saw an owl!' exclaimed Euryclea, her eyes expressing wonder as she placed a hand on his. 'Did you see it clearly? Was it a white owl?'

'Yes, white, as far as I could tell.'

Euryclea was silent for a time then said, 'Let's speak of this no more, young master. Explain to me what you wish me to do.'

'Euryclea, what I need is for you to find two or three men of our household you know can be trusted. Tonight, when my mother's suitors are fully occupied in the dining hall, have our men carry down to the harbour a few days' provisions from our stores ready for Noemon to take on board his vessel. Include flagons of red wine and mill-crushed grain. Should anyone notice have them think we are trading these for goods brought ashore by pirates. I must also have gifts of value for those I intend to visit if I'm to be taken seriously. Try to have the appearance of our stores arranged so the removal of the more precious items is not obvious. No one else is to know about this, including my mother.'

'But,' countered Euryclea, 'Lady Penelope will realise something is amiss when you're not seen for more than a few days. Her anger will fall upon me for this deception and rightly so.'

'No, tell her you were also deceived. Tell her you were unaware and that I must have been planning this for a long time. I've been away for days on end before now so it will be a good while before she asks any questions and that goes for our unwelcome guests. I informed them someone had put the idea into my mind but that I didn't take it seriously.'

'But,' she insisted, shaking her head and wringing her hands together, 'once they know you've left Ithaca those damnable men will press your mother even harder for her consent in marriage – and all this in their certainty of your father having departed this world. Why do this when you yourself agree with them over his being dead and gone? I wonder who really put the idea into your head.' Then she added under her breath, 'Perhaps I need not wonder at all.'

'Well whoever it was,' said Telemachus, 'I've decided and that's that.'

'There is so much at risk here,' she sighed. 'So much.'

'It's a risk I will take,' he replied softly. 'And I know Thoas will keep an eye on her.' Telemachus reached to take her lean hand. 'Euryclea, will you swear by the gods to do as I ask?'

'Yes, I swear by almighty Zeus and all those above who preside over our lives - I will do as you ask though it will grieve me to have you gone from Ithaca as it will your poor mother.'

Alone once more in the silence of her room, Euryclea stood before her window to gaze out at the stars. Her eyes were moist with tears as she whispered softly. 'Athena hear me. Watch over and protect Telemachus on his journey. Have him return safely to this house no matter what dangers await beyond our shores.'

The flames of her lamps brightened momentarily but because she stood facing the window she did not notice.

The horizon was faintly blushed by sunlight when the figure of Mentor appeared at the door of Telemachus' chamber. Telemachus was already dressed in plain tunic and leather sandals, his bronze razor and flask of olive oil laid aside by the water bowl. He turned from the window in surprise as the old man spoke. 'Young sir, the supplies you ordered are taken down to the harbour and are being placed aboard Noemon's boat. Your crew will soon be ready to sail and Noemon sends word that he will accompany you. You should join them without delay if you are to avoid hostile eyes.'

'I doubt any of them will be sober enough to leave their beds this early,' responded Telemachus. All the while he stared hard at Mentor with questions flooding through his mind over that evening by the water and his presence here today. Could the old man really have walked to the harbour and back again before daylight this morning?

'I'll head down there now,' Telemachus informed him, buckling on his sword belt and adjusting the plain blue band that held his hair in place. 'You, my friend, have done enough and you should not have climbed the stairs to fetch me when you could have sent a slave. You must return home. You must rest and say nothing.'

'I'll do that, young master,' smiled Mentor, as they reached the narrow stairs leading down to the megaron.

Telemachus watched him negotiate each step with stick-tapping caution, his free hand grasping the guide rope threaded along the stone wall through bronze rings. He felt reluctant to assist the old man or to say anything at all because Euryclea's words of that previous evening still played on his thoughts. Yet, potent as the gods were believed to be, the idea was ridiculous: how, he asked himself, how could anyone doubt this was really his aged tutor? No, it was the prospect of breaking the impasse after so many years of fruitless longing for the return of Odysseus that had awakened Mentor's hopes and given new life to the old man's step. At the base of the stairs awaited the cumbersome leather bag containing the gifts Telemachus intended to present at Pylos and Sparta. At the main door of the palace he turned to Mentor, saying, 'You have opened new opportunities for me. Goodbye for now my friend and take good care.'

'Young master,' Mentor smiled, 'I have served only as a means to reveal that which already stirred within you.'

Crossing the palace courtyard then the marketplace he encountered no one until reaching the town gate where the murmurs and sporadic snores of the dispossessed emerged from the shadows. Once outside the city wall he paused to observe the vague glow of dawn spread over a clear eastern sky. With a pleasantly cool breeze on his cheek and the weighty bag slung over his shoulder, Telemachus set off toward the harbour. He carried on further then, before the path began to descend, looked around to ascertain whether or not he was being followed. Somewhere in the bushes close by a bird was singing and he continued at a brisk pace down the rocky path, free hand resting lightly on the hilt of his sword. The path descended more steeply and when he caught site of the small harbour backed by rugged hills the sky had brightened enough for him to be certain the way ahead was clear.

Strong odours of fish, wood-smoke and pitch drifted on the morning breeze as he drew closer. And there must be his vessel as there was no other in the harbour to match her; a lean black craft, her prow brightly decorated with a pair of large eyes and swirling colours as she swayed on the water with men scampering over her deck. The fir mast was set in its hollow box amidships and they were already hoisting the white linen sail with plaited oxhide ropes. There were a few other men visible but none appeared to be townsfolk and even an inquisitive loiterer would have little opportunity to guess the vessel's purpose that day.

His loose, pale gown flapping as a wind-blown sail, portly, balding, round-faced, bushy-bearded Noemon hurried along the quayside cobbles to greet Telemachus with a broad, gap-toothed grin. 'You're most welcome, young sir,' he declared, 'and we'll soon be ready to sail under your command.'

'Friend Noemon,' replied Telemachus as each grasped the right arm of the other, 'command of the vessel must be entirely yours. Any vessel I tried to command would be destined only for Poseidon's realms, of that I'm sure. All I ask is a safe voyage to Pylos from where I'll afterwards make my way overland to Sparta.'

'A safe voyage, young sir, is what I'll promise,' he responded, waving his arm toward the vessel. 'And though she's modest in size you'll have as swift and trustworthy a craft at your disposal as could be found anywhere about Ithaca and the islands. She is my favourite boat, yes, and her name is *Amphitrite*. She could accommodate more crew but we also need space for goods. Those men we have are sufficient and I can vouch for each one personally. Some are my own sons, some my sons in law and others my nephews. They will sail wherever you wish and they'll do so with good heart. You must come aboard at once in case you are recognised by someone you'd rather not be seen by.'

'*Amphitrite* - ah, yes,' remarked Telemachus as they reached the waterside steps, 'the goddess who rules the waves. One of the Nereids is she not, the sea nymphs who aid mariners in distress. I trust we'll have no need of their services on this voyage; drowning at sea is not what I had planned.'

'Trust!' enthused Noemon as he assisted Telemachus and his precious bag down onto the stout timber gangway running part way along the centre of the vessel. 'I trust her with my life and I believe the gods look upon her with the greatest favour. But we will as always make a small offering once we're clear of the harbour. If you'll follow me past the chests and wine jars to the stern you will find as comfortable a seat as my dear *Amphitrite* is able to offer. I will take my place at the steering oar. There we can talk.'

Telemachus liked Noemon. Here was a straightforward and honest man; a man he was sure he could depend upon.

With minimal fuss and noise, *Amphitrite* was heaved away from the harbour wall and her bow swung seaward. The rough-hewn, stubble-faced men, each in linen kilt, had clambered to their oars

– eight per side, and now worked to manoeuvre their gently rocking vessel clear of the harbour itself. As he made his rope-grasping way awkwardly behind their captain, each man of the crew acknowledged Telemachus with a nod. Telemachus responded likewise, noting their arms bundled on several layers of dry sacking spread along the bottom of the boat but part hidden by the gangway. There were spears and swords, powerful bows waiting to be strung and quivers of deadly, bronze-tipped arrows. Further on were stacked circular, boiled oxhide shields with metal rims or burnished copper facing, smaller and lighter than those employed for combat on land. There, too, clustered the helmets of bronze or boar's tusk and oxhide armour to protect the upper body. As he set down the bag Telemachus reflected upon the fact that his only asset for combat was the short sword at his waist.

The breeze picked up as *Amphitrite* turned south from the headland into the open waters of a morning sea kissed by rays of the rising sun. Her sail drum-thudded in a fresh breeze, ropes tightened, thwacked and quivered, spar, mast and timbers creaked and the men drew their oars onboard. Waves slapping her hull, *Amphitrite* scudded proudly forward, rolling on a modest swell. Noemon's boat was a lively craft and already Telemachus sensed she was blessed with a personality all her own, perhaps as her owner had suggested, the spirit of the sea goddess herself. He savoured the salt air as a fine wine, forgetting for the moment those troubles afflicting the House of Odysseus. This was a new day in his life; the start of an adventure he was confident would reveal the answers he sought.

'This will be much the longest voyage I've taken,' he confided to Noemon as the breeze whisked hair across his cheeks. 'The one question I must ask is how long will we spend at sea?'

'If this northerly wind holds,' replied the captain, 'we'll have Pylos in sight on the morning of our second day but as we'll never be far from an island or mainland coast we'll rest ashore at night. Should the weather turn against us during the day we can put ashore wherever looks to be safe.'

'Safe?' queried Telemachus. 'D'you mean a harbour? Surely pirates have not been seen hereabouts though I've heard they're on the increase elsewhere.' As he spoke his attention was drawn to members of the crew. Their lips moved in silent invocation as they poured libations of red wine into the sea from small, rough jars which were then discarded overboard: offerings to Zeus, to Poseidon and to Athena. Were they also asking the gods to keep pirates at bay? Telemachus pressed Noemon for an answer.

'Pirates are not yet a problem in our waters,' assured Noemon, 'but there have lately been reports of strange vessels. They've been encountered further south, off the Peloponnese, and in much greater numbers to the east. I'm told some speak a dialect different to that of the settled Greeks. It's said they are driven westward by the advance of other peoples from lands far beyond Troy. Travellers report of late how these invaders now occupy the lands of Troy itself.'

'But I understand piracy *was* once common here,' said Telemachus.

'True, young sir, but that was in the time of our forefathers and those pirates were Greek, north African or from lands further to our west. The Cretans put an end to most of the problem in the days of King Minos. He ruled over his island and many others from the great palace at Knossos. He built a navy able to range far and rid the seas of this pestilence. That navy was well maintained into your grandfather's days by his son, Deucalion but the power of Crete has declined greatly since those days and the seas are no longer hers to command. Deucalion's son, Idomeneus, fought most bravely at Troy in spite of his advanced years. As for the pirates we hear of now, I'm told they operate with single vessels and occasionally in small fleets. There are reports from our merchants and others of large scale raids on Attica and upon the territories of Megara, Corinth and Epidaurus. It's claimed only Athens has proved successful in defying them. Yes, they tell how Athens stands as a bulwark. They say it was her king, Theseus, who strengthened and part rebuilt her walls to resist her enemies.'

'Troubles at home and abroad,' sighed Telemachus, 'but I expect our men are well prepared for whatever we may encounter.'

'True enough they are proven warriors in combat as well as excellent seamen. And being Cretans, they are the finest archers you'll ever meet. They are masters of their skill even from the deck of a rolling ship.'

'Then I consider myself most fortunate to have such men in our service,' said Telemachus, aware of a chorus of wind and waves and feeling the warmth of a newly risen sun on his cheek.

Amphitrite ploughed on through lively waters with the pennant of Ithaca fluttering at her mast as if nothing in this otherwise troubled world could ever mar their voyage.

'Mentor emphasised the importance of your journey,' said Noemon. 'He holds your interests and that of your father's house as close to his heart as any man could. He insisted I offer you my finest craft and crew though I would anyway have offered them willingly to a son of Odysseus.'

'The old man's been well occupied for one so frail,' responded Telemachus. 'Until lately he had difficulty in walking even a short distance, let alone all the way along that rough path from the palace to the harbour.'

'Oh, he didn't come down to the harbour,' replied the captain. 'He'd never make it there and back nowadays, I realise that. He sent a slave to summon me and I took myself to his home at night.'

Telemachus stared out to sea and thought it better to say nothing more on the subject.

Ithaca lay to their left. To the right side of the channel arose the much larger island of Kephallinia. Telemachus eyed its sunlit coast, steep and rugged, and Noemon said, 'I well remember when Kephallinia and other islands were under the firm hand of your father. He also controlled cattle grazing territory on the mainland that others saw fit to occupy after his departure.'

'Euryclea took me to Kephallinia when I was a small child,' said Telemachus, 'It's the furthest I ever sailed though I remember little of it – apart from being seasick. Whoever my mother married would expect to assert his authority by arms over Kephallinia and all those regions once controlled from Ithaca. There could be bloody conflict throughout these islands if others challenged the new man.'

'That is so,' said Noemon. 'And I doubt it would be safe for us to go ashore on Kephallinia during the day as things are.'

'Probably not: Leiocritius, one of the wealthiest of my mother's suitors holds power there. He regards much of the island as his own with no allegiance to whoever should rule Ithaca.'

***

The seas remained benign, the wind favourable in its southerly course. The men occasionally broke into raucous song; their usual subject being women. When later in the day they cleared the southern tip of Kephallinia, the lesser island of Zakinthos was in view, rising stark from a glinting blue sea. The boat pitched gently as she buffeted her way through the waves and now some of the crew had completed a spell of fishing. Tinder and scraps of wood had been brought in readiness and soon the smoky odour of cooking wafted from the small wood-fired grill suspended to swing in a metal frame between *Amphitrite's* mast and bow.

Telemachus had watched fascinated as they made the fire with a piece of flint that threw off bright yellow sparks when struck hard against a pebble-sized, grey object Noemon referred to as his "fire stone." Telemachus had heard of this method but here was the first time he had seen it done. There were always fires burning at Ithaca, in the taverns and in most of the temples. Should a fire go out it was easy enough to acquire a flame to remake it from the hearth of another.

'We enter wider waters after Zakinthos,' Noemon informed him, 'and we'll have the Peloponnesian coast on our left. I know of a small cove accessible only by sea where we can eat and rest ourselves until morning. I suggest we go ashore there rather than reach Pylos during darkness as we'd not be quite so welcome when most of the palace sleeps.'

'As you wish,' smiled Telemachus.

'Thank you, young master, and it will give me chance to describe to you more of Pylos and its people. Next morning we approach Sphacteria and there sail by the long island until passing around the south where we enter calmer waters of the bay. You'll find the city and palace of King Nestor much to your liking.'

'I hear it's quite splendid,' said Telemachus.

'That it is but you'll see for yourself before long and there is a festival due, so I'll say no more.'

'And you, Noemon, will you be going there with me?'

'I will if you wish it but I think you'll find nobler company than mine up there. My time would be better employed with our own men and my good *Amphitrite*.'

'Your good *Amphitrite*, your dear *Amphitrite*,' laughed Telemachus. 'You regard her the way some men regard a woman.'

'I most certainly do,' he replied with exaggerated seriousness, 'and I assure you she serves me better than any woman could; always

71

ready and willing when I need her and never to this day has she raised a complaint – oh, except when her timbers are rotten and have to be replaced!'

'Ah, most reassuring,' grinned Telemachus, peering intently along *Amphitrite's* hull.

Telemachus found the cove into which they entered less than assuring. The narrow beach afforded sufficient space for their needs but the rock walls enclosing this rose almost sheer to the land above. Anyone abandoned there would have little hope of escape.

***

It was close to mid-morning when, in a brisk wind beneath a benign blue sky, they rounded the fragmented southern tip of Sphacteria to enter the sheltered waters of the great semi-circular bay where ahead of them lay Pylos. Telemachus had slept fitfully on the narrow beach of the cove, yet his eagerness for the journey had never faltered. On the contrary, as they sailed by sunlit, forest-edged shores his enthusiasm was fired to even greater measure.

'Two of my lads will set off and let 'em know we've arrived,' said Noemon. 'It will avoid any confusion and I wager they'll send out an escort once they know who you are.'

Before their vessel beached, two of Noemon's crew sprang over the side to wade ashore with spears raised and there found themselves surrounded by prancing, babbling children and yapping dogs. Both men sprinted across the sand, covering the modest distance to a well-smoothed path that passed the thatched dwellings of fishermen and their families before disappearing into the pinewoods. With the vessel fast ashore, Telemachus took up the leather bag now containing only those precious ornaments and items of jewellery selected as gifts for the King of Pylos. The remainder, intended for Sparta, were secreted beneath the sacking where lay the crew's weapons. *Amphitrite's* captain and the rest of his men set about preparing a fire for their second meal on dry land since leaving Ithaca. Telemachus had little appetite for food but much for what lay ahead in Nestor's realm.

The sun was past its zenith when Noemon's two men emerged from the forest striding briskly toward *Amphitrite*. Ogled by excited children, Telemachus had paced back and forth along the beach to occupy his time and at present stood some distance from the boat. Gladdened to see the men approach, his attention was next drawn to the sight of an ornately gilded, two wheeled light chariot pulled by a pair of plume-bobbing chestnut horses that emerged some distance behind them from amidst the trees. He observed close behind the chariot a quartet of horsemen bearing spears and round shields. The harsh midday sun glinted from bronze blades and gilded cuirasses. Tall red plumes swayed above gleaming helmets as they would before the eyes of an enemy. The riders' panoply of arms proclaimed them warriors of noble blood.

Noemon's returning men had not reached the shore when they were obliged to move aside to let the chariot and its escort pass by. Clearly a high noble of Nestor's court, the chariot's driver reigned in his sinewy horses before reaching softer sand where he stepped from his carriage. Having Telemachus pointed out to him by Noemon's men, the newcomer strode purposefully toward him. The escort advanced further onto the beach, drew to a halt ahead of the chariot and there waited.

Noemon and his crew turned to face the charioteer in silent deference as he trudged by them bearing the gilded staff of authority in his left hand. His rich maroon, gold-edged gown was colourfully embroidered and at his belt was fastened a short sword in ornately gilded scabbard similar to that worn by Telemachus himself. He was a man of early to middle years, dark-haired, clean-shaven and possessing the resolute aspect of a seasoned warrior. He stepped smiling up to Telemachus, reached out a hand in greeting and announced in a tone of regal authority, 'I am Pisistratus, youngest son of King Nestor. I'm told you are Telemachus, son of Odysseus who once ruled over Ithaca and her islands.'

Encouraged by the man's amiable manner, Telemachus seized the hand with enthusiasm, saying, 'I am the son of Odysseus. I come with modest gifts in the hope that King Nestor will assist me in learning something of my father's fate.'

'He will greet you with pleasure and he'll see to it that your captain and crew are amply provided for during your absence. Noemon and his men are well known to us and your arrival is suitably timed. We're beginning our feast in honour of Poseidon and as custom demands a black bull has already been taken for sacrifice. Come with me now and speak with my father. You will afterwards be a welcome guest at our celebrations.'

The man was slightly taller than Telemachus. He exuded a calm self-confidence as they walked over to the chariot where the armed escort drew aside to allow both men through. Telemachus, clutching the bag but fearing at this point youthful naivety might be to his disadvantage, said, 'Lord Pisistratus, I've had little enough opportunity to meet kings – in fact none at all since no king has visited Ithaca during my lifetime. Your father is known to everyone through the accounts of his deeds so in what manner am I to greet him?'

As they clambered aboard the creaking chariot, a lightly built conveyance of woven basketwork draped with lion skins and gilded ornament as befitted its owner's status, Pisistratus replied, 'If you're the son of a king then you show subservience to no man. You address my father with respect for his great age and he will, of course, fully honour your own status once he is satisfied of it.'

Taken aback by those last words, Telemachus was nevertheless reassured by the continuing good-humour and, by now, easier manner of his royal companion. They proceeded to a thump of hooves along the gently rising path in tree-shaded light, passing amidst pine trees then through olive groves before savouring the tang of orchards. Telemachus compared the attitude of this man, a prince of his realm, to the high-handed coarseness and lack of respect displayed by his mother's suitors.

By mid-afternoon they were passing through a small village of clustered stone houses where craftsmen and potters worked when the palace buildings of King Nestor came into view against a backdrop of low hills. Telemachus was surprised to see there were no walls of gaunt, cyclopean masonry. Instead there appeared a complex larger and more colourfully embellished than anything to be found on Ithaca. Telemachus could discern little sign of initial planning; rather the layout of these buildings appeared the result of random enlargement over many years. To counter the effect of earthquakes the walls, as at Ithaca, had been constructed with frameworks of massive wooden beams infilled with polygonal stone blocks. Ranged along many of the parapets were stone-carved, stylised bulls' horns similar to those to be seen at Ithaca's royal palace but here ranged in far greater number. Immediately to the west of the main structure Telemachus noted a smaller block that showed evidence of considerable damage and looked to be abandoned.

'There was a fire many years ago,' confirmed Pisistratus, aware of his passenger's interest. 'Our newer workshops and buildings for the storage of grain and trade goods lie at the other side of the palace. And there is our library, claimed by my father and others as the largest and best in all Greece.'

'Noemon tells me women play a greater role at Pylos than they do at Ithaca and the islands,' said Telemachus.

'That's right, and so it is at Sparta as well as most larger cities. They form a considerable majority among our artisans and almost the whole of our priesthood. They conduct their own businesses; they own land, yes, even estates. I think you confirm what I'm told is a less liberal situation on Ithaca.'

'My mother owns land and farms but it seems our customs are otherwise more conservative. You must think of us as a backwater.'

Pisistratus merely smiled.

On regarding the main building, parts of which rose to a third storey, and admiring the familiar but here more externally abundant rows of russet and sand coloured columns, Telemachus said, 'I see no fortifications. My father's palace and Ithaca town have defensive walls whereas you seem not to need them.'

'That was true enough in earlier days,' replied Pisistratus. 'My grandfather built much of what lies before us. He aided the Cretans in suppressing raiders from the sea. Unlike many of the cities further north we had no enemies of importance in the Peloponnese once my father had subdued the region. Things are changing now and we are obliged to reconsider our situation. We've organised detachments of armed men to keep watch along our coastline day and night. They will light warning beacons and summon us to arms should an enemy approach. Noemon's vessel was reported when out at sea but of course our men recognised him as a friend.'

'These are the largest buildings I ever saw,' remarked Telemachus, gazing fascinated as they drew closer to the main portico along the stone-paved road at its south side. 'I guess my father's palace would fit inside them several times over.'

'It's claimed there are over a hundred rooms on the ground floor alone,' said Pisistratus. 'Neither I nor anyone I know of ever felt the urge to go around counting them so I suspect there may be fewer than people think. But I tell you from personal experience, what you see around you is less than the great palace of Knossos on Crete. That is said to possess eight hundred rooms. To those who have never been there as well as those who have, Knossos has rightly become a legend.'

'I was taught about Knossos as a child,' said Telemachus as they slowed to a halt. 'I was told how Theseus the Athenian went there to slay a monstrous creature claimed to be half man and half bull. I'm not sure if I believe that.'

'Our world is awash with strange tales,' responded Pisistratus, eager to expand on the subject. 'Beneath Knossos there exists a dark labyrinth where they say the beast was confined. Their priests took me to see the shaft down which they claim its victims were pushed. I assure you, my friend, it exuded the very breath of evil and no one, not even their priests care to enter the place despite the passage of many years. They assured me the remains of the creature, the Minotaur they called it, are still down there together with what's left of its victims, their flesh long since devoured by rats and other foul things. But here we are at my home and you'll find no such abomination lurking beneath Pylos.'

Hung between a massive pair of fluted columns, the great bronze-banded cedar doors of the entrance stood wide. They passed with their escort through the echoing portico whilst hard-faced guards in ceremonial cuirasses of tooled bronze stepped back, spears raised in salute above gleaming, plumed helmets. Only then did the escort leave them.

To an echoing clatter of hooves they entered a courtyard, a larger version of the main one at Ithaca. Behind the colonnades he glimpsed brightly painted scenes that depicted hunters and stags in a style similar to those of his homeland. Beneath these, also familiar but here in far greater abundance, were ranged great terracotta storage jars, many tall as a man, with moulded sea creatures swarming over their surface. Cats slinked in the shadows but there was not the sight or smell of dogs.

Seeing his interest in the painted scenes, Pisistratus said, 'I believe most royal courts have over the years employed the same body of travelling artists.'

'I think so,' agreed Telemachus, admiring the frescoes, 'these same men have probably worked at Ithaca. They must see much of the world.'

'Yes, they see much of the world but I doubt they ever get involved in its tribulations. They come and go with their skills as the seasons of the year.'

They stepped down as two slaves trotted dutifully over to remove the chariot and horses. Telemachus and Pisistratus walked through another, lesser portico into a richly painted ante-room where odours of smoke and cooking flavoured the air. That portal opened into a great, galleried megaron ringing with the laughter and revelry of celebration. The heat of braziers spaced along one wall was at once tangible as they entered. At its centre, supporting a dazzlingly embellished ceiling, stood four great columns forming a square within which sat a circular hearth of much greater size than that in the hall of Odysseus' palace, its surrounding stonework decorated with flame patterns. A

79

multitude of finely attired diners occupied ornately carved and inlaid tables. Telemachus marvelled at the splendour of these surroundings and at an atmosphere charged with a measure of well-being long since banished from the palace of Odysseus.

Peering down from the galleries as well as conspicuous within the hall, the gem-flashing, bare-breasted, crinkle-haired female courtesans appeared even more striking than those of Telemachus' court. Children played tag amidst the colonnade supporting the galleries. Attendants and slaves, young and old, careered here and there with dripping flagons and precariously poised dishes while others carved the sizzling flesh of ox, sheep and pig that were turned on spits to roast above cracking flames. Late afternoon sunlight shafted through high windows to illuminate rising smoke as miniature storm clouds ascending through a spacious square shaft above the hearth.

Telemachus appraised the many colourful images enlivening the walls of the megaron. Not here in the great hall of Pylos was he confronted by the militaristic figures so familiar in the palace at Ithaca though the spears and great shields were present. Painted charioteers paraded by in gaudy attire, exotic creatures peered from amidst flowers and woodlands, and here again were displayed hunting scenes in a peaceful land of plenty. This was a kingdom of wealth far beyond anything he had encountered.

'Many of the men we see around us,' explained Pisistratus, gesturing across the hall, 'are my father's sons, my several brothers that is, and his grandsons. Most of the rest are our kin or nobles of our lands.'

On a scallop-edged, brightly cushioned alabaster throne at the far side of the hall, Nestor, the renowned King of Pylos sat festooned in regal glory with golden goblet in hand. His abundant hair, held in place by a jewelled band, was as white as any Telemachus could recall and his beard considerably longer. A carved wooden seat next to the throne was occupied by a man not quite so aged but almost as richly robed who Telemachus assumed must be a royal companion of considerable importance. Bald on top though he was, his ruddy face was girded by a grey, bushy beard. The court musician, a pale-bearded long-haired spectre of a man was perched close by strumming his lyre.

To the left of the throne Telemachus observed a long bench replete, as were the other tables with precious goblets and vessels, but occupied solely by women - a situation he had never witnessed at Ithaca. All of the women looked to be of high status and all appeared to enjoy the same service from attendants and slaves as did the men. They were attired in an even more sumptuous manner than the flirtatious younger girls and certainly more so than older females at the palace of Ithaca. At the head of this table was seated a richly gowned, bejewelled woman of advanced years with a plain-robed male attendant hovering close by.

Noting Telemachus' interest, Pisistratus smiled, 'I'm assured our customs are more relaxed than those of your homeland and certainly more so than at the court of Mycenae. The lady at the head of the table is Eurydice, my father's wife and my own mother. The other women are mostly her sisters and daughters.'

Nestor spotted the new arrivals, placed aside his goblet and acknowledged their presence with raised hand and gap-toothed smile. His action was noticed by several of those assembled, prompting a general decline in the noise and bustle so that, as the two approached to stand before him, the king's voice could easily be heard.

Pisistratus conducted his charge between avidly curious diners toward the throne from which this all but legendary ruler surveyed his court. Telemachus was struck with amusement at the king's beard which, laced with gold and silver wire, was divided as a fork down the middle to reveal food stains on his lavishly embroidered gown. His eyes, pale and glistening, fixed upon Telemachus but for a time he said nothing. Now everyone in the hall was peering at the newcomer who, with Pisistratus at his side, stood with the leather bag clutched in one hand.

At last Nestor exclaimed, 'You are taller than I remember your father was but you most certainly have his features!' Assisted at his arm by his companion, Nestor arose and took a pace forward. Telemachus let the leather bag down so as to accommodate the king's welcoming embrace. 'Yes, I doubt it not at all,' Nestor enthused, 'you are indeed the son of my old and dear friend Odysseus. And, yes, I swear you carry the expression of fortitude and determination he wore when planning Troy's defeat – though perhaps you have yet to acquire his deviousness and cunning!'

'King Nestor,' smiled Telemachus, once freed from the bony grip, 'I'm honoured to meet you.' He collected up the bag, adding, 'May I offer you gifts from my father's palace. There are jewelled amulets and small vessels of gold and silver. Modest as they are, I trust they will be of good service to you.'

'I thank you, young man,' responded Nestor, 'but your presence here is gift enough.' Returning to his seat of authority he announced to all those assembled in a voice notably loud and clear for one so advanced in years, 'The feast we hold in honour of Lord Poseidon shall also be in honour of Odysseus' son, the noble Telemachus who has crossed the seas to visit us here at Pylos.'

Telemachus smiled. Never before had he been addressed as "noble" except as a term of derision by his mother's suitors.

Turning back to his new guest Nestor queried, 'Why have you not made yourself known to us sooner? I understand it is your mother who at present holds the throne. Ooh – and that I fear is a precarious situation indeed.'

The man positioned close by who had assisted him up from his throne nodded in agreement.

'Precarious, yes,' responded Telemachus, 'but circumstances occurred some years back that prevented my attaining rightful authority. It is time I responded to the situation; hence my coming here.'

'Very good, my boy – then sit by me a while, take food and drink and we will discuss whatever you wish.' Gesturing at his grinning companion Nestor added, 'This is Broteas, commander of my vessels all those years ago. He threw many a spear I wish I myself had been able to cast but I don't complain since he managed to skewer a fair number of Trojans. Now, together, we savour memories of our past as we savour the good wines of Pylos.'

The hazy-eyed Broteas, seated to the king's right, raised his goblet and grinned wider still to reveal a mouth occupied by a diminished number of discoloured, uneven teeth. Telemachus, before seating himself at the king's left, had noted the lurid scar running from above Broteas' cheekbone to his mouth.

'I am informed by Noemon and others trading with both our lands,' continued the king, 'about the situation prevailing within the House of Odysseus. The suitors who beset your mother and feed off your possessions are a disgrace. If what I hear is true then I say it ought not to continue.'

'That's true enough,' responded Telemachus, 'but it's a situation I in part grew up with. For some time I have known I cannot allow it to go on but of late there are greater dangers. Perhaps matters have gone too far – perhaps not.'

'No, my boy, perhaps not. But at least your father did not return to meet the fate of Agamemnon. On that day the gods turned their backs upon the court of Mycenae.'

'Maybe the gods were preoccupied with other matters,' reflected Telemachus.

Nestor turned to his own son who remained standing before them. 'When we have finished talking I'll ask you to take charge of this young man as our honoured guest.'

'I'll do so gladly,' smiled Pisistratus. 'I'll leave you now and return when I see you are ready.'

Conversation had resumed for the rest of those gathered in the hall and the bard began once more to strum. Nestor's servants manoeuvred into position ornate bronze tripods bearing dishes of meat and bread then hovered at a respectful distance awaiting their venerable lord's further requirements.

'Tell me, then,' asked the king, stabbing a gilded knife into one of the bowls, 'what have your enquiries over your father achieved so far?'

'I've made very few until now,' replied Telemachus, accepting a goblet of wine from the hand of a plainly attired serving girl. 'The majority of people on Ithaca would welcome his return but many doubt he still lives. I doubt it also but our affairs have reached a point where confirmation must be had one way or the other. I intend to visit Sparta for the same reason I came here. Any knowledge you possess over what happened after Troy would be of interest to me.'

'Ah – Troy,' he sighed, closing his eyes as images of those distant days in a distant land seeped into his mind. 'Such days of glory they were. What memories the name conjures up, imperfect though they are. So much bravery there was – so much bloodshed. Some of our best men fell before the city wall and by our own ships. There was Ajax, there was Achilles and there was Patroclus his squire and staunch companion – and yes, there was Antilochus - one of my own sons. He lies buried in a hero's grave on that accursed shore.'

Lowering his goblet, Broteas affected an appropriately saddened nod as Nestor went on, 'I was even then considered too old to cast a spear or swing a sword but I gave my advice and support whenever and wherever it was requested – as it often was.'

'Oh, very often,' agreed Broteas.

'And not until the tenth year,' Nestor continued, 'was this conflict resolved, as you doubtless have learned. In the end it was Odysseus who devised the answer, guided so it was said by Athena to whom his house was always devoted. It was to her he offered sacrifice and though he'd departed Ithaca while you were still a babe in arms he was convinced the goddess would watch over you. Your father was a man with whom I never exchanged nor felt I ever could exchange a word in anger. That's more than could be said for our illustrious leaders, Agamemnon and Menelaus. Always there was discord.'

'As I witnessed for myself,' put in Broteas with an alcoholic slur. 'Always discord.'

'But you departed in victory,' said Telemachus, inwardly amused at the sight of grizzled old Broteas gurgling down more wine.

'We did indeed,' responded the king. 'We departed in victory but too great a number of our men were drunk with more than just success. I'm surprised as many survived that terrible storm as did after the amount of Trojan wine they had consumed. I could hardly blame them, though – not after ten years of hardship and frustration. But it was the last I saw of my dear friend Odysseus. After that storm the gods gave me favourable winds and so we returned without further incident to Pylos. That was not so for others of our company. It took -.'

He was interrupted by a deep belch from Broteas but appeared otherwise unconcerned over his companion's lapse of courtly manners. 'It took Menelaus seven, no – eight was it?' continued

Nestor. 'Yes, eight years to get home though in his case it was not the result of misfortune. He returned to Sparta a wealthier man than ever he was before setting out to Troy. Then, his house did not suffer the problems that beset yours. And while speculation over your father's fate must be at very least as common in Ithaca as it is here, Menelaus may cast more light upon the matter.'

'Having a better idea of what became of him after the storm will determine my actions in the future,' responded Telemachus. 'That's what I'm hoping.'

'Ah, the future,' sighed Nestor. 'Yes, as we grow older the real future matters less because looking back upon our past becomes ever more our future. In all those years since Troy I wonder that the gods still preserve me. But my reminiscing is of no value to you.' Nestor gulped his wine then added, 'I will have envoys leave tomorrow for Sparta carrying news of your intended visit. That will alert Menelaus in advance of your arrival and will also give him time to make enquiries - if there are any to be made.'

'I thank you for that,' replied Telemachus, taking his share of the food on offer. But tales of Agamemnon's fate loomed darkly in his mind. He was here face to face with the first man he had met who knew the affairs of Mycenae and its royal house well. Nestor could recount the death of its king better than anyone he was likely to meet – including Menelaus. Hoping the time to be appropriate, Telemachus opened the subject. 'I have only a rough idea from others with second or third hand knowledge of what happened at Mycenae when Agamemnon returned - and why it happened. I was only ten years old then and other rulers rarely send envoys to my mother because they disapprove of our situation. Is there more you could tell me?'

'Indeed there is,' replied Nestor, 'and I gladly will. It is a dark and a confusing tale so I trust it will not try your patience as I relate it.' He gestured for an attendant to replenish all three goblets, though only that of Broteas was actually empty.

'The royal House of Mycenae,' he continued, 'had as bloody a past as could be imagined. There was disorder and violence as far back as anyone could recall and certainly before the days of King Atreus. Atreus was father to both Agamemnon and Menelaus and in those days Mycenae ruled the land. She was at the height of her wealth and power though I'm sure you know that much.'

Nestor gestured for Telemachus to shuffle closer then, as Broteas rocked forward to hear what he must well know, Nestor began what would prove to be a lurid account.

'Atreus had a brother called – called – er – Thyestes.'

'That's him, Thyestes,' agreed Broteas after another rattling belch.

'Of course it was, yes - Thyestes, a brother who was also his sworn and bitter rival. This Thyestes ruled Mycenae until Atreus drove him out. Aegisthus, the man who would later slay Agamemnon, was Thyestes son – born a few years after the father had been kicked out of Mycenae. Whilst Thyestes was away from home involved in some petty conflict, his mother abandoned Aegisthus. Yes, she left the child in a field with warm clothes and a sword. I don't recall where the woman ended up but I imagine she wanted no more of the strife and bloodletting that would have dominated her life had she stayed to bring the child up in Thyestes' wretched house.

Little Aegisthus and the sword were found by shepherds and brought to Mycenae where they were put on show in the marketplace to see if anyone could say who the child belonged to. Atreus' wife happened to be passing by, felt pity for the boy and took him in. Atreus recognised the sword for the fine piece of work it was – not at all the weapon of a common man, so they agreed to adopt the child. Atreus retained the sword and presented it to Aegisthus once the boy had reached manhood.'

'So,' commented Telemachus, 'Atreus unknowingly raised the son of a brother who hated him.'

'Should have left the brat out there to die,' mumbled Broteas, downing more wine.

'Yes, raise him he did,' concurred Nestor, 'but no one at Mycenae had any idea who the boy's father was, though it may have been some family resemblance that persuaded Atreus to accept him – who can say. Years later, Thyestes returned to Mycenae in disguise and began plotting against his brother. Atreus found out where Thyestes was hiding and ordered Aegisthus, by then a strapping youth, to go out one night, run him through with his sword and bring back his head.'

'Why did Atreus not have one of his true sons do it?' asked Telemachus.

'Because in later years Atreus regretted having adopted Aegisthus. The boy had by all accounts become arrogant and insolent. Atreus usually had him do this kind of sordid business to save putting his own flesh and blood in mortal danger. Perhaps he hoped Aegisthus and Thyestes would kill each other, it's the way their happy household did things. Well the plan didn't work out because when Aegisthus found his way into the room where Thyestes was sleeping the man woke up in time to grab his own sword. They must have had enough light in the room since before they came to serious blows each recognised the sword the other was intending to use as being from the same workshop. In fact the swords are said to have matched very closely in style and ornamentation. In the secrecy of that place they laid aside their weapons and revealed their respective identities – father and son. So there we have it – *both* now had a strong grudge against Atreus and rather than Aegisthus killing his true father, Thyestes persuaded his newfound son to murder the king instead. This he did by creeping into Atreus' chamber at night and cleaving his skull with one blow of the very sword that was earlier intended to slay Thyestes.'

'I'm surprised anyone felt safe in bed at night,' observed Telemachus. 'As you say, a happy family.'

'Quite, dear boy, and so it went on. With his brother out of the way Thyestes called in a gang of hired thugs from outside, ordered Atreus' retainers butchered and had himself declared King of Mycenae for a second time. He doubtless would have turned his baleful gaze upon the dead Atreus' real sons, Agamemnon and Menelaus, had not his own wretched offspring, Aegisthus, decided that he, rather than his father, now had a legitimate right to the throne since he'd been brought up in the royal house and his father was little better than a brigand. It was during their time of squabbling, plotting and counter plotting that Agamemnon raised a strong following within Mycenae and found an opportunity one night to do away with Thyestes by having him - er, having him -.'

'Having him hurled down from the c-city wall,' mumbled Broteas, almost sliding from his seat as he glanced up and down with a dramatic sweep of his free hand.

'Quite so,' continued Nestor, 'heaved over the edge. So now, with his father dead, Aegisthus took flight to save his own skin and for a while that was that. Mycenae was always rich in gold and despite the turmoil of its royal house the city continued to grow in prosperity through trading and raiding. Agamemnon was called upon as, by that time, the wealthiest and most powerful ruler in Greek lands to lead the expedition against Troy - even though it was his brother, Menelaus, who had the grievance. It was Paris, a prince of Troy, who ran off with Menelaus' wife, Helen.'

'And is that what started it all?' queried Telemachus. 'I mean the long war with Troy.'

'Whether it was or was not, it was a good enough excuse since they'd had designs upon Troy years before that. Oh, and what a mighty undertaking it was! There were those who claimed the Mycenaean fleet alone numbered a hundred ships though I never reckoned it as being that many.'

Broteas frowned, shook his head and gulped the remains of his wine as Nestor continued. 'It was claimed that Pylos supplied ninety vessels but er, I don't want to disillusion anyone; it was more like - well never mind, I can't quite recall the number.'

'S-still a good few,' put in Broteas, wagging his cup for a refill.

'I'm told my father supplied twelve vessels,' said Telemachus.

'Oh, er, ten or twelve,' agreed Nestor, draining more of his own wine as Broteas growled under his breath, 'Pah - more like seven or eight.'

'But,' continued the king, 'our departure heralded further troubles for Agamemnon. The fleet was held up by adverse winds and heavy rain at the port of Aulis on the south-east of the Greek mainland opposite the island of Euboea. The storm prevented them from entering the Aegean Sea and before long the crews were getting restive and our supplies were running low. Some were threatening to go home, wanting to return to their farms, and it looked as if our whole enterprise might fail until Agamemnon's soothsayer, an old charlatan called – called – Cal -.'

'C-calchas,' blurted Broteas, his goblet once more brimming, his grin fixed.

'Yes, yes, yes – Calchas, I know who it was. Calchas came up with an answer. I don't say *the* answer because I for one didn't believe a word of it. Calchas maintained that Agamemnon, while out hunting, had offended the goddess Artimis by killing one of her sacred stags. He claimed the only way out of the situation was for Agamemnon to sacrifice his own daughter, Iphigenia, in recompense. You can imagine the quandary that left him with because so much hung upon that enterprise and what Calchas had said found its way into everyone's ear.'

'Hm,' agreed Telemachus, swirling his wine. 'A tricky situation.'

'A tricky situation indeed but Agamemnon had to be seen to comply with the prophecy because many believed Calchas had a good reputation when it came to making predictions. Agamemnon came one night, utterly distraught, to ask my advice, which I gave to the best of my ability. As a result he sent a party of horsemen dashing back overland to fetch Iphigenia on the pretext of marrying her off to Achilles, the very man everyone regarded as his finest warrior. Achilles had always fancied the girl even before she was of marrying age. Agamemnon prayed hard every day and made sacrifice hoping the weather would change before his daughter showed up – but it didn't.'

'I still say we could have sailed,' mumbled Broteas. 'I've s-set out in worse weather.'

Nestor shrugged then continued his narrative. 'The girl did arrive but to Agamemnon's horror so did her mother, Clytemnestra. This was most unfortunate but in spite of it we organised the ceremony to take place after dark at the shrine of Artimis. When Clytemnestra discovered the alleged purpose of her daughter's summons she pleaded hard with Agamemnon not to go ahead with the sacrifice. Ah, but you see, he had to keep up the pretence. Our men were kept too far away to witness exactly what happened when Iphigenia was taken to the temple. The fact that we were beset by howling wind and pelting rain also helped. Actually, it was bad weather that saved the situation altogether.'

'But I s-saw it all!' declared Broteas, a distant look in his eyes as he waved his goblet back and forth. 'Oh - oh yes, and the poor child was convinced they were going to slit her throat.'

'True enough, she was at first,' agreed Nestor, 'but then it *had* to look convincing. There were screams and sobs when Agamemnon raised the knife – by that time with the connivance of the girl herself, but it sounded genuine enough to her mother who'd been held back forcibly with the rest of the crowd. When it was over Agamemnon intended to tell his wife what had really happened and assure her that Iphigenia was perfectly safe, but before he could, Clytemnestra flew off in a rage back to Mycenae with her attendants. Agamemnon dared not send anyone after her in case the deception got out.'

'So what had really happened?' asked Telemachus, now so absorbed that he was hardly aware of the continuing bustle and chatter throughout the megaron.

'Ah, yes – what actually happened! I had two of my own men whisk Iphigenia out of harm's way. There was plenty of blood to be seen on the altar because a small deer had been slaughtered there as substitute. Agamemnon had it roasted and served up later to the leaders of our various contingents as part of the feast in honour of Artimis and Poseidon. He'd placed an armed guard on that old fraud, Calchas. He'd have needed to flee for his life if his prophecy had failed. Amazingly however, the rain did stop, the winds calmed and soon shifted in our favour. Within two days the fleet was heading out to sea once more. Meanwhile I'd had two of my men escort Iphigenia to a desolate, out of the way place called Tauris. She was supposed to stay there at another temple dedicated to Artimis until after her father had sailed off.'

'So you fooled even the gods and got away with it,' said Telemachus.

'I was none too sure about fooling the gods,' Nestor mused. 'Rather I think one of the gods stepped in on our behalf. Iphigenia, meanwhile, was made a child priestess of the temple. She insisted on staying where she was rather than go back to strife-ridden Mycenae – and who could blame the poor girl. That left her brother, Orestes, and her sister, Electra, without the support of the older girl. Orestes was too young by far to assert his authority so Clytemnestra ended up in a situation rather similar to that of your own mother - except that, strong willed as she certainly was, the gods had never blessed her with the same high principles.' Noting one of his young, bare-breasted courtiers hover nearby with her eye upon Telemachus, Nestor hesitated. 'Have I said enough, dear boy? I feel I may be diverting your attention from, er, other matters.'

'Not so,' answered Telemachus, unaware of the girl's presence as slave and jug loomed close by to top up their goblets including the once more empty vessel of a now aimlessly mumbling Broteas. 'You're dressing the meagre bones that have haunted my thoughts all these years with flesh and blood – yes, and there seems to be plenty of that. Please go on.'

'Yes blood!' responded Nestor, 'and there's no shortage of that to come. Clytemnestra was back in Mycenae when news arrived that the fleet had departed Aulis and was sailing for Troy. Aegisthus summoned up enough courage to return to the city with the rabble who were his followers, intending, I dare say, to make a grab for the throne. There was not much to keep him out, either, since Mycenae had been all but drained of her best fighting men – a bigger risk than most cared to admit at the time. But there was still the palace guard to hold him back so Aegisthus worked out a more subtle approach than force of arms.

He began by paying court to Clytemnestra who, anyway, was regarded in her day as a great beauty. She at first refused to see him and Electra did all she could to keep him away because in spite of her tender years the girl realised what Aegisthus was up to and quite rightly detested the man. She wasn't terribly close to her own mother, either, since Iphigenia seemed to have been the most favoured in every way. Some people made out that Iphigenia had been the daughter of Clytemnestra's first husband who Agamemnon killed in battle before forcing her to marry him.'

'So she could never be the devoted wife my mother has been all these years,' reflected Telemachus.

'No she could not. But then she was obliged to scheme in order to protect herself from the inevitable palace intrigues. She'd had no love for Agamemnon but on the face of things treated him as a wife ought until the assumed sacrifice of Iphigenia. After that she loathed his very name and made no secret of it to those close to her. She didn't think much of Aegisthus, either, but he persisted in charming her and she in turn came to regard him as means of taking revenge on her husband. Aegisthus also helped preserve her status as ruler of Mycenae because people came to look upon him as her consort and therefore suitors never became a problem. Even so, four years passed before she let him move into the royal suite though soon after that, so it was rumoured, he chased out the slave boys she entertained at night, even had some of them killed, and was soon in her bed.

Agamemnon, as I later learned, was back in port with his surviving ships and men within days of my own arrival here at Pylos. He, of course, possessed the lion's share of booty from Troy since his had been the greatest contribution of men and ships. His surviving vessels were loaded with Trojan gold and other precious objects as well as all the female slaves he was able to accommodate.'

'He must have expected quite a welcome,' put in Telemachus.

'And he had every right to,' responded Nestor. 'Clytemnestra was informed of Agamemnon's return well in advance by one of her slaves and long before he set foot in the palace his dear wife had Aegisthus hustled out of sight and forbade all mention of the man's name on pain of death. She pretended to be overwhelmed with joy at seeing Agamemnon and ordered a welcome banquet and a hot bath prepared. She plied him with wine and insisted her doubtless tired and begrimed husband went off to bathe and make himself presentable to the court in advance of the celebrations. I've no doubt that given half a chance he would have taken her to one side and enlightened her over Iphigenia's fate – but he was never given that chance.

It was while he bathed in an ante-room they struck. I learned this as well as much else from a servant who saw the whole thing and fled in fear of his own life for having witnessed it. As Agamemnon rose from his bath, Clytemnestra approached to offer him a robe inside which she'd concealed a dagger. Pretending to help him dress, she drove the blade into his heart. As he fell, Aegisthus appeared on the scene, flew at him with an axe and split open his skull.

Clytemnestra had three of her slaves clean up the mess but once news got out the palace was in uproar. She played off the king's death as a seizure followed by drowning and kept Aegisthus well in the background. Those three unfortunates who knew the truth she had executed as thieves before they could reveal anything. The servant who witnessed what had happened fled to Electra's chamber and told her everything. Electra concealed the man and soon afterward helped him escape to a vessel bound for Pylos whilst swearing she would one day avenge her father's death.'

'Utterly, utterly shameful,' muttered Broteas, quite unable to focus on the finger he circled in mid-air.

'And was Orestes not in danger as heir to Agamemnon?' asked Telemachus.

'He most certainly was. Aegisthus was afraid the boy would eventually plan his downfall and death, so Orestes, now into his teens had good reason to fear for his life. He saw what his own fate would be should Aegisthus become king - or even if he didn't. With Electra's help Orestes departed those grim walls early one morning to obtain refuge in some town or other on the mainland near Corinth. Electra ended up treated no better than a servant and simmered deep resentment. Clytemnestra tried to win her over by insisting Agamemnon's murder was justified by his sacrifice of Iphigenia but the girl would have none of it. She was adamant her father would never have allowed that to happen and suspected the truth of it, that he'd not been given an opportunity to explain himself.

Electra accused Aegisthus and her mother openly of murder and debauchery. Aegisthus would have had the girl killed as well, or done the deed himself, but even for Clytemnestra that was too much. Convinced she'd already lost one daughter she forbade him or any other man to go near Electra. Yes, young as she was, Electra had her male admirers and was regarded as a most desirable young woman, but for a time she was allowed only the company of her mother's female slaves. Even so she remained in real danger and had to spend much of her time confined to private rooms in the palace.'

'F-female s-slaves,' mumbled Broteas with a stupefied smile.

'One of the slaves took pity on her,' continued Nestor, 'and helped her get secret messages out to Orestes. Seven years after the murder of Agamemnon she rightly considered her brother would have reached full manhood and so she begged him repeatedly to come home and put matters right. Orestes returned in disguise to Mycenae to meet up with his sister. Electra got out at night and took him to the grave of their father where he made sacrifice and swore revenge upon Aegisthus and Clytemnestra. But as you know, it has always been a heinous crime before gods and men to slay one of your own kin and so he wavered. Well that didn't worry Electra any more than it had other members of their house - not after all she'd endured. Her desire to see an end to Aegisthus and to punish her mother had become a blood lust that demanded only one outcome so in the end she prevailed upon Orestes to do the deed.'

'Don't forget to tell him what Or-Orestes did,' mumbled a glazed-eyed Broteas, dribbling wine from his goblet onto his gown.

Nestor stared at him in exasperation. 'I haven't forgotten anything! I'm in the middle of telling him if only you'd pay attention.' Turning back to his guest the king resumed, 'Orestes entered the palace next day after dark. Somehow he got past the guards and made his way up to Clytemnestra's chamber with sword at hand, hoping to find Aegisthus asleep in her bed. Electra followed but kept in the shadows. Orestes encountered his mother outside her chamber but it evidently took her some moments to recognise who he was. When she did, she realised why he was there and begged him not to harm her. He might well have spared her life had she not backed toward her room. Orestes thought she was going to warn Aegisthus so he struck her through the heart and she died without a sound. He entered her chamber to find Aegisthus lounging on a couch naked with wine cup in hand. Before the man could get up Orestes drove the sword repeatedly into his body then severed his head as Aegisthus had severed the head of Orestes' grandfather, Atreus. The head was later fixed high above the palace gate where the rats and the dogs couldn't get at it though I dare say it kept the birds happy.

On that bloody note ended the torment for so long inflicted upon the House of Atreus at Mycenae, though the guilt of what he'd done seems to have affected Orestes' mind. He fled the city, imagining he was pursued by the Furies who do that sort of thing when you murder a parent - and in reality he may well have been. He later returned, of course, to assume the throne of his father.'

By now Broteas, the empty goblet cradled in his hands, eyelids closed but twitching, was beginning to snore.

'And what of Electra?' asked Telemachus.

'Oh, there's little else to tell of her. Once that particular episode of bloodletting had passed she married, had children and lived on in Mycenae. At last she was able to enjoy something akin to a normal life - whatever a normal life happened to be in that blighted town.'

'It seems Orestes made a pretty good job of it,' commented Telemachus. 'Listening to your account makes me all the more determined to sort out our problems on Ithaca. The sooner I get on with my journey the better.'

'I'm sure you'll succeed in the end, my boy,' smiled Nestor. 'Now let Pisistratus entertain and introduce you to others of our household and our court.'

101

He gestured to a slave boy to call his son and the smiling Pisistratus soon reappeared. 'Telemachus, if you're done with my grousing old father and his boozy captain you must join me for the remainder of the evening?'

'I'd be delighted,' replied Telemachus, rising from the seat. 'I'll be happy not to hear of any more violent deaths for a while.'

He spent time in conversation with Nestor's son and others of the court, eventually leaving the megaron with Pisistratus on a pretext of seeing more of the palace. When they were alone Pisistratus turned to him. 'I'm sure you have your choice of fine young women at Ithaca but there's no reason to abstain because you're with us. There are apartments set aside for bathing and the discreet entertainment of our guests should you wish to take advantage.'

Pisistratus noted the light of enthusiasm in Telemachus' eyes when his guest answered, 'Yes, my good friend, I'll not insult your hospitality by declining such an offer.'

'Then let's return to the hall – the ladies preening themselves there will welcome the attentions of a prince of Ithaca since it is their duty to please. One of them was sent as a gift to the court of Pylos; she's the daughter of a Libyan ruler – some desert lord with a quite unpronounceable name. My father couldn't pronounce her name either so he decided to call her Polyxena. You'll recognise her sitting at the nearer end of the gallery because she still retains the attire of her homeland.' As they stepped back into the great hall, Pisistratus added with a smile, 'She's one of the most beautiful women I ever encountered and no one would object if you were to make her acquaintance. She'll bathe and oil your travel-worn limbs - and much else. Oh, and er, don't expect too much by way of meaningful conversation. She's not been here long enough to learn Greek.'

Telemachus looked up at the girl indicated by his royal companion: her full, sensual lips and dark eyed beauty he found impossible to ignore. Noting his interest she smiled down at him and teased raven hair from her cheek.

'Make her acquaintance?' he breathed. 'Maybe I'll do that.'

***

The chamber to which the girl conducted him was pleasantly cool and illuminated by a trio of small, flame-fluttering pottery lamps placed upon a table close to a bed draped with coloured woollen blankets. Except for the bed, most of the room was in near darkness though an uncovered window in the thick stone wall revealed a star-scattered night sky. She reached to tug a cord, releasing the leather blind suspended from a wooden lintel above the window. Once both were naked, her slim curves had presented, even in those dim surroundings, a feast of sensuality to his eager eye. He at first complied with her gestured wishes and stood before her as she rested on a wooden stool to soothe his body and limbs with olive oil, massaging him with the greatest intimacy until he drew breath at her every touch. Telemachus understood little of what she said because of her strange accent though her words flowed as honeyed wine. But this would not curb the fulfilment of their desires as through his mind

103

drifted the thoughts, 'A beautiful woman is a beautiful woman no matter what her language.'

Polyxena sustained his passions late into the night as no other woman had. Her repertoire of arousal was beyond anything he had experienced with the more homespun girls of Ithaca, even with the palace courtesans who flaunted a degree of wit and sophistication as a part of their feminine assets. This girl had no pretensions, no false affectations. She was herself and needed to be nothing more. They had writhed together as serpents locked in a frenzied contest of pleasure, their laughter and their cries rising as panicked birds until both were exhausted. When her fingers caressed his cheek and she whispered, 'You good man. We sleep now?' Telemachus rolled onto his back, sighed aloud then muttered, 'Yes, I think we better had.'

***

The girl still lay by his side when he awoke, her breathing soft, her expression one of peaceful contentment. She slept even though morning sunlight spilled from around the edges of the blind. Her hair, black as polished obsidian, not contrived in the elaborate palace style, fell loose over her shoulders. With memories of their lovemaking vivid in his mind, Telemachus eased quietly from the bed where he stood in silence to gaze down at her.

Stepping into the ante-room where the window admitted full daylight, he marvelled at the luxuries of Nestor's palace: luxuries unavailable to anyone in Ithaca and, for all he knew, even at Mycenae. The walls of both rooms swarmed with colourful frescoes – here exotic animals and plants, there marine creatures depicted in fluid motion. There was fresh water piped in for bathing. Fresh water! No need for slaves to attend with pitcher and olive oil. All that was required was the twist of a small bronze lever and water issued from a pottery tube set into the wall as if sent from above by the gods themselves. It drained away via an aperture in the base of a polished stone bowl fitted into a wooden bench. Another, larger receptacle set into the floor, also supplied with water, served as a convenience for the most basic of bodily functions. How the water was delivered intrigued Telemachus and he asked himself if such a facility could ever be acquired by the House of Odysseus.

He sat by the open window, taking a bronze razor to his cheek before a silver mirror, peering through the window at tranquil countryside, across lush orchards, groves and vineyards basking in the newly risen sun. Birds were singing, ox carts cast long shadows and people were going about their varied tasks in field and meadow. For a time the troubles of his world seemed very far away.

When Telemachus returned to the bedchamber the girl was gone.

***

Another day saw him set out on horseback with spear and sword to hunt antelope in the company of Nestor's son and three of the royal companions. Telemachus had wanted to depart sooner but diplomacy overruled his eagerness to continue the journey. For the first time in his life Telemachus saw what traders and travellers in Ithaca had so often described: lions. The party drew to a halt to observe three of the big cats lounging idly some distance away amidst the bushes on a gentle rise – a male, two females and their prancing cubs. The male of this seemingly innocuous trio of adults regarded the onlookers then effected a languid yawn.

'They look placid enough,' said Telemachus, shielding his eyes so as to study the animals.

One of the men laughed as Pisistratus declared, 'Placid until they see you as game. They're best avoided when you're out alone.'

'The lions regard you not as a man,' added another of the companions, 'but as their next meal. Just as they would a wild deer.'

'I take it there are no lions on Ithaca,' remarked the third man.

'We have no lions on the islands,' responded Telemachus. 'No, on Ithaca we have predators of a two-legged kind!'

Chapter 4 - The Plotters

Amidst the babble of the great hall Pisistratus asked him, 'D'you look forward to leaving for Sparta in the morning.'

'That I do,' confirmed Telemachus, goblet in hand. 'I had little idea how I was to undertake this journey through a strange land but your father has organised armed men and chariots with ample provisions for the journey. He assures me his men know the best routes and if we travel unhindered from dawn until dusk it will take us no more than three days to reach Sparta.'

'True enough but some of it is rough going and we'll need to manhandle the chariots since we really cannot show our faces at Sparta without them. Ah, what I'm saying is that you'll have to suffer my company as well unless you've had enough of it here. The fate of Odysseus always fascinated me and a break from the affairs of Pylos will do me no harm. Then there's my chance to meet old Menelaus again: it's two years and more since my last visit.'

'Suffer your company?' grinned Telemachus as each grasped the arm of the other. 'I'll welcome your companionship as I'd welcome no other.'

'You may be glad of it for other reasons, Telemachus; it's not only the sea that breeds pirates. Brigands have been reported of late within a day's ride of Pylos when before there were none. The last thing you need is to have them take the gifts you are carrying for Menelaus even if they spared your life - which I doubt they would.'

Telemachus retired that evening to share pleasures once again with Polyxena. She stayed with him until morning but this time remained until both were bathed and dressed. He was soon to leave their chamber of sensual delights and looking into her dark eyes he now regretted his journey could not be set aside for longer. He placed a hand on her shoulder and whispered, 'Will you be here for me when I return?'

The girl smiled and kissed him. Her breath tingled his ear as she whispered, 'You good man. I like.' Her fingers lingered on his cheek then she drifted as a breeze from the room, smiling as she went. He was not sure how much of his words she had understood but the memory of her touch and of her smile, and so much else, would remain long after he had departed benign old Nestor's kingdom.

***

They set out eastward in the sweet-smelling, cool half-light of a still morning, well before the sun had risen to glorify the wide land. There were eight in the party. Telemachus and Pisistratus each occupied a creaking, two-horse light chariot that carried gifts for Menelaus from the houses of Ithaca and Pylos. Each had at hand his sword, a pair of spears lashed at an angle to the side of his chariot and a circular shield, this last slung from his shoulder. Behind each chariot was led a stocky packhorse carrying helmets, bows, quivers charged with arrows plus barley bread, goat's cheese and fruits in linen bags. Adding to the burden were two jars of pale wine and a cluster of small pottery cups.

Their escort of six men had been chosen by Pisistratus in person from amongst Pylos' fittest warriors. Mounted on horseback, these men, wore brightly plumed helmets of bronze or of interlocking boars' tusks and over their woollen tunics, body armour of boiled and elaborately engraved oxhide. Telemachus recalled his royal companion's earlier remarks about bandits though he and Pisistratus were yet to put on armour of their own.

During the first half of warm but breezy day they rode beneath cloud-streaked skies. The going was uneventful with no more than casual conversation passing back and forth but when the sun was past its zenith they halted for a light meal. While the rest drank, two of Pisistratus' men set off with bow, arrows and spear, returning in due course with a freshly killed wild pig. The flesh of this they deftly removed with sword and dagger for use that coming evening.

Conversation had ebbed when later, in the growing heat of the afternoon, they encountered more rugged country intersected by streams flowing roughly southward. Here they took the opportunity to bathe, refill their leather flasks and water the horses. The chariots were taken across with some difficulty. Though light, such conveyances were not well suited to this terrain but as Telemachus now understood, they were much preferred for the carriage of royal gifts and men of status.

Toward the end of that day, following the coastline of a great gulf with the sea lying to their right, they made their evening encampment. He watched fascinated as one of Pisistratus' men crouched to make their fire; not in the manner he'd witnessed on Noemon's vessel but here by the use of a small bow and stick, the latter twirled rapidly against a block of wood until friction generated the precious flame needed to ignite their tinder of dry pine needles. Gathered about spitting flames and acrid smoke they prepared their meal, always with one of their small party standing aside to keep watch.

Telemachus found camping beneath the stars a more pleasant experience than expected in a land so unfamiliar to him. One of the men had brought along an ivory flute and after they had accounted for skewered meat and vegetables he began to play the instrument with admirable skill. The men clapped and sang to his tuneful notes, their voices soaring upward on warm night air with the smoke and sparks of their campfire. He did not join the small chorus as such team spirit was unfamiliar to him but, much contented in this novel setting, Telemachus sensed the evening possessed a benign spirit and he wondered if Athena herself was watching over them. As when he sailed out to sea with Noemon and when he gazed across the fertile vistas of Nestor's kingdom, the troubles of Ithaca might exist in another world and another time.

But while Telemachus felt at peace with the night he sensed Pisistratus and his men were not altogether so. Their singing finished, their chatter subdued, none spoke of danger but each, by his expression and occasional glance into impenetrable darkness, betrayed an unmistakeable caution. Before they slept the fire would be extinguished and a man chosen by lot to remain alert and keep watch until daybreak.

***

Sunrise of the second day found them riding across rugged country beneath a cloudless sky with

110

the coast still to their right. A cluster of deserted huts closer to the water Pisistratus described as an intended lookout post recently ordered built by his father. By late morning, with the gulf falling behind, more thickly wooded land appeared with a range of higher hills looming in the heat haze some distance beyond.

'There are few routes ahead of us where a chariot may easily be taken,' explained Pisistratus. 'There is a settlement called Pharai where the coast turns south but we must go north of it. In several places we will need to dismount. Once over those hills, we descend toward the Eurotas river making its way to Sparta.' As they continued over rising land he warned, 'Camping in dense woodlands may not be in our best interests. We should keep to open ground whenever possible then we can see what is going on around us.'

'So there really may be brigands to deal with,' smiled Telemachus now the subject had been touched upon.

'Well, let's say we should keep our eyes open now we've ridden this far to the east.'

There was ample meat remaining in the panniers to roast above their fire and they still had fruit from Pylos' orchards when they rested a while to eat and drink under a harsh early afternoon sun. They were preparing to leave when one of Pisistratus' men, staring toward the nearby pine woods with a hand raised to shade his eyes, turned to their captain. 'We're being watched from among those trees.'

They looked in the direction indicated, peering hard, but Pisistratus shrugged, 'I see no one.'

111

'Nor do I,' added Telemachus.

'But he *was* there,' insisted their companion. 'I saw a dark-bearded man holding a spear. He was on foot and backed into the trees when he knew I'd spotted him. There will be more of them.'

'I don't doubt your words,' said Pisistratus. 'Your eyesight is keen – I know that. We proceed with caution.'

'Bandits, perhaps?' queried Telemachus.

'Quite possibly, my friend, and I don't care to have my father's guest fall into their hands.'

One of the men gestured ahead. 'I see the way we're heading but the land further to our right is more open and level. It will add little to our journey and it might offer some advantage if we take ourselves that way?'

'Yes, we should do that,' agreed Pisistratus. 'Let's get mounted and move off. Keep your eyes wide until we're sure there's no threat. We should be in those hills before sunset.'

To the snort of horses, the steady thump of hooves and creak of chariots they rode on, seldom speaking, ever watchful but seeing no one. When by late afternoon they had reached higher, more open ground with a busy stream chattering through a gully close by, Pisistratus announced, 'The sun's not quite low enough for us to make camp but here we have a good view and fresh water to hand.'

When they had dismounted, Telemachus said to him, 'I begin to see why making this journey alone might not have been in my best interest.'

'No, my friend,' smiled Pisistratus, placing shield and spear on the ground by his chariot. 'My father and I would have prevailed upon you more forcibly had you not accepted the offer of our company as you so wisely did. Two or three years ago it might not have mattered but –.'

The horses were being tethered when he was interrupted by one of the companions. 'See – toward the woods! There are riders heading this way!'

Shielding his eyes, Pisistratus looked aside. 'There are nine – no, ten of them,' he observed. 'They don't look to be traders - nor are they shepherds.'

For a time no one spoke then Pisistratus said, 'They're all armed though I doubt they're as well prepared as ourselves. And I see a number of them carry oblong shields.'

'Armed as footmen rather than as horsemen,' commented one man.

'Ready your bows, lads!' ordered Pisistratus, gathering up his bronze helmet. 'Let's see if a few well-aimed shots will persuade 'em stay clear of us. The position of the sun favours them no more than it does ourselves.'

Pisistratus' men were already squatting low to string powerful reflex bows while Telemachus and their captain each assisted the other in fitting on his cuirass before taking up his own spear.

As the mounted party drew closer Pisistratus said, 'They're as rough a crowd as ever I saw – brigands for sure.'

'With those shields they'll need to dismount if they intend to fight,' said one man, drawing an arrow from his quiver. 'They may be Greeks but they're not men of our own lands.'

The approaching band was now within earshot and it was clear that their bushy, beard-fringed heads were clad in helmets of boiled hide and boars' tusks.

Pisistratus stepped forward, plume swaying defiantly above his helmet, round shield at his side. 'Come no closer!' he called, raising high his spear. 'Tell me your purpose!'

There was no reply as the horsemen drew to a halt.

'They're dismounting,' observed Telemachus, joining him.

Watching the strangers group in front of their horses Pisistratus said, 'Once we've given 'em a taste of our arrows we could mount and head off along the stream until nightfall. Then we can seek out cover close to water. What d'you say, Telemachus? This is your enterprise. Do we retreat and look for safety further along or do we stand our ground here?'

The six companions stared at Telemachus, waiting for his reply.

'Retreat!' he exclaimed, turning to face them with a broad smile. 'No, better we settle matters here rather than have them close in on us after dark.'

'Exactly what I hoped you'd say,' declared Pisistratus, 'so let's get it over with!'

His companions, eager to draw their bows, voiced agreement.

The unwelcome party was moving forward with determined stride and it was clear that most were dressed in tunics of hide, some fitted with metal disks or plates. Sunlight glinted from spearheads with each man appearing to carry two. Those with shields held them at the ready. They hesitated only to break their silence with coarse verbal challenges and insults in Greek of an unfamiliar ring. A powerfully built, bear-like man with plaited beard and black bush hair, evidently their leader, strode boldly ahead of his companions then stopped to call out, 'Leave your goods and your pack horses behind and we'll give you no trouble!'

'Come and take them!' responded Pisistratus. 'We're waiting!' He turned to Telemachus, 'They're hoping we'll run with our tails between our legs.'

Laughter and further insults issued from amongst the brigands. Then darker threats. Pisistratus' companions remained still and silent. The opposing group broke into boastful chatter and, advancing confidently once more, appeared to lower their defences.

On his command Pisistratus' six men suddenly drew their bows and let fly a swarm of arrows to speed through the air with serpent hiss. The brigands hesitated to stoop behind the shields of those who had them and it was into those shields most of the arrows harmlessly embedded themselves. One of their company was not quick enough. A shaft pierced his head above the right eye. He let out no sound but spun, arms swinging wildly, and crashed to the ground. None of his companions spared the stricken man glance. With wild shouts the brash, disorderly gang lurched forward, only hesitating to hurl a first spear with raucous cry before continuing on. And although that act lightened their burden and speeded their lumbering advance a little, their first volley of spears achieved nothing – some falling short, all denied flesh and blood by the hard earth.

Telemachus and Pisistratus held back, the latter warning, 'It's the spear you don't see coming that'll kill you! If it's heading your way it's no more than a speck in the sky!'

Telemachus recalled the tale of Orestes at Mycenae and through his mind passed the words, 'He first killed because there was no other way. Now I will equal him and more.' Then breathing, 'Athena be with us,' he readied his spear.

Others of the enemy pushed closer, still encumbered by the shields behind which most of them stooped, some emerging only to hurl a second spear. Pisistratus' men, more agile with their lighter arms, spread apart to avoid the missiles. The spears hissed by, most gouging earth or clashing against rock, their lethal purpose thwarted. One glanced from the shield of a man of Telemachus' company, spinning him to the ground with a cry though he was soon clambering back to his feet unhurt. With bows set aside and spears at the ready, Pisistratus' companions stepped forward as one to raise and hurl their shafts at close range.

Two more spears flashed by as the howling brigands lumbered closer. But they had not bargained for the skill and determination of Pisistratus and his cooler-headed men. One of the enemy was struck full in the chest, his sword spinning to the ground as, with a blood-rattled shriek he staggered, fell, then sank to the ground. With a cry Pisistratus hurled his own weapon then with barely a heartbeat passing, Telemachus cast his. Pisistratus' spear found its mark in the wooden shield of the closest man, piercing it and the wearer's corselet to penetrate deep. Its victim fell backward to the ground, his expression one of startled disbelief as, thrusting away the shield that all but covered his torso, the bloodied weapon was wrenched from him. His men hesitated momentarily as he writhed, kicked and choked in death agony. Telemachus' shaft also struck home, not piercing a man's shield far enough to disable its owner but rendering it useless to him. The brigands' leader charged on, an image of fearsome, unstoppable wrath, bellowing as an enraged bull with his grim band, their eyes glaring murderous intent, pressing close behind. Recognising Pisistratus as captain the brigand hesitated to bawl aloud, 'I'll cut off yer balls then I'll make you eat 'em!'

Brothers in arms, Pisistratus and Telemachus strode forward. Further shouts cleaved the air on both sides as the combatants, blades flashing, fell upon one another. Sword clashed with shield and sword with sword in the chaos of a mêlée frowned upon by the lowering sun. Pisistratus struck his man, slashing deep into his sword arm, severing it to the bone, before running the blade through his adversary's poorly protected side.

Thrown off balance by a fierce strike against his shield, Telemachus recovered quickly enough to avoid a second blow. He leapt aside then sprang forward plunging his blade beneath the man's exposed jaw as easily as he would one of the straw effigies upon which he had for long practised, feeling a hot spatter of blood as the other, blurting gore, let fall his weapon and toppled aside.

Telemachus was possessed by a cold, remorseless urge to dispatch any man who might confront him.

The brigands' leader hurled his shield with a roar at one of Pisistratus' companions, causing him to stagger back then, eyes ablaze he hacked down his opponent, cleaving the man's helmet with a savage blow of his sword. His face a mask of grim triumph he thrust aside friend and foe to close upon Pisistratus who, engaged blade to blade with another of the enemy, was unaware of his approach. He would have struck Nestor's son down from behind but Telemachus darted forward to deflect the swing with his small shield, in the same instant driving his blade hard through the oxhide cuirass to penetrate deep between the man's ribs. Sword again raised high but with his right arm blocked by the shield, the big man tottered with a wide-mouthed cry, his expression one of stark surprise. Face to face, he glared at Telemachus, hair-framed lips quivering as if to demand a reason for his being pierced through. In that glaring instant Telemachus saw beneath the man's hair. The ears were gone. The mutilated head bore livid, inflamed gashes where the ears had been brutally sliced away; a punishment for some crime committed against the community of which he was once a part. Eyes fixed upon his, Telemachus, using the shield as a lever, wrenched the blade drizzling red from his opponent's body then with ruthless efficiency plunged it in again. Letting fall his sword the brigand glanced down as Telemachus withdrew the blade a second time. He staggered back, spluttering course laughter then thudded to the ground as an axe-cleaved beast, jaws agape, eyes fluttering, his head rocking from side to side until death imposed a final stillness.

Seeing their leader struck down, the brigands lost heart, broke off and turned away. Those still clutching shields threw them aside as they scurried in panic toward their horses. One was not so agile as his fellows and paid the price. His head was all but severed from his body by a flashing sword as he blundered by one of Pisistratus' vengeful men. Even as the fallen man twitched and jetted hot blood, Pisistratus' gore-spattered companions, fired with victory, were eager to dash in pursuit and complete the business forced upon them - but their captain called aloud, 'No – stay as you are!'

Telemachus had not considered pursuit. Brief as the encounter had been in this, his first experience of true combat, it was obvious to him that the men of Pylos possessed greater skill in arms than did the marauders. The latter, after all, would expect to harass only merchants and traders, not seasoned warriors. Five of the enemy lay sprawled and twisted grotesquely in death and another, having fallen some way behind the fleeing survivors, was obviously wounded. One of Pisistratus' companions was also lost; his skull split by a sword blow from the man Telemachus had in turn brought down.

Drawing a sleeve across his brow to mop the sweat, Odysseus' son gazed in silence at the slain, his breathing calm, his thoughts numbed, his shadow cast across bloodied ground by the lurid glare of a soon to vanish sun. The bandits' leader, though a grounded corpse, remained one of fearsome aspect, eyes staring in blind defiance at a placid sky. A hand fell to Telemachus' shoulder and there was Pisistratus at his side. 'By the gods you accounted for yourself well enough. You settled for their leader and you saved my skin. And there was I thinking you a novice!'

They stood together, staunch companions, their lengthening shadows merged as one.

Telemachus took a deep breath but there was no elation in his reply. 'I practised hard in the use of arms and it seemed little more than a game. I never before killed a man - now I have ended the lives of two. I felt no more anger in doing it than I did in training. Strange, don't you think?'

'Strange - I think not!' exclaimed Pisistratus, grasping his arm. 'No, by Zeus, you made a damn good a job of it. We'll strip their dead of whatever is worth taking and collect up our spears and arrows. Anything of real value must be yours.'

'And what of our own man who lies there?' asked Telemachus as the remaining five of their companions gathered around. 'We surely cannot leave him as he is.'

'We've no means of burying poor Epios in this rocky ground,' breathed Pisistratus, eyeing their comrade who lay sprawled face down on blood-soaked earth. 'He was a good man. We'll collect brushwood and make a pyre for him. We'll burn the brigands' arms and armour on it as well since they'd be little more than a burden to us. Their bodies can stay as food for the crows and whatever creatures pass this way. We can find a place down by the stream to wash ourselves and our weapons - yes, and make camp before the daylight is altogether gone. I doubt those oafs will care to bother anyone for a long time. And you, my good friend,' he continued, grasping Telemachus' arm, 'I'll not forget what you did today. When my father hears of it he will reward you well and since you never knew your own father he will accept you as a son of his own and as my true brother. I give you my word on that.'

Telemachus placed a hand upon Pisistratus' shoulder. 'It was your presence and that of your men preserved *my* life. As for rewards – no, to be accepted into the House of Nestor as your brother is the only reward I would wish to accept.'

The sun had vanished below the horizon when they set themselves to gathering up spears and arrows. Once more gazing upon the pallid dead, Telemachus pondered over what had happened and under his breath declared, 'Well I'm sure mother would approve.'

***

Later that same evening in the great hall of Odysseus' palace, Phemios played his lyre though his voice was silent. The chamber was less noisy than usual after the suitors had indulged their unwelcome round of feasting. Close to the steps beneath the now unoccupied gallery sprawled Iros the fool, as so often at this point in the proceedings, quite senseless. A number of men had strolled outside because the air within the dining hall was oppressively humid – a situation worsened by acrid smoke from the cooking fires that, reluctant to rise, lingered in swirling eddies above the tables. Several men had made their choice of slave girl or courtesan and had retired elsewhere to take their pleasures. Four had gathered away from those remaining in the hall to engage in subdued conversation. They ceased talking only for the time it took a flagon-clutching slave, a boy who dared not look any of them in the eye, to refill their goblets. The boy hoped it would be the last of his many calls as two of the men, sated with wine, were sullen and as he well knew, liable to vent their anger upon the likes of him.

'If I'm not mistaken,' said Antinous, slowly, eyes fixed upon a piece of mutton that teetered on the point of his knife blade, 'that – that damned son of hers should be on his way to Sparta by now unless he's already there. Without him skulking in the shadows his precious mother will find it difficult to maintain her authority over the palace for much longer.'

'Very true,' agreed soft-spoken, well-groomed and not so well imbibed Amphion, splaying out bejewelled fingers as focus of his thoughtful gaze. 'As you say, a woman alone should not occupy such a position. On the other hand the boy may have given up his quest. He may return to Ithaca sooner than you expect – perhaps tomorrow. You cannot rule that out – if, of course, he ever left. He could be keeping out of sight, waiting to see what happens, don't you think? Maybe he's hiding somewhere in the palace. Has anyone considered that possibility?'

Inserting the meat into his mouth Antinous lowered the knife and chewing slowly, regarded the effeminate hand. He wondered if its owner would know what to do with her should Penelope single him out as her would-be husband no matter how remote a possibility that might be. He raised the knife then stabbed it hard into the tabletop causing the startled Amphion to jerk back his hand.

'Yes,' growled Leiocritius with slurred voice emerging through his thick beard, 'some of us did consider it but I'll wager the bugger did leave Ithaca as I said all along 'e would. Still, 'e just might show up sooner than we think. Yes, 'e just might. We need people on the lookout to make sure 'e doesn't reach the palace. I'll 'ave my men cut him down if we catch 'im outside the city wall then it'll be over and done with.'

'Oh, yes – a lookout,' agreed pot-bellied Eudorus in a high voice. He, like Amphion, appeared less under the influence of wine. 'That's a good idea all right.' The man's eyes glinted as two glass beads pressed into a dough of blemished flesh. Leiocritius, easing further back to avoid the other man's breath, regarded him with silent but ill-disguised contempt.

'It's already dealt with,' remarked Antinous. He peered up then lifted the goblet unsteadily to his lips as if there was nothing more to be said on the matter.

'What is?' slurred Leiocritius, stirring upright in his seat. 'What's already dealt with?

'I already have men keeping watch,' replied Antinous. 'We all know what needs to be done should our dear prince return, so I'm ready to do it. Simple enough.' His dismissive manner hinted that the question should never have been asked.

'Oh, we've men keeping watch 'ave we!' rumbled Leiocritius, leaning forward with an angry thump of his goblet on the bench, this time causing Eudorus to jerk back. 'Then some of us, including me, yes me, should 'ave been informed of it. We're in this together – or maybe you'd forgotten!'

Antinous regarded him with a humourless smile. 'Of course we are my friend, on the face of it. But let's be realistic; many of the men who come here have long since abandoned the idea of marriage to Odysseus' wife even if they entertained it in the first place; and a lot of 'em never did.' Turning to Amphion and Eudorus he added, pointedly, 'Am I right?'

Eudorus looked from one to the other but said nothing. Amphion shrugged with a whimsical, 'Mmm - perhaps you are. I've no real interest in the woman.'

Eudorus nodded his complaisance as, glancing at Amphion, Leiocritius muttered under his breath, 'Nor in any woman as I've 'eard.'

'Of course I'm right,' Antinous breathed. And whilst his expression barely concealed the contempt he harboured for Eudorus and Amphion, to neither of them could he ever ascribe the threat Leiocritius posed. 'It comes down to this,' Antinous continued in matter of fact manner, 'regardless of how well-off he was, would any man -?'

His words were interrupted by a shriek followed by a howl of laughter from across the hall as two men, their discretion flushed away by a surfeit of wine, had seized a dark-haired slave girl and were attempting to bend her over their bench whilst wrenching her long dress above her thighs.

'You assume too much,' glowered Leiocritius, ignoring the commotion. 'I've as big a stake in this as anyone, including you and our pal Eurymachus -

and I intend to win both the woman and that fucking throne she's been resting 'er pretty arse on!'

'How I admire your confidence,' said Antinous, tapping his knife blade lightly on the bench, 'but there's no need at present to disagree over who keeps watch is there? That's the way I look at it.'

'Then you'd better look a bit 'arder,' Leiocritius growled. 'I want to know exactly what's goin' on. I want to know what those men of yours are up to or I call over men of my own!'

Shrieking laughter and the rapid banging of goblets on benches echoed across the hall as Antinous, leaning closer to Leiocritius, smiled coldly. 'That, my friend, is not a good idea. If you call out men of your own to do the same job it could result in a confrontation - or worse.' He relaxed, lifted his goblet and continued, 'Let's discuss this some place well away from here and I'm sure we'll reach an understanding. Better still, I'll show you exactly what I have prepared should that son of hers return. I think you'll not disapprove.'

'Yes, let's do that,' rumbled Leiocritius, with too little thought for caution. 'When and where?'

'Join me tomorrow evening by the main gate before we're due in here. I'll be alone and,' he glanced aside at Amphion and Eudorus whose attention remained wholly diverted by the drunken antics of those milling about the now naked slave girl, 'and, my friend, my - our intentions may be compromised should anyone else hear of this.'

***

The sun had vanished below the hills and the first stars glinted in a deepening sky when Leiocritius, attired in his embroidered robe of court,

125

approached the monumental stone gate leading from the market square. With no slave to light his way he passed beneath, hardly aware of those rejected souls who slept fitfully in deeper shadows with their mangy dogs huddled beside them. Outside the gate he came upon Antinous leaning casually against the wall. Dressed in plain, belted tunic, Antinous appeared unarmed. But the sword and the corselet of boiled hide Leiocritius had concealed beneath his robe expressed deep mistrust of someone he secretly hated no less than he in turn was despised by Antinous.

'I take it there'll be just the two of us,' said Leiocritius. 'If you've other men, I'll call on some of my own.'

'I've a couple of menials from outside Ithaca to keep an eye on approaching vessels – nothing more. They're little better than vagrants.'

'A couple of menials,' repeated Leiocritius. He hesitated, thinking however, that should trickery be afoot then he, Leiocritius, a big and powerful man, would be more than a match for Antinous and those he described as menials would doubtless flee. There was no one to overhear their brief conversation, no one to witness Leiocritius disappear with Antinous into a night illuminated only by a half moon. They carried on, treading a path negotiable during darkness only by those familiar with the route.

'Why've I seen none of these men of yours in the town?' asked Leiocritius, following two steps behind. Beneath the gown his hand rested firmly upon the sword hilt. He now regretted agreeing to meet Antinous yet to retreat now would diminish his credibility in the other man's eyes.

126

'Because,' came the reply, 'I want none of them getting drunk in the taverns and talking out of place. Once you see what I'm doing there'll be no further disagreement between us; of that I'm sure.'

They said little more but carried on along the winding path that led down to the sea. By tumbled rocks at one side of the small, sandy cove a spark-spitting brushwood fire danced in the night. Three men stood behind the flames. 'We're here!' announced Antinous as he and Leiocritius approached the group.

Firelight revealed a lean and bedraggled, wild-eyed pair with long, swept-back hair; not the sort of men Leiocritius would have expected Antinous, a noble like himself, to depend upon for so clandestine an enterprise. Such men as these were fit for only the basest of tasks; how could anyone trust in their discretion? One of them stepped around the fire, raising a hand, calling out gruffly, 'Lord Antinous!' The other remained where he was.

Leiocritius gripped the sword hilt tightly, hesitating several paces from Antinous who stood to converse briefly with the man. The ensuing silence was accented by the crack of burning wood and by water gurgling amidst the rocks. Leiocritius eyed Antinous and the two figures with intensifying suspicion yet he could see no weapon about them. 'Well?' he asked as Antinous stepped back to stand close at his right side.

'Those men,' replied Antinous, 'will make short work of Telemachus if and when the dear boy returns. It's the sort of thing they're good at – they and their kind.'

'Is it now,' growled Leiocritius. 'Well 'e's not going to land back on Ithaca alone is 'e, and not right 'ere. How are these damned mongrels going to take on -?'

'Oh, it'll work out in the end,' responded Antinous, slipping the dagger unseen from within his left sleeve. With startling suddenness he grabbed Leiocritius' right arm with his left hand, swung around and struck hard at the man's stomach only to find the point of his blade checked by the hidden corselet before penetrating far enough. As both sprang apart, Antinous' two men seized weapons from where they had lain concealed behind a rock close to the fire.

Leiocritius wrenched the sword from its scabbard within his gown and, crouching, raised it in readiness. With grim determination he faced Antinous but his two men moved no closer. 'So you and these sheep fuckers 'ave it all worked out do you!' he roared. 'We'll see about that!'

Braced to engage with his opponent, Leiocritius was confident that he would cut Antinous down and the others would run for their lives. Closing upon Antinous, who backed toward his men, he was unaware of two more figures emerging at his rear, silent spectres from the night, swords at the ready. Too late Leiocritius heard the sigh of bare feet on soft sand. He twisted around as the first man drove sharp bronze hard through the corselet beneath his ribs whilst the second thrust his blade in from the other side. The pair, of similar appearance to the other two, wrenched out their weapons and stepped aside as Leiocritius staggered, his howls of agony rising on the night air. Antinous stepped calmly over to complete this bloody violence, plunging his dagger beneath the man's thick beard and deep into his throat. Letting fall his sword Leiocritius, eyes rolling wildly, reached out to grasp Antinous, his death rattle muted by gore welling copiously from his mouth. He reeled toward the lurid glow of the fire, swung about, arms flailing then pitched to the ground with a muffled thud. They watched their victim heave, quiver, then become still.

Antinous strode to the water's edge where he stooped to rinse the murdered man's blood from his hands and his blade. Maintaining an air of calm, he returned to the fire where his four hirelings waited in silence. There he observed the flesh of one of Leiocritius' arms blistering where it had fallen against glowing wood. He stooped over the bloody corpse, pulling the arm away from the fire, tugging gold and silver rings firstly from the fingers of this hand then from the other. These valuables he slipped into a small pouch at his belt.

Firelight reflected in his eyes as he addressed his accomplices in a tone that suggested nothing out of the ordinary had occurred. 'There's plenty of brushwood around here. Build the fire high. Burn the body and all the clothing – and I do mean *all*. It will require some time but there are no fishermen out tonight and your fire won't be visible from the town. When that's done, take whatever remains and throw it into the sea. You'll want to keep his sword but it must not be seen again on Ithaca. I want to see no trace of this man by morning, or of the fire that consumed him. D'you understand – no trace at all! At first light tomorrow you'll return to the mainland until I send for you again.' With that he handed them a small leather purse containing silver, then stepped away into darkness.

***

The days following their encounter with the brigands offered Telemachus and his companions little challenge other than the hills themselves, where too often their chariots proved more a burden than an asset. They netted fish from the streams and acquired wild boar through the skills of Pisistratus' excellent archers. Having negotiated a difficult pass through the Taygetus Mountains they rode over rocky ground to the snort of the horses and rattle of chariots, the latter often needing to be manhandled until they reached the banks of the Eurotas on its southerly course toward Sparta.

That last evening before reaching Sparta saw them encamped by the river. The fire hissed, spat and cracked in the warm breeze of a calm night as Pisistratus turned skewers of hare meat over the flames. Telemachus sat facing him whilst their companions busied themselves tending the horses, after which they would roast their own food. It was at this point Pisistratus remarked upon the subject of the Spartan court. 'I take it you've a few tales regarding Menelaus' wife.'

'Tales of her live in the very air we breathe,' replied Telemachus, 'but the truth behind them is just as intangible as far as I'm concerned. Will we see her; will we meet the famous, or is it infamous, Helen of Troy?'

'Oh, I'm sure we will. As his queen she occupies her place at the king's court and enjoys considerably more freedom than most women regardless of much ill-informed gossip.'

130

'Menelaus must be a very forgiving man if all we hear is true.'

'The closer you get to them,' informed Pisistratus, 'the less certain her tale becomes – or so it seems to me. I dare say you'll form your own opinions but you should avoid mention of Troy. Better if you wait until the subject is offered.' He placed carved meat on a bed of leaves then continued, 'Tomorrow we'll pass the sanctuary of Athena in her guise as Lady of the Road. I'm informed your family has strong associations with Sparta and with this shrine.'

'Yes, my mother occasionally mentioned it. I recall her telling how my father founded and helped build the sanctuary and that it was in Sparta where she actually met him. It seems he entered a cross-country foot race with the rest of her suitors, as custom demanded, to determine who was the fittest man. Tyndareus, who was king at the time made sure my father was declared winner because of important advice he offered him. He and my mother were married in Sparta by Tyndareus himself in spite of objections from the rest of her suitors. They claimed Tyndareus had told him of a short cut through the woods and he'd accepted this as a sure way of winning. My mother always insisted it was quite in order because she wanted my father to win. I have no idea how much of her story is true but I gather from it they were already lovers.' This was a fleeting picture of Odysseus' youth but it had always amused Telemachus. It had endowed the vague image he had of his father, a warrior king, with a touch of humanity.

'I believe what Lady Penelope told you is largely true,' said Pisistratus, poking more wood into the fire. 'But did she tell you also what this important advice of your father's was?'

'I've no knowledge of that,' answered Telemachus. 'Perhaps she herself was unaware of it but if you're able to enlighten me then I can think of no better time to hear it now we're so close to Sparta.'

'Very well, you sat through my old man's account of Agamemnon's house of misfortunes so this briefer tale shouldn't weigh too heavily on your patience. Tyndareus was the father of Helen, in spite of ridiculous claims by the priestesses that she was a daughter of Zeus. Tyndareus also had two sons but because they died before reaching maturity he adopted and named Menelaus as his successor to the throne of Sparta. Menelaus' own father had been killed in battle when the boy was only twelve. Tyndareus admired the young man's unquestioning loyalty and prowess in times of conflict even though he was something of a tearaway and unpredictable at times. He wanted Menelaus to marry Helen so as to secure the continuation of his house and by all accounts Menelaus was eager to do that since the girl was regarded by everyone who saw her as a remarkable beauty. Even as a child of twelve she was at one point sought after by no less than Theseus, that same great hero of Athens. And true or not, Theseus was accused of trying to abduct her while visiting Sparta after the death of his own wife, Phaedra.

At fifteen years old Helen was of marriageable age and there were suitors arriving at the court of

Sparta from many parts of Greece. That made things difficult for Tyndareus when you consider the lure of such a woman is hardly less than that of conquest and wealth. You can imagine what it must have been costing him to entertain them no matter how many gifts they handed over.'

'I don't need to imagine it,' muttered Telemachus, 'except at Ithaca we don't get the gifts.'

'No, of course you don't,' agreed Pisistratus. 'And at least he only had them for a month – maybe less. Anyway, it was your crafty old father who solved the problem. He suggested Tyndareus have the suitors swear an oath to protect from harm whichever of them was chosen to marry his daughter.'

'And I take it they all agreed,' said Telemachus, savouring the meat. 'But why did they?'

'They had to agree or risk being disqualified. Once that was done Tyndareus nominated Odysseus to draw the chosen name from a jar of pottery shards. Naturally, it was Menelaus.'

'Oh, naturally,' grinned Telemachus. 'I take it Menelaus' name was on all of those shards. And the girl - was she happy about it?'

'That,' replied Pisistratus, 'was and still is a matter of speculation. Having the attentions of so many men made her restless. It was suggested from the beginning that whoever Helen married she would consider it ought to have been someone else – even if it was someone else! And she soon had acquired a reputation for giving her favours to anyone who took her fancy.'

'Was my father also attracted to her?' asked Telemachus.

'Hmm, I'm not sure. If he was it never gave rise to any rumours but the suitors' interest in her is said to have persisted long after she was married and the number of slaves she had in attendance, all fit young men, caused no end of whispering. After Tyndareus' death and Menelaus' succession the Trojans sent one of King Priam's sons, Paris, as envoy to Sparta. His business with Menelaus was to sort out growing disputes over trade and taxes imposed upon our shipping by the Trojans, but he and Helen began meeting in secret when Menelaus was away hunting and more rumours began to circulate. It's said Paris was quite bewitched by her and contrived to outstay his allocated time.'

'But Menelaus must have had some idea of what was going on,' said Telemachus.

'You'd think so, wouldn't you,' smiled Pisistratus, 'but after entertaining the Trojan and his three companions handsomely for several days he surprised people outside his immediate circle by sailing off to Crete early one morning to attend, or so it was said, his grandfather's funeral. There was also talk of a Cretan princess and some kind of alliance on offer. He left with as little fuss as he might for a routine day or two's hunting. No doubt he looked forward to being entertained amidst the luxuries of Knossos and the pleasures of its women.'

'Members of the Spartan court must have suspected what might happen,' observed Telemachus.

'They did indeed and the king's ship had barely put to sea before the court discussed openly what his wife and the Trojan had been up to. Gossip spilled into the town that same morning and in the afternoon an armed mob showed up at the palace threatening to murder Paris if he didn't quit Sparta. He fled in secret the very evening of the day Menelaus departed – taking Helen with him.'

'They must have wondered at how easily Menelaus was fooled,' said Telemachus.

'Hm, I don't think he was to begin with. He'd always known what she was like and maybe expected her liaison with Paris would fizzle out like all her other affairs if he ignored it. He can't have expected her to run off with the Trojan but if the man had still been there when he returned from Crete Menelaus would have kicked him out.'

'Yet after the defeat of Troy, Menelaus took Helen back.'

'He did,' replied Pisistratus, reaching for his wine flask. 'Another man might have had her flogged, sold into slavery or worse, but though a formidable leader in times of conflict, he still seemed to be in her power. With Paris dead and gone he chose to accept it when she insisted she'd been led astray by the gods in allowing herself to be kidnapped. Well maybe he just wanted an easy way out.'

'The gods,' sighed Telemachus, looking up at the sweep of stars. 'Yes, people can excuse whatever they like by ascribing their actions to the gods. They serve us as well in folly as they do in wisdom, no matter to what depths of vileness men sink.'

135

'Wise words my young friend,' smiled Pisistratus. 'Best not to let Sparta's priestesses hear you say that - though I am inclined to agree.'

'Then,' said Telemachus, 'I'll try to avoid first mention of the gods as well as Troy.'

'You'll probably hear other tales from Menelaus. And I'll say now; Sparta may not be blessed with the light and colour of Pylos but I know for a fact their banquets can be quite as sumptuous and the women of the court just as accommodating – well, almost. And there's good hunting to be had there so we'll see who can bag the first game: I wager I'll beat you to it.'

'We'll see about that!' grinned Telemachus. 'I'm no novice when it comes to the hunt so you'd better not wager anything of value in case you lose – or in case *I* lose since I have little of value with me other than the gifts for Menelaus.'

It was time to rest but Telemachus' thoughts returned to Pylos and to the girl, Polyxena. Images of her beauty, memories of her voice and her kisses stirred him deeply until, eventually, sleep prevailed.

***

The night breeze sighed and in the sighs were voices. Disembodied whispers hovering in the darkness. They called his name. Telemachus opened his eyes, reached for his sword, pushed aside the sheepskin cover and peered into the cool night. The fire still smouldered. He watched its vapours spiral steadily upward but there was only silence. His companions were asleep, except for one man who he vaguely glimpsed sitting on guard by the chariots and horses. Telemachus closed his eyes and would have drifted back into slumber but the voices

136

returned, clearer than before. Again they spoke his name. He remained still, though beneath the sheepskin his hand returned to the sword.

Now a single voice. 'Telemachus, hear me.'

'Do I know that voice?' he murmured, propped on one elbow. 'No how could I - but who -?'

Soft laughter and the voice was now closer. 'Telemachus, hear what I say.'

'Who speaks to me?' Telemachus found himself surrounded by a night profoundly altered. A night when secret portals open and the spirits are abroad. He peered again into darkness; a darkness so profound his companions, the chariots and horses were no longer to be seen and the stars themselves were gone from the sky. The fire had become a flame upon an altar within the deep shadows of a temple sanctuary.

'Who are you?' he breathed, 'What d'you want of me?'

Once more it spoke his name but the voice was moving closer, reaching to him, the whisper of a woman – clear and beguiling.

'But who – who are -?' Telemachus sat upright, his gaze fixed upon the fire that blazed afresh as though replenished with dry straw. Smoke from the fire thickened. It swirled in the air, growing ever paler and in its vortices a face began to form. A face! And it was becoming clearer! The spectral figure of a woman materialised, rising, shimmering. It – she resolved, ever more real and there was nothing else but the image to dominate his vision. On her head rested the gleaming helmet of a warrior. In her right hand a spear was raised high and at its bronze tip flared and danced silent lightning. She grew in stature, large as life, radiant, and her gaze, crystal sharp, was fixed upon Telemachus until at last he knew. The figure reached a hand toward him. Again her voice, and her words swirled within his mind. 'Telemachus, now you are close to Sparta you must sacrifice at the shrine built by your father. Make an offering on your way to the city of Menelaus and again after you leave to begin your journey home. Remember to do this.'

'Y-yes, I will do it,' he murmured hoarsely.

The apparition hovered a while longer, eyes still upon him. It grew larger, becoming diffused, then began to dissipate until once again there was only languid smoke from a dying fire. Telemachus lay back, eyes closed, the name of the goddess uttered by contented lips.

The night was in retreat and the sky brightening. Pisistratus and four of his companions were readying themselves in cool morning air for the day ahead. The fifth man, who had remained on guard through the night, was busy remaking the fire for their morning meal. He looked up and, seeing Telemachus awake, said with a grin, 'You were dreaming, young sir. You were restless for a while. I heard you talking in your sleep but I understood not a word of it. Was it a good dream you had?'

'Yes,' replied Telemachus, rubbing a hand across a stubbled cheek then stretching limbs that ached from the chill of night and the hardness of earth. 'It was a very good dream. As for being restless - yes, perhaps I was.'

'And I saw a white owl,' the man continued, gesturing upwards. 'I watched it circle above for a while then disappear into darkness. Maybe that was a good omen.'

Telemachus glanced up at the clear blue sky but said nothing.

Pisistratus, fixing his sword at his belt, remarked, 'I dreamt we shot wildfowl by the river for our breakfast but now I'm awake and up I see that we still have to do it.'

'Yes,' said Telemachus, 'and I'll ask our archers to bring down one more bird than we need – one I must offer at the shrine of Athena.'

***

'Master,' croaked the voice of one who hardly dared utter the word. It came from beyond the heavy drapes that closed off Antinous' private chamber. The comfortably furnished room he occupied belonged to a supporter of his cause; a merchant of Ithaca town. Light spilled from the sides of the leather window blind to confirm the sun had already risen.

Antinous slipped from beneath the woollen blanket and sat up, a hand instinctively fallen upon the sword that rested by his bed. The young girl of the tavern who lay naked at his side opened her eyes but remained still. Having recognised the voice from beyond the room, Antinous laid aside the sword, pulled on his gown and stepped over to drag aside the curtain. 'What d'you have to tell me?' he demanded.

'Master,' repeated the youth, a curly-haired, sinewy figure; a slave of Antinous' house who backed away to stoop in subservience, hands clasped at his chest, 'you ordered us to watch who came and went from the palace.'

Antinous' face clouded with impatience. 'I *know* what I ordered, dammit! What have you seen?

'T-two men of Lady Penelope's household,' replied the youth. 'They departed at first light. They carried with them, I think, food and water. We followed them to the harbour. We watched as the sky lightened. We saw them go on board a fishing boat and we watched them sail south. The vessel sailed on until it could no longer be seen.'

'Just the two of them you say?'

'Only two, master, I swear.'

'Then get back down there,' responded Antinous, 'and one of you report immediately to me if they return during the day.'

Flinging back the curtain, Antinous stepped back to the bed where the girl waited. She pushed bedraggled hair from her eyes, watching him with apprehension as he dragged the blanket roughly from her and ordered, 'Get dressed and get out!'

***

Within a back street tavern below the citadel and palace of Ithaca three men sat huddled in subdued conversation. An enclave of secrecy. Their only source of light in the small, austere room, and it was all they desired, was a single pottery lamp whose swaying flame cast their shadows large upon roughly plastered walls. Between them on the pitted wooden table rested plain pottery goblets and a crudely fashioned pitcher containing rough wine. Noise from the alleyway beyond was muffled by an oxhide curtain spread across the small window. Occasional shouting and laughter drifted by from the main room together with the odour of roasting meat.

'And that's what I know so far,' breathed Antinous, lifting his drink. 'Those men reported by my slave this morning have not returned. I suspect they won't be seen on Ithaca for a good many days.'

'And what might we conclude from this?' asked Amphion. His goblet remained full and untouched by his manicured fingers. The wine was much inferior in quality to that of his own estate or to that of Odysseus though Eurymachus seemed not to have noticed. Nor was the mean tavern with its disagreeable odours to Amphion's liking in spite of the privacy he imagined their venue offered.

'What *might* we conclude?' mocked Eurymachus with a dismissive flutter of his hand. 'What the fuck d'you think we conclude? She's sent the pair of 'em off to find her pretty boy. It'll be to give 'im news of what's going on here.'

'Exactly,' said Antinous. 'We must assume they'll succeed and that our beloved prince will return with his crew, and possibly with men from Pylos to back him up. I'm assured Nestor was a close pal of Odysseus in the old days. On the other hand they may never make it back to the harbour. It wouldn't surprise me if the pirates have 'em.' He relaxed back in his seat, adding quietly, 'Not in the least I wouldn't.'

'Fine,' said Amphion, glancing warily at Eurymachus, a man he had always deplored as an uncultivated oaf. He stared at his goblet, saying, 'I thought Leiocritius would be in on this.'

'Not been around for a while has he,' shrugged Antinous. 'Maybe met up with some tavern woman – more his style.'

'So, in the meantime,' asked Amphion, 'what are you proposing?' The question was put even though he regarded his own involvement in their affairs as superfluous as that of others, including the presently absent Eudorus – except that out of base curiosity both he and Eudorus wished to remain party to the intrigue. And should Antinous or Eurymachus seize the throne of Ithaca, both Amphion and Eudorus would expect to gain from having supported them.

Eurymachus drained his goblet, muttering under his breath as Antinous replied, 'Not much at present – except that we check on how many fighting men we and some of the others can muster should the townsmen here in Ithaca be against us.'

At last this was an opportunity for Amphion to manifest some measure of commitment. 'A good few of my men are well versed in the use of arms,' he offered. 'They'll be available if needed.'

Antinous ignored him. Eurymachus grinned.

'And now,' breathed the inebriated Eurymachus, peering with glazed eyes at Amphion's slim hands, 'we start putting real pressure on her ladyship to make her choice and quit that fucking throne.'

Antinous' expression remained impassive.

Chapter 5 - Menelaus of Sparta

The grey edifices of Sparta came into view through a mid-afternoon heat haze. Further along the dusty track, now well–defined as it snaked toward the city, stood a neglected, unpretentious square stone structure little higher than a man. It was part obscured by tall grass and flower-decked bushes and over it birds flitted and sang in bright sunlight. It was pointed out to Telemachus by his noble companion as the very shrine built by Odysseus. 'There are several shrines between here and the city,' Pisistratus added, 'but no other like this.'

Telemachus jumped from the chariot and strode over to stand before the monument. He could find no inscription on the shrine but the image of a wide-eyed owl engraved above the small, recessed altar left no doubt as to whom it was dedicated. He remained a while in contemplation, gazing at the handiwork of a father he never knew but whose name was on the lips of so many and whose unknown fate had brought him this far. He reached out to brush fingers against the rough stone of the altar. 'They say you built this monument,' he whispered. 'Did you stand on this very spot? Did your fingers rest upon this altar as mine do now? Do these stones hold your words and something of your spirit?'

With his own words spoken, with his modest offering of the sacrificed goose laid upon the flat stone, Telemachus felt an all but overwhelming urge to remain where he was. Had his companions not been waiting he would have sat in warm

143

sunlight on the low embankment close by, listening to the buzz of insects and call of birds, to rest there in quiet contemplation until the sun was low in the sky.

Seeing him lost in thought, Pisistratus and his men waited in respectful silence a while longer. When their captain called for Telemachus to return, the party moved on.

Like Pylos, Sparta was unfortified but its buildings were plainer and rugged in their forbidding dark exteriors of solid polygonal masonry. In area, the town appeared nearly as large as Pylos and here, too, were the ranks of stylised bulls horns marching across the walls and parapets of its buildings. The squares were not as spacious but when the new arrivals were escorted by guards through the courtyard further similarities to Nestor's palace became evident.

Pisistratus and Telemachus, followed by their men, passed through the entrance hall to enter the megaron of King Menelaus. Set about the crowded hall were glowing, spark-showering braziers and at its centre the great circular hearth. Spaced away from the braziers were gilded tripods bearing exotic vessels, ornaments and statuettes, an opulent display unlike any Telemachus had seen even in the palace of Nestor. Many of the items on show appeared to be encrusted with precious stones and inlays, and the more Telemachus looked the more objects of value did he observe to fuel his wonder. The ubiquitous odour of cooking lay on the air as smoke coiled by the stout columns of the galleried hall and up to the high windows. Above the windows spread a ceiling brightly decorated with rich geometric patterns almost as grand as that of Pylos.

More vessels of gold and silver, again many set with gemstones, were arrayed upon the tables to be used as though they were of no more value than common baked clay pots. Telemachus hesitated. If this amount of wealth was on casual display, what greater treasures must be hidden out of sight in Sparta's vaults and could there be even more at Mycenae? He noted the weapons arrayed about the walls and the colourful frescoes: marching soldiers and chariots so familiar at his father's palace though here once again in greater number. These he found oddly reassuring. The new arrivals had by now attracted glances of interest from the diners and there soon followed a lull in conversation. The slaves whose job it was to serve held back in anticipation.

Menelaus had, of course, expected his visitors and as members of a noble house the banquet would have been prepared in their honour as custom required. The king was seated on his alabaster throne and by his side his regal consort, the woman whose name everyone throughout Greece knew for good or for bad. Telemachus assumed others sitting close by must be the royal daughter and three sons as they appeared not much older than himself.

The king arose as they approached. His lithe figure held a slight stoop but the sharp, dark eyes and weathered features of an angular face suggested a man with much experience of the world. He was of considerably lesser years than the aged king of Pylos. His long, copper-coloured hair and short, neatly trimmed beard were unadorned but his attire, a black gown far plainer in style than that worn by Nestor, and unsullied by food, boasted an ornate gold chain bearing a jewel-inlaid pendant of the same metal. Nestor's son was greeted by Menelaus with a vigorous hug and broad smile. 'It's good to see you again, my boy!' he declared. He next turned to Telemachus grasping him by the arms to announce in a deep, commanding voice, 'So, I have before me the true son of our intrepid Odysseus; the very Odysseus upon whom so much depended after those ten long years in the final days of Troy!'

'I guarantee it is,' smiled Pisistratus, 'and we bring you gifts from Ithaca as well as Pylos.'

'I'm honoured to meet you, Lord Menelaus,' said Telemachus. 'You may be the last hope I have of discovering my father's fate.'

'Oh, really,' laughed Menelaus as conversation around the hall resumed in full and the slaves continued their duties, 'this is the first time I've heard myself described as a last hope! I'll tell you all I can in good time but I fear afterwards you may consider your journey less than fully rewarded.'

'If there's little or nothing more to learn about my father then I'll continue as I must and regard him as dead and gone forever. That being so I will set my mind to solving the affairs of Ithaca by whatever means are at my disposal.'

'Well said,' responded the king, 'but before we discuss matters more fully let my attendants conduct you and your companions to chambers by the courtyard. There you may bathe and avail yourselves of fresh tunics. Then Pisistratus, Telemachus, you both must return here and sit with us to enjoy our feasting while your five companions mingle with the other guests.

Telemachus liked this man. As with Pisistratus and Nestor, instinct assured him Menelaus could be trusted as a true friend.

When they returned, refreshed, to the dining hall Pisistratus said, 'The king will take no offence if I sit with you for a short time then re-join our own men over there. Whatever he may have to say will be largely for your ears rather than mine since his account has long been familiar to me.'

The younger members of Menelaus' family had been dismissed to join the main company, leaving space to sit for Telemachus and Nestor's son. Whilst their wine cups were being filled, Telemachus was able to satisfy in part his curiosity, to see at close hand the woman whose alleged abduction all those years ago was said to have launched a great fleet and brought down a mighty kingdom at the cost of countless lives.

Telemachus judged Helen as roughly twice his own age. Unlike most women of the court she was not bare-breasted, crinkle-haired or heavily rouged. Slim and curvaceous, she needed no such enhancement. Her features hinted at the stresses of those calamitous times through which she had lived yet she remained strikingly attractive with full, sensual lips and large, blue-grey, feline eyes. Fair hair swept over the shoulders of a long, deep blue gown, richly embroidered and interlaced at its edges with gold and silver wire. The woven gold headband, set against a soft loop of black fabric, boasted a large, brilliant sapphire. Telemachus

147

wondered if this single gemstone could be worth more than half the livestock on Ithaca.

Silver goblet in hand, Helen regarded him with steady gaze as if searching into his thoughts, as if peering deep into his soul. She compelled his attention as might a goddess appearing before worshippers at her shrine. He quickly understood how this woman had sparked the desires of so many men of influence and power. Telemachus delved hard for suitable words with which to address her but could muster none. To his relief it was Helen who spoke first.

'Yes, you are the son of Odysseus,' she said in an alluring voice, a voice expressed in words of intimacy intended to caress no other ear but his. 'You are much as I remember your father, except for the colour of his hair. It was almost as red as my dear husband's.'

Telemachus grinned boyishly; glad of the opportunity she had opened for him. 'Then I'm pleased that so far no one has considered me an impostor.'

Helen smiled discreetly, raising a free hand to brush a wisp of hair from her cheek. Menelaus laughed, declaring, 'Impostor! Never! At least not until another like you shows up before us claiming to be a son of Odysseus. My dear wife,' he continued with thinly disguised irony, 'will I'm sure relate some of what your father did at Troy. She encountered him there under circumstances of considerable risk to them both.'

Helen, lips slightly parted, glanced warily at her husband. The silence that followed, their silence, loomed larger than the chatter and bustle that continued throughout the megaron. Telemachus, sensing a need to prompt further dialogue and relieved that the subject had so soon been breached, asked the king, 'Did you see war with Troy as inevitable?'

Knowing Pisistratus was familiar with the circumstances, Menelaus nodded his approval when Nestor's son politely excused himself.

'It would have happened sooner or later,' resumed Menelaus. 'Even so, when we first arrived at their city gate your father and I tried a little diplomacy to secure the return of my wife, not to mention a number of, er, trade concessions.'

'Concessions?' queried Telemachus.

'Oh, yes, the Trojans were imposing ever higher taxes and restrictions on trading vessels as they passed through the straits on their way to the Black Sea so Agamemnon, as our leader, considered a show of force might help matters. That was not, I must add, to play down our other concern; the rescue of my dear Helen.' He glanced at his wife with a moderately forced smile but Helen showed no response as he resumed. 'We were allowed into Troy under an armed escort but confronted by a rabble who would have murdered us and hung our corpses from the city wall if Priam himself hadn't enforced the laws of hospitality - with the backing of his palace guard. Then as nothing could be settled by peaceful means we got out of the town that night by a side gate to avoid the mob. Next day the city gates were barred and Priam's men lined the city wall. I challenged his son, Paris, to single combat outside the main gate one afternoon, hoping we could resolve the dispute in an acceptable manner without undue bloodshed.' Menelaus paused then added with a smile, 'unless of course it was *his* blood. Until confronting Paris I never quite experienced my older brother's killer instinct but then I never experienced the family bloodletting Agamemnon had grown up with at Mycenae.'

'But as joint leader of the expedition with Agamemnon were you not taking too great a risk in challenging Paris?' asked Telemachus.

'Oh, I didn't think so,' shrugged Menelaus, 'I was quite confident I'd kill him – and rather quickly. He was a pampered philanderer rather than a true warrior. I'll admit he was handy with a bow and arrow - especially when he was out of harm's way perched up there on the city wall.'

Telemachus noted the brief tightening of Helen's expression and aversion of her gaze as she muttered, 'Oh, yes, he did kill men outside the city wall.'

Seemingly unaware of the comment her husband, eyes bright with enthusiasm, continued his narrative. 'The main gate opened and the dear boy came sauntering out in fancy cuirass and plumed helmet to meet me with several armed retainers who stood aside shouting the usual insults at us as they goaded their so-called champion on. We each stepped forward to cast a spear and each dodged aside just as expected to avoid the other's shot. But that was little more than a gesture. Once we closed with sword and shield I was soon getting the better of him. He was giving ground and all that concerned me was that I finish him off before we got too close to his own men. Hmm - had that happened they would have dashed in with every intention of cutting me down.

Our men guarding the boats had got to hear of it so most of them hurried over to witness the contest, leaving our campfires unattended. That in turn brought more armed men out of Troy. There was a strong breeze coming in from the sea and it carried burning embers low across our camp from one or more of our own cooking fires. A wagonload of animal feed was set ablaze and clouds of choking smoke drifted everywhere. The alarm was raised but a number of Trojans and our own men had already dashed forward to set about each other. It was difficult to tell who was who but the whole scene must have been a lot clearer from high up on the city wall because one of their archers took a shot at me from there. He missed by a whisker but I suspect it was one of the options they'd planned if I'd gotten the better of their fancy man.'

Menelaus reached aside for his goblet. This was a modest vessel of bronze decorated with intricate scrollwork but of no great value when compared with those items gracing the tables of the great hall. Noting Telemachus' interest he said, 'Oh, I used this at Troy and I've been loath to part with it ever since. Mere sentiment, my boy - you'll suffer from it one day.'

He drank deeply then resumed his account of the battle.

'Because of worsening visibility each side backed off but when the smoke thinned out the Trojans realised some of our men had retreated to the beach in order to prevent the flames spreading to our ships. Seeing an advantage in this they raised

151

their battle cries and were on us again, this time calling heavily armed men out in chariots. Spears flew with groups of men becoming engaged in close combat with sword, lumps of rock or whatever they could get their hands on. There were a number killed or injured on both sides but I rallied my Spartans and we dashed in like lions to drive the damned Trojans back. It gave us chance to strip arms and armour from their dead but I regret to say Paris wasn't among them. Meanwhile our men at the camp had the fire under control and were soon returning.'

'So,' commented Telemachus, 'I take it by that time diplomacy was no longer an option.'

'Absolutely not! Priam never intended an agreement since he was convinced we would be forced to give up the siege and withdraw. We were a long way from home and camped outside a strongly fortified city with their allies on hand to help and our own territories many days distant. Well we couldn't defeat them, nor could they defeat us so the conflict went on seemingly without end, often with months when little happened other than trading insults. For the best part of ten years we were getting supplies in by sea and by foraging, though some of what we needed was supplied by people closer to that part of the world who didn't see eye-to-eye with the Trojans. At first it had seemed like an adventure but after a year and more the prospect of Trojan loot and slaves appeared less attainable. It was your father who kept our spirits up when things went badly. On one of those occasions when our men were becoming restless Agamemnon himself spoke of quitting but your father wouldn't have it.'

Menelaus turned to Helen, adding, 'Then later, Odysseus entered Troy in disguise to reconnoitre did he not?'

Her eyes fixed wide on Telemachus she leaned forward, seized by this opportunity to relate in her own words a tale that must be of great interest to the son of a courageous man she once knew. 'Yes,' she declared, 'later on in the siege he did and, oh, what a brave and resourceful man your father was. An escaped Trojan slave explained the layout of the city and Odysseus memorised it all. He scourged himself. He befouled his body with sheep's blood and dressed himself in rags. The Trojans allowed him into the city after darkness because he was unarmed and claimed he was an escaped slave willing to help them. He gave them to believe Agamemnon and his allies were demoralised, short of supplies and might soon give up and sail away if only the Trojans would be patient.'

'Which I must say was, on a number of occasions, close to the truth,' added Menelaus.

'They cleaned Odysseus up and fed him,' Helen continued, 'but that night he broke into their main temple and stole the Palladium from its shrine. When the priestesses who were supposed to be in charge of it found out they were horrified but dared not inform Priam for fear of a flogging or death.'

'The Palladium?' queried Telemachus. 'I've heard of it but -?

'Yes, it was a sacred wooden image of a maiden said to be given by Zeus himself. It was believed to protect Troy from evil as long as it was kept safely there. Odysseus threw it over the city wall then made his way into the private apartments of the palace looking for me. Paris, who had abducted me by force, was by then dead, killed by a poisoned arrow so I was told, and I had been compelled against my will to marry another of Priam's sons. Everything from the very beginning – *everything*, was done against my will!' At her emphasis on the word, "everything," she glanced aside at Menelaus who merely smiled.

The ensuing pause threatened to become an eternity until, much to the Queen's relief, Telemachus asked, 'And what resulted from your encounter with my father?'

'Odysseus burst in while I was trying to console Hecuba, Priam's wife. She had lost several of her sons in battle yet still she blamed Paris as well as her husband for all that had happened. She took one look at Odysseus and screamed for the guards. There were none to hear her because by a signal from Odysseus, a light waved from the city wall, Agamemnon's forces had launched an attack on the main gate and all Troy's fighting men had been summoned to deal with it. Hecuba's personal attendants had been dismissed because she wanted to confide her sorrows to me without being overheard. When Odysseus made it clear who he was and that he intended us no harm she said nothing more. I gathered by then she no longer cared what he or anyone did. Odysseus had seen all he needed to see of Troy's situation and left us promising I would soon be freed. He was true to his word.'

'I'd no idea my father had accomplished all that,' admitted Telemachus.

'Oh, but he did,' Helen replied with enthusiasm, 'and much, much more. He later claimed building the famous wooden horse was his idea and I believe it was even though others said not. He was certainly one of those brave men who concealed themselves inside it.'

'I will also vouch for his bravery,' offered Menelaus. 'He and those others being closed up inside the thing risked much.'

'Did the Trojans not see you building this enormous horse?' asked Telemachus.

'We never tried to hide it!' laughed Menelaus. 'In fact we couldn't have done so because of all the sawing, hammering and banging, and because the thing was so big. It had to accommodate several men and their weapons. And it didn't look to be a very good horse – no, more like an ox without horns, but then it did need a roomy belly!'

'I heard several among his court advising Priam to leave the wooden horse where it was and have his men break it up,' added Helen. 'Some wanted to set fire to it rather than allow it into their city but the gods were against them. Most insistent was Cassandra, one of Priam's own daughters. She begged her father to destroy the horse where it stood but he ignored her. She'd often prophesied future events but in the months leading up to this, no one believed a word the poor girl said. The priests claimed it was because she had offended Apollo but when Priam saw Agamemnon take to his ships and set sail he and the majority of his court accepted the wooden horse must be a genuine parting gift in recognition of a much respected enemy.'

'Yes,' added Menelaus, 'a gift was a gift and whatever they thought it looked like they evidently regarded the thing as a worthy offering. The citizens of Troy came out in force with stout ropes and heavy wooden rollers to drag it through the main gate, which it barely cleared, and into the marketplace where it was positioned as a trophy of war. Priam suspected a number of his own peoples' adverse intentions regarding the horse so he had guards placed there to protect it. That night the whole city was celebrating what its people believed had been a great victory and the guards keeping watch over the wooden horse had no intention of missing out. When, long before sunrise, your father and his men opened the hatch and lowered themselves by rope down to the ground, the guards were so full of Trojan wine they were long past caring where or even who they were. They never saw the death that descended upon them from that wooden carcase.'

'Alas for them the power of good Trojan wine,' Helen added somewhat coolly.

'Our warriors,' continued Menelaus, 'had sailed back and landed ashore fully armed during the night, so when Odysseus unbarred and threw open the main gate they poured like braying hounds into the city. Few Trojan men were sober enough or had time to arm and rally themselves so there was much slaughter well throughout the day. Even now I see the fear in their citizens' eyes and I hear their cries for mercy. But after ten years of hardship and frustration our men had little time for compassion.'

So saying. Menelaus lowered his head as though contemplating regret over the memory of those final, bloody days at Troy. His queen remained impassive, her eyes closed, her memories alight.

'From your accounts,' said Telemachus, 'I see in my father a greater man than I once did and I wonder if he reached the very end of the world in his travels. Perhaps he even sailed to lands beyond.'

'Well let us hope,' remarked Menelaus, 'that if he still lives he has gained material profit from his wanderings. Yet I wonder how few mortals have anything to show for their years of hardship – apart from that small number blessed by the gods.'

'You have many objects of value here,' said Telemachus. 'I never dreamt there could be so many precious things gathered in one place. There must be a good deal more I do not see.'

'Ha – there is!' boasted Menelaus, 'and much of it safely hidden away. I confess openly the greater part of it is loot, though a modest quantity was gained by trade in those enclaves where the river Nile enters the sea. It began when we separated from the main fleet and met with another storm. This was not as severe as that which struck us after Troy but it was still bad enough. Four of our undamaged ships continued on home with my dear wife, our booty and a number of slaves, while the rest of us went ashore for repairs.'

He hesitated to have a boy slave top up their goblets whilst Helen engaged in conversation with a female courtier. Menelaus' face glowed with enthusiasm as he leaned closer to Telemachus for the continuation of a tale he obviously relished.

'That's when we saw an opportunity to make up for more of the losses incurred during the expedition. There were the old allies of Troy for a start – several along the Aegean coast of Asia and the islands. Most of them were easy pickings because many of their fighting men were tending their land or had never returned from Troy. There were pirates even then in those parts but no one expected battle-hardened, well-armed men with seagoing vessels as sound as ours.

We attacked from the sea wherever the Trojans and their allies had trading colonies - Cyprus, Phoenicia, the Nile delta and Libya. Seven years of wandering we had before we decided to make our way back to Sparta.' Menelaus raised his hands, adding, 'Ah, how time flies by when we keep ourselves gainfully occupied. I miss those days – oh, yes how I miss those days.'

'I had scant knowledge of your own adventures, said Telemachus. 'After hearing all this, I'm more determined than ever to find out what became of my father.'

'I wish I could throw more light on the matter,' said Menelaus. 'I cannot tell you where he is nor will I speculate upon what might have happened to him. Yet because of rumours I heard on my own travels, and because I knew the nature of the man himself, I tend to believe Odysseus still lives. Meanwhile you must stay with us here in Sparta as long as you wish. And when you leave us, because I hold such fond memories of the man and the key part he played in our victory, I will offer to the son of my old friend three fine horses and a chariot from my own workshops. I hope these gifts will be of service to you and to your father should he return.'

'Lord Menelaus, I hardly deserve such generosity but as time is not on my side, staying long in Sparta is out of the question. Noemon, captain of the vessel that brought me as far as Pylos is waiting there with his men. As for horses and a chariot, we'd never find room on Noemon's modest boat and Ithaca is too rocky by far to allow full use of a chariot. I hope I do not appear ungrateful.'

Menelaus smiled, 'Ah, a small boat; yes, and rocky Ithaca, of course! Odysseus once described it to me as such and I confess I had forgotten his words. But you'll not leave Sparta without gifts of value; the memory of your father and the presence here of you, his son, demand it.' With a wave of his arm he added, 'You must choose whatever you consider suitable to carry home before you leave us - except, of course, the chain I wear. That once belonged to a nobleman of Troy who only relinquished it when he parted also with his head! But for now enjoy our excellent wine and find entertainment with one or more of our palace girls.'

Telemachus smiled yet his thoughts turned once again to Polyxena: memories of her image, her voice and her warmth conspired to possess him.

***

The sun was in decline when on the following day two horsemen arrived at the gate of Menelaus' palace. To facilitate speed they were lightly armed, each carrying only a sword and small shield. They were much fatigued and wildly dishevelled, their dusty mounts close to exhaustion. Challenged by the guards they asked if Telemachus, son of Odysseus, was in Sparta and learning that he was they demanded to see him. Once dismounted they were escorted into the courtyard and obliged to wait while Telemachus was summoned.

'Prince Telemachus!' burst out one, striding urgently to meet him as Telemachus emerged from the palace entrance. 'Lady Penelope sent us to find you in all possible haste! We sailed in secret from Ithaca to Pylos! We spoke with Noemon there and we've ridden hard with little rest to find you!'

'Then give me your message!' Telemachus demanded on recognising both men as trusted servants of his father's house.

'We are to inform you of what is happening at the palace,' responded the first man. 'Some among your mother's suitors have proclaimed that because you are absent and may not return, your father's throne should now be regarded as vacant. They insist that by custom any man may claim it if proven worthy. Several among them are pressing her to make a choice and we were told one of them, Leiocritius, had approached your grandfather, Laertes, intending to bribe him into sending Lady Penelope back here to Sparta, but Laertes would have none of it. Leiocritius then boasted he would send messengers to her own father, Icarius, intending to bribe him also into calling her away and keeping her out of Ithaca for good. We're told Leiocritius changed his mind once he knew you were on your way to Sparta but now he's disappeared. It's rumoured Antinous murdered him to further his intentions though he still has others to contend with. Some of this, My Lord, I overheard them discuss in one of Ithaca's lower taverns when they thought no one was close.'

'Sending men here would have gained him nothing,' said Telemachus. 'Icarius died years ago.'

'We saw dead men as we rode here,' added the second messenger. 'They were part eaten by lions or wild dogs. We feared the brigands had set upon you until we looked closer.'

'Those men *were* the brigands and they did set upon us,' responded Telemachus as Pisistratus stepped over to join them. 'Now, what else d'you have to report?'

'A number of the suitors spoke of a contest to decide who will rule Ithaca,' replied the first man. 'The majority of them agreed to this so all have to comply. What that contest will be they had yet to decide but there is one man determined to seize the throne of Ithaca, contest or no.'

'I take it that is Antinous.'

'It is Antinous, My Lord,' the horseman replied. 'But Eurymachus tells others he is an empty boaster and another man among them urges restraint.'

'Another man you say?'

'Yes, his name is Amphinomus. He has weighed the scales for a time against Antinous and Eurymachus.'

As they spoke Telemachus recalled Amphinomus as being the only real gentlemen among the suitors as he said, 'So I gather Noemon will remain waiting at Pylos with his men and vessels'

'Yes,' the man replied, 'he assured us he will be there when you return.'

'You both have done well. I'll ask that you're given refreshment and the chance to rest. We will

161

leave Sparta at first light tomorrow and I'll make sure you both are better armed.'

'Lord Menelaus will see these men are looked after,' said Pisistratus. 'All our goods can go on the packhorses. The chariots we can leave behind and I'm sure Menelaus will provide fresh horses for ourselves.'

'Good,' agreed Telemachus. 'And our numbers should deter any bandits on our way back.'

***

Menelaus ensured his guests and their companions would leave Sparta with fresh horses and provisions. The king, gilded staff in hand, his sons and members of his court assembled by the palace gate to bid them farewell but his consort, Helen, was not among them. Her face veiled, she watched their departure unnoticed from an upper window of the palace. What men, what adventures, what tribulations the fates had determined for her yet there were many who still held her accountable for what the gods themselves had decreed; the hardship, suffering and deaths at Troy. Within her own court the scathing whispers of menials might still be overheard. What realms, what great exploits could such as they ever encounter from within the barred cages of their petty lives? She had witnessed great and tragic deeds, she had consorted with kings and with exalted men, she had been desired by mighty heroes and warriors who would kill for her. Tears from a well of memories rolled down her cheeks – memories of all that had transpired and all that might have been.

***

Shadows of an early morning sun fingered the land when they reached the roadside shrine of Athena. Here they halted and Telemachus leapt down from his horse. A white goat, tethered to one of the packhorses was led by the two horsemen from Ithaca to where Telemachus waited by his father's monument. Sacrificing goats was a duty Odysseus' son had until then managed to avoid but with their help he slew the animal with a flash of his knife, spilling its lifeblood freely over the stones. Once the goat lay still he offered a silent prayer to Athena. As on the day of his first visit, Telemachus wanted to loiter in reverential thought by the shrine. A silent call of those brooding stones drew him in. He closed his eyes, imagining himself quite alone in a distant place of dreams.

'Telemachus! You have a mission but you'll not attain it standing there!'

The cymbal clash of Pisistratus' voice shattered his thoughts. Close by at a busily bubbling stream, Telemachus knelt to wash the blood from his knife and hands, cleansing them of corruption in pure water before re-joining his party to continue their journey. With the horses stamping forward he glanced over his shoulder at his father's overgrown and once more bloodied shrine. He alone saw the white owl swoop down from a tree by the stream to alight on the roof of the monument. It remained there watching as they departed.

During the return journey they came upon the more level ground where they had engaged in deadly combat with those men who had seen fit to assault them. Beneath a cloudless sky they rode close to where the bandits had fallen. The corpses, partly devoured, lay sprawled beneath a hot sun, the black sockets in their pallid heads witness to eyes long since eaten out by birds. Their jaws, agape in silent rage, served as portals for noisome, scurrying creatures. The stark white bones of their ribs stood exposed amidst rotting flesh that quivered with vermin and in places glistened black with a bustling turmoil of flies. Tasting the noxious odour of putrefaction that assailed them on warm air, Telemachus and his companions were not inclined to linger.

'Hardly the most pleasant thing I've seen today,' commented Telemachus, glancing over his shoulder at Pisistratus.

'Better get used to such sights, my friend,' responded Nestor's son, drawing close alongside him. 'You're a fighting man now and a damned good one!'

Chapter 6 - Challenge at Sea

Pisistratus, Telemachus and their companions had continued on as quickly as the rugged land would allow, starting each day at a first hint of light in the eastern sky, ever alert but meeting no challenge from man or beast. After a final day's riding, stopping only to eat, the western horizon was no more than a dim swathe as they passed through the outer domains, the sprawling farms and vineyards of Nestor's kingdom. Night ruled the land when, fatigued by the length and hardships of the journey, Pisistratus led his party through the palace gate. After sending one slave to announce their arrival and another to inform Noemon of their return, he insisted they first bathe away the dust and aches of the day before formally presenting themselves.

On entering the great hall they were warmly greeted by Nestor with Broteas propped up and sound asleep at his side. Several members of his court still loitered in the megaron though the feasting had ended with many of the assembly retired to their beds. Gone, too, were the women of the court, although the bard, resting upon cushions by a column, plucked languid notes.

The gifts from Menelaus were placed before Nestor who gestured for his attendants to display them on a vacated table. Food and drink were gladly accepted by the newly returned but their captain and Telemachus were not soon to find rest. Both were obliged to give the king an account of their journey and in particular their interview with Menelaus. Nestor listened intently with a fixed smile, hands from time to time fondling his divided beard. Broteas, his empty goblet laying on the floor where it had fallen, was quite oblivious to their presence. He remained in his seat, head bowed, eyes fluttering, his snores rising and falling like the rumble of a potter's wheel.

A young woman of the court stood watching unobserved from the shaded gallery above. Light from a wall-mounted firebrand shimmered on her cascade of raven hair. When Telemachus retired to his darkened chamber Polyxena was waiting, clad in a diaphanous white gown of fine Egyptian cotton that left her firm breasts exposed. Light from a cluster of small oil lamps shone in her eyes. Tired as he might have been, the sight of her was a newly risen sun and the burden of the journey slipped from him as the shades of a bad dream.

As he began, 'Oh, I wondered if you -,' she arose from the bed, arms outstretched in greeting, enveloping him in her sensual warmth, uttering words from her meagre fund of Greek. 'With me – yes. You with me this night.' It seemed in his absence she had acquired little more of the language of Pylos but there was a ring of confidence in her speech.

'I know what you're trying to tell me,' he smiled, pulling her close. 'But there's no need to say anything. No, not another word.'

Polyxena clasped and kissed him avidly. Sleep would not intervene for some time.

***

Telemachus was up and dressed before daylight. In near darkness Polyxena slept soundly and he wondered if she would remain so until after

166

he had gone because the men and horses would be waiting in the courtyard below. Would it be right to leave her and say nothing? Should he not try to explain why he had to go? He was aware how intense her feelings had become for him and there was no denying he was conflicted with emotions new to him. He was standing by the door when she stepped naked from the bed to confront him and grasp his arm, saying in her strange accent, 'With you, yes – I with you?' He guessed the girl somehow knew he was soon to leave Pylos, perhaps for good.

'You want to come with me,' he breathed. 'And I wish you – but no, I'm afraid you cannot.'

She gazed into his eyes, her expression one of innocent pleading. In spite of their short acquaintance his feelings for her ran far deeper than those for any woman he had yet encountered. Telemachus thought hard then took her hands in his. 'No, it's too dangerous. You don't understand – the voyage, the risks we'll be taking, the dangers at home. Ithaca is not like Pylos. You'd never be happy in Ithaca, though - though I'd surely have you with me if I was certain we'd make it safely back. Yes, by the gods I would.'

Polyxena understood the essence of his words. Lowering her head, she began to weep softly and Telemachus, though anxious to be on his way, endeavoured to console her as best he could. 'Listen now – please understand. When this – when this mess is sorted out I'll return or send for you but I can remain at Pylos no longer.'

On the stairs leading to the courtyard he hesitated, regretting the manner of their parting and wishing it had not been that way. Had he stayed with her longer, had there been more time, he might have given way and requested from Nestor and Pisistratus that she be allowed to return with him.

The previous evening Nestor had allocated his gifts for the House of Odysseus so Telemachus and Pisistratus rode out in a single chariot, accompanied by the two horsemen from Ithaca and a pack animal festooned with hemp bags containing the valuables. During that short ride they spoke little. Telemachus thought hard about Polyxena but did not mention her name. Nor did Pisistratus. The girl's image wavered as they emerged from the trees and into the wide bay where morning sunlight glittered on the water and a sea breeze parted the curtains upon a new day. Noemon could be seen with two of his men standing by his cherished *Amphitrite*. Soon they would be at sea.

But there was another boat – one too large to draw up onto the beach. She was being unloaded at a wooden jetty some distance along the wide bay where asses jostled together, waiting for their loads. Drawing closer, Telemachus observed a number of Noemon's men in casual conversation with the crew of the other ship so there appeared no need for caution. Portly Noemon himself spotted their approach and trudged with swaying gait over the sand to greet the party. 'Young sir!' he called with a bushy-bearded grin. 'Welcome back! Has all gone well?'

'As well as might be,' replied Telemachus, stepping down and striding from the chariot so that each man met to grasp the arm of the other. 'Friend Noemon, you and *Amphitrite* are a most agreeable sight. I'll tell you soon enough what's happened but first I must say goodbye to my companion.'

Pisistratus remained where he was until Telemachus returned, then leaned out smiling to grasp the other's hand. 'I'll be on my way, Telemachus, my good friend and my new brother. I pray the gods are with you and I'll ask that whenever the time is right they will have you find your back to Pylos. When you return you can give me an account of what has happened at Ithaca. We'll ride out hunting once more, we'll drink good wine together and we'll be entertained by the girls. I know there's one among them especially who would welcome your return. I'll make sure she is well cared for. Yes, she will be personal attendant to my mother and no one else.'

'You've been a good and true friend to me,' replied Telemachus, 'and your father now treats me as one of his family. Yes, it would please me greatly to meet with you again once my affairs are in order. And I hope the girl you speak of will also be waiting.'

Pisistratus swung the chariot around and departed, leaving Telemachus to watch him head back along the path that led to his city and his people. Nestor's son turned once to raise a hand before disappearing amid the pine trees.

'Farewell my friend,' Telemachus breathed. 'And were my feelings for her that obvious?'

Noemon had summoned two of his men to help collect up and carry into his ship the gifts and provisions given to Telemachus by the rulers of Sparta and Pylos. The two messengers from Ithaca stood with their own possessions by their mounts until Telemachus said, 'Let the horses go, lads – they'll return on their own to Pylos town.'

'Will you join us by the boat, young master?' asked Noemon, glancing across to see his men treading their way back across the sand from the other vessel. 'We'll make preparations to sail; there's a good breeze and my men are as keen as you must be to return to their homes.'

'Yes, but whose vessel is that by the jetty?'

'They are Taphian traders. I have spoken to several of them and they seem more agreeable than their reputation would suggest. They bring cotton, spices and luxury goods from Egypt for Nestor's palace. I asked if they had any knowledge of your father but they could offer nothing. It seems the rumours are in short supply at present.'

'So be it,' responded Telemachus. 'While you're making ready to sail I need to think over what has happened. I'll re-join you soon enough.'

He set off across the beach to where a broad, flat slab protruded from the rocky embankment on the landward side. There he sat, his head lowered in contemplation, a warm breeze brushing hair against his cheek. He recalled the words of Nestor and Menelaus, those too few nights of intimacy with Polyxena and images of that bloody confrontation with the brigands. His thoughts turned once more to Ithaca, to his mother and to the suitors; to one man in particular who by now could well have moved to depose her and seize his father's throne. Whether or not that had happened Telemachus knew there would be among them those with mischief planned for his homecoming. Deadly mischief if Antinous or

Eurymachus were involved as surely one or both of them would be.

He was oblivious to anyone's approach until a falling shadow and a voice invaded his thoughts. 'Young master, I find you here all alone and lost in contemplation.'

Telemachus glanced up, startled. 'Mentes the trader!' he exclaimed, half rising. 'So that's *your* vessel! I should have walked over to her instead of wasting my time sitting here.'

The sturdy, weather-beaten figure blotted out the sun as he peered down at Telemachus. 'No matter,' he smiled, 'being a Taphian ship is no guarantee that I'll be her captain. Let me sit by you.'

'Of course,' responded Telemachus, shifting aside. 'I'm pleased to see you once again, my friend. Noemon tells me none of your crew has news of my father. That's a pity.'

'What can I say, young sir. It was on my advice you called the council of citizens and from what I hear it was this in the end caused you to make your journey.'

'And now I'm on my way back to greater uncertainty with no more answers than before I left.'

'In your absence I returned for a short time to Ithaca. What I gathered there will be of great importance to you.'

'Oh, and what did you learn?'

'Nothing that pleases me, friend Telemachus. Some of those who intrude upon your house have hired men from beyond Ithaca to confront you at sea. They have a boat and a crew awaiting sight of your vessel at an otherwise deserted headland on the southeast of Kephallinia. They know you will pass that point of the island on your return home. They'll be hired brigands so should you or anyone else survive the attack it's hoped there will be no connection to your mother's suitors.'

'I thank you, Mentes, but how did you find this out? Those men would have no wish to impart their plans to anyone – not even when entertaining themselves in our hall.'

'I was never present at the palace,' replied Mentes. 'No, I spent my time in various of Ithaca's taverns where some of them gather during the day. I kept myself out of sight but not out of earshot. After too much wine, men's wits are dulled and their mouths take on a life of their own. Apart from that, their hirelings needed to stay a while at the port of Ithaca to gather their instructions. I had my own men drink with them at the tavern, and most liberally, until one of their crew was no more able to hold back his words than he was his piss. Another of my lads followed them in a small fishing boat when they sailed. He watched them go ashore the next day at Kephallinia. You must be prepared, young sir, you really must.'

'I thank you, my friend,' responded Telemachus. 'I don't ask why you are doing this for me but I owe you a great deal and I'll repay you in good measure when the time comes. I will inform Noemon and our crew; they're all fighting men. And you – where are you sailing to from here?'

'It's not yet decided,' Mentes replied. 'I'll walk the beach a while and think over it.'

172

Mentes arose, his hand falling to Telemachus' shoulder. It was a comforting, an oddly reassuring touch, not the grip of a hardened seagoing trader. He strode casually along the sand with a seaman's gait, not to the Taphian ship but further along the bay where pine trees marched down to the sea. Telemachus watched him for a time then made his way back to *Amphitrite* where he discussed with Noemon and his men what Mentes had revealed. Whilst they listened to his every word it was evident that Noemon and his crew were most eager to set out on the return voyage.

The good ship *Amphitrite* swayed gently in the water, wavelets slapping her hull, her oarsmen preparing to ease the vessel clear of the beach before raising her sail.

'And do you trust this man?' asked Noemon as they stood by her bow. 'The Taphians trade very much by their own ways. They're not always what they seem.'

'Maybe they're not,' responded Telemachus, 'then how many people *are* as they seem, but the man evidently knew my father and has no grudge against our house - at least none I'm aware of. I believe he was speaking the truth since what would he have to gain otherwise.'

'Well truth or no,' declared Noemon, 'we'll be prepared for any vessel that comes against us and being prepared is to our advantage. Now if you're fit, young sir, I'm keen we get on our way. It's a time of the year when foul weather arises and the wind may not favour us on the journey back as it did on the way here.'

'Noemon, before we sail I must thank Mentes once more for his advice today and in the past. I promised him a reward when next he came to Ithaca but from those gifts given me at Pylos and Sparta, there's some small item of value I'll offer him before we leave. It may bode well for the future when it comes to trade with Ithaca.'

Ignoring Noemon's impatient frown, Telemachus strode back onto the beach, leather satchel swinging from one hand. He glanced across to the rock where he had been sitting when his visitor appeared. Apart from children and their mongrel dogs splashing in the water there was no one to be seen there or along the curve of the bay, so he hurried to where the Taphian ship was moored.

Noemon strode back and forth in growing agitation, his feet splashing shallow water until at last Telemachus was seen hastening back. The bag he carried still appeared to be weighted with the contents he had declared he would offer the Taphian captain. Telemachus' bore a troubled expression as he clambered aboard *Amphitrite*. He made his way along the boat, past her captain, saying nothing, placing the bag below the catwalk then perching in the stern as Noemon's men heaved away, moving *Amphitrite* from the shallows into open water, chanting aloud to the sweep of their oars. When the sail was unfurled and gathering wind, when the timbers sighed, Noemon stepped along to sit by Telemachus. With the steering oar in hand he asked, 'I find you perturbed, young sir. Was your visit to the Taphian not as you expected?'

'I'm mightily puzzled,' Telemachus replied after some thought as their ship headed for open water. 'No, my friend, not puzzled,' he added, glancing across at the Taphian vessel then shaking his head from side to side, 'totally mystified! The man I wished to find was nowhere to be seen so I assumed he'd returned to his ship. When I went to the jetty and asked to speak with him they – well they told me Mentes wasn't their captain at all though a couple of them claimed to know of him. I tried to explain how I'd just been in conversation with the man when another man jumped down from the vessel insisting *he* was the vessel's captain. It became clear soon enough that this man - that all of them, were telling the truth. Clear enough, too, they thought I was not in full control of my wits.'

'I never had sight of this Mentes,' said Noemon, 'though I, too, have heard of him on occasion. But I saw no third vessel in the bay that might have been his or anyone else's.'

'No, as you say, there was no third vessel.'

'Then might the gods not be at work here? Only the gods could deceive a man that way.'

Telemachus gazed out to the horizon. 'The gods?' he said at last. 'Perhaps things will become clearer when we reach Ithaca. Meanwhile, if Mentes - or whoever it was spoke to me - proves to be right then we have an interesting voyage ahead of us.'

***

Skeins of white smeared an afternoon sky. The sea blinked light of a thinly veiled sun. *Amphitrite's* rigging clattered in a less than favourable blustering wind as she ploughed on with the southernmost tip of Kephallinia rising at their left. Two of Noemon's

175

men occupied themselves in manipulating spar and sail to make better headway. Others rowed hard and Ithaca was visible as a muted daub on the horizon to the north. A few small boats were spotted close inshore but none had made to approach Noemon's vessel. None, that is, until the first promontory of Kephallinia loomed directly to the west. One of Noemon's men, standing at the bow called out, 'Look at that ship sailing from the bay!'

Telemachus peered across the water to observe a vessel of similar size to their own with high, decorated prow. Having emerged in full sail and with oar blades flashing, she was turning to catch the fluctuating breeze. For some time it appeared she intended to parallel *Amphitrite's* northward progress but as they continued to watch it became obvious the boat was converging on their course.

'She's no trader as far as I can tell,' said Noemon as he and Telemachus studied the vessel. 'She's not sailing as if she carries cargo. Nor is such a vessel out to catch fish.'

'The men on board are armed,' said Telemachus, shielding his eyes. 'There's sunlight glinting on bronze and they're rowing pretty hard.'

All of *Amphitrite's* crew were taking notice, their oars quickly drawn in, some already reaching for helmet, corselet or tunic with overlapping bronze scales.

'How many d'you count and how well are they armed?' asked Noemon as the other boat drew ominously closer. 'I fear my eyesight is not what it used to be.'

'They number more than we do,' replied Telemachus. 'Twenty at least I'd say. A few look to be wearing light armour - some with helmets. They'll have advantage over us if we let them approach too close.' He glanced aside at Noemon's men then added, 'I'd say your Cretans are unlikely to allow that, nor am I of a mind to!'

'Quite right, young sir,' he confirmed, 'though the breeze is strengthening and the sea getting livelier. I hope Lord Poseidon has noted our libations but I fear bad weather is closing on us.'

High mists were already obscuring the sun. Noemon's men, anticipating his instructions, were crouching to string their powerful bows. 'Be ready to pick 'em off, lads!' he called 'I'll keep us steady as I can!' Turning to Telemachus he added, 'My boys are well used to shooting in open waters. They take account of the wind as well as the waves When sea birds hover above our ship, that's when you find how accurate they are. Those buggers heading our way won't expect it.'

'I won't claim skill in archery from the deck of a boat,' responded Telemachus, feeling the vessel roll, 'but I'll stand ready with my two men and we'll set about them as we know best!'

'You'll not find my lads lacking there, either,' declared Noemon, observing how much closer their adversary now was. So close that raucous jeers could be heard above the rising sound of wind, sea and creaking timbers. 'Can you make out which one of 'em's their leader?'

Steadying himself to peer harder, Telemachus replied, 'Maybe, maybe not. Two of their men at least are wearing horned helmets but we should aim at the steersman!' He turned his head to the crew and called loud enough for all of them to hear, 'Get their steersman, lads!'

'Er, yes - the steersman,' responded Noemon, uncomfortably aware of his own position at the tiller. 'You heard that, lads!' he cried. 'Let 'em have it before the spray catches your bowstrings!'

Soon each side would be close enough to attempt a spear shot but the approaching vessel was well within range of Noemon's archers, twelve of whom, their number divided fore and aft of *Amphitrite's* mast, rose up suddenly to draw their bows. The boat pitched but as she steadied, their first volley sped as a hissing, vengeful flock over choppy water. The would-be attackers did not expect a shower of well-aimed arrows and the result was much to Noemon's satisfaction. The man at the steering oar of the enemy vessel was hit in both neck and shoulder. He released the tiller, attempted to rise then fell aside, visibly choking blood. Three other men were struck, one full in the face as, with spear raised, he clung to their vessel's mast yelling insults, a second when boiled hide failed to protect his chest from speeding bronze. Both tumbled overboard whilst the fourth, pierced through the right arm, lost his spear over the side. His companions raised their shields against an anticipated second volley but with their steersman lost the rising angered waves rolled their boat which then veered away, her sail thumping hard, until another man grasped the steering oar in an attempt to bring her around once more. Some of the enemy, taking shelter behind the shields of their comrades, took up their own bows. A few arrows sped from their vessel but were not so well aimed, one striking *Amphitrite's* hull, the rest claimed by the sea.

'Weather's getting worse!' declared Noemon, noting how much the sky had darkened.

With each vessel now within spear shot of the other, those men intent upon attack determined to cast their weapons first. They behaved as if expecting Noemon's men to do likewise at such short range and were obliged to lower their guard so as to take as good an aim as they could from an unsteady vessel. In a strengthening wind, with each vessel rising and falling, Telemachus and his two Ithacans braced against the roll of the boat to hurl their spears as Noemon's crew, each man with a foot planted against the timbers, loosed a second volley of arrows.

Spears and arrows sped in both directions, a lethal flight beneath an ominous sky. One spear flashed in to strike a man of Noemon's crew. It pierced his corselet between the metal plates, precipitating him overboard where he was swept away with a cry to vanish beneath the water. Another Cretan was bleeding at the left arm from the glance of a spear that had embedded itself in timbers close to the mast but the man would soon rally, wrap the wound with a cloth then wrench out the enemy's weapon for his own use.

Their opponents had suffered greater loss with another three men struck and tumbled overboard and others collapsed inside their boat, injured or dying, including one of their horn-helmeted crew. As waves slammed against *Amphitrite's* hull it was Telemachus' spear shot, hurled with all his strength, that disabled the newly appointed steersman when

179

his lance impaled the man's thigh causing him to bellow aloud as he grasped the shaft. Again the enemy vessel veered. Again another took the stricken man's place whilst others, careless of the victim's sobbing agony, heaved him pitilessly overboard.

'A truly fine shot, young sir!' called Noemon.

'Could be,' muttered Telemachus, hand dropping to his sword hilt, 'except it wasn't him I was aiming at. Just anybody.'

Shouts of defiance from both sides rose above the confusion. The clouds were lowering and both vessels shuddered with the hammer-blow impact of ever more forceful waves. Noemon's crew hastily unstrung and put aside their bows, now rendered ineffective through contact with spray. As they took up their swords he declared, 'Those buggers have had the worst of things - surely now they'll return to wherever they came from.'

'I think not!' responded Telemachus feeling chill water sting his cheek as the enemy boat continued to close. 'They'll have been offered a great deal to ensure we never make it to Ithaca! And there'll be more gold for each man now there are fewer of them!'

Weapons were readied to strike now the vessels were separated by little more than the measure of a man's outspread arms. Men on both vessels hard-eyed their adversary, each shouting encouragement to his own side as masts swayed, as yardarms swung violently to crack one against the other. Telemachus studied the enemy as a grappling hook was flung from their boat to seize on *Amphitrite's* timbers close by him. One hand firm on the trembling spar, his distance well judged, he swung forward with a second spear as the boats were drawn together, piercing the side of a man who, clinging onto a mast stay with sword raised, was intending to leap aboard Noemon's vessel. A second grapple caught, its cable snapping tight so that timbers demon-screeched against each other and the two boats rose and fell as one. Men clambered with grim intent to thrust and strike, each side determined to board the other while sea-spray scurried over the decks and loose sails boomed. If the enemy had a leader who still breathed he had yet to make himself known. Sword poised, Telemachus, steady and determined amidst blustering chaos, plunged the blade beneath the jaw of another man attempting to gain foothold on *Amphitrite*. A crack of thunder swamped the man's death cries, rain swirled and a boisterous sea threatened to overwhelm both vessels.

The hireling foe, used mainly to fighting on land or against the crews of trading vessels, were proving no match for Noemon's seafarers in this foul weather. Telemachus, followed closely by his two companions, sprang aboard the enemy amid a tumult of voices that contested with the storm and grinding protest of lashed-together hulls. A searing glare burst from the heavens to freeze for the blink of an eye a scene of growing carnage. A number of men attempting to board *Amphitrite* were cut down or hurled back, one by Noemon himself who having relinquished the steering oar plunged his blade into soft flesh beneath an aggressor's corselet, causing the man to fall, to become trapped between the sterns of the two vessels until his faltering cries were consumed by the sea. The sky-beast raged, timbers protested agonies of their own, spars clashed and swung wildly. Hacking swords took their toll, soaking decks proved treacherous, lightning flared and the rain intensified, making it hard to determine who was enemy and who was not until men of both sides could no longer fight effectively.

'Back on board, lads!' called Telemachus above a howling wind. 'Back on board and cut their boat loose!' Treading bloodied water he paused to sever two mast stays of the enemy vessel, threw his gore-streaked sword into Noemon's boat then clambered with some difficulty back onto her deck. Noemon hacked at the nearest grappling rope with a man of his crew slashing through the second. Two of the enemy still grasped the rigging of Noemon's ship but realising their plight they dropped their swords and scrambled to regain their own vessel as it and *Amphitrite* sprang violently apart. Both men plunged into foaming turmoil, one clinging in desperation to the enemy ship as the other, bleeding from a sword thrust administered as he tried to escape, was dragged beneath the water.

Amphitrite heaved as an angered beast, her sail pounding wildly until Noemon brought her about in an attempt to regain control. The sail alone was no longer able to keep her stern to the waves so two of Noemon's crew deployed knotted warps to slow and stabilise their vessel while four of his men bailed furiously with leather bags to clear water swilling within the hull. Others attended to sail and rigging until, with the boat steadied, they were better able to make sense of their situation. Of Noemon's sixteen crew, two men had been claimed by the sea and one sat aside, stunned by a blow to the head that had failed to penetrate his helmet, though he would survive. Telemachus had seen one of his own companions cut down on board the enemy vessel. Two of the enemy lay crumpled in *Amphitrite's* bow, one with a broken sword blade still protruding from his ribs.

'We routed 'em and no mistake!' declared Noemon through a thoroughly drenched beard. He glanced aside to see the other boat pitch and roll in the grip of the sea.

'Yes,' responded Telemachus, brushing rain-matted hair from his eyes, 'they hoped to destroy us and now they're fighting for their lives!'

'I tell you,' declared Noemon, both hands grasping the tiller, 'they'll need the gods on their side if they're to make it ashore in this sea!' The skies growled with menacing voice as his men heaved the two enemy corpses overboard. With *Amphitrite* somewhat steadied Noemon glanced again at the receding ship then called, 'I can hardly see them now, young sir! Can you make out what's happening?'

Telemachus peered through shifting mists of rain at the vessel of those who had set out with such fierce determination to end his life. 'Their mast is down,' he replied. 'They look to be foundering.'

Hands firm upon the rigging, others of Noemon's crew straightened up to follow his gaze.

'So,' responded Noemon, 'those of their men best able to handle her must be dead or wounded. The gods have decided.'

'With the help of my sword,' muttered Telemachus. He watched the enemy boat pitch violently. The seas were driving her as a wind-blown leaf. A wave struck her broadside and within moments she was lost from sight. 'They're gone!' Telemachus declared, 'and I know for sure who'll be disappointed!'

'We must offer sacrifice for our own lads who were lost!' called Noemon. 'We'll do it when we land. They were the best of men.'

Amphitrite ploughed on and though the winds eased, the sea calmed and the rain lessened to a drizzle, Noemon considered the bad weather would not fully abate until close on nightfall. 'Our sail is in need of repair,' he said as Telemachus joined him to sit close by. 'We must put ashore along the coast of Kephallinia before darkness. There's a small harbour where we can shelter until morning. We can dry ourselves and our arms before returning to Ithaca. Meanwhile, young sir, let me say you proved yourself as fine a warrior as I ever saw. You stayed your hand until each moment was precisely right then you took your man.'

'Thank you my friend but my good fortune was to be as one with such excellent company as we have here - though I confess the wrath of the sea worried me more than did that of the enemy. Yes, and right now I'd like nothing better than to be warm and dry again.'

'Maybe so, young sir,' added Noemon, 'but give the storm credit for purging ourselves and my good ship of all the violence and bloodshed forced upon us this day.'

Chapter 7 - At the House of Odysseus

'It's in everyone's interest but yours in particular,' declared Antinous, 'that we settle this matter now.'

Draped in the elaborate gown of a noble he stood, hands placed assertively on his waist and sword hilt before white-gowned Penelope who, in the otherwise deserted megaron, sat on the cushioned throne that the man poised before her regarded as his for the taking. Antinous had already offered his word perfect greeting of respect but she regarded that formality as of less substance than a passing breeze. The words, 'You have no right to be here!' threatened to burst from her lips but she checked them, determined not to have him think she was intimidated by his presence. She glanced toward the main entrance, wondering why she had not seen Thoas that day and why he was not present now to deter this intrusion.

'We all know Odysseus will never return,' Antinous continued. 'With your son also gone from Ithaca your position is untenable and your house beset with growing problems.'

'I will not give in to you, Antinous,' Penelope replied with bright-eyed anger. 'No it is entirely in your interest to leave me alone – you and those others who gather here each evening as hungry jackals poised over a stricken beast. *That* is the manner in which my husband's house is beset! But this house is not a stricken beast. It has survived these troubled years despite my limitations as a mere woman. Telemachus is my true and only heir. He is of age and by long established custom he is head of Odysseus' house until my husband returns as I and many others believe he will. And should Odysseus not return then my son will rule Ithaca as our true king – that is *his* right!'

'Not so!' insisted Antinous. His voice had until then remained dry and free of emotion. Now his words were coloured by impatience. 'For nigh on twenty years Odysseus' throne has been vacant. True, for half that time our glorious king was away at Troy and there was his father to consider. But Laertes is too old now to play any part in your affairs and that – that ridiculous farce with the shroud – d'you think any of us were taken in by it for long? Well maybe Laertes *will* be needing it and that could be sooner than you imagined. As for your son, he may be of age but is no longer here and might never return. These are dangerous times, particularly at sea as I am often assured.' Penelope regarded him coldly. Antinous eyed her with darkening expression. He waved a gold-ringed hand before her. Anger honed his words. 'In the absence of your son our customs must be followed – the customs you have so often quoted to me and others. Empty words now, I say. Another man has to take the throne of Ithaca and that is the *only* custom that matters at present! I offer the security you hardly now possess and soon will no longer possess if you continue as you are!'

'You seem convinced Telemachus will not return!' she retorted. 'I wonder why that is!'

'Wonder whatever pleases you, madam!' snapped Antinous, patting his sword hilt as he turned to leave. 'But think hard on my words. Time is no longer your partner in folly!'

As he stepped away Penelope called after him, 'Thoas remains loyal! He will support me until Telemachus or my husband returns!'

'Oh, yes, your precious captain of the guard,' laughed Antinous, turning briefly, 'D'you imagine he'll stay around much longer the way things are going? I think otherwise – no matter what inducements you offer to maintain him in the line of duty!' On reaching the door he turned a second time. His voice rang through the hall with mocking echo. 'Maybe you should ask him!'

Penelope remained in solitude, her head bowed, fingers clutching the edges of her cushion. The big circular hearth smouldered. Charred wood settled, cracked and sighed. Smoke from incense pots set between the columns coiled upward into obscurity. Under her breath the words, 'Telemachus, come home to me. Athena I beg you, bring him back soon.'

In the shadows of the colonnade opposite the throne a dark figure waited, silent and unseen.

**

Afternoon light slanted through the high windows. Attendants waited idly by as Penelope and her female companions gathered in subdued conversation. They looked up to see a familiar figure enter the great hall, a dark-haired, stubbled, stocky man of early middle age, attired in thick linen tunic, gleaming cuirass and greaves of engraved bronze. Under one arm he cradled a horsehair-plumed bronze helmet. At his side was fixed the ornate scabbard of tooled leather in which nestled his sword. He halted before the throne to offer a slight bow. His voice was deep and gruff. 'Lady Penelope, you wish to see me.'

Penelope's women rose to their daintily sandaled feet and bustled away, eyeing each other with discreet smiles they did not intend their mistress to observe. At her gesture the slaves also left.

'Yes, Thoas' she replied once all had made their exit, 'I called for you because we have spoken little since my son left Ithaca. Those men see for themselves greater advantage now Telemachus is absent. Although I had forbidden it, Antinous was here this morning, standing where you now stand. He is pressing me harder for a decision on marriage and I – I'm fearful of what might happen if I continue to refuse and equally fearful of what will happen if I were to agree. It would result in my becoming a slave in my own house. I would have thought your presence and your support might have been more in evidence yet it was not. That is what I wished to discuss with you.'

Thoas lowered his gaze. Penelope sensed a deep unease as she continued, 'I believe those men intend to murder Telemachus before he returns then one of them, probably Antinous, will assert his right over my husband's kingdom. Should matters so demand I will require you and your men to drive him and his like from the palace, yes, and out of Ithaca town by force if necessary. I know how risky that will be. I know it will mean bloodshed. Are you prepared to do that for my sake?'

Her captain glanced up as if to speak, then stared uneasily aside, saying nothing.

'Well,' she demanded, 'why don't you answer me?'

'I will answer, lady, but I fear what I have to say will not please you.'

'Oh, not please me - then explain what you mean. There's little enough to please me at present.'

'Custom permits,' he began, 'that the strongest of them is entitled to claim Odysseus' throne in the absence of a legitimate heir.'

'Nonsense!' exclaimed Penelope. 'I have made this clear to Antinous - Telemachus will claim the throne of Ithaca as is his right until his father returns. Those men who help themselves to our wine, our food and yes, on occasion to our livestock, should no longer be here. What I suggest we may have to do surely cannot be contrary to our customs.'

Thoas remained silent, his head once more bowed.

Penelope leaned forward, her voice lowered though her words bore an abrasive harshness. 'Thoas, what are you keeping from me? I demand to know. I have placed all my trust in you these last years. I have rewarded you well and I have allowed you privileges offered to no other man. I hear rumours to my shame - rumours I find difficult to endure. When my husband returns those rumours will still be there but for your sake as well as mine I will maintain they are but groundless mischief spread by the suitors. If I do not, if I say I consented to what I so foolishly allowed to happen in order to keep your loyalty, which I suspect is nearer the truth, Odysseus will surely slay you.'

Thoas raised his head. 'Lady Penelope, there is more to this than you know and what I have to tell you is to *my* shame.' Again he hesitated; his next words were summoned with difficulty. 'After Telemachus departed I - I was approached by Antinous. He offered me gifts of great value if I would vacate my farm and sail with my family away from Ithaca. What he offered was more than enough for me to buy livestock and set myself up again in a place of my own choosing.' Penelope sat back to regard him in perplexed silence as he continued. 'I refused out of loyalty to yourself and to your husband's house though Antinous has approached me twice since and -.'

'You've said nothing to me about this,' cut in Penelope. 'Why?'

'I have said nothing because - because I felt it would burden you with further anxiety, but other things have happened – are happening. I have returned home of late to find my wife and our children stricken with fear. They report men close to my farm during the night when I'm on duty here. They shout insults, threats of rape and murder. Of late my farm hands have been threatened, my livestock has been attacked – several of my sheep have had their throats slashed and two of my pigs have been speared. I know Antinous is behind this. I approached him and demanded he account for what is happening. At first he denied all knowledge of it but when he saw I might draw my sword, when he thought I might cut him down, he implied that should I do so, those men of his would return after darkness to carry out their threats. They are evil men bought here from outside Ithaca by Antinous' wealth. They land on our shores unseen. They would slaughter my children and burn down my home - they would carry away my wife and use her as they pleased. If I kill Antinous, they will surely carry out his wishes with the backing of his kin.' He sighed deeply then added, 'I cannot sleep at night. I'm driven as chaff in this damnable wind. I see no option other than to do as he says for the sake of my family. With the wealth your suitors possess I could never be sure if my own men were not bought off as well. I say this to you with all deference; it is happening because there is no strong hand within the House of Odysseus to govern Ithaca. That alone is what is needed and I believe, as rumour suggests, they plan to ensure Telemachus does not return alive.'

Several heartbeats passed before Penelope spoke. 'You have explained yourself well, Thoas. You must do as you see fit. Please leave me. Go! Go now!'

Thoas hesitated as if to speak again then, with a slight bow, he turned and walked away.

Penelope lowered her head, placed a hand over her eyes and sat bowed in a silence of despair. After a while she gazed across the smouldering hearth to the warriors' frieze on the column-shadowed wall opposite. A sliver of doubt pierced her thoughts for the first time. What if her husband, what if Odysseus was after all dead? 'No,' she whispered. 'No, I will never give in to those men. They will have to slay me first. Telemachus – when will you come home? Telemachus!'

***

It was a morning of disquiet. Through that fretful night she had dreamed. There were armed men, hordes of armed men swarming darkly over the land. Who were they? She had arisen to a world of desolation and lay now on cushions close by her forsaken loom in near darkness, drowning in thought, her eyes closed. The steady flames of two small oil lamps would not have allowed enough light for her to work on Laertes' shroud but that no longer mattered. Draped over her table its only purpose now to remind her of folly and abandoned hopes. She was unaware of footsteps until a voice from beyond her chamber called softly, 'Lady Penelope.'

It startled her though the voice was familiar.

'Yes,' she sighed, rising to her feet, 'you may enter.'

The curtain pushed open and a dark-skinned figure in white linen kilt hovered cautiously at the door. 'I beg to speak with you,' he whispered, hands clasped in deference at his waist.

'Have the suitors sent you, Medon? Is that it? You were in the service of Odysseus once but you seem to have forgotten that.'

'I have not forgotten but Odysseus and the young master are not here, and for many days you have given me no duties.'

'No,' she replied, sitting on the edge of the bed, 'I've not sent for you because you spend too much of your time with those damnable men.'

'If I do not obey them they humiliate and abuse me. They have abused me on occasion for their own amusement when they were drunk. Lord Odysseus always treated me as a man and not a chattel. When

I needed to tell him my troubles he would listen. He never raised a hand against me in anger.'

'Very well, Medon, say what you have to say; I am weary.'

'Lady Penelope, they demand my presence and they take it for granted, but when their tongues are loosened with wine I stand discreetly by and they often forget I am there. Since the young master left us there has been bolder mischief in their conversation.'

'Even more mischief than before? That hardly surprises me.'

'Yesterday,' he continued, 'I was in the great hall when Antinous spoke with you. I heard what that evil man said. Because of it I must tell you what else I have heard.'

'What – you were there! Then why did you not show yourself? Why did you not speak to me at the time?'

'I - I was afraid he might return or that he might see me leaving the megaron so I waited in shadow by the columns until you yourself had gone. Only then did I feel it safe to leave. They planned to slay the young master if he tried to return; I believe you know of this. But it was not to be done by any of the men who gather here each evening. No, because they feared our citizens might rise against them before they were able to call upon their own supporters. I heard them boast how they hired men from beyond the kingdom – brigands and pirates. Their names may never be known but it is they who are to be rewarded should the plan succeed.'

Penelope arose to face him, fingers clutching at her gown. 'This surprises me no more than it would if you were to say who was behind it. Say it anyway.'

'Antinous and Eurymachus,' he replied, looking about nervously. 'A few other men know their intentions but are not so deeply involved, if at all.'

'Antinous and Eurymachus,' she repeated. 'And what of that vile man, Leiocritius – I've not noticed him in the dining hall of late? He's at least as bad as any of them.'

'Leiocritius has not been seen for many days. Others have remarked upon it. Some make out he has been slain at the hand of Antinous.'

'I've heard such rumours, yes, as I hear much else. As for their plotting to murder my son - is it then at sea they intend this should happen?'

'Yes, they sent out men to watch for his ship in waters to the south of our island. They determined he should be attacked in open water so there would be no trace of its happening. They have waited these past days for news of success but now they are growing impatient because there has been no news at all and their men have not returned. I will attend their tables and I will continue to listen until I have more to tell you.'

'Be careful, Medon,' she sighed, 'if they find out how much you've told me already they will most certainly kill you and I have no means of stopping them. You should know that I - that I can no longer rely upon Thoas and his men. Go now and return with more news whenever you can.'

'I only wish the master would return,' he said, nodding from side to side. 'Always, always I have wished it as do you yourself. May Athena grant our wishes.'

As he turned to leave Penelope whispered after him, 'Medon, take care.'

Medon was gone and the small flames wavered in a vortex of air to cast swaying, teetering shadows through her room. She imagined the shadows as portents of the future. But what were those dark forms telling her? Penelope lay back on her bed. Her pillow was soon wet with tears.

***

Phemios had strummed though the night but no longer sang because tiredness afflicted him and the darkness outside would before long give way to dawn. He stopped playing, struggled to his feet then with the precious lyre clasped in his arms he hobbled away, no longer caring if his presence was or was not required. The bare-breasted girls were long gone though Iros the fool lay in one corner as a discarded sack of offal, snoring loudly in drunken abandon. The clamour of voices had ebbed away though smoke still rose from metal grilles where meat had earlier cooked and mongrel dogs scavenged beneath the benches for the cast off remains of food.

Servants and slaves, some of tender age, still awaited the call of those few suitors remaining in the dimly illuminated dining hall. A small group of slaves loitered sullen in the courtyard, sheltering from a chilly night beneath a colonnade until it was time to escort or perhaps carry their overindulged masters to their lodgings in Ithaca town.

Antinous had been joined by Eurymachus away from others at the far end of the chamber, close to where hung the great bow of Odysseus. One day soon he intended the bow and quiver of arrows would be removed for good and some device of his own installed in their place to show all who came there who ruled Ithaca and her kingdom of islands. Lifting his half-filled goblet to drink, Antinous' attention was caught by the sight of three hair-matted, bruised and barefoot men pushing in through the side door opposite the gallery, their bedraggled tunics hanging damp with sweat. Eyeing them steadily, Antinous lowered the goblet. One of the men peered furtively across, spotted Antinous then limped cautiously forward with hands clasped at his front. His companions remained by the entrance, staring in anticipation along the hall.

'Lord Antinous,' the man announced not daring to approach too closely. 'I've returned from Kephallinia with two of our men.'

'So I see,' breathed Antinous, noting how visibly agitated the man was. 'And -?'

'My Lord,' he continued, 'we watched your vessel set out when Noemon's boat appeared. They were closing upon her when the storm came over. We watched them join in combat but we were not able to see what became of this because of the rain. When the air cleared there was no sign of your boat and her men. No, there was nothing at all. All we saw as daylight faded was the other vessel sailing close to the shore of Kephallinia.'

'What!' exclaimed Antinous with alcoholic slur. 'You say you lost sight of our vessel! What kind of fucking message is that to bring me at this time of the night?'

'I'd say it's getting on for fucking morning,' mumbled Eurymachus staring down at his goblet where it lay overturned in a pool of wine.

Backing two steps away from the table, the messenger raised his hands. 'S-sire, we think it possible Noemon and his crew will have found refuge on Kephallinia. We rode hard as we could to the port of Sami. From there we sailed at great risk in darkness to reach the coast of Ithaca. Had the sky not cleared to give us the light of a full moon we might also have been lost to the sea. We seized horses then rode hard again to bring you news. We did what you asked of us and you - you promised us good reward for doing this.'

Antinous slammed his goblet down, spattering wine across the table then turned to Eurymachus. 'Am I hearing right? Is he saying that bastard son of hers might be on his way back here?'

'Sounds like it to me,' grumbled an indifferent Eurymachus, unable to focus his gaze. He followed the remark with a loud belch then added, 'I've had enough. I don't give a fuck what any bugger's doing. I'm off for a shit and then to bed.'

He raised a swaying arm and two slaves hurried over. Antinous remained silent as they helped Eurymachus struggle up from the seat then guide him staggering to the main entrance where a third man waited to light their way with burning firebrand. Eurymachus was gone from sight but moments later could be heard throwing up violently a short way beyond the door.

Antinous struggled to stand, oversetting his seat with a crash that echoed as thunder throughout the near deserted hall. A hand fell to his sword as he moved unsteadily around the table, hard-eyeing the wretched messenger. 'Reward!' he growled. 'I'll give you a fucking reward! A length of bronze through your lousy guts – that's what! Get out of my sight!'

The man staggered back, turned and fled to the door. His two companions were already gone.

Three other suitors were left in the dining hall. Two were slumped over their table in drunken collapse; the third rose up, steadied himself then made his way with uncertain step over to Antinous. Antinous, meanwhile, dragged the seat upright, sat once again and looked up. 'Ah – Amphion – what a surprise; not getting yer beauty sleep?'

Amphion dropped with a thump into the space vacated by Eurymachus, a jewelled-ringed hand clicking on the table amidst the pool of wine. He withdrew the hand, peered contemptuously at the pool and the wetted sleeve of his colourfully patterned robe before speaking. 'W-what's happening now dear fellow - anything?'

'Huh – got 'emselves fucking drowned.'

'Drowned? Who?'

'Those brainless sheep fuckers we took on to catch his fucking lordship at sea, that's who. Drowned!'

'Oh, drowned are they,' mumbled Amphion, preoccupied by the wetness of his sleeve. 'Such a pity. What now?'

Antinous drew fingers down a stubbled face, stared with thinly-disguised contempt at Amphion then replied, 'If they've hung out for the night on Kephallinia then that fat old bugger Noemon is going to be back here some time tomorrow, or do I mean today, and her precious son will be heading this way unless he's stopped.'

Amphion chose not notice the other's expression. 'So we make use of our own men - is that what you're saying?'

'No choice is there? We've not enough time to pull in more outsiders.'

'And Leiocritius?' mumbled Amphion, a questioning finger raised. 'Haven't seen the dear fellow in − in, oh, I can't remember. Has he lost interest in the throne of Ithaca?'

'I dare say he has,' breathed Antinous. 'Lost it altogether.'

A torch on the adjacent wall to his left spluttered out, its extinction inviting deeper shadows to encroach upon their table. Antinous looked up at the smouldering brand. 'I'm getting out of here. I've still got a few lads in the town. I'll go back. I'll get things organised then catch some fucking sleep.'

Both departed, each with a steadying hand on the shoulder of the other. Within the obscurity of the colonnade a darker shadow stirred.

***

The rain had ceased and the sky cleared though the sun had long since vanished behind steeply rising hills when *Amphitrite* was hauled onto the narrow, rock-strewn shore. Noemon's familiarity with this small harbour was fortunate as by the time they were ready to leave their vessel the sky had darkened and they groped their way inland with much difficulty in spite of a full moon. They struggled on, carrying their weapons and goods, up a steep, pitted track to where a cluster of small,

199

deserted houses hugged more level ground. They entered the first of the houses whose rough stone walls and thatched roof seemed intact enough to keep out bad weather should the rain return. Stumbling, reaching about in near darkness they discovered kindling and chopped timber, abandoned by whoever once lived there, and after much tactile effort one of Noemon's men had the beginnings of a lively fire spitting yellow flames. Apart from the benefit of illumination the fire would help dry out their clothes and the archers' precious bowstrings. With the blessing of their humble light they discovered another, smaller room and a small loft area above, so each man would find enough space to sleep. Much heartened by the modest warmth and light they chatted, adding more wood to their fire until smoke weaved upward into the beams and thatch, finding exit via to the single small window.

Apart from their fire there was little physical comfort to be found so Telemachus and two of the Cretans, aided by moonlight, scrambled cautiously back down to their vessel, each returning after a while with a flagon of the wine donated by King Nestor of Pylos. Though hungry – most of their remaining food had been spoiled during the storm - the men knew their final destination was not far away and, insisting Telemachus accept first draught from one of the flagons, they sang cheerily to help alleviate stresses of the past day. They sang not of past conflicts and long vanished heroes but of the women who now featured high in their imaginations. Telemachus joined them for the sake of companionship yet in his thoughts was the image of one in the kingdom of Pylos with whom he had spent so little yet such precious time. But for now warmth and humanity had returned with the fire so with good conversation and laughter they drifted, a focus of light and life in a dark night of emptiness.

Telemachus slept fitfully, propped in discomfort against cold stone, his mind a turmoil of thoughts; the encounter at sea, his friend Pisistratus and their fight with the brigands, of Menelaus and Nestor and again of dark-eyed Polyxena. He awoke suddenly to the tang of wood smoke from a fire that had settled to a placid glow. He imagined someone had called his name as had happened that night on the road to Sparta. He waited. He listened. The room was utterly silent. Odd because there was no breathing, no snoring from his companions, none of those sighs, nor those slight sounds of movement people often make in the night. But there was light. The smoke from the fire thickened, writhed, glowed, and for a second time her form began to materialise from shimmering coils of vapour. The image became more distinct, once again the helmeted female figure holding up her spear. She arose as before against the darkness, higher as if there was no roof above but only the blackest of starless skies. Gone were the walls of the cottage, replaced by a fathomless infinity with only her image to command his attention.

'Am I so affected by the wine?' breathed Telemachus. 'By the gods what next?'

'Telemachus, hear me,' came her voice, soft and compelling. 'When you reach Ithaca's harbour go first to the dwelling of Eumaeus and there for a time remain.'

'Eumaeus, keeper of our pigs? This cannot be right. No, I must return to Ithaca town. I must see to my mother's safety.'

'Telemachus, hear me' the image repeated, though now it was diffusing, fading into vague smoke. But her voice was nearer. It swirled, vortices of whispering, until very close to his ear, until mingling with his thoughts. 'You must go to the dwelling of Eumaeus. There you must wait. Do this and much will become known to you.'

Then silence. The image and the voice were altogether gone but persisted a while longer in his mind. 'Become known to me,' he sighed. 'If only.'

There were sounds. Breathing, light snoring. One of the men turned in restless slumber. The fire spluttered and reddened. He stared mesmerised at living embers then drifted into oblivion as though laying upon a bed of feathers.

Telemachus blinked awake. Morning light showed vaguely through the small window. He arose stiffly to join Noemon and those of his men who were already preparing to leave the cottage. The yet unrisen sun blushed a cloudless eastern horizon as, in cool morning air, the small company made its way in silence down the rough path. The sea and the wind had calmed and soon enough, with repairs to her sail and yardarm completed, the good ship *Amphitrite* was eased into deep water and ready to sail.

'We've not the breeze I'd hoped for,' said Noemon as they cleared the headland, assisted by the sweep of oars, 'but we'll make Ithaca soon enough unless the gods decide otherwise.'

'Don't be surprised if news of what happened yesterday has found its way there before us,' commented Telemachus.

'D'you think that likely?' asked Noemon.

Some of his crew had shipped their oars and now busied themselves arranging spar and sail.

'Those men on Ithaca,' replied Telemachus, 'will have had others waiting ashore to report what happened regardless of the outcome. At least that's what I'd do.'

'Then, young sir, if they anticipate your return they'll have resumed their plotting with greater determination than ever.'

'Quite so, my friend. I doubt they'll be waiting to greet me with good wine and a merry song.'

'You'll have the backing of my lads should you need it,' said Noemon as the sail filled and *Amphitrite* coursed along to the splashing rhythm of a lively sea.

'I regret not having discovered what happened to my father. I'm as sure as I was before we set out that he died long ago regardless of what Menelaus had to say. But when we reach Ithaca you must put me ashore at a deserted bay to the south of the harbour. I'll explain why later.'

Noemon took the steering oar but Telemachus remained deep in thought for some time before resuming conversation with him, 'During the night I awoke and I saw -.' He hesitated with the name of Athena on his lips, decided it would be better not to reveal what he had, or imagined he had experienced, then continued, 'I thought over what happened during the storm yesterday and on my way overland to Sparta. I never in all my days training with sword and spear so keenly desired to take the life of another man and it was not so difficult as I once thought.'

'Young master, killing their enemies is what all men must learn to do or face death before their allotted time is passed.'

'Of course – only I imagined most people must hold the same values as I once thought I had. I treated my days of training with Thoas' men as little more than another diversion - like hunting wild beasts.'

'Surely you must have considered how one day you might apply those skills against your mother's suitors,' said Noemon as *Amphitrite's* spar was swung across to better catch the breeze. 'And soon you may have to. I cannot imagine their values ever matched any you or I hold dear.'

'Yes, now I've killed other men I feel much inclined to treat Antinous and his pals in like manner. In fact, my friend, I rather look forward to it.'

'It's the true warrior stirring within you again, young sir. I see Odysseus returning to Ithaca in the guise of his own son.' Telemachus smiled discreetly as Noemon added, 'My one regret at present is the fickle nature of this breeze. Still, I intend to make our island long before the day is out then we'll have you ashore unseen just as you wish.'

Chapter 8 - The Beggar

She was half asleep and imagined she was dreaming until the voice came again. Subdued, almost a whisper, he spoke her name. A single lamp burning fitfully on the far side of her chamber offered insufficient light to penetrate dark corners so caution was uppermost in her mind as Penelope slipped from her bed. She pulled the gown about herself, stepped across the room, eased the curtain aside and peered out to find him waiting wide-eyed with apprehension in semi-darkness. 'Ah, Medon,' she whispered. 'Come inside. Is the sun risen yet? I wanted no light in my room unless the morning brought good news. What have you to tell me?'

'Lady Penelope, the sun is not yet risen and I do have news. I listened in the dining hall through the night. A messenger came to speak with Antinous and Eurymachus, a man who had travelled far with two others. They appeared greatly fatigued as if they had -.'

'Yes, yes, Medon! I don't care what they looked like - what did you learn from them?'

'The man reported how assassins tried to kill the young master at sea but had failed. He said they were defeated, he said their ship with all the men on board was lost to the storm – yes, all of them drowned. That is what the man said, my lady. Antinous expects your son will be on his way home and that his ship will arrive at our harbour this coming day. Antinous may have armed men hiding by the path to ambush and kill the young master when he leaves the harbour to make his way here.'

205

'Antinous,' she breathed, 'he is a fiend. He is the most evil, the most despicable of men.' She remained in silent thought before stepping over to hitch aside the leather curtain that obscured her window, then she blew out the wavering flame of her lamp. With light from a brightening sky flooding into the room she turned to him, her voice animated by fear and anticipation. 'Medon, when Telemachus returns you will have your freedom; that I promise, and I'll ensure you are well rewarded for your loyalty. But now I want you to find Euryclea and send her to me. Let no one see or hear you but do it quickly.'

***

Penelope sat by her idle loom, listening for footsteps. She heard nothing until the voice announced softly, 'Madam, I am here.'

'Euryclea, come in.'

A wrinkled hand eased aside the curtain. Penelope stepped across to face Euryclea then glanced beyond to assure herself no one loitered in the corridor. As the old woman entered she whispered, 'Euryclea – good news, I believe the gods may be with us; Telemachus will arrive at Ithaca soon, perhaps this very morning. I'm informed he was attacked at sea but I think he is unharmed. Now they plan to fall upon him as he makes his way to us from the harbour. He must be warned. I will go in disguise to meet him if you will bring me suitable clothes.'

'Lady Penelope, no, that would be too great a risk! If the suitors have hired men from outside Ithaca they will not stop at killing you also.

Antinous and others would claim it was the work of bandits and none of their doing.'

'But who would believe them?' Penelope asked as they sat close together. 'I've heard nothing of bandits here on Ithaca.'

'True but they have been reported on the mainland and that's not far away. People say their threat is increasing and should not be ignored, especially as there is no lord and master here at present, if you will pardon my saying so.'

'Euryclea,' insisted Penelope, 'someone has to alert Telemachus even though he must expect there will be dangers ahead.'

'Then why not send Medon to warn him?'

'I cannot do that. Antinous and the rest of those men treat Medon as one of their own slaves. If any of them were to see him leave the palace they might become suspicious. There must be another we can trust; someone whose coming and going will cause no comment.'

'Well there is Leucon, the slave of my own household. He's hardly known to the suitors. I treat him well enough and I know he can be trusted. He has no sympathy for what is happening here and no connection with any who wish us ill. I often send him on errands – he brings fish and other goods from the harbour so no one will comment on his being seen there.'

'Leucon – yes, of course. Then send him at once. Give him food and drink. Tell him to wait all day and through the night if nothing has happened. Have him keep watch until Noemon's vessel comes in.' Penelope hesitated then added, 'Whether Telemachus arrives in the day or after darkness falls, have Leucon warn him not to take the path unless he does so with armed men. He will understand.'

'Why not have Telemachus go to the house of Eumaeus,' Euryclea suggested. 'He may be overseer of our pigs but he is a worthy and responsible man with his own holdings and he lives alone. I speak with him often at the market and he accounts to me over the state of those animals under his care. He was always a staunch supporter of Odysseus and holds Telemachus in highest regard. The track to where Eumaeus lives is some way from the harbour route leading here so there is no reason why it should be watched.'

'Of course, Eumaeus' farm. Telemachus can remain there until we get further word to him. I will make offerings at Athena's shrine. I will pray to the gods for his protection.'

'And, Lady Penelope, I must inform you - we have a stranger at our courtyard gate.'

'Oh, and what's the significance of that? D'you suspect he is one of Antinous' men hired from beyond our island?'

'I thought so at first but having troubled to walk by him I suspect he is not. I saw him at first light when there were few people around the square. He looks like a beggar but I'm not so sure he always was so. Unless he's gone away you should be able to see him from your window.'

Penelope arose and, followed by Euryclea, stepped over to observe morning sunlight already spilling over the courtyard walls and traders setting out their wares. 'I see him, yes, but I've never set eyes on the man before.'

'He's loitered there a good while,' said Euryclea. He's been watching people come and go as if he expects something to happen.'

'How ragged his clothes are,' said Penelope. 'His hair and beard are unkempt; the cowl he wears hardly conceals that. But you think he was not always a beggar. Why?'

'That is so, mistress, he looks to have fallen upon hard times but he appears sound of limb. He possesses a manly bearing we'd not expect in one of his situation and he's not asking for alms.'

'Where is he from, I wonder; some distant place, perhaps?'

'Who can say,' replied Euryclea. 'He may not understand our language. Perhaps that is why he speaks to no one.'

Penelope continued to stare as the figure in the courtyard strolled casually about, glancing here and there from beneath the cowl, sometimes passing a hand down his unkempt beard as if deep in contemplation. 'I'm most curious,' she said. 'People seem wary of his presence though he's not pestering anyone as far as I can see.'

'He doesn't look the kind of man people would care to approach,' observed Euryclea. 'More like a man from some wild place beyond Greece if you ask me. Shall I go down and try to speak with him? Shall I see if he understands? I doubt he'll pose any threat to an old woman.'

'Euryclea, we cannot let this opportunity pass if there's a chance the man knows anything – anything at all about my Odysseus. If he's wandered far abroad he might have heard or might know something. If he will talk to you, bring him into the

209

palace. Take him out of sight into the servants' quarters. Offer him food and rest. Call for hot water and have Leucon bathe his feet. No one will question such an act of hospitality, will they?'

'Lady Penelope, such hospitality was common in the days of Odysseus but things now are different. Those who need to beg are largely ignored. You would see a few of them if you were to go down to the main gate though I would advise against your doing so. And, remember, Leucon is to go to the harbour as we agreed and may not return for some time.'

'Oh, how foolish of me; of course he is – then who may we trust to attend to the stranger?'

'Do not concern yourself over what may be a trivial matter; I'll appoint someone else to deal with him as soon as I have sent Leucon on his way.'

Then I'll stay by my window. If that man understands you then get him to reveal anything that may be of interest to us. Who knows what tales he might have to tell.'

Euryclea got up, saying, 'I understand, my dear, but don't let this trivial matter raise your hopes too high.'

With gentle touch Penelope squeezed Euryclea's rough, bony hand, saying, 'No one could better serve my husband's house or myself than you and dear Mentor have for all these years. I thank the gods for having sent you both.'

Euryclea smiled meekly and left the chamber. Penelope remained at the window to observe Leucon, basket swinging at his side, cross the square, followed a short while later by her aged companion with stick in hand. The stranger had

210

wandered over to the outer gate and now stood watching traders, artisans and other citizens come and go. He appeared interested in those even less fortunate than himself; those huddled within the gate; the wretched vagrants, the lame and the blind; those unable to fend for themselves. Those who might not witness another dawn but for the diminished charity of Ithaca's citizens.

Euryclea made her aching way across a courtyard still pooled with shadows the morning sun was yet to dispel. Close to the gate she stopped and called, 'Stranger!'

The man turned to look at her, his dark eyes gleaming bright from beneath the cowl and unkempt growth of sullied copper hair and beard. His hands were concealed within the sleeves of his tattered gown and the sandals laced about his begrimed feet appeared close to disintegration.

'Do you understand the Greek of our land?' she asked.

He regarded her for some moments then replied calmly, 'I understand it well.' His was a firm voice that belied his straitened appearance, a voice she at once considered must belong to a man cast down by the gods for reasons he may or may not be inclined to reveal.

'Will you come with me?' Euryclea asked. 'It was once our custom to attend to the needs of those such as yourself who are careworn and who have travelled far. But let me say, we expect you in return, as we would of any traveller or trader, to say where you are from, where you have been and what you know of people and events in lands beyond our kingdom. Otherwise, you see, we live in ignorance of affairs that may one day affect our own.'

'I have few words to give,' he answered. 'An account of my wanderings, my years of living from hand to mouth are too meagre to offer in return for your kindness.'

'Never mind, you must rest a while.' Euryclea sensed an uncommon dignity within the man, a tantalising yet elusive familiarity in his manner. She planned on escorting him to the servants' quarters where a slave would be summoned to undertake the ritual washing of his feet. That would have been acceptable enough. 'You do not appear to be starving,' she continued, 'but it looks as if those feet of yours demand acquaintance with hot water and olive oil. There will be food and wine later should you wish to accept it. Please - follow me.'

He walked with measured slowness several paces behind her, as if unwilling to draw attention to his lowly status. At the servants' area he followed her into a plain, unoccupied room where he was invited to sit on a sturdy wooden stool and place aside his all but ruined sandals. A female slave was summoned, instructed to prepare hot water and to bring a copper basin in readiness. The basin was placed at the stranger's feet. It would be a while before the water arrived but Euryclea, thinking it not yet appropriate to question her charge, stood aside to gaze in silence through the window, hoping he would soon feel at ease enough to offer conversation. He did not. From the corner of her eye she observed him do nothing other than stare down at the basin.

The slave at last returned, accompanied by a small boy. Each carried a dripping copper jug of hot water, the adult with a woollen towel and cloth draped over her arm. The boy scurried away, returning almost at once with a small ceramic jar containing olive oil. When the water was poured the boy was dismissed and the woman, having placed the towel before the bowl, stood in expectation of an order to wash the stranger's sullied feet. Euryclea dismissed her also then with one hand grasping the edge of a nearby table for support, she sank with considerable difficulty to rest her pained knees on the towel. The stranger gazed down at her and began to rise, saying, 'Madam, this is no task for you.'

'It's a task for me if I decide so,' she replied, tugging at his reluctant right foot until he relaxed and lowered it into the water. 'I was born and remained a slave through my early years so washing the feet of another is no great shame and I must never allow the favours bestowed upon me to dismiss those memories. I remain as I was born.' His skin was hard and rough, his toenails broken and discoloured as those of any peasant working the land though he did not exude the unsavoury odour of such a man. Euryclea pushed aside the hem of the stranger's gown to avoid it dipping into the water then plunged the cloth into the bowl.

'I'll wager these feet have done more than their fair share of wandering,' she remarked, busily applying the cloth with her right hand, hoping he would at last reveal more about himself. 'The oil will soothe them once they're dry.' The stranger remained silent but with his calloused right foot cleansed as well as she was able, she turned her attention to his left.

Still the man said nothing as she lifted the cloth a second time and remarked, 'It seems to me you must once have – must once -.'

Euryclea hesitated. She dropped the cloth and stared in numbed confusion, her words stillborn. There was a scar on the outside of the man's leg a short way below his knee. It was a curved, pale crimson blemish no longer than the hand with which she had held the cloth; the visibly trembling hand that reached slowly upward with outstretched fingers to touch the scar. The sight of it kindled a flame that blazed uncontrollably through her! Euryclea caught her breath. She peered up at him wide-eyed and open-mouthed. He had incurred the wound whilst out hunting as a youth. She had attended to it with honey and bandages. The stranger who had to be no stranger at all stared intensely down at her.

'Oh, but -!' she gasped aloud. 'It cannot be! It cannot! But yes – yes, the gods be praised, it is you. It is -!'

His hands fell to her throat, gripping to stifle her words. 'Do not utter my name!' the man hissed close to her ear. 'Say nothing of this! Nothing at all! Do you understand?'

The hands slipped from her but Euryclea continued to stare up at him, her lips quivering, her eyes welling with tears. 'But you - you have come back to us,' she stammered, clasping his knees. 'After all these years you have returned. Oh, I thank the gods – oh, how I thank them now they have answered our prayers.'

214

He placed a kindly hand on her shoulder, saying quietly, 'I should not have allowed you to do this – it was foolish of me.' Pushing aside the bowl he stood and helped her to her feet where, stooped and shaking, eyes closed tight, she leaned against the table clutching her gown. There he gazed upon this gentle, fragile, desiccated woman who in her years of youth and beauty had joined his father's house then later nurtured and cared for Laertes son. Tears streamed down her cheeks as he took her by the shoulders, raised her higher and whispered, 'Euryclea, dear, dear lady, I have shamed myself. I did not wish to hurt you. I ask you humbly, no, I beg you to forgive me. I have seen terrible things and -. You must tell no one of my return. Swear you will not. You *must* swear to it!'

Clasping his arm in both her hands she continued to tremble before answering hoarsely, 'Oh – oh, dear - I – I swear, yes. But you have come home to us as a beggar – as an outcast dressed in rags. Why like this? You are our lord – you are our king. Oh, why like this? What will you do?'

'I need time,' he replied, easing her arms away, glancing from side to side, collecting up the towel then sitting to wipe his feet. 'I came to assess the situation on Ithaca, to find out all that has happened during my absence. I'll take myself away from the town before midday. I know a place where I'll be able to learn more and where I can plan what I have to do. Believe me - this is only the beginning.'

'But your clothes – your hair and -?'

'I have to remain as I am for now; it is *vital* I'm not recognised. I've learned something of the situation here simply by loitering in the streets and

215

taverns. Rumours alight everywhere as wild birds. I know the plight my wife is in because of those who appear each evening at the palace and I hear my son, Telemachus, has left Ithaca to find me. I gather my mother died after I departed but I've heard no mention of my father though I spotted Mentor in the market and know he at least is still with us.'

'Oh, sir, Laertes has withdrawn from our affairs and keeps to his farm. He has endured a growing sadness these last ten years not knowing what had become of you. He resents deeply what has been happening here and is angered because there is nothing he can do to alter things.

'I can hardly blame him,' breathed Odysseus. Not a man of his age, though he never was interested in affairs of the palace. 'So - I will leave you now but I'll be back when the time is right. That I promise.'

As he turned to go she asked, 'But Lady Penelope – is she not to be told?'

His expression hinted at anger as he stared back at her. 'No one is to know until I am ready. No one at all!'

He left Euryclea in a state of near collapse, her mind in turmoil. She remained leaning against the table, unable to move. After all the years of waiting, Odysseus had returned to Ithaca, not as the shining hero they prayed for but as an anonymous vagrant. How could she face her mistress and say nothing? Yet she must keep her word as promised.

***

That morning found grey-haired, full-bearded Eumaeus seated on a three-legged stool before his wooden bench. He was busy in the warm sun with

216

hammer, strips of leather and copper rivets. The pair of sandals he was making for himself ought soon to be finished. Close by, the wood of his fire hissed with the dripping fat of skewered pork that would be ready to eat before his work was done. Three of his men had set out earlier to pasture their droves of pigs whilst a fourth had left for the palace with a hog destined to supplement the revellers' feast that coming evening. People unfamiliar with his situation might have expected the swineherd's social status to be little better than that of his charges. This was not so for Eumaeus. The stone-built cottage was of modest size and though furnished with little more than basic necessities it exceeded in comfort a peasant's earthy hovel.

There were better places than rocky Ithaca to grow wheat, better places to nurture cattle and breed horses. The importance of sheep and pig as sources of meat was far greater here than on much of the mainland. The standing of Eumaeus' himself was therefore higher than that of the herders of sheep and goats who wandered over those parts of the island best suited to their purpose. Eumaeus could read and write so that, as in the days of Odysseus, he continued to tender his accounts directly to the palace on tablets of hard-baked clay.

His mongrel dogs began to yap. Eumaeus called for them to stop but they persisted in yapping and yapped ever louder, leaping to paw the low wooden fence that surrounded his farmhouse. Eumaeus looked up. A cowled, shabbily gowned man was approaching from the direction of the city; a man with firm and purposeful stride though in appearance he could be no more than a destitute wanderer. Eumaeus put aside his work, rose to his feet and called again to his dogs for silence. The dogs circled in anticipation.

The stranger, on passing by the well and vegetable gardens, reached Eumaeus' fence, halted at the wicker gate and stood silent. A hand brushing his sword hilt, Eumaeus stepped across then asked, 'Yes, my friend, what is it you want?'

'I'm a traveller,' replied the man. 'I was in Ithaca town this morning. I ask for somewhere to rest a while and a scrap or two of food if you've any to spare. If you can't then I'll be on my way.'

Eumaeus eyed him cautiously then declared, 'Well, stranger, the track you're following leads down to a small bay where few people go: I doubt you'd find anythin' there to satisfy your needs. So, what do I say to you? You don't look like a bandit – more like the victim of one.'

'I'm no bandit,' said the stranger.

No, maybe you aren't; we've suffered little from bandits in this part of the world, unless I count those bloodsuckers who descend each evening upon the palace of Odysseus.'

Eumaeus was confident the stranger had no ill intent since, had he wished, he could easily have kicked down the gate and quite possibly killed the dogs had he possessed a weapon. He therefore concluded the man carried no weapon; at least not a belt, scabbard and sword as these would have been difficult to conceal under his frayed attire. Eumaeus opened the gate, saying, 'Come inside, you can share my bread and what I'm roasting over there. I'll fetch you – no, I'll fetch both of us a cup of wine. If you want somewhere to rest your head through the night there's my outhouse and clean straw. I'll offer you that and a blanket to keep you warm. My dwelling lacks a few of the refinements you'd find in the town though I don't expect that'll bother the likes of you.'

'I thank you,' responded the stranger.

Eumaeus tried to assess the stranger's age but managed only a vague guess at his being of middle years. They stepped to the fire where Eumaeus pulled over another stool, adding as he shifted aside his work, 'And should you decide during the night to offer me mischief or help yourself to any of my belongings, the dogs will 'ave you. They'll let almost anyone in but they'll not let 'em out unless I allow it.'

'I'll give you no trouble,' said the man, easing himself down opposite Eumaeus.

As they ate and drank, Eumaeus, thinking the stranger would prefer to relish a meal he must have long craved, thought it better not to distract him with conversation. He noted, however, that the man dealt with the food and wine in a restrained manner rather than the animal gusto of someone used to a life of hunger and deprivation. When the heat of the day was at its most intense, the stranger said, 'I thank you for your hospitality, sir, and your offer of a bed that I'll gladly accept. But at sunrise tomorrow I'll return to Ithaca town.'

'And what'll you do there?' asked Eumaeus.

'If I'm obliged to beg, sir, then begging's what I'll do; it won't be the first time by any means, though I'd rather earn my bread by working.'

'And tell me what work will you seek? What skills have you to offer?'

'I'll handle and I'll slaughter any beast, I'll chop wood and I'll break stones, and I'll carry a burden great as any man. If I can get myself cleaned up and out of these damned rags then I'll offer myself for service at the palace I hear was once ruled by Odysseus.'

'Yes, my friend,' sighed Eumaeus, refilling their rough pottery goblets from an earthenware jug, 'as you say, once ruled by Odysseus though I fear these are uncertain days now.'

'Uncertain days, sir – why is that? I've heard rumours on my travels but as I'm not familiar with these parts I'd be grateful if you'd tell me more then I'll know better what to expect.'

'Oh, I'll tell you what 'appened: our king sailed off to Troy with King Agamemnon gettin' on for twenty years ago and he's not been 'eard of since. Some say 'e'll never return whereas many 'ope 'e will, though twenty years is a long time. His good wife insists 'e'll one day come back to Ithaca and she 'olds onto 'is throne by the skin of 'er teeth. When those men from families once Odysseus' subjects decided 'e'd never return they became 'er suitors even though a few of 'em are younger than she is. Some of the buggers 'ave wives of their own but they'd dismiss those women soon enough. Like wolves they consume 'er food, much of which I'm obliged to supply to the palace kitchens. Their demands of late 'ave increased with their numbers of 'angers-on so that my own stocks are now in decline. They press Lady Penelope constantly to choose one as 'er 'usband so as to take his throne but she'll not accept any of 'em. It's her own wiles, the palace guard and the fact that she 'as a son of twenty years that's 'elped her remain where she is. But as I see it, time's runnin' out and worse things are ahead. I'm told the captain of her palace guard cleared off when they threatened to murder his family and she can't be certain 'ow many of his men are loyal or in the pay of the suitors. No woman should suffer such a burden - but then, as all agree, no woman should occupy a king's throne.'

'Can this son of hers not take his father's place?' asked the stranger, 'A king's throne, as you say, is surely no place for a woman.'

'She's done 'er best over the years to keep the boy away from palace affairs for 'is own safety. Perhaps it was the right thing to do before 'e came of age but now 'e has, things have gone too far and those men will never back down. Ah, if only Odysseus 'ad returned. Many of us pray to the gods that 'e may yet do so but our words seem to fall upon deaf ears and fate casts an ever longer shadow. If 'e ever does return I tell you, my friend, I'll be there with my sword and there'll be no fancy work in it - no, I'll treat those buggers as meat for the slaughter!'

'So where is this boy of hers?'

'Telemachus set out some time ago for the mainland to discover if his father still lives. It became known a short while back that his mother's suitors 'ad plotted to ambush 'im at sea on 'is return from Pylos to Ithaca but I 'ear the would-be murderers were themselves slain or drowned.'

'How can you know this?' the stranger asked. 'Surely such matters would be kept secret by those involved.'

'Secret! Very little is secret nowadays it seems to me. It was 'eard said by one of the men who reported to Antinous, the worst of 'em, because he was responsible for the ambush. The hireling received so much abuse when delivering the news he got 'imself drunk in one of the taverns next morning and revealed what 'e never should 'ave. I don't rate his chances of seein' many more days in this world if that rogue Antinous or any of his men find out what 'e said.'

'Well, sir, this boy, Telemachus – what might he do next?'

Eumaeus hesitated before replying. 'For a vagrant with little experience of these lands you seem to 'ave an uncommon interest in our affairs. What am I to make of this?'

'I mean no harm,' the stranger replied. 'Listening to other people's tales colours my own life.'

'Hmm, I don't suppose it'll matter what I tell you,' shrugged Eumaeus, adding wood to the fire. 'There's no news of the boy but I 'ope 'e still lives. I worry that 'is travels may have taken 'im further east into lands where it's rumoured great troubles are afoot.'

'And if this Odysseus did return,' asked the stranger, 'what then?'

'What then? I'll tell you what then, my friend; there are few people on Ithaca and beyond who'd not welcome 'im back. Yes, this would be a grateful land. As for the suitors, it would surely be the end of 'em, though they'd do all they could to prevent 'is reclaiming 'is rightful throne.'

'I heard tales of this man on my travels,' remarked the stranger casually, clasping the goblet of wine in his hands. 'It wouldn't surprise me if this Odysseus was to return to Ithaca.'

'What – an' I thought you knew nothing about 'im! Are you now tellin' me you do know somethin'? If so I'll 'ear it now as payment for the food and the comfort I've offered you.'

'It's hardly more than hearsay – the odd account from people who claimed to have seen him. It's possible I myself saw him but much of the time I had other things on my mind.'

'Saw Odysseus, you say?' responded Eumaeus. 'You must 'ave travelled and seen a great deal whereas I've seldom left Ithaca because of my responsibilities. I sometimes wonder - do I rule the pigs or do the pigs rule me - I'm never quite certain. But as I've been open with you, now you can tell me somethin' of *your* past.'

'My past?' mused the stranger as Eumaeus stared at him in anticipation. 'Well, sir, I – I was born on Crete, yes, I was bastard son of a landowner, a nobleman at the court of Knossos who played free and easy with any woman who was unable to avoid him.'

'Knossos!' exclaimed Eumaeus. 'I've 'eard people speak of Knossos. It's supposed to be the wealthiest kingdom in the entire world.' He eyed the stranger dubiously but allowed him to continue.

'The wealthiest, aye – there's nowhere else as prosperous as Knossos, except for Egypt. But at Knossos I was one bastard too many, at least for the man who fathered me. Idomenius had become king but gone were the days of glory and there was a lot of infighting at the palace. I was one of its victims. I was banished to a humble estate out in the country. I was no farmer and that I made clear. I wanted to get away so I thought I'd struck lucky when the king put me in charge of a ship to search out pirates.'

The stranger downed more wine then continued, 'But the old days when Crete ruled the seas were gone and we ourselves took to preying on other vessels around the Aegean Sea. More ships joined us as it suited them until we became a small fleet. We acquired much of value but that was our undoing. We entered the Nile and raided into Egypt where we believed there was a lot of gold to be had. The captains of other ships decided to carry on upriver by themselves, forgetting that Egypt was a powerful nation and well able to deal with the threat. Aye, sir, most of them were soon killed or taken prisoner. That left us without our strength in numbers but still we carried on.

One day we were sailing in the Aegean, heading for the shore where we'd set up camp. We thought no one knew our whereabouts until we were intercepted by a vessel from Athens full of armed men. Our ship was overloaded with plunder and we were outnumbered so our only escape was to run her onto the beach. Well the rocks took us instead so we had to swim for our lives. I alone got clean away but I was left with nothing of value. I ended up as you see me now, a homeless wanderer. I drifted wherever chance took me, often not knowing where I was, often in lands where they spoke a different language to my own.'

'Why did you not find your way back to Crete?' asked Eumaeus.

'I, er – yes, I suppose that's what I should have done. Yes, maybe I'll go back to Crete.'

They continued in conversation but the stranger was reluctant to enter into any but the most superficial details of his past. The dogs were little disturbed when three of Eumaeus' men returned from the pastures. The men acknowledged their master and the stranger seated with him then, having lifted burning wood from Eumaeus' fire they lit another at the far side of the enclosure in preparation for their own meal.

When the dogs began to yelp again it was not as aggressively as when the stranger arrived but in tail-wagging anticipation of another visitor. A figure walked along the rough track but this time from the seaward side of Eumaeus' house. Glancing aside, Eumaeus recognised the carefree but confident walk and shoulder length, fair hair framing a broad yet much stubbled smile. He jumped up, knocking over his stool as he exclaimed, 'By the gods!'

One hand gripping the hilt to steady the sword swinging at his waist, Telemachus placed the other on a post and vaulted nimbly over the fence. Each of Eumaeus' men arose to acknowledge him with raised hand and the dogs circled enthusiastically as he approached their astonished owner.

'Eumaeus, my friend!' Telemachus greeted aloud, glancing aside at the huddled stranger, 'it seems I caught you by surprise! That's no bad thing since it's the way I hope to catch a few others!'

The stranger remained as he was, one hand on his goblet, his head lowered.

Eumaeus, arms raised high, declared with bright-eyed enthusiasm, 'Young master, you're back with us safe an' sound! I and many others have prayed and offered sacrifice for this moment!'

Still the stranger did not rise but with cowl pulled forward he studied their new arrival with a discretely searching eye.

'Here and glad of it,' smiled Telemachus, 'and in need of food and drink, a damn good wash and a shave!' He peered for some moments at the vagrant whose face was now hidden by the cowl.

'I'll offer you food and drink at once,' beamed Eumaeus, 'then while you eat I'll draw water from the well and see that it's heated over the fire. And I'm sure hidden away somewhere I've an ancient razor and a stone to sharpen it with. There's even a bronze mirror though it will be dull since I've not 'ad the courage to polish it and look at myself these past years. But 'ave you come up straight from the sea? Will you be makin' your way to the palace?'

'I have come straight from the sea and I will go to the palace,' answered Telemachus, brushing a wisp of hair from his cheek, 'but not until tomorrow morning.'

At last the stranger turned his head and spoke. 'Give this lad the bed you offered me. I'll sleep out here if you'll allow it.'

'This man's a wanderer and far from 'ome,' explained Eumaeus, gesturing toward his ragged guest. 'I've offered 'im food an' shelter. All 'e wants is to find work in the town.'

Telemachus eyed the stranger then, stepping closer to Eumaeus he said in a lowered voice, 'You're a good man, Eumaeus, but I'll ask another favour.'

'Ask anything, young sir.'

'I want you to go to the palace before dark. Inform my mother I'm alive and well and say I'll be with her tomorrow. Also, see if any of Antinous' thugs are on the lookout beyond the city wall. No one will question your coming and going.'

'I'll do that, young master and I'll return 'ere early as I'm able in the mornin' with whatever information I can glean.' He gestured to the stranger, adding, 'This man will 'ave the space I promised 'im and you are welcome to my own modest and, I must add, clean bed. My men'll soon return to the fields to gather in our pigs. After that they'll go to their own 'omes.'

'Then I'll have your wandering man's company for the evening,' said Telemachus, glancing once more at the stranger. The stranger appeared not to have heard.

'But may I ask in turn,' said Eumaeus, ''ave you gained anythin' from your travels that will 'elp solve our problems?'

'Not materially,' he replied, 'but I have learned much and fought hard to preserve my life. I see the world differently now and my resolve is strengthened more than ever I could have imagined. Somehow we will prevail over those men.'

'Then I am much gladdened, young master – that I am!'

His three men were long gone when Eumaeus departed for Ithaca town but Telemachus, stepping bathed and shaved from the house with flagon of wine and goblet as darkness fell, was not to have his anticipated company. The stranger, rising from his seat by the fire, avoided acknowledgement as he retired, shadow-like, to his allocated place of comfort.

**

'I watched Noemon's ship enter the harbour,' said Leucon, maintaining a respectful distance from the enthroned Penelope. Her female attendants had retreated to the far side of the great hall and to the strumming of Phemios' harp they occupied themselves in idle chatter. 'I went down there,' he continued, 'but the young master was not to be seen. Noemon informed me he was alive and well but had sworn not to say where he had gone. He insisted I speak to no one but you about this.'

'So we don't even know if Telemachus is on Ithaca,' she sighed.

'Lady Penelope, it may be for the good he did not return with the others. There were five armed men loitering amidst rocks above the harbour. I'm sure they were waiting for Noemon's ship. They would not have been visible from the harbour but they had good sight of it and I had sight of them on my way down there. They may have realised I intended to inquire after the young master and would have known as did I that he was not on board the vessel. When I left the harbour they were gone.'

'Did you recognise any of them?' she asked.

'Two, my lady, I have seen in the taverns, sometimes with your suitors. Of the other three I could not be sure but I'm certain the young master is safe and that the gods watch over him.'

'Yes, he must be safe and well. Oh, he must. Leucon, go back to Euryclea and if she's alone tell her what you've told me. Make sure no one overhears you – oh, and have Niobe come to me with her perfumed oils and her comb.'

***

The night was clear with a river of stars glowing above Eumaeus' farm. The dogs slept as dogs usually sleep, with an ear for the slightest noise. But they hardly stirred at all when the stranger left his bed.

Telemachus had slept well but now he awoke because there were voices seeming to drift from the realms of darkness - voices swirling within in a vortex of sounds. Thinking he heard his name called he sat up to ask, 'Who is there?' His hand was already at his sword, drawing it partly from its sheath as he listened intently to the whisperings of the night. The whisperings receded until there was only the sound of his own breath, drawn then held in anticipation.

In total blackness vague images are sometimes perceived floating in the air, drifting, evolving forms that have no meaning. Except that, for Telemachus, one of them was acquiring human form. It was the spectral likeness of a man, a well-built, short-bearded man of middle age with shoulder length, muted red hair held in place by a gilded, gem studded band. His eyes were bright and alert, his richly embroidered tunic was that of a noble and his belt, sword and scabbard could belong only to a warrior of royal standing. His lips moved in soundless speech as he reached outstretched fingers to Telemachus, but the apparition was already fading before they touched. Heartbeats later it had dissolved into blackness.

Convinced at last that he was fully awake Telemachus slipped from the bed and peered into obscurity. There was no lighted oil lamp, no flame to illuminate the room though the stars appeared bright beyond the small window above. He reached for his belt. It lay close by the bed with the sword still nestled undisturbed within its scabbard. 'Hmm,' he muttered, 'did I also reach for my sword a short while ago? Maybe not. It must be the effects of Eumaeus' country wine.'

He returned to the bed, drew back the sheepskin and was trying once more to relax when -.

'Telemachus.'

This voice was undoubtedly real. It came from beyond the oxhide cover suspended across the doorway. Telemachus was on his feet and reaching for his tunic he stood listening for tense moments, pulling on the tunic before calling aloud, 'Who's there? Answer me!'

'I wish to speak with you,' came the reply. It was the voice of the stranger, calm but assured. 'I carry no weapon. I intend you no harm.'

'Wait and I'll be with you! Stand back from the door!'

Telemachus seized up his scabbard and hastily fastened the belt about his waist. With a hand resting firmly on the sword hilt he wrenched aside the curtain and emerged cautiously into cool air. The fire only smouldered but the soon to wane stars and the light of a half-moon enabled each man to vaguely assess the other. The stranger stood several paces away, arms folded. The cowl no longer concealed his head.

'So,' Telemachus asked. 'What have you to say that could not wait until daylight?' He glanced aside wondering for a moment why the dogs remained silent and seemingly undisturbed.

'Most of the night has passed and we move closer to dawn,' replied the stranger. 'I intended to speak with you at sunrise but impatience harassed me through the night and I can wait no longer. I have been unable to sleep for thinking over it because it is something you have to know before Eumaeus returns. Perhaps the intimacy of darkness will favour my words. We should sit at Eumaeus' bench and take some of our good host's wine. When you hear what I'm to say you may need it.'

'Very well, I'll hear you,' Telemachus felt this was no trivial matter, yet what of any consequence could this destitute man have to reveal?

They sat opposite one another; their cups filled brimming from the pitcher Telemachus had placed on the ground to one side of the bench. On the eastern horizon was resolved a dim, hazy light that promised soon to brighten into morning. The stranger drank. Telemachus drank. Telemachus waited with stirring impatience for him to speak. Still the man said nothing. He continued to gaze at Telemachus as if unsure as to how he ought to gather together his words. When he at last spoke his voice was calm yet to Telemachus his words might have fallen as a crash of thunder.

'I am Odysseus. I am your father.'

Telemachus, held in perplexed silence as the words coursed through his mind, continued to regard the figure sitting motionless before him. Should he respond to this declaration with scorn or laughter? He did neither but, drawing breath he looked hard at the stranger and at length said, 'Oh, really? And what makes you think I or anyone else would believe such an unlikely claim?' But even as he spoke the image that had appeared in the darkness of Eumaeus' house not so long before loomed clearly in his mind. The man's eyes possessed that same intense look and Telemachus wondered if the gods might be at work here. Perhaps for mischief.

'I can hardly blame you for doubting me,' came the reply, 'for I know you do, and I in turn am ill prepared to prove the truth of it – other than the fact that I possess a knowledge of affairs at Ithaca I think no other man could match even after the passing of so many years. Euryclea alone knows my true identity though she has sworn to remain silent for the time being.'

'Does she really,' responded Telemachus, yet the blood pulsed through his veins. He was unable to suppress the notion that something of momentous import might be happening. He tried to remain aloof, to sound unimpressed, but was barely able to contain the emotion in his voice. 'I hear what you say and if this is a game then we can both play at it. Yes, let's try – let's see where it gets us! You can tell me about our nursemaid who you say believes you, and the duties she performed over many years - and about the man who tutored us. Oh, yes, and the palace vaults: what you recall has lain in there since before you, or should I say my father, left for Troy and – and, yes, how and where did he meet my mother? I'm waiting.' Telemachus sat upright on the stool, prepared to rise and draw his sword while adding, 'And if this *is* some stupid game you're playing you'd better be ready to leave here much quicker than you arrived because I'm in no mood for it! And I don't intend you'll be going back to the town, either!'

The stranger smiled. He proceeded calmly to address the questions with which Telemachus had challenged him and did so in even more detail than had been demanded. To end his account he added, 'Should you still doubt me then Euryclea will confirm how she discovered the truth when Eumaeus -.'

'Better if you relate it *before* Eumaeus returns!' interrupted Telemachus.

'Very well: I carry the scar of a wound she dressed when I was four years younger than you now are.' He hesitated, drained the contents of his cup and concluded, 'There's little more evidence I can offer at present. Should you choose not to accept me for who I am then I'll have to plan accordingly. I will return to the palace I once commanded whether you like it or not and there I'll see what support is to be had in Ithaca. I doubt you'd kill an unarmed man.'

'Very convincing!' exclaimed Telemachus, rising to step aside from the stool, 'especially the scar. But lots of people bear scars. I've a few small ones of my own as a result of hunting, not to mention a small episode at sea a couple of days ago. If you are who you say you are, why have you ended up here at Eumaeus' farm and – and looking like –?'

Again there was silence. A long, charged silence as Telemachus continued to stare at the man, his mind awash with half-formed questions and conflicting notions. A hiss from the dying embers of the fire prompted Telemachus to announce at last, in little more than a whisper, 'Yes, I - I'm thinking I could almost, and I say *almost*, accept your claim as true. Not just because of what you've told me but in part because I believe Athena gave me a sign before you called me out here. And I - I ask myself what could you hope to gain by lying. Then I also have to ask why it has taken the best part of ten years for you to return from Troy. Ten years, throughout which my mother has endured the uncertainty of our situation and the attentions of those men who have so recently attempted to kill me. And as for your appearance – it's hardly that of a returning hero.'

'No it is not,' agreed Odysseus, standing to face him, 'but I wished no one to recognise me until I gained some idea of what had transpired on Ithaca. Aye, all I had to guide me until these last few days were the rumours offered by people I listened to in the streets and in the market. As for the ten years after Troy - let me tell you that after the storm we were separated from the rest of Agamemnon's fleet, we were driven into strange waters and far stranger lands. I will explain it all in good time but there are the affairs of the palace to be discussed. What I ask now daylight approaches is that you relate to me certain matters.'

'Certain matters,' breathed Telemachus, his doubts over the man reasserting once more. 'By Zeus this has to be the strangest day I've yet encountered. I have taken up residence at the home of our keeper of pigs through warnings of my own assassination and now I stand confronted by a vagabond who claims to be the missing father who I was convinced died ten years ago. Very well, let's say I go along with this – at least for now. My mother always hoped her brave Odysseus would one day march into the palace clad in flashing bronze with a bright plume swaying above his warrior's helmet, sword at the ready and men at his side to drive out those ill-bred oafs who descend upon us each night. What d'you imagine she'd think if she were to set eyes on you? Tell me – whatever is to happen next?'

Again Odysseus smiled, his manner ever more relaxed and reassuring. 'Whatever is to happen next is what we must discuss. Let's hope the risen sun will illuminate a clear path for our thoughts.'

'I'll await the risen sun with considerable interest,' breathed Telemachus. 'Perhaps by then I'll know better what to make of what's passed between us. For now I'll outline what was happening within the palace when I left, then whatever else you wish to ask can wait until Eumaeus returns. I very much look forward to *his* response.'

After relating what he considered relevant, Telemachus stepped back to the house, determined to be alone with his thoughts. Seated on Eumaeus' bed he pondered over what the coming day might have in store. He wondered, too, if the vagrant who claimed to be his father would still be there when Eumaeus returned from Ithaca town, as soon he must.

Chapter 9 - The Traveller's Tales

Telemachus re-emerged from the house to find the rising sun spreading bright fingers over the land. To his surprise a newly restored fire cracked and hissed and the stranger stood by the fence gazing across the morning landscape. Telemachus stepped back into the house to acquire one of the clay-capped flagons of well water set aside by Eumaeus. On hearing his footsteps Odysseus resumed his former place at the table. Telemachus filled the goblets but so far no word had passed between them.

Raising his goblet to drink, it was Odysseus who broke the silence. 'Even now I cannot believe so many years have passed since we conquered Troy. No, in spite of all that has happened, in spite of all that I've witnessed and the dangers I and my men faced, it seems as though everything took place in some domain fashioned by the gods for their entertainment. And now - now at last I'm fully awake to the affairs of our own world.'

'Pity you weren't awake a few years sooner,' commented Telemachus. The wonder of his father's materialising as a being of flesh and blood had surged back and forth during his brief retreat into isolation. Belief hounded disbelief in a whirlwind of uncertainty. Could this man have been companion to the long dead Odysseus and the information he had so convincingly imparted earlier have been gathered through that association? Could he have met with Euryclea yesterday for the first time and fooled her with the same tale?

Telemachus looked sternly at him. 'The palace is infested each evening with men who consume the wealth of our estate with little more thought or manners than pigs at a trough. And as they also contrived to murder me at sea they will surely not have abandoned the idea once they realise I'm back on the island. Yes, mother always insisted her husband would return but I couldn't imagine anyone of his standing would treat his responsibilities with such disdain.'

'Disdain, boy!' Odysseus cried angrily, his features darkening as he sprang up to knock aside the stool and slam down the goblet from which a spray of water erupted.

Rising to face him, Telemachus' hand dropped instinctively toward his sword but stopped short of grasping the hilt.

'There was no disdain!' Odysseus declared. 'None! The very gods who seemed at first to favour us turned against me because of what happened at Troy, aye, because of that damned wooden horse I created to bring about the city's ruin. You might ask how could the men of Troy have been so stupid unless the gods were against them as well. But whatever action I took in my bid to return to Ithaca the gods thwarted. They seized hold of me - mind and body! They set lures, false trails and contrary winds wherever I went! They drove me here and there until I often had no idea where I was and on occasion who I was!' He calmed, lowered his head then added, 'And yes, I confess it freely, I failed to account for the passing years.' He leaned forward to reach across the bench, placed a rough hand upon Telemachus' shoulder and said, 'I - I cannot blame you for doubting all I claim. All I ask is that you give me a chance. Allow me some trust and I promise by Zeus I will prove myself your true father or die in the attempt.'

Telemachus pondered over his words. Perhaps this man's arrival really was one of the most important moments in both their lives and if so then the future of Ithaca might depend upon it.

Odysseus pulled the stool upright and said, 'It would be better if I lay low here for a day or two. We'll have time to spare and I've already made clear there's a great deal I have to relate. So if you care to hear me out, boy, I'll -.'

'Do not address me in that manner!' cut in Telemachus. 'Late I might have been in getting there but I have taken on tasks and responsibilities that, if I'm to accept your account, were by rights yours. I have the blood of men on my hands and it isn't going end there. I have risked and still do risk my life to maintain what's left of a kingdom that you, if you *are* my father, failed to reclaim.'

Odysseus eyed him angrily, relaxed and splashed more water into his goblet. 'I was wrong to address you that way,' he sighed. 'Telemachus, you are my son and I'm sure by now I have good reason to be proud of you.'

Telemachus returned to his own seat and again was convinced this man could well be his father. With suspicion giving ground to a measure of sympathy he said, 'As we're going to be here for some time it might be a good opportunity, when Eumaeus gets back, to relate in full what did happen after Troy.'

'I'll do that, aye, I will' agreed Odysseus. He stared into his goblet, swirled the water around then asked, 'Have you found yourself a decent wench – I mean anyone special, or are you still as free with the palace girls as most men would be at your age?'

Telemachus drank from his own cup then replied, 'I claim no degree of self-restraint inside or outside the palace but when visiting Nestor I met someone who – someone who I found more to my liking than ever I imagined I could. I wish it had been possible to bring her back to Ithaca and she also desired it. She spoke very little Greek and we spent little enough time together but that was of little importance. I felt t the gods intended us to meet.'

Odysseus smiled and also drank, saying, 'Aye, women; such snares they set for us as I'll soon enough relate. But as for this girl of yours - maybe, if things work out as we wish, you'll be able to get her over here. Tell me, what was she like?'

'What was she like? What justice can a mere description do? She was beautiful, of course, and at the time I thought she was a gift from the gods.'

'Aye,' muttered Odysseus, 'well not all gifts from the gods work out as we'd wish.' He tipped away the contents of his goblet then added, 'And as for water, I have good reason not to value it as I once did so next time you pour, let's make it wine again.'

'As you wish,' Telemachus replied.

They continued in amicable conversation but soon enough the dogs became agitated.

'They want their food,' remarked Odysseus, glancing aside at the tail-wagging mongrels.

'They do,' responded Telemachus. 'And it may not be long before they have it. I see their master heading our way.'

'So Eumaeus returns. Then I'd better explain myself to him as I have to you though I expect it will be easier.'

'I expect it will,' agreed Telemachus. 'He once knew the King of Ithaca whereas I never did.'

Eumaeus, staff in hand, entered the enclosure and strode over to address Telemachus as he and Odysseus rose from their seats. 'Young sir, all is as well as it might be. Lady Penelope is overjoyed to know you are safe but will inform only those closest to her.' He eyed the other man, adding, 'She expressed her unease over our wandering friend here. She believes he told Euryclea something the woman will not divulge – something that she suspects might concern yourself or your father.' Eumaeus regarded the stranger with visible unease.

'Yes,' breathed Telemachus, 'it has to be now.' Then he announced, 'This man, friend Eumaeus, may not be the vagabond we thought. I suggest you take a closer look at him. Better pour yourself a cup of wine first.'

Odysseus pushed back the long, bedraggled hair that had obscured part of his face.

Eumaeus stood confused, glancing from Telemachus to the stranger. When he shrugged, Telemachus placed a hand on his shoulder and asked, 'Look closer. Is there anything about him you recognise? He may soon be leaving us if you don't.'

Eumaeus peered closer with a hand raised to shield his eyes, muttering, 'I don't understand.'

Several heartbeats passed whilst he gazed intently at the stranger's face, then, 'Wait –!' he gasped. 'Oh – oh but I –! Yes – no! It cannot be!'

'I believe it might be,' said Telemachus, adding under his breath, 'And if I find I'm deceived he'll pay for it.'

Trembling uncontrollably Eumaeus stepped back a pace then fell to his knees with hands clasped at his chest. 'Lord Odysseus, it is – it is you! Really you! The gods have answered our prayers. After all these years you have returned and – and I have shown you no respect at all! Why - why did I not know?' Hands raised to his cheeks, Eumaeus continued to stare up in astonishment.

'On your feet, man,' insisted Odysseus, stooping to take Eumaeus' arm. 'I didn't want to reveal myself until now, but let me tell you one thing if nothing else: I know you have kept faith with my house and I trust there are a good many like you. You are a loyal man, Eumaeus, and if I succeed in my intentions you and others will gain much from my homecoming – that I promise.'

As Eumaeus stood in perplexed silence, hands clasped tightly at his front, Telemachus asked himself if the man's memory could be so clouded by the passage of years that he had fallen for a deception. It seemed most unlikely yet the spectre of doubt, though driven close to extinction, was not entirely exorcized.'

'Wh-what now, sire,' asked wide-eyed Eumaeus, stepping back another pace to appraise the one-time stranger's image. 'What is to be done now you are with us?' He continued to stare at

Odysseus as if the image was that of Apollo materialised within a radiant shaft of light.

'There is much to be worked out,' replied Odysseus, 'but the guise I have as a vagrant has to stay with me until the time is right.'

'Now it seems he's back from the dead,' confirmed Telemachus, 'we'll remain here as long as we have to. It will give us an opportunity to plan what has to be done but for now, friend Eumaeus, you must continue to come and go from the town without raising suspicion. First attend to your dogs then sit with us so we both can hear what my newly resurrected father has to tell us of his travels. Oh, and maybe a bite to eat would help.'

'That I will prepare for us now,' enthused Eumaeus in a voice cracked with emotion. 'Then I'll not miss a word of it! No, not a word! By Zeus I will not!'

'Better if we continue indoors,' cautioned Telemachus, peering beyond Eumaeus' fence. 'The suitors may have scouts roaming the island. It wouldn't help our situation if I was spotted by one of them. At least not yet.'

'And my lords,' offered Eumaeus, glancing up at the sky, 'the day will not continue as it began. I look at those gathering clouds and I feel it in the newly risen breeze, the weather may soon change for the worse.'

***

The stools had been pulled close to a solid, age-assaulted wooden table and Eumaeus placed honeyed oatcakes onto three dishes. A fire spluttered and danced in the hearth where skewered meat sizzled. Soon enough, with three cups and a recharged flagon of wine on hand they huddled beneath the beams, secure within the shadowed intimacy of Eumaeus' dwelling. Eumaeus remained awestruck of the newly revealed Odysseus and seemed unable to speak until Odysseus himself did so, beginning with an account of how his small group of ships sailed from Troy in the company of Agamemnon and his allies.

'…The storm grew rapidly. It struck us in open water and was worse than any I ever knew. When it cleared we, that is my small company of six vessels, found ourselves quite alone with no idea what had happened to Agamemnon and the rest of the fleet. I'd lost none of my own ships but all were damaged. The wind drove us northwest toward Thrace but it was not until we made land, not until we spoke to someone ashore that we discovered exactly where we were and that it was safe to go ashore. We spent several days repairing our ships then, refreshed and ready to deal with whoever challenged us, we sailed along the coast to attack and plunder the town of Ismaros. We did this mainly because its people had allied themselves to Troy and their men had fought against us. Ismaros was a town of no great size but was one of considerable wealth.'

'Wealth?' queried Telemachus. 'Had you not just looted Troy?'

'Yes but the Trojans had hidden or sent out of the city so much that was valuable only Agamemnon and Menelaus could claim to have left with all the plunder their vessels could carry.'

In the half-light bounded by those confining walls, his words grew in substance. His eyes shone as he unleashed memories of flashing blades, swaying plumes of the warriors' helmets, the shouts and the cries of victor and vanquished.

'Aye, we laid into 'em and were flushed with an easy victory because within the town itself there were not so many fighting men. I went to make sacrifice at Apollo's temple and their priest presented me with a cask of the very best wine of the region because I'd ordered his shrine and those of other gods to be left untouched. Alas their wines are highly potent and many of my crew indulged themselves for longer than they should have – yes, and without bothering to water the stuff down. Unknown to us the people of Ismaros had summoned outside help then rallied to attack us when it arrived. We were badly outnumbered; a few of my men were too drunk to fight or flee and were killed, and one of our boats was set ablaze before we managed to get ourselves clear.

After that we were determined to head for home with the plunder we'd loaded aboard our vessels. We made good progress across the Aegean, never far from land, intending to round the southern Peloponnese after which we'd steer north toward Ithaca. Then the gods sent down mists; impenetrable mists that descended about us like a shroud. We managed to stay together but lost all sense of direction and drifted before an ever-increasing wind. When the mist lifted we were again in open water with no sight of land. The wind continued but with the sun and stars visible it was obvious we were being driven far to the south in unknown seas.

After nine days at sea and with our fresh water almost gone we had a welcome sight of land. The wind had calmed so we sailed in to haul our boats onto the beach in a place that appeared deserted. There were date palms along the shore and an abundance of flowers. The air was warm and carried an exotic perfume. We located a freshwater stream and came upon a village but the people we encountered were an oddly placid lot with big, soft eyes. They weren't in the least bothered when we explored their village though it proved all but devoid of material possessions. Yes, if they owned anything worth taking it must have been well hidden because we looked hard and discovered nothing of value. Each family lived in a hut with little comfort other than a bed of straw. Their utensils were made of wood or baked clay because they had no bronze. Somehow they made themselves understood to us – aye, smiling all the time as if their world lacked all the troubles that beset ours. Their diet included a plant they called the Lotus. It was sacred to them – so sacred they worshipped as well as ate the thing. In fact they seemed to eat little else apart from fish, which they readily offered us.

Several of my crew wanted a change from fish and mouldering bread and were tempted by the Lotus Eaters – aye, that's what we began to call them - to sample their damnable plant. It must have contained some kind of drug because not long after eating the stuff those men fell into a state of apathy and expressed no interest whatsoever in returning to the ships. They forgot they had a home and even who they were. If it had gone on any longer they'd have ended up devoid of willpower like the natives. I ordered my other men seize them, yes - seize and drag them back to the ships where I had 'em tied to the rowing benches until we were well out to sea. Only then did they shake off whatever it was had a hold on their senses. I tell you, a man of our own world could go insane in that place unless he fed himself on Lotus leaves. But if he did then - then he'd no longer be a man.'

'But you were still lost,' put in Telemachus.

'We were, though I figured we had to be somewhere along the coast of Africa. That meant we needed to head north or north-east if we were to find our way back to Greece.' He took a draught of wine then added, 'But the danger we'd faced in Lotus Land was nothing compared with what lay in wait for us. No,' he sighed, gazing into the fire, 'nothing at all.'

Beyond Eumaeus' house heavy clouds had risen and spread to obscure the sun. The land had become shrouded. The skies began to growl.

'We've another storm on the way,' said Eumaeus, adding new wood to his fire.

The fire cracked and grew bright in his hearth. Wood smoke swirled into the obscurity of the beams and blackened thatch above. Rain began to fall and the world beyond Eumaeus' darkened house might have ceased to exist - except for thunder rolling above like the drums of war. Wine cups were raised and Odysseus continued his tale.

'After many more days at sea we approached a steep coast with several islands offshore. We'd no idea who or what lived there - hostile tribes maybe, so we located a natural harbour at one of the smaller islands where there were no signs of occupation. On the mainland we could see smoke and flames rising from a distant mountain but there was no visible danger. I took twelve men and sailed over to the mainland, thinking we'd obtain fresh water, hunt game or trade for food. But when we landed we could see no people and no farms, let alone any sign of a village although there were plenty of sheep to be seen in the distance. Had we taken more notice of those sheep and seen what we should have seen, we'd have gotten back to our boat and sailed away pretty quick.'

He gulped more wine then carried on. 'The land rose before us and higher up there were three caves in a sheer cliff face with well-worn tracks leading to them so we headed for the nearest. It was further away than we'd reckoned and when we got there, larger than we'd at first thought. We passed through a great arched entrance into a grim, echoing cavern the likes of which I'd never seen and never want to see again. The place was dank and foul smelling. It reeked of evil yet it was obviously lived in. It went back quite a way and widened further to a stony chamber. At the back where lamps burned we discovered huge cheeses and animal carcases stored on rock ledges. There were tall jars we thought must contain wine and oil, and there were great ingots of bronze. Everything in there looked much larger than several men could handle. That ought to have alerted us. Regrettably it did not.

Some of the lads wanted to help themselves to whatever they could. One of 'em proposed hacking chunks off the cheeses and carcases with their swords then getting out of the place but I said no. I insisted we wait to see who lived there so we could discover where we were and maybe trade a few

247

goods. We had with us some small items of value to barter and I'd taken along the cask of wine handed over by the priest on Ismaros. I thought it better to bring that as a gift for whoever we encountered rather than leave it behind where some of my crew might have been tempted to open it. Most people will trade for good wine except in Egypt where they make enough of it to drown themselves.'

He took another drink then added gravely, 'Hah - I've made my share of mistakes in life, that I'll admit, but lingering inside that damned cave has to be one of the most regrettable.'

The fire flared and hissed. It threw their shadows large against the walls. Eumaeus glanced aside at the hearth, saying, 'My lord, young master, the skewered meat is ready if you'll allow me to share it out – and there's plenty more wine. My men brought it by wagon from the town yesterday so you may find it preferable to my own.'

'I've had worse offers,' smiled Odysseus.

'Where are your men today?' asked Telemachus, turning to Eumaeus. 'I've seen none of them.'

'I told them to stay away because I had other matters to attend,' answered Eumaeus, 'They'll see nothing odd in that. Each will take a drove of pigs to his own farm for the time being and encounter no one from the town.'

With ample bread and meat in earthenware bowls and the wine cups replenished, Telemachus turned to Odysseus. 'Please continue, father - there must be a good nine years to go.'

Telemachus' sarcasm was not well concealed. Odysseus eyed him sternly then ate and drank a little, as did Telemachus and Eumaeus, before resuming his narrative.

'We remained there,' he went on. 'We waited all that afternoon within the cave until the sun was well down and we helped ourselves to whatever food and drink we were able to get at. Around sunset we heard a heavy, ponderous plodding like the beat of a big drum. Those footsteps hesitated then sheep began to enter, driven inside by the being we had yet to see. We were filled with wonder at the sight of those animals. Some of my men cried out in alarm. They were huge, lumbering beasts, high as a man. They took not the slightest notice of us but we needed to keep well back to stay clear of their hooves. Aye, we were now to realise in full the consequences of my decision to loiter there.'

Odysseus stared hard into his goblet before continuing. 'A shadow darkened the ground as the keeper of the beasts entered the cave. His breathing came loud and harsh as that of a labouring ox. He blotted out the daylight from outside the cave and his shadow fell over us. High as the cave entrance was, he had to stoop low to pass beneath it. He rose up and before us stood a nightmare conceived of flesh and bone, a fearsome travesty of a man - almost three times the height of any mortal and in proportion even broader. His arms were long. His naked skin was rough and bristled like that of a hog but it was his face that caused us to reel back in horror. It was squat, fleshy and bore one great, round eye that shimmered like a jellyfish. It darted from side to side above his wide nose and flaccid mouth. I tell you, whichever of the gods created this monstrosity must have done so out of malice to all mankind. As he ushered in the last of his sheep we thought to make a dash for the entrance but there was no room to do that without pushing close by him. Then he spotted us. He scowled in a voice like - like slabs of rock grating one against the other, 'Oh, strangers is it? And what are *you* called for what it's worth?'

We all understood his speech, more or less, though it was of little consolation. 'Once I'd summoned the wit to reply I told him I was Nobody. It seemed a good idea in case he'd somehow heard of me and for whatever reason sympathised with the Trojans. I told him I and my men were shipwrecked traders looking for shelter.

"Oh, shipwrecked sailors are we," he growled, then heaved a great round boulder, much higher than a man, across the entrance. "You have entered the dwelling of Polyphemus," he informed us. Then he began to laugh – a hollow, mocking laugh that echoed about the cavern and chilled each man of us to the bone and I somehow knew he intended none of us were to leave that place alive. Rays of the setting sun shone through the gap above the boulder but I could see there was no way any of us could climb up there and push through. We had to remain where we were as he drove the sheep to the far end of the gallery. We could only stand and watch as he built a great fire in the centre of the cave, much of the time staring at us with that damned hideous eye of his. Not once did I see it blink. Then there was his shadow: the fire threw it up against the wall, huge and menacing as its owner. That shadow was a black demon in its own right.'

'I was once told about these beings,' said Eumaeus. 'A traveller referred to them as the Cyclopes, three giants who live apart from one another and herd sheep. He said they were favoured by the gods. He said men familiar with that part of the world avoided their land even in the fiercest storms, though I myself never met anyone who actually claimed to have seen them in person.'

'Aye, well you've met one now,' breathed Odysseus. 'We spread out but there was nowhere to hide even though darkness was falling outside and a deeper gloom had descended within the cave. The smoke from his fire rose up and disappeared into the high ceiling. I looked up hoping there might be some way of escape there but I could see nothing within our reach.

He started laughing again then suddenly reached out to grab one of my men. He picked him up like a child's doll then smashed his head against the wall by the entrance, spattering blood and brains. He squatted opposite to where we cowered in mortal fear and began to eat parts of the man raw, crunching bones and flesh, all of which he swallowed.'

'By the gods!' gasped Eumaeus, 'this is the most fearsome tale I ever heard!'

Telemachus pushed the hair back from his cheeks but remained silent.

'I've seen what men can do to one another in battle,' continued Odysseus, firelight dancing in his eyes. 'I thought I'd seen outside the walls of Troy all the bloodshed and suffering any man could endure but, I tell you, nothing could ever match the horrors we experienced in that grim, stinking cavern. Nothing. I've witnessed fear but never did I see men piss or shit 'emselves as did some of my own crew. That beast dropped the remains of his first victim onto the flames, leaned toward us then reached with unbelievable speed to seize a second man who struggled screaming, calling to us for help until he was likewise slaughtered and partly devoured. Polyphemus killed those men as casually as we would a goat or a pig. To him we were nothing more than a gift of food.'

'Surely you were armed,' put in Telemachus. 'Could the rest of you not have risen up and killed him?'

'We discussed that among ourselves but realised those of us he didn't kill before we did for him would be trapped inside his cave. We could never have moved that rock and even if we'd formed a human ladder the gap didn't look big enough for a man to push through. No, we'd have made a tomb for ourselves though maybe we'd have lived on for months eating his damned sheep and provisions. The creature still gnawed at what was left of his second kill, growling as he ate, and by then we'd decided there might be no way out for us other than to fall on our own swords: better that than share the fate that abomination doubtless intended for us. But it seemed he'd eaten his fill and was going to leave us alone until morning when his appetite for human flesh returned. He consigned what was left of his last victim to the flames, showering sparks across the floor, then he sat staring at us, grinning from a bloodied mouth full of teeth that were large, sharp and very white. We watched him arrange his bed of brushwood and sheepskins then I had an idea - born out of desperation I fully admit. I called out to him: "Are you going to murder the rest of us? Is that your intention?"

"Oh, naturally," he replied, as if this was taken for granted. "The gods now and again send humans as a gift to me. They are much leaner than sheep."

"Then," I said, "you may as well have the gifts *we* brought since they'll be of no use to us. I have here a cask of the finest wine. Will you share this with us and allow us in return to take our own lives as we see fit?"

I had the cask raised in my hands, hoping he'd drink enough of it to make him sleep soundly. He growled at me, leapt up, reached over the fire with one of those grotesque arms to seize the cask. He squatted back against the wall, broke away the clay seal, sniffed at the contents then proceeded to drink the lot, grinning insanely at us between gulps. It was the respite we needed. Soon he was grumbling to himself and rocking back and forth. At last he settled down on his bed then after what seemed half the night had gone by, he began a rattling snore with his gore-fouled mouth hanging wide. His eye was still open but fixed staring upward. We prayed to Zeus and to Athena, begging for the wine to have rendered that bloody, insane creature senseless.

I'd earlier noticed a cluster of olive-wood stakes propped against one wall so I crept across and took one of them. A couple of my men held the stake so I could sharpen one end with my sword. I did it quietly as I could then I hardened it in the fire, turning it, all the time watching in case Polyphemus began to stir. He did not. And now!' Odysseus raised and thumped down his fist. 'Yes, now it was time to act! There was a rock ledge at the side of him onto which I was able to climb, though twice I almost slipped and might have fallen onto him. In the lurid glow of that cavern, bathed by his foul exhalations, I held the stake poised smouldering above his head, ready to strike, then - then that bloated eye turned to look at me! He was about to rise when I plunged the stake down until it sizzled in the eye - but not so hard as to kill him.'

'By Zeus what courage you had!' exclaimed Eumaeus.

'Courage? No, I'll not claim it was courage! It was sheer desperation drove me to it. What did I or any of us have to lose? Polyphemus lashed out to seize me but I leapt aside, got clear of the ledge and dashed over to re-join my lads. The man-beast roared louder than any lion; so loud it shook the very air and walls of the cavern until we feared his cries would bring down rocks from the ceiling. We watched him writhe in agony as he wrenched the stake drizzling from his eye. He rose up, lashing out, almost stumbling into the fire, bellowing and cursing in a voice that thundered about the walls. We dodged about the cave to keep clear of him. We pushed among and underneath his sheep to avoid being caught. The sheep became restless and started bleating. That further confused him because he could no longer hear us moving about. He groped around the walls until finding his bed again and there he sat with his head in his hands wailing in agony.

Eventually the light of dawn began to show above the boulder. He somehow sensed this because he was on his feet, quiet now and feeling his way along the wall until he reached the entrance. He yelled out through the gap above it, fingers clawing the rock until a voice like his own called back from outside to ask what all the fuss was about. "I am blinded by Nobody!" he answered. "Nobody has done this to me!"

He repeated it several times and it became clear that not one but two more like him, waited outside the cave. We heard them laughing. They seemed to think he was drunk. One called, "Well if nobody has harmed you then we'll leave you in peace!"

Then they walked off, so we assumed, to attend to their sheep. Polyphemus groaned and cursed but could do nothing.'

'But still you were prisoners,' said Telemachus as Eumaeus refilled the cups.

'Aye, so we were, but because the Cyclops was alive I knew he and his sheep would sooner or later need to leave the cave. Still cursing he part shifted the boulder then stood by it. Out of habit the sheep began to move toward the exit but he'd left only enough room for one at a time to pass. As the first went by he ran his hands along its back to make sure none of us had clambered up on top to take a ride for freedom. But this was our chance, our only chance, and we saw what we had to do.

There was myself, ten of my men and, another fourteen or fifteen sheep. We each chose one of the beasts and clung hard to the long fleece under its belly. It was precarious and it was our only hope - but it worked! He hadn't the wits to check underneath so each of us made it out of there. We dropped to the ground as soon as we were clear of the cave and headed towards our ship and I tell you, the air never smelled so good. As his sheep wandered off to pasture we hesitated to watch from a safe distance as Polyphemus groped his way outside. He rolled back the boulder, certain we were still trapped inside his dwelling. He stood leaning against the rock so I called out to him. I told him I was Odysseus and that I and my men were free. It wasn't the best idea I'd had that day, no – not when he started to bellow for his neighbours.'

Odysseus sat upright and gestured aside. 'Aye, we saw a first, then a second, appear over the hill. They spotted us and came bounding toward us quicker by far than any man could run, including me! I tell you it took us little time in getting back to that boat. Even so, even as my men cast off and rowed for their lives those two monsters were closing on us like the Furies. They waded into the water, roaring aloud, raising great waves, trying to seize our boat! Well – I thanked the gods they couldn't swim.'

Odysseus relaxed, closed his eyes for a time as the memories paraded large. After downing more wine he resumed. 'When we re-joined the rest of our men our vessels still numbered five though the smallest was in tow since I'd not enough men left to fully crew her. After a day's sailing we approached our next landfall, one we believed from travellers' descriptions might be the island of Aeolus. It rose upward bleak and steep-sided to a high summit from where dark smoke belched into the sky. Aeolus is familiar in name to travellers abroad as keeper of the winds. And though they say he was a friend of seafarers no one could ever agree on quite where his island was located. It was claimed to move from place to place on tide and current.'

'An island that floats,' muttered Telemachus.

'We found only one spot to beach our ships,' continued Odysseus, ignoring the remark, 'and that was a small, sheltered cove beneath what appeared to be entrances built into the slope higher up. After our last experience the sight of caves was far from welcome but these were of more modest proportion. We were again short of supplies and more repairs were needed to our ships. We struggled up the path to find a man waiting for us at the main entrance and we knew this was the one we sought. The dark-clad, shadowy Aeolus greeted us and accepted our modest gifts with detached courtesy. His palace was a dismal looking affair within a series of interconnected caves, but he and his court entertained us well enough. It was reassuring to be among people who behaved without hostility – except they appeared more shadow than substance and hardly spoke at all. I hoped Aeolus would tell us how we might best find our way home but he claimed not to know because his island was always on the move. Hah! - I didn't believe a word of it but what could I do? In return for our gifts Aeolus ordered provisions sent down to our vessels and presented me a bag made from the hide of a flayed bull. This he claimed held all the winds we would need to find our way back to Ithaca as long as we kept the bag sealed. It sounded as far-fetched to me as it must to both of you but after what we'd already witnessed I thought it better to reserve judgement.'

Telemachus looked from Odysseus to Eumaeus then back again with an expression of doubt his father appeared not to notice.

'We set sail,' Odysseus continued, 'and true enough, with fresh breeze and clear skies, we were having as fine a journey as we could have wished for though we expected it would be an exceedingly long one. Things went well over the next day in open water so I saw no harm in it when the men aboard my boat asked to open one of the wine casks. They drank too much as usual and one of them, convinced Aeolus' bag contained valuables that were to be shared among us took it on himself to open the thing whilst I was asleep in the stern.

Some might regard what happened next as co-incidence but I say it wasn't. The bag shot from his hands in a shrieking blast of air that had me stark upright. It spun upward and disappeared into the sky then the winds arose and another storm was upon us. We were quick enough to take down our sails before they were ripped apart but the gods were not sympathetic. With a night and a day of high winds and tumultuous seas we were again plunged into despair. When the storm did abate we found our vessels had been driven back to Aeolus' island. He wasn't happy to see us a second time. No, we'd disobeyed him by opening the bag. He assured us we were blighted by the gods, closed tight his gates and left us to continue on our way empty-handed.'

Thunder rolled above Eumaeus' roof and they became aware once more of beating rain. Odysseus drained the contents of his goblet and stared solemnly into the fire before resuming his tale.

'It was after that episode,' he sighed, 'that I lost most of my men. We sailed for six days in weather so calm we were obliged to row much of the time, again running low on fresh water, until we encountered another bleak isle whose name I have no wish to recall. Rounding a headland we observed a town built around a bay with a high-walled but oddly narrow harbour. Our hopes were at first raised. It looked peaceful enough under a bright sun though much neglected. There were sparse orchards with but a few stunted trees beyond. My men were exhausted through rowing and they saw here a chance to rest and refresh. But as my other captains headed for the harbour with the pennants of Ithaca flying, I began to feel all was not as it ought to be. I'd spotted people ashore running as if to get out of sight. I'd no means of summoning our men back so I had my vessel stand a short way out to sea.

My caution proved well founded. Once moored in the harbour our ships were attacked without warning. The natives had watched them approach and lain out of sight with murder in their hearts. They poured out of the buildings surrounding the harbour, all of them roughly dressed much as I now am but armed with all manner of crude weapons. They hurled stone blocks onto our ships from the harbour walls, splitting timbers, crushing and killing the crews who had no chance to manoeuvre their vessels out of harm's way. They whooped like wild animals revelling in the kill then they descended upon those of our lads who survived the initial onslaught with spear and sword. Aye, the harbour waters churned red with the blood of my men and I could do nothing. Only much later did I learn from other travellers why this had happened. These people hated all Greeks but worse – much worse – because their land was infertile and possessed no timber to build ships, they had become cannibals.'

'Well here I am thinking I was getting to know the world,' commented Telemachus, 'What *have* I been missing.'

'There are realms into which men ought never venture,' countered Odysseus, ignoring the scepticism in his son's remark. 'The world most of us know is bad enough.'

'But,' asked Eumaeus, 'with most of your men gone and only one ship left, what then?'

'Yes, my friend, what then? Late in the day we approached yet another island. There was no sign of life here, though it looked pleasantly green and partly forested. My thirty or so remaining men were too fatigued to journey further so we hauled our vessel up on shore to take a much-needed rest and there we made our camp by a small stream. We rested well, without sight of man or beast, and next day before sunrise I strolled off alone armed with sword and spear to see what lay inland. It was a truly pleasant island with alder and pine groves. From a higher vantage point I could make out smoke rising so I walked on a short way to investigate. There was a clearing with a few modest houses, partly overgrown, and a handsome stone building that looked like a small palace. It appeared innocent enough but I decided not to approach any closer.'

'A wise decision indeed,' Eumaeus remarked.

'And so it seemed at the time,' responded Odysseus. 'On my return I speared a young stag and managed to haul it back to where my men waited. They already had fires going so they set to preparing the animal for the first decent meal we'd had in many days. Before midday I sent eight well-armed men to locate more provisions for our vessel and warned them not to make contact with the inhabitants. They first drew lots to see who'd go because they were afraid of what might be waiting to confront them in this unknown land. Well, I couldn't blame them. One of my best men, Eurylochus, led them off into the woods. We were getting our ship ready for departure when, in the middle of what had become a very hot afternoon, Eurylochus returned alone in considerable alarm and with a very strange report.'

'Can these tales of yours get any stranger?' queried Telemachus.

Eumaeus glanced at him uneasily.

Odysseus frowned. 'D'you or d'you not wish to hear me out!' he snapped.

'Lord Odysseus,' put in Eumaeus, 'please go on - I beg you.'

'Yes, do,' added Telemachus though his comment was not charged with equal enthusiasm.

'Very well, they had chosen to ignore my warning and out of curiosity approached the village. On entering the clearing Eurylochus and his men had been alarmed by the appearance of lions, wolves and bears and stood ready to defend themselves from attack. But far from being aggressive these creatures behaved much as pet dogs and were totally at ease with my men. As they approached the building a young woman stepped out to meet them. She informed them her name was

Circe and invited them to join herself and her friends for food and wine. Men being men they followed her. Except, that is, for Eurylochus. He suspected all was not as it should be and after they disappeared inside he made his way around to the rear of the building. He watched through a gate as they stepped out into a courtyard. Her attendants, all attractive young women, offered the men cheese mixed with barley-meal and honey and wine in golden goblets. Once they'd downed the contents of those cups she touched each man on the head with her fingers. They collapsed in turn then rolled on the ground as if possessed by demons. Eurylochus swore they were changing shape before his eyes and then – and then they were pigs, grunting, jostling each other with their clothes and weapons strewn aside.

'Pigs indeed!' exclaimed Eumaeus, eyebrows raised.

Telemachus breathed in and glanced up at the rafters.

'I didn't believe a word of it either!' Odysseus snapped on noting Telemachus' expression. 'I thought he and they must have picked poisoned mushrooms or fruit, or encountered vapours from beneath the earth that had addled their minds. They say it's what happens to the priestess at Delphi when she makes her prophecies. The rest of my men were all for quitting the island there and then but I was having none of it. I ordered Eurylochus to take charge then I set off fully armed to find out what had happened. I encountered the beasts just as Eurylochus had described them. I also saw someone watching me from amidst a pine grove - a youth who seemed to have materialised from nowhere. I say materialised because he was not of flesh and bone – more a spectral figure from the world we often encounter in our dreams. I feared that whatever had afflicted my men was now taking hold of me. I was thinking to return to our vessel when he stepped forward and offered me a black-rooted plant bearing white flowers. "Take this," he said. "Breathe its perfume and they will have no power over you."

To say I trusted him seems nonsensical after all we'd witnessed, but I did – or maybe I no longer cared. Nor did I consider it odd when the figure vanished before my eyes, so many nightmares had I already lived through. I shrugged, sniffed the plant, noted a delicate perfume, then carried on, convinced the gods must be at work here.'

Telemachus remained impassive. He could not deny his own other worldly experience on the road to Sparta, nor that second time after the combat at sea on his return to Ithaca. He thought, too, of Mentes and Mentor. There was much he could not explain.

'I approached the palace,' continued Odysseus, 'a pretty rustic affair overgrown by climbing plants. There I came upon three of the girls in conversation by the main door. In appearance they were utterly captivating, slim and golden-haired, and I understood how easily my men must have been won over by their charms. One of them stepped forward to greet me in a most soothing and seductive voice. She introduced herself as Circe and offered me in a golden cup what I suspected she'd given to my crew but I refused it. She smiled and reached out to touch me but when nothing happened the smile quickly faded. I drew my sword, held it at her throat and demanded to know what had become of my men.'

'Would you have killed this amazing woman?' asked Telemachus.

'Aye, I might have. I was in no mood to fool around even if some part of me believed this was all some crazy dream. She looked at me with alluring green eyes and promised to restore all my lads to human form. And by the gods, in that courtyard I stood there and watched her do it! Before my eyes they twisted and thrashed, reforming until they were men again, but quite naked. They were stupefied, as was I, but struggled to their feet, managed to gather up their clothes and their weapons and straighten themselves out. With that I thought her influence over us was broken but it wasn't. No, it was not. We were on the point of leaving when they approached us and turned on their charms. She and her girls promised to entertain my crew the way men desire and when she invited me to her private chamber with one of her attendants it was an offer I felt ill inclined to refuse.

'But this pretty enchantress may have been plotting another trap,' said Eumaeus. 'Did you not consider that?'

'Oh, I considered it,' Odysseus replied, eyes closed in blissful recollection, 'but if the gods were determined to do away with me I thought it better to end my life in Circe's bed rather than Polyphemus' cave or on the dining table of those damned cannibals. If any woman lived up to a man's wildest desires I tell you she and her companions did. We hunted during the day but wined and dined each evening with Circe and her girls. The pleasures they offered us each night were sublime. We forgot our homes as surely as we would have with the Lotus Eaters so what passed to us as uncounted days added up to a year and more. I realised it only after visiting our vessel and those of our crew who had remained with her. They'd concluded we would never return and had no intention of following our trail. Some had wished to leave the island but Eurylochus had persuaded them to stay and build dwellings as there was much food to be had and too few of them to man the ship. I saw how badly our vessel had fallen into disrepair – a situation I determined to put right as quickly as possible.

The day before we sailed I remarked to Circe about the dangers we might have to face before reaching home. She said she would help me understand what was to come but didn't make it clear how – though I was soon to find out.

In her bed that final night she sent me on a dream journey that was too real for comfort. I descended into Tartarus, that part of the underworld where the dead and those who have sinned are held for judgement. It's said only Heracles and Theseus the Athenian ever went there and returned. I had to make blood sacrifice of a ram and ewe to call up Tiresius, the blind prophet who would foretell what dangers lay ahead for us. He appeared before me, reluctant, as if he had better things to do down there, and mumbled on to the effect that our troubles were far from being over. And why? Because I had managed to offend Poseidon by blinding Polyphemus! I protested it had been done to save our lives but he was quite unconcerned, making out it was not his problem. He went on to say the many dangers we'd have to face would soon be made clear to me then he drifted away into darkness. I saw, or thought I saw, the ghosts of others including Agamemnon and Achilles. None of them seemed to notice me and I was of no mind to attract their attention.

I woke up wondering why I'd been sent to consult that old fool, Tiresius, but perhaps his powers of prophecy flowed into Circe because it was she who warned me of the fatal Sirens, of monstrous Scylla and the watery hell of Charybdis. She described the islands we might encounter and their dangers in vivid detail so I had some idea of what we could be in for. She also cautioned that if we went ashore to rest on Trinacria, the island where the cattle of Helios the Sun were pastured, we were not to harm them as doing so would call down yet more tribulations. I knew nothing about Trinacria or the cattle of Helios nor, as it turned out, did any of my men. But I had to take Circe's warnings seriously: I'd long since concluded she and her companions were set upon this earth by the immortal gods themselves. What I desired above all else was that we find our way back to Ithaca. More tribulations we didn't need.'

'And we've still over eight years to go,' breathed Telemachus.

The thunder was subsiding but beyond Eumaeus' house rain fell steadily from a sullen sky.

'Maybe we have,' frowned Odysseus, 'so you'd better say now if you don't want to hear more.'

'Until recently,' Telemachus replied, 'I doubted your very existence, yet here you are and all Ithaca, with a number of predictable exceptions, will be glad of it - so do go on.'

Eumaeus dispensed more wine, saying, 'I, my lord, 'ave more years behind me than yourself although I've seldom travelled beyond our island. Even so, in my dialogue with strangers from other lands I've 'eard many a story that leads me to believe almost anything is possible. I've 'eard 'em speak of the Sirens, of Scylla and Charybdis. And are we to doubt the exploits of such great heroes as Jason, Heracles or Theseus – or indeed the powers of the gods themselves?'

Telemachus raised his goblet in polite agreement as Odysseus resumed his narrative.

'With the pleasures of Circe's court in our thoughts this was no easy departure for some of my men. Three of the younger ones needed more than just words to convince them. Nevertheless we departed her island with spirits high, our vessel in good order and well supplied for the voyage home.

Days later we approached the isle of the Sirens in a lively sea. Apart from Circe's warning I'd heard travellers speak of it but dismissed their tales as spawned more by the effects of strong wine than real experience. Yet the island had been described in enough detail to make the sight of it almost familiar – a smallish, treeless island of chaotic black rock formations where, from its midst, arose clouds of a sulphurous grey smoke that scurried seaward before the winds. Ahead and to our right we spotted a shallow inlet with a dark, boulder and driftwood strewn beach. We had to sail in close because further out the currents were hard against us. It was then we noticed figures moving behind the rocks.

Circe's warnings had truly determined my actions and I followed her advice when I might have ignored that of others. I had my men lash me securely to the mast with spare cordage and plug their own ears with wax to block out all sound. I had to see and hear for myself what truth there was in the tale of the Sirens. My crew were to deploy their oars, look straight ahead and row hard until we were well clear of the place. A part of me wondered if the tales were unfounded rumour because I would have looked a damned fool insisting upon those precautions had they been so.'

Telemachus for once appeared to listen intently as Odysseus drew breath to recall memories of this latest challenge.

'We sailed closer to the beach. I saw them clearly and my first impressions had me thinking maybe I had been deceived. They stood part hidden behind the rocks, fair-haired, young and seductively beautiful. They smiled, they swayed as saplings in a breeze, they drew fingers through their hair and over their naked breasts. They raised their arms and beckoned us to join them. Then they were singing. Aye, they were singing more sweetly, more enticingly than ever I could have imagined. It was surely music of the gods – music to be cherished by Apollo himself.'

Odysseus pushed aside his goblet, clenched his fists and closed his eyes tightly.

'Oh, their voices! Even now I -! Their voices were honey-laced wine. Their words drifted over the water to tingle my bones. They caressed my very soul; they enticed me as no earthly woman ever could. With the wind filling our sail, my men rowed with vigour but so close to the bay I feared we might be grounded or worse. The Sirens' voices closed around me. They banished the splash of oars, the sound of the wind in our rigging and the waves buffeting our hull. I was fighting to get free of my bonds. I wanted only to leap overboard and swim ashore. I pleaded with the crew to cut me loose but of course they couldn't hear a word and they rightly ignored my struggles. Aye, had they done as I so desperately begged during those moments of possession it would surely have been the end of me. But we had a brisk wind and my crew strained at their oars as if pursued by the Furies.

As we hauled past the beach the Sirens' voices faded, my vision cleared and I caught sight of the horrors we had avoided. I tell you, I saw what no man should ever see. There were shattered wrecks of vessels amidst those rocks. The remains of their crews lay strewn over the sand. Some were corpses still rotting, still picked at by the birds. Others were the scattered white bones with wide grinning skulls: those seafarers who had succumbed to the Sirens' call then been torn apart by those fearful creatures. I say creatures for that's what they were. They stood upright, revealing themselves fully to glare at us in baleful anger. Their flesh was pallid, their eyes large and red. Below the waist they possessed the legs and clawed feet of great birds! They howled bloody malice, they scuffed and scattered sand and stones, outraged at being denied human victims! Then they shrieked in laughter – laughter, I say! From what depths of evil those things came or what god created them I hardly care to think. Once clear of that island I was freed but though the men questioned me I was too dismayed to describe what I'd witnessed. All I could manage was, "You did well, lads. You did well."

We continued on for more days and nights living off our stores of food, off netted fish and a diminishing supply of fresh water. At length we were driven into a channel where another trial was to test us without mercy. We expected it, we had been warned, but this time there was not the opportunity to sail on by. To our left we approached a fiercely roaring torrent, the great foaming whirlpool driven by Charybdis. It's said she was struck down by Zeus himself and condemned to the depths where she raged and stirred the sea. She could drag down far larger vessels than ours then disgorge the wreckage and the bodies of their crews in calmer waters, but we had to go on. The whole thing, a vast greenish, rotating turmoil of water threatened to consume our fragile ship but my men rowed with great determination and the gods summoned a brisk following wind to assist us on our way. Then – aye then, perhaps they didn't consider Charybdis offered sufficient punishment.'

A tense silence followed. Eumaeus gripped his goblet. Telemachus stared into the fire, imagining he saw within it strange forms much in keeping with some of those described by his father. Then Odysseus resumed his account.

'Ahead of us and to our right arose something that confirmed our worst fears. The place was bleak and there were few sea birds. It was the great sea cliff where I'd been told Scylla waited to leap upon passing boats from the mouth of her cave. She was said to have a craving for human flesh surpassing even that of the Cyclopes. After the trials we'd endured the prospect of this struck us with mortal fear but the current was strong and we could never have turned back without falling into the grasp of Charybdis. But I steered well and my crew, driven by a desire to survive, rowed as men possessed. In avoiding the whirlpool we had to sail close beneath Scylla's rock, a pitted, almost sheer black precipice with caves like gaping dark jaws that opened above the water no higher than our mast.

I thought we'd made it past the cliff unharmed when there arose a piercing hiss louder by far than the wind and sea and she appeared as if from nowhere. In those fearful moments I saw – by the gods I saw what seemed a glistening black form swoop down at us. The thing had six necks, each one like a snake with a fang-toothed, hair-covered head and blazing yellow eyes! Each head plunged into our boat too quickly for anyone to avoid it, seized one of my men in its jaws, piercing him through with dagger-teeth and tearing his innards. In the blink of an eye they were wrenched screaming from their seats, oars flying into the air, their blood and entrails scattering across the boat and over us. The shrieks of the thing, a howling of mad dogs, cut through the air like a keen blade. Those men who were left rowed in blind panic to distance our vessel from that – that unspeakable creature. But the sound followed us, screeches of triumph, mocking, as did the dying cries of the men she had seized, until we were clear and heading into open water.'

Telemachus glanced at the open-mouthed, ever-credulous Eumaeus but offered no comment.

271

Odysseus gulped more wine, took a deep breath then added quietly, 'Yes - sudden death had become a way of life. After that I – I began to doubt my own sanity. The presence of my men, at least those who were left, together with the wind and cold spray from the sea, kept me from thinking I had lapsed into madness.'

Looking utterly crushed by those memories he stared long into the fire before turning to relate his next encounter.

'We eventually made it into calmer seas but there was little food or drink left aboard to sustain those of us who had survived, nor were there enough of us to properly man the boat. We needed to cleanse it and ourselves; we had to remove all traces of blood and human remains before sailing on. So numbed were the men, so dismayed over what had happened, not a word was spoken until night closed over us.

We drifted another day, exhausted, utterly disheartened, before being driven by adverse winds toward Trinacria - yes, the very island where I'd been told cattle sacred to Helios were kept. I had little doubt over that as the beasts could be seen grazing in placid green fields, their golden hides bathed by warm sunlight and shielded from the elements that had so afflicted our vessel. I had reservations over landing there but Eurylochus prevailed upon me on behalf of our men and I had to agree. The winds were strengthening and we sorely needed fresh water and rest. We made for the calm waters of a leeward bay and once ashore we set up camp. The men eventually had a fire going and we shared out the few remaining morsels of food. A clear spring from the hills ran not far away so for a time it seemed our troubles might be ended. We at last had sanctuary and I anticipated we could stay there a few days before continuing our journey. There was also the condition of our vessel: in the two and more years since we'd left Troy she'd been battered and patched up again and again. Now, with good timber to hand we had an opportunity to undertake further repairs.

The night was kind to us so the following morning, much refreshed, I went out foraging for game. I had given strict orders that the cattle were not to be touched but during my absence, with their minds afflicted by all we'd been through, three of my crew had seized and slaughtered one of the cows. Realising they should never have done it they dragged the beast out of sight beneath a rock ledge. They were busying with their knives to skin and carve up the carcase when I returned and discovered what had happened. They tried to justify their actions by claiming it was also a sacrifice to Poseidon. I berated them for their stupidity but even as I looked on the carcase began to squirm as a living thing. Yes, like - like a blood-sodden sack full of dogs it writhed and shook, spattering gore. It bellowed aloud and was struggling to its feet – another stark horror none of us cared to face! My men fled in panic to the ship and I hurried after them with that blood-drizzling abomination trotting not far behind.

We departed the island fully aware we had yet again offended the gods – and those much-needed repairs had not been made to the boat.

We ended up in turbulent waters with a strongly blustering wind, not knowing where we might be driven. We were too few and when our sail was ripped away from the spar we had not the strength to manoeuvre our vessel with the oars. Then came the final blow. The heavens darkened almost to night, the drums of thunder rolled, the sky flickered with the gods' anger and Zeus struck our vessel with a bolt from above. For an instant sea and sky lit up as though a hundred suns glared. The rain froze before my eyes, suspended in the air as gleaming jewels. The face of Eurylochus and of my men were pallid masks of dread then all was darkness again. Our boat was shattered and I was hurled into the sea. I was in danger of drowning until I grabbed onto a broken piece of the hull. I feared the currents might carry me back toward Charybdis but after what seemed an eternity I found myself in calmer waters.'

'And the rest of your crew?' queried Telemachus, adjusting his position uneasily as if to ask for how much longer the narrative might go on.

'Lost to the sea,' he answered, dryly. 'I saw none of those men again. How long I drifted I cannot say but it must have been days. I felt close to death and was barely conscious when I was washed onto an unknown beach at nightfall. I recall struggling some way up the sand before I passed out. When later I awoke I found myself in calm air under a warm sun. I could hear birds singing. I lay there dazed, asking myself if what I had witnessed had been no more than a cruel nightmare sent by the gods. The sun grew very hot and I craved fresh water. I struggled to my knees and saw three white-robed people approaching along the sand. I couldn't tell if they were men or women nor could I swear they were flesh and blood. I still had my sword but not the strength to stand and use it. I simply waited as they drew close, expecting this might be the end of me.

I was relieved to see they each had two eyes and only one head; they didn't look at me as if I was their next meal nor did they attempt to charm me with some fatal song. They helped me to my feet. They gave me sweet water from a leather flask and guided me inland a short way from the beach to a splendid dwelling sheltered beneath a great stone arch. All about lay colourful gardens and fountains with exotic birds fluttering among the trees. The building was fronted with columns much as our own but these were white and gold rather than russet or black. There was a pureness, an air of innocence about the place. Though much afflicted in body and mind I felt there a sense of peace unlike anything I'd known. I wondered if I'd departed the world of man but this certainly was not Hades. When I thought to ask where I was, my guides were gone. They'd spoken not a word.

At the entrance a woman stood waiting as if she'd been expecting me. She was young and beautiful, her hair long and golden brown. Her long gown was white and translucent as a morning mist She smiled but said nothing so I remained silent, not knowing if she would understand me.'

'Another beautiful woman?' mused Telemachus. 'Your lucky day, father – yet again.'

'Aye, another beautiful woman!' retorted Odysseus tersely. 'And even in my dazed condition the sight of her uplifted my spirits when they were at their very lowest.'

'But, My Lord,' asked Eumaeus, 'did you not consider this might be another trick?'

'I no longer cared,' Odysseus replied. 'I was alone with no means of escape - weakened by exertion and hunger. I'd made sacrifice to the gods whenever possible and begged their forbearance but it seemed their attention was ever somewhere else - even Athena to whom I had dedicated a number of shrines so many years ago.'

'Ah!' exclaimed Telemachus, 'I made sacrifice at your altar on the road outside Sparta. As we left a white owl settled upon it.'

'A white owl!' exclaimed Odysseus. 'A white owl is always a good omen.'

'And sacred to the goddess,' muttered Eumaeus.

'So,' asked Telemachus, 'what was the outcome as they obviously didn't kill and eat you?'

'She spoke to me and I to her in Greek. Her voice passed through the air as a whisper but was clear within my head. She told me I had arrived on an island called Ogygia, a place I'd never heard of, and her name was Calypso. She took me inside her dwelling where I was offered food and wine. When I'd recovered somewhat I was bathed and my face shaved clean by girls whose existence seemed as vague and ephemeral as those who brought me there, though it won't surprise you if I say their touch was most pleasurable.'

'Doesn't surprise me at all,' muttered Telemachus over his goblet.

'Calypso herself was certainly real, as from time to time were her companions, yet her world was not of ours - more a realm of dreams and I could never be quite sure if that's where I was or not. She told me I could remain with her forever and like her I would be immortal. Well I wasn't planning on immortality. I thought maybe a few days to sort things out would be enough then I'd be on my way again. But by the time I'd regained my strength this goddess, for surely that's what she was, infused me with desires I was unable to quench – desires for her and her companions. Time became meaningless. Day and night went by and it seemed she willed the passage of light and dark as she saw fit.

Telemachus suppressed a groan as his father continued. 'I'm aware a man might be sated by too many pleasures but in the company of Calypso and her girls I never was. Aye, we revelled in the pleasures of the night and in the sunlit days that followed we wandered by the purest of streams and through exotic glades where coloured birds, the likes of which I never saw before, darted from tree to tree. The air was heavy with perfumes, fine as those of Egypt. I marvelled at orchards where the fruit glittered like coloured jewels hanging from gold and silver tendrils. She revealed to me ancient statues and temples, overgrown amidst the trees and I gazed upon the shrines and images of long forgotten gods. Some days we strolled secret pathways of the island or set out to hunt small game. In the evenings, beneath the stars, we sang, we laughed and danced before the fire. Ah, such contentment I had - such utter, glorious contentment

- pleasures denied to mortal man. The evils I'd witnessed, the dangers I'd encountered became no more than vague memories. Maybe I was drugged as were those of my men among the Lotus Eaters yet often, in the depths of night, when the world seemed more real, I knew I had to resume my journey home. In my mind were thoughts of Ithaca and the wife and son I had left behind. I prayed to Athena for guidance. But whenever I tried to speak of it with Calypso the words faltered on my tongue and were driven from my thoughts. That's the only way I'm able to explain it.'

'Most unfortunate,' breathed Telemachus, while in his mind hovered the smiling image of Polyxena and the pleasures she had bestowed upon him at Nestor's palace.

'One day in the garden,' Odysseus continued, 'I spotted someone talking to Calypso. It was the spectral man I'd encountered before I met Circe. I heard what was said because he wanted me to hear it. The gods had sent Hermes to insist upon my release. My prayers at night had at last been acknowledged. Calypso reluctantly agreed and over the following days I found her influence over me waning until I was my own man once more. But how was I to leave? I searched the island for means of escape but there were no boats and no tools so I decided I would construct a raft. I'd lash together fallen branches with whatever cordage I could lay my hands on. I'd make a sail with linen from her mansion. I'd stock the thing with provisions from her gardens and orchards. She watched me at work and pleaded with me to change my mind, saying that if I knew what lay ahead I'd give up all thought of leaving. But she said no more of this because she knew how determined I was to make it back to Ithaca.

Calypso stood alone wiping tears from her cheeks when we parted. She was there as I set off toward the rising sun working a pair of crude oars but when I was clear of the surf and looked up again the beach was deserted as if she'd never existed. A fair wind filled my sail, the warm air was welcome and I wondered how long it would be before another man landed by mischance on Ogygia. And if he did, would he encounter Calypso and her realm of pleasures or nothing more than a deserted island?

If the weather stayed as it was I hoped I would reach our own waters within a few days. But that few days turned out to be many. Seventeen I counted by making notches in the mast. I followed the coast as best I was able, coming ashore whenever I could to rest, to tighten up the cordage holding my raft together or to find game and fresh water. Aye, all seemed to be going well, but Poseidon had not finished with me. No he had not!

Early one afternoon a familiar island came into sight – Kephallinia. I was certain of it though the air was hazy, and Ithaca would be within reach before dark because I had a mild southerly breeze. Then the wind gathered strength once more and the seas turned angry. I lowered sail but those meagre provisions I still had on board were swept away and it was obvious my raft would soon break up. When it finally did I was in the water clinging onto a length of wood, my arms and body battered by loose branches, not knowing if I was to live or die. When night came I doubted I'd see another sunrise

279

but still I clung on, rolling, choking on seawater, unable to see anything other than foaming water. I swear I heard laughter amidst the tumult – aye, a man's laughter. Poseidon himself was mocking me and I called out in despair to Athena! I could see nothing even when the log struck against a rock and my feet touched sand. All the time the sea tried to claw me back, to drag me under, but in the darkness I struggled onto dry land and there I collapsed. As I lay sprawled on the sand a mist swept across, much like that which enveloped my ships after we'd departed Troy. Half-conscious as I was, it felt as if one door had opened before me and another had closed behind. That's the only way I can explain it.

I awoke in morning sunlight, bruised, grazed and caked in sand. I got up with difficulty, worried in case I'd broken any bones. I was devoid of clothes - even my precious sword was gone. Some way along the beach there were several women bathing. They spotted me and one of them walked over, pulling a robe about herself. She was young and even in my sorry state she struck me as most desirable.'

Telemachus glanced at Eumaeus, eyebrows raised, as his father continued, 'Her image even now fills my thoughts because she reminded me of nothing more than my own dear wife on the day I sailed for Troy. She was soft-spoken, aristocratic in her bearing and confident in her manner. She asked me who I was and how I had ended up there so I told her I'd been swept overboard from a trading ship during the storm. I asked where I was and she informed me this was the island of Scheria and that she was Nausicaa, daughter of Alcinous, king of the

Phaeacians who ruled that place. At last I knew exactly where I was! Aye, at long last! Scheria, though never a part of my domains, lay off the mainland to the north of Ithaca. I'd once been familiar with the Phaeacian court but these names I did not recognise. She indicated a freshwater stream flowing into the sea and told me that if I would wash there she would have her companions fetch me a tunic and sandals. She was as good as her word and though sore and aching mightily I soon had myself clean and presentable enough, though only just, to stand before her.

"You should go alone to my father's palace," she advised. "We must be discreet because he doesn't care at all for strangers. Present yourself first to my mother, Arete. If she greets you with food and a small gift of welcome then father will accept her decision. He leaves such matters to her."

I set off limping like an old cripple along the path she'd indicated. This island reminded me of the Ithaca I'd left behind. The landscape, the steep path up to the palace and the palace itself; all were of a similar scale to the Ithaca I once knew. On entering the megaron I was conducted by attendants to stand before Arete who sat enthroned in her gilded royal robes. She was somewhat younger than I'd expected - a graceful, smiling woman. She spoke to me kindly in spite of my appearance.'

'But not an irresistible beauty,' grinned Telemachus.

By now accustomed to his son's attitude, an attitude verging upon scorn, Odysseus smiled, 'No, not an irresistible beauty this time – and before you pass further comment, I didn't end up in her bed.'

Eumaeus sighed with relief and Telemachus grinned widely as Odysseus continued. 'Their great hall was of similar size to that of Ithaca but it's walls displayed little of the arms and armour I hope is still on display in our own megaron. There were depicted sea vessels engaged in trade rather than in combat. Their bard played and recited like our own Phemios but was blind. He sang of Troy and of the wooden horse with an infusion of colourful embellishment I found quite amusing. It seems I'd already become the stuff of legend and – oh, I must ask at this point; is Phemios still with us? If so he must have reached a fine old age.'

'Yes, he's still with us,' replied Telemachus. 'Mother has him sing of the heroes who returned from Troy and of those who did not. She does it to annoy the suitors.'

'Ah, I'm glad of that and I look forward to hearing him again. But as for my stay on Scheria – the Phaeacians nursed me back to health. They fed and cared for me until I was feeling fit and strong as before. They were at the time holding ritual games, which I was invited by my hosts to watch on level ground outside the city gate. I was anxious to leave but did not wish to insult those who had shown me such charity, so I agreed to stay and watch. Seeing me there, some of the younger men, none of 'em looking particularly fit for combat, remarked over my appearance because I still bore signs of the many hardships I'd endured. They suggested that in spite of my stature I'd never be able to match them in any aspect of their sports. Aye, they regarded me as a rough old seafarer unfamiliar with civilised pursuits – opinions they voiced when Nausicaa and her mother were present. I said nothing because I had no wish to cause offence. Their athletes began to compete in discus throwing with discs of increasing weights and sizes. Now and again one or more of them would look in my direction, grinning as if to suggest the likes of me would have little chance of matching their skills. The two women expressed their disapproval and apologised, saying how unfair it was that men so experienced in sport should treat a guest of their court with such discourtesy. Well that did it!

I excused myself. I stepped out onto the field. I marched across to where those soft-faced youths were gathered and grabbed the largest discus. The boys backed off, not sure what to do. The target they were aiming for was a stone pillar within easy reach of the lighter shots. I drew back the discus and hurled the thing as I used to in athletic games here on Ithaca and the mainland. I watched it glide close by the post and disappear into a vine plantation some way beyond. The lads stared in the direction of the pillar, at each other then at me. I challenged any of them to stand against me in boxing or running, or whatever they liked, but they just stood in silence. Arete and her daughter were amused and much impressed and offered their congratulations. I had evidently broken their distance record.

Later that day I decided to reveal who I was. I related to Arete and her companions, enough of what happened at Troy to convince them of my true identity but I said nothing about the saga of my return. Instead I maintained I'd been blown off course, which was no lie, and had used the opportunity to explore much of the world seldom visited by the Greeks then finished up totally lost in foreign lands. I felt they believed little of what I said but were too polite to openly express their doubts. At the time I did not understand why. They continued to treat me well – as a curiosity, maybe. They insisted I went hunting with their young men and I felt obliged to further extend my stay. By day I found myself steeped in the easy-going atmosphere of their court and at night Nausicaa paid me the sort of attentions no man can resist.'

'Well I never,' breathed Telemachus. 'And so close to home.'

'Yes, and so close to home! I was unbearably restless. Ithaca was within reach and I could be with my wife and a son who I thought by then must be thirteen years old. I was eventually granted an audience with Alcinous, a gaunt, slim, grey-eyed man who stared at me long and hard before saying anything. When he decided to talk I questioned him over events since the fall of Troy and asked what he knew of affairs on Ithaca, still certain little more than three years could have gone by since I set out on my return voyage. Aye, it was then and only then that the truth dawned; a truth that struck me like a bolt from Zeus himself. Only then did I realise how much time I must have spent on Calypso's island. Seven years, by Zeus! Seven years that had passed as if they were only months! Thirteen years would have been bad enough but now it was twenty! My mind was plagued with visions of the calamities that might have descended upon Ithaca during that time. Aware of my anxiety and by now, in part because of my skill with the discus, they seemed to accept that I was at least of noble birth. They offered a vessel and crew to carry me to Ithaca together with generous gifts though I of course had nothing to offer in return.

I had no wish to be seen so I had them land me after sunset on a rocky beach I considered safe from prying eyes. I was unsure at the time what next to do so I determined to rest there until morning and think matters over. There's a small cave where I sometimes played and hid as a child. I recalled it was dry and not obvious to anyone who might wander down there. I scrambled inside and concealed the gifts as far back as I could. The one thing of value above all others in that bag was a sword given me by Alcinous – as fine and as sharp a weapon as I ever set eyes on, its ornate scabbard inlaid with silver and lapis-lazuli. I eagerly await the opportunity to use it!'

'Why,' asked Telemachus, 'has so little word of the things you encountered reached us through the travellers who come and go from Ithaca and her markets? The Cyclopes, Scylla and the Sirens: should they, as well as Circe and Calypso and their enchanted islands, not be better known rather than vague hearsay repeated by people who have witnessed nothing of the sort? And the marauders who are reported to be encroaching upon lands to our north and east and upon the lands of Troy itself - had no word of them reached you?'

Odysseus lowered his head in thought then looked up at Telemachus. 'Since my return I have listened to gossip in the marketplace and, yes, I have thought very hard on these matters. On leaving Troy, when the mist I spoke of enveloped us, it was as if a portal had opened, a portal through which I

285

and my men were inexorably drawn by the will of the gods. I believe Poseidon overruled the rest in his desire to punish me. Once I was cast ashore on Phaeacia, all links with this other world were severed. I can offer no other explanation.'

As Eumaeus replenished their cups from the wine flagon, Odysseus' son remarked, 'Very well, as you were so recently conveyed to Ithaca fresh from the luxury of the Phaeacian court I wonder how it is you turn up here now as an unshaven vagabond.'

Eumaeus grimaced and glanced aside. Odysseus regarded Telemachus with bland expression, saying, 'I realise your credulity is sorely tested but you have also witnessed the goddess' image and heard her words have you not?'

'True enough I have, but briefly and while I was dreaming. And when I woke up I looked very much the same as I did before I went to sleep.' But through his mind passed images of old Mentor and Mentes the Taphian trader, both of whom had appeared as men of flesh and blood when they must have been elsewhere.

'Yes,' continued Odysseus, 'and I also was dreaming as I slept by that cave – so I thought. Athena appeared to me shining in all her glory. Her light bathed the walls as though the sun blazed in. She told me I must not reveal myself until I'd seen with my own eyes and heard from others what was happening on Ithaca. I awoke as you see me now and – and I was ashamed of myself until I saw the wisdom of it. This guise has served me well and will do so until the time is right.'

Telemachus hesitated before responding. 'I'll make my way to the palace after sunset. When the suitors set eyes on me it will be interesting to see their expressions, especially that of Antinous.'

'I beg you be careful, young sir,' said Eumaeus.

'The rain has finished,' said Odysseus, rising from his seat, 'I'll go down to the cave and recover my valuables. I'd prefer to keep them here now you know who I am.'

From the doorway of Eumaeus' house they watched him set off toward the inlet. The sky had cleared, the morning sun asserted itself over a glistening land.

'This account of my father's exploits,' said Telemachus as the figure of Odysseus disappeared below the rise, 'how much of it, if any, are we to accept as true? Can it all be the fault of the gods? All too easy, I think.'

'The gods are fickle and deal with us as they please.' offered Eumaeus. 'And do not other travellers speak of the things he encountered?'

'They do but none, as I said earlier, can claim to have witnessed them directly. People who travel abroad and some who never have, pass on rumours as though they were known facts. As for the number of eager young women he claims to have encountered – ha - if only! Is it possible he's lain low all these years, living as an outcast on some other island? Could his reason be so undermined by hardship that he's lost touch with the real world? You may offer a contrary opinion my friend and I will respect it, but I believe hardly anything he's told us even though I cannot deny my own more modest encounters.'

Eumaeus appeared ill at ease. 'Young sir, it is not for the likes of me to question what your father says but may I tell you something?'

'Please do.'

'When I was a boy, more years ago than I care to think, there was a tale we were all familiar with and regarded without question as genuine; your father will know of it.' Eumaeus raised his hands and looked up in awe at the sky. 'Two men were seen flying through the air on feathered wings. It was said they escaped imprisonment from the tyrant Minos, ruler of Knossos on the island of Crete, and that they intended to fly over the water to Italy. Even their names were later revealed to us: Daedalus and Icarus, father and son.'

'Some events at Knossos,' said Telemachus, 'were explained to me by a noble and brave companion I met when I visited Pylos. He spoke of a monstrous creature half bull and half man said to have been slain by Theseus the Athenian, but he said nothing of flying men – though I vaguely recall my mother speaking of it many years ago.'

'Well, young master, reports of this wonderful event reached Ithaca from travellers on land as well as out at sea by people who spoke different tongues and could not have known one another. The crew of one vessel, trading with our island, reported seeing the younger man fall to his death from the sky before reaching land. Now that is quite as strange as some of your father's tales but with so many witnesses who could doubt it?'

'Perhaps so but my father can offer no witnesses as they were all conveniently murdered or drowned. Still, we must give him our full support. It is he the people wish to have restored to the throne of Ithaca rather than me.'

'Yes, your father is our rightful leader with yourself his rightful heir. He was always a strong and for the most part a good ruler of our lands. I wish only to see him once again in firm control over Ithaca and its dominions even though the strain of his long journey may have coloured his memory somewhat.'

'I think the strain of his journey has done more than that. But now he's returned we must plan what is to be done to reassert in full the House of Odysseus.'

***

The air was heavy with incense when he entered the megaron to find his regally gowned mother seated on her throne of tenuous authority. Penelope was surrounded by her gaudily attired female companions, twittering as agitated birds. Phemios was perched upon a wooden chair close by, strumming leisurely notes. At a discreet distance waited two male slaves and in the shadow of the colonnade opposite, five members of the palace guard lolled in silence, their attention occupied by the palace girls. Telemachus approached the throne in a manner so casual he might only have been absent since that morning. Phemios spotted him first, ceased playing and raised a hand to alert his mistress. As the chatter of her girls ebbed Penelope sprang to her feet. 'Telemachus! Oh, I thank the gods you're back with us at last! What's been happening? What news d'you have and why did no one announce your return?'

Standing before her he replied quietly, 'Mother, we must speak alone.'

Penelope looked around anxiously at her intimates and attendants. 'Please leave us. I will call for you when I'm ready.'

Her companions, followed by Phemios left the hall with three men of her guard positioning themselves just beyond the main entrance while the other two stood outside the door to the corridor, all of them out of earshot.

'I see Thoas is keeping a few of his guards close at hand,' said Telemachus. 'That's good.'

'Yes, those men in the dining hall have become more aggressive. I know they've plotted against you and – I - I've been so very worried. Please, Telemachus - please tell me what you've found out. Tell me everything!'

'Now, mother, I want you to sit down and try to remain calm.'

'Calm – how can I be calm the way things are?' Penelope nevertheless sat and raised jewelled fingers to her cheeks. 'Telemachus, what has happened that I should know about? There's been so much whispering, so many rumours since you left.'

'Now listen to me,' he replied, stepping closer, 'your husband – my father, is alive and -.'

She drew a sharp breath, gasped, 'Alive!' and stared at him in wide-eyed astonishment.

'Yes, he's here on Ithaca but -.'

'Odysseus here!' she exclaimed, leaping once more to her feet. 'Is this true? You mean he's come home to us! Oh, I thank the gods! Telemachus, where is he? Take me to him now!'

'Soon, mother,' he responded, glancing from side to side then holding her by the arms. 'Please sit down and lower your voice. You have to be patient. He will reveal himself when the time is right and quite soon, I assure you. Should those men find out before then he and I will be in mortal danger. After what's been going on here these past years they'd not dare see him back alive.'

Tears welled to stream down Penelope's cheeks. She grasped Telemachus by the shoulders. 'Athena has answered our prayers. My Odysseus is home at last. At last, at last, at last! Euryclea knew, didn't she? I thought something had happened. How could my own husband make himself known to her and not to me after all this time? Was it that filthy vagabond who told her? And how did *he* know?'

'It was never my father's intention to tell anyone,' replied Telemachus, lifting her hands away. 'Euryclea found out by accident and he made her swear upon her life to tell no one – not even you. She bears no guilt whatsoever.'

'But Euryclea *did* see him!' she exclaimed, trembling visibly, 'is that what you're saying? And just *where* was this? And where exactly is he? How can you just stand there and – and -? Telemachus - I demand to see him now! Take me to him at once! At once, I beg you!'

'Mother, keep your voice low. I cannot say more and it was foolish of me to tell you down here. He will come to you very soon, I promise, but not yet as a returning king. You must play your part in order for him to regain his rightful place.'

'Play my part! What part? His rightful place is here with me. I want to see my Odysseus! It's been twenty years! Is he unharmed? Please tell me the truth!'

'Yes he's unharmed and as fit as any man. Now, mother, you *must* remain calm and say nothing to anyone unless it's in private to Euryclea. And make sure those guards keep an eye on you – whatever you have to pay them.'

Penelope wiped her cheeks with a sleeve of her gown, clasped fingers together before her chin and stared down at the floor. 'Odysseus is alive and I cannot see him.'

'You will, and soon. Trust me.'

'I trust you, yes, but Telemachus, there's – there's something you should know: you mentioned Thoas just now but he fled Ithaca with his family because Antinous' men threatened to do them harm. I still pay in silver those of his men who are willing to keep watch here but I can't be certain how long they will stay. I think some are still loyal but others may be in Antinous' pay and spying on me. The suitors will soon know you are home.'

'That's inevitable. All the more reason for us to act quickly.'

'Then - then tell me what I have to do and how soon I'm to see Odysseus – your father.'

'That's better. Now let's go up to your chamber.' Telemachus held his mother firmly by the arm and guided her still shaking to the narrow stone steps leading to her private rooms. 'We'll take wine and discuss matters in detail. Afterwards come back down, recall Phemios and the rest of them and behave as if nothing important has happened apart from your need to question me over my absence. Tell them I travelled far but brought no news of my father. I know this won't be easy but assure me you'll do as I say.'

'Yes,' she answered, again wiping her cheeks as she gazed up at him with beseeching eyes, 'Yes, I will try my best. If it means I'm to see him soon then - then I'll do whatever you wish.'

***

Darkness had fallen across Ithaca town when the suitors gathered to once more establish themselves in Odysseus' palace. The feasting had been underway for some time and the wine flowed liberally when Telemachus arrived at the entrance from the megaron corridor. He halted to peer across but did not step down into the smoke-laden bustle of the dining hall. Against the wall, close by the base of the steps, sat the ragged Iros in wine-induced torpor, at present ignored by those who had adopted him as buffoon of the dining hall. The black mongrel dog nestled close beside him looked up at Telemachus. Standing some way from the braziers stood Medon, Penelope's slave, ever alert to what was being said. One of the first to observe the newcomer was pot-bellied Eudorus. About to drink from his goblet he lowered the vessel and hooted shrilly above the noise, 'Watch out, friends - he's back!

The noise subsided. Heads turned. Grizzled Eurymachus slammed down his goblet, glared with contempt from beneath birds-nest eyebrows and exclaimed, 'By the gods so he is – all scrubbed and prettied up. Well, boy, we're still enjoying mummy's hospitality in case you were wondering!'

Antinous glanced coldly at Telemachus then carried on drinking. Iros opened his eyes, looked around in alcohol-hazed confusion and attempted to rise from the floor.

'And we thought our worthy young prince had drowned at sea,' remarked someone. 'Pity.'

'Do tell us what news you have on our beloved king!' sneered one. 'We don't see him standing there to back you up!'

'If the old bugger was on the island,' scoffed another, 'we'd know it by now!'

Softer spoken, finely attired Amphion had been seated with his back to their visitor. He swivelled about and, closer than the rest, asked, 'Did you by any chance encounter our dear friend Leiocritius on your travels?'

Antinous swirled wine casually inside his goblet and smiled.

Telemachus ignored their comments, grinned broadly and raised a hand. 'Gentlemen – I regret having interrupted your evening's enjoyment. I called by to make sure you had everything you needed. I'm unable to share the pleasure of your company right now but I will be back in due course.'

'Will you now,' muttered Antinous, pushing his goblet aside.

Someone passed wind loudly. Raucous laughter followed. Goblets thumped on benches. A bone spun across the room to be pursued by a pair of scowling mongrels. By the time laughter had subsided, Telemachus was gone.

***

He left the palace before any hint of dawn, passing prostrate beggars beneath the town gate, causing dogs to stir and rats to scamper then setting off into the cool, clean air of night. Some way on he turned aside from the harbour path then crouched by a bush, hand on sword, waiting to ascertain if anyone had followed, eyes searching in case shadow forms rose up against the starlit sky. There was no one so Telemachus continued along with only the unseen shades of night as company.

The faintest band of light smeared the eastern horizon when he approached the house of Eumaeus. The dogs were yapping, tail-wagging and circling before he reached the gate then the door creaked open to reveal Odysseus and Eumaeus emerging, each with sword at the ready.

'It's me!' called Telemachus pushing open the gate.

'How is your mother?' asked Odysseus, sheathing his sword. 'Have you told her I'm back?'

'I have.'

'And what was her reaction? What did she say?'

'She's pretty desperate to see you.' Telemachus replied. 'She was distressed because you hadn't gone straight to her.'

'And did you explain why? Did she understand what we have to do?'

'I didn't go into detail no, she was too emotional, but I promised you'd go to her soon. You really have to do that.'

'Yes, very soon I will,' responded Odysseus. 'And you should travel only at night to avoid being seen. After midday today I'll go into the town and keep out of people's way until the suitors show up. I'll wander into the dining hall and see for myself what they've been doing these past years.'

'That's quite a risk,' responded Telemachus.

'No, they'll not recognise me. Most of 'em were playing games with wooden swords the year I left Ithaca for Troy. Maybe they'll think I'm a leper.'

'But what of Phemios?' Eumaeus asked. 'Will he not know you?'

'Highly unlikely,' answered Odysseus. 'His eyesight wasn't too good even before I left but I'll not get too close to him if I can avoid it. I doubt even Euryclea would have recognised me had it not been for that old wound on my leg. No, I want those men to see me only as I am now, before things come to a head. I want to look into their faces. I want to hear their words and I want to know their thoughts.'

'So be it,' said Telemachus, 'but I'll not be far away.'

***

In the oppressive heat of early afternoon Odysseus breathed the odours of the marketplace. His ragged gown was pulled close like that of a man afflicted by cold and hunger. He ambled amidst milling crowds, ruddy-faced, demonstrative stallholders, whooping, dashing children, frantic dogs, bleating goats and cackling geese, and as so often the cowl was drawn to part conceal his face. Few acknowledged the beggar as he casually perused the wares of Phoenicia, Egypt, Crete and lands further to the west. Perfumed oils, rare herbs, trinkets, furs, hides and fabrics, small ornaments in gold, silver or bronze caught his eye – some of them vain luxuries for those with enough gold or silver to make a purchase.

Perceiving a man whose fortunes, whose dignity and bearing had been blighted by poverty there were among Ithaca's citizens a small number who offered Odysseus wine and bread. A little of each he accepted though his appearance and his sullen manner deterred anyone from holding other than the briefest of conversations with him. Later that afternoon he observed Mentor and Euryclea enter the market square, strolling at their aged pace, so he shuffled casually behind a stall displaying jars of olive oil to avoid being noticed as they passed by. The stallholder said to him, 'I've seen you 'angin' about 'ere before. What's your business if you've got any an' where d'you come from?'

'I've no business other than to see out the day,' replied Odysseus. 'But of late I feel there's a change in the air. What d'you know of this king they tell me never returned from Troy?'

'He left when my father traded 'ere,' replied the stallholder. 'My old man 'oped he'd come back as most of us once did but it doesn't look that way – no, not after twenty years. As for a change in the air - I feel no change in it today or any other day. I only wish there was.'

'But what if he did return?' pressed Odysseus.

'Well, "what if?" That's anyone's guess unless the gods themselves know. It's a poor state of affairs as things are but I don't see it 'appenin'. No, 'e'll not come back though I dare say 'e'd still 'ave most of the people behind 'im if 'e did. His son might try 'is luck, mind you, but as I understand things there are too many powerful men set against 'im. All from well beyond this island as far as I know and few if any of 'em worth the fancy clothes they show up in. There's one or two of 'em struts about the market as if they own the place. Anyway, what's it matter to the likes of you?'

'Nothing at all, my friend,' Odysseus muttered, and walked away.

Dusk fell across Ithaca, the traders had packed their goods onto donkey or ox-drawn wagon and the market square lay almost deserted. Odysseus waited amid the shadows of the palace colonnade to watch and listen as the suitors crossed the inner courtyard with their retainers and slaves. Among the first of them strolled Antinous in lordly garb and, a short distance behind him, the less pretentiously attired Eurymachus whose course laughter rose above the general chatter to echo about darkening walls. Their amusement was heightened by the spectacle of Iros who, wearing a studded collar and towed along by a leash held by Eurymachus, yapped and mimicked the antics of an excited dog prancing on its hind legs. Odysseus watched them and a cold vengeance stirred within.

They continued to arrive in small groups, their slaves holding firebrands aloft to guide their masters' way as far as the narrow side passage that led to the dining hall. There the slaves halted before drifting off to occupy themselves in sullen conversation. Odysseus was not concerned if the slaves saw him loitering there or what they might think. The slaves of noblemen were better off than beggars. Better off even than many of the peasants who worked the fields, unless they fell short in performance of their allotted tasks.

Odysseus waited a while after the last of the suitors had arrived before continuing on by the main entrance which all those years ago had been a king's designated route into the palace. It led via an antechamber into the megaron from where he once ruled but he did not care to be confronted by any of Penelope's staff. Had he ascended the steps there might have been an armed guard to challenge him. Certainly in his day there would have been guards. He proceeded through the side passage taken by his wife's suitors.

It was seldom accepted now for a stranger to enter the dining hall at night and during times of celebration although the customs of charity were occasionally observed when a man of lowly aspect arrived to proposition alms. Such a man they would consider harmless and might tolerate for a while so few took notice of Odysseus when he stepped casually through the doorway into what had become a lurid enclave of rowdy chatter, scurrying slaves, wavering firebrands and the drifting smoke from braziers where meat sizzled and spat. He glanced up to observe the bow and quiver of arrows hanging where they had been since before he left for Troy. Listening, he gathered from their conversation that Penelope was yet to make her appearance despite the fact that her sequestered slave, Medon, had been sent to demand her presence. The bard Phemios was seated below the galley, close to the passage leading to the floor above where Penelope's suite lay. He strummed and sang as circumstances required but his notes and his voice made little impression amid the suitors' babble.

Clutching his frayed gown, Odysseus approached the nearest of the diners lounging at a table with five others. 'Pardon me, sirs, but might I beg from you a morsel of food. I've not eaten these last three days.'

'Who's this?' asked one of the men. Six faces turned to stare in disapproval at the intruder.

'Is there nothing left over in the marketplace?' asked another.

'If you mean scraps of food, sir,' replied the stranger, 'the dogs, the cats and the rats have taken all there was left out there. No, I can find nothing. Can you not spare a little?'

'Clear off and annoy someone else!' retorted the man he'd originally addressed. 'We've already got one of your sort scrounging for food here.'

'Try performing a few tricks like that shitbag Iros,' grinned another, gesturing across the busy room. 'He earns his food and drink that way.'

Odysseus peered across to see the one in question attempting a handstand close by the table occupied by Eurymachus and his companions. Their laughter welled up as Iros collapsed into a heap. His head appeared moments later above Eurymachus' bench where the latter offered him a piece of meat impaled on the tip of his sword blade. Iros took the meat in his mouth whilst someone called out, 'Now's your chance! Skewer the filthy bugger!'

Odysseus stepped along to the next group and again asked for food. Others had begun to notice the intruder and to comment on his rugged yet unkempt appearance. The children of some female serving women were pointing and chattering. His request for food at this table prompted the same response he'd received at the first, though more aggressive. Except there was one man, slim, sharp-eyed and fair-haired, who looked up at him, saying, 'Show your face properly, my friend, and I'll give you food and wine.'

Odysseus pushed away the cowl. The man was true to his word, offering the stranger a pottery dish of bread, lentils and pork and a finely wrought bronze cup of wine.

'Don't let 'im too close, Amphinomus,' grinned one of the companions, 'something might jump out of that fucking beard!'

Amphinomus responded, 'Hm - our friend here doesn't look to me a life-long beggar – more like a man of substance fallen on hard times.' Turning back to the stranger he asked, 'Is that so? Were you a trader, a craftsman in some other land, maybe?'

Odysseus accepted the dish and replied, 'It's too painful to relate, sir. Really - too painful.'

'Really *toooo* painful!' mocked one of Amphinomus' companions. 'Well bugger off and be painful over by the wall. Better still out of sight before you get a boot up your arse.'

'Don't wander away with that goblet,' another added, 'or you'll taste cold bronze instead of good food!'

'Yes, my friend,' advised Amphinomus, 'maybe you should make yourself scarce. Earlier tomorrow evening might be better for you but if you're still around here later and the mood is less heated I'll see to it you have more.'

Odysseus thanked him and backed away to stand by a column. There he ate and drank a little. There he watched and listened as servants and children swept by with flagons and dishes. Another figure had arrived from the corridor leading to the great hall. He remained discreetly back amidst the shadows at the top of the steps to observe his father.

There were shouts and cheers from across the hall as Iros, in begging-dog posture, attempted to seize with his teeth a portion of meat dangled from a cord by one of the male slaves. With each attempt the meat danced tantalisingly out of reach until with a surge of effort he managed to seize it. Jumping up to applaud himself wildly he spotted the stranger on the other side of the hall. He calmed and still chewing, peered hard with a hand raised above his eyes. 'Who's that?' he demanded in a voice akin to the creak of a bronze gate. 'Is 'e trying to steal my fuckin' patch?'

Heads turned and someone eyeing the stranger, called, 'That's it Iros you lump of shit - you'll have nothing more tonight! The wild man over there's getting the rest of your share!'

Antinous watched with amused interest from that end of the hall where hung the bow.

'That's right!' declared Eurymachus, waving his sword close to Iros' dough-like nose. 'That old bastard's in 'ere for what was yours! Go sort 'im out or I skewer yer damned guts!'

Laughter rang out and someone shouted, 'Go for it, boy! Go on, boy! Go get 'im!'

Iros leaped onto the bench, knocked over a goblet, wagged his hands like paws in the direction of Odysseus and yelled aloud, 'Bow-wow! Here I come! Bow-wow! Bow-wow!'

The chatter ceased. The painted ladies milling on the gallery above stared in silence across the hall to where the stranger waited. Odysseus returned his plate and goblet to the table.

Tables were promptly cleared in anticipation of Iros bounding across their tops which, whooping loudly, he proceeded to do with surprising agility, his dishevelled mop of black hair flapping like bird wings with each jump. Wooden seats and benches scraped on stone flags. Diners swivelled around to witness what they were certain would offer an entertaining spectacle while those further back stood up or clambered onto their seats for a better view. His round face a mask of eye-bulging frenzy, Iros landed with a thump between two benches several steps from the stranger, his insane grin exposing a gappy array of uneven, discoloured teeth. And though Iros was not as tall as Odysseus he crouched low, appearing much wider in his shabby, billowing gown as he approached, prancing from side to side, a great fluttering beetle with palps raised in readiness to seize his opponent. Odysseus waited calmly as, lurching from side to side, Iros closed then hesitated to voice aloud, 'Come on sheep fucker – let's 'ave you!'

He was poised to spring when Odysseus stepped forward and struck him on the jaw with a suddenness that caused the closest of the onlookers to flinch. Iros reeled into a nearby bench where the diners grabbed and prevented him from sprawling over their table. Goblets banged repeatedly on wood. Shouts of, 'Back on yer feet!' rang out. Other less than complimentary remarks arose throughout the hall, scraps of food flew across at Iros as, a hand clamped to his throbbing chin, he steadied himself and glared with teeth-gritting hate at this man of so little worth who had humiliated him when only those of higher status had a right to do so.

Silence returned. Iros crouched, growled like a wild beast, raised his fists ready to swing and lurched forward shrieking, 'Right, you shit-head! Right – right - right!'

They were the last words of abuse Iros would issue for some time. Odysseus parried his right-handed blow, drove a fist hard into the man's ribs then as he staggered back gasping, administered a left-handed punch to the side of his head that resounded through the hall as a sharp crack. It would have been enough to lay out any man but Odysseus grasped Iros beneath the chin to prevent him falling then thrust him against the wall where more savage blows were delivered to the man's body and head. Fool or no, Iros was one of the suitors if only by association and so he would suffer accordingly.

Those not already standing leapt from their seats. Some pressed forward and cries of, 'Finish 'im off!' and 'Feed 'im to the dogs!' rang out accompanied by thumping goblets.

But for the time being Odysseus had settled his account and stood back to watch his wretched assailant, glaze-eyed, battered and bloodied, slide down the wall into a shapeless heap and there remain. Laughing aloud, the suitors were returning to their places though several, in particular Antinous, kept their attention hard upon the stranger as he made his way leisurely toward the door through which he had first entered. Odysseus reached the exit but stopped on hearing someone call out, 'Where's her ladyship? She was sent for, wasn't she?' Their attention turned to the doorway beneath the gallery. Goblets banged, bones and scraps of food spun through the air and demands arose ever more loudly for the appearance of Penelope. Deep in thought, Antinous resumed his wine.

She was seated in her chamber when Medon appeared at the doorway with his gnarled stick. 'Lady Penelope, their mood is roused by an excess of wine and there has been a fight. The vagrant we have seen and spoken about – he beat Iros to the floor and now their sport is over they are demanding you appear before them.'

Penelope sighed, 'So that's what all the shouting was about. I have no wish to go to the dining hall, but the vagrant – what was he doing down there?'

'I don't know, my lady, other than that he begged for food and by now may have gone away. Please – I think you should go. They have become most unruly. Your presence may calm them.'

'All right, Medon, I'll go now but I won't stay long, no matter what they say.'

She descended the dark stairs from her room to open the door and stand where all could see her. The men quietened then calls rang out for her to confirm her commitment in choosing one of them for marriage. Eurymachus stood up to address her. 'Madam, there's been no news of Odysseus so it's clear enough - the man is long dead and gone! So -.' Here he looked around at the rest of the company. 'We're not prepared to have this drag on any longer! You must decide very soon and if you don't then it will be decided for you!'

'Hold it!' called Antinous, pushing his way between the tables to confront Eurymachus. 'We all

305

know this affair is coming to an end. We'll sort it out amongst ourselves soon enough but not here and not now.'

'Says who?' responded Eurymachus, glowering at him. 'Since when did you make the fuckin' rules around here!'

Antinous' hand fell to his dagger. Eurymachus stepped back, a hand slipping across to his sword hilt. Seats scraped, rattled and thudded over as each man's supporters pushed forward, hand on sword or knife ready to do bloody business. Slaves and their children retreated to the wall where the braziers stood and excited dogs added to the growing tension.

Amphinomus, the man who had offered the stranger food, stepped across to intervene exclaiming, 'Let it rest! Let's decide once and for all who really has a chance of marrying the woman and who hasn't then approach this issue later with only those men present.' He turned to Penelope with upraised hand. 'There is greater choice among us than you may have once thought. I possess land and resources equal to most men here but I will treat the house of Odysseus, you and your son with due respect. I will be at your service when it comes to your making a choice.'

Penelope regarded him with far less distaste than she did the rest of them. He had been a latecomer but had never caused offence nor had he pressed so hard for a decision.

Antinous and Eurymachus cold-eyed Amphinomus as well as each other then moved apart without further comment. Their companions returned to their benches. Antinous looked up at

Penelope. 'You heard that. Go back and think it over. Your time on that throne, lady, is soon to end!'

Telemachus stepped into view at the head of the stairs. 'Mother, go to your chamber. I'll join you shortly.'

Penelope glanced up at him but on the point of withdrawing she spotted the stranger at the door opposite and hesitated.

'Mother,' repeated Telemachus, 'Do as I say!' Turning to the suitors he declared, 'The answer you all deserve will not be long in coming! That I promise!'

Antinous threw a dismissive wave and strode back to his table. Eurymachus scowled and spat.

Penelope backed into the shadows of the staircase, closed and bolted her door. Telemachus retreated from the dining hall and hurried back along the corridor. From there he passed through the megaron, through the ante-room and out from the unguarded palace entrance then, checking to ensure none of the suitors were present, to the passage that led to the side door of the dining hall. There he re-joined his father who had also emerged into the night. 'Now is the time,' Telemachus declared. 'You must present yourself to mother then she will play her part in full.'

Odysseus placed a hand on Telemachus' shoulder. 'Yes, it is time.'

They entered the palace, strode through the ante-room into the megaron and from there made their way to the floor above where a single firebrand wavered against a wall. Odysseus stayed concealed in shadow whilst Telemachus dismissed the lone male slave standing by to await Penelope's summons.

In her darkened bedchamber Penelope lay restless and fretful, propped against a richly woven pillow, consoled by the soft humming of her slave girl Niobe who sat beside her holding her hand. Two small oil lamps served to keep total darkness at bay. The demands of the suitors were final. There was no more to be done until -.

Both looked up in surprise when Telemachus appeared at the door to announce, 'Mother, I need to speak with you. Niobe, go and join the other women.'

The girl arose, pausing momentarily to gaze into his eyes as she pushed by. Penelope eased wearily from her bed while Telemachus watched Niobe's slim form merge into gloom as she descended the stairs. Telemachus peered into his mother's bedroom. 'You need more light in here. See to those other lamps before we go any further.'

'What's happening?' Penelope asked as she took up and lit three more lamps from those already burning. This accomplished, she stood in anxious anticipation of Telemachus' answer, hands clasped at the front of her pale gown. He turned, gestured toward the columns, watched the figure emerge from obscurity and approach before moving aside to let the stranger enter. Penelope stepped back in dismay. 'Telemachus,' she demanded, angrily, 'why have you brought this man into my chamber? What business has he here?'

'He has business with all of us,' replied Telemachus. 'Look at him, mother. Look closely.'

'Look at him? Why are you asking me to look at him? I can see him from where I'm standing!'

'No, mother, you can't. You won't see him at all unless you try harder.'

Penelope, with undisguised reluctance, moved closer to peer at the stranger. She stared into his eyes, moved closer still and suddenly the eyes were all that mattered. She stared and in her mind the mass of disarrayed hair and unkempt beard were gone to reveal the rugged, neatly trimmed features of twenty years ago. She stared, held her breath, and it seemed the sun had arisen within her room to light his features. Penelope knew his eyes and when he smiled she knew his smile.

'Oh!' she gasped, one hand over her mouth, the other clutching her breast. 'Oh, by the gods!' Eyes wide she reached out a quivering hand to touch his bushy cheek. 'Is it? It is - it is you! You have returned to me. You have come home – you are here with me at long, long last.' She closed her eyes and would have slid to the floor but Odysseus reached to hold her in his arms. 'Yes,' he whispered, 'I've come home to Ithaca and to you.'

Telemachus withdrew discreetly from the chamber, whispering to himself, 'Well there's a weight off my mind. It's definitely him.'

Penelope grasped tightly the stranger who was no longer a stranger, and her cheeks glistened with tears. 'Oh, my love - this is a cruel dream. Soon I'll wake up and my Odysseus will be gone. What will I do?'

'No, sweet lady,' he breathed, 'this is no dream. I have returned and I'll still be here when you open your eyes - I truly promise.' He helped her back to her bed and sat beside her with an arm resting tenderly about her shoulders. Penelope wept profusely, her right hand clutching desperately upon Odysseus' left as if to prevent herself sliding over a precipice. For a time she dared not open her eyes.

'I'll pour wine then I'll say what needs to be said for now,' he assured her. 'Later I will explain more. Much more. Yes, I'll explain everything.' Even as the words were spoken he knew there was much he could never explain.

Penelope opened her eyes to stare at him, unspeaking, still struggling to convince herself all was real. At last she relaxed the grip of her hand on his, saying hoarsely, 'I - I have watched you wander the marketplace as a beggar. Why do you appear the way you are? Why? You are my husband, you are home again and you are king of your people.'

'I needed to know what had been happening on Ithaca. I had to look upon those men in the dining hall. I had to know who had remained faithful to this house throughout my absence. There can be no resumption of my kingship as it once was. There can be no peaceful outcome. Our son returned home in spite of their attempt to murder him and they must know he is aware of who was behind it. Should they suspect who I am they will rise against me before I'm able to gather my own forces. Telemachus, myself and others have devised a plan to defeat them but it is you who must initiate it.'

'Me?' she nodded, tearfully, 'I – I can no longer think straight, no, I cannot. May we not discuss this in the morning? May we not sit here together so you tell me about – about yourself, about everything? Now, not later, so I know you are really home. You must not leave me – no, you must not. If you do I'll think the gods have punished me with a cruel illusion and that things are as they have always been these many years. You must stay here with me. Say you will! Please, say it!'

'Aye, I'll stay,' he whispered. 'I'll be with you through the night and I'll be here when the sun rises - as long as you don't mind the company of a ragged vagrant, though I admit I did bathe at Eumaeus' well before coming here.'

'Ragged vagrant!' she exclaimed, throwing an arm around his neck then reaching to tug his unkempt beard. 'I'm going to keep a hold of this and never let go!' Laughing even as her tears continued to fall she pulled him by the beard toward the bed. Her chamber was once again their chamber. It was all that mattered. The world outside its walls had ceased to exist.

***

Another day passed and when the skies had darkened over Ithaca the suitors gathered in anticipation of further developments. Conversation in the dining hall was subdued, with children and dogs excluded, as were the flirtatious women of the court. Phemios strummed gently. Servants and slaves spoke in whispers or not at all and gaze met questioning gaze. Only the crack and spit of braziers refused to recognise the significance of the occasion.

The suitors' eyes were upon the door beneath the gallery but when Penelope, in flowing white gown, hair fallen loose, emerged to face them it was not from where they expected but from the corridor connecting the dining hall to the megaron. There she halted at the top of the steps. Telemachus emerged to stand next to her. Phemios laid aside his harp, voices fell silent as Telemachus addressed them. His expression betrayed no emotion though his voice was firm as he surveyed the host of waiting faces. All were eager to hear what was to be said so even those without serious aspirations ceased talking and laid their goblets aside. Servants and slaves retreated to gather in silence close to the braziers. A bruised and battered Iros hovered amid column-cast shadows beneath the gallery.

'The situation created by my father's long years of absence is at last to be resolved,' declared Telemachus. 'My mother agrees we must soon determine by contest which man among those gathered here would prove best qualified to take the throne of Odysseus and so gain the kingdom of Ithaca.'

'Contest?' some of them muttered, glancing one to the other.

'Most of you,' continued Telemachus, 'never held any such ambitions but have enjoyed the largesse of this house to the full. Hear her with respect. Let her decision be final.'

'That'll depend what her decision is!' sneered Eurymachus.

Before anyone could respond, Antinous stood up at the far end of the hall to declare, 'Well, dear prince, she can marry only one of us so I will certainly agree to her terms whatever they are - as must we all!'

Muttering an oath, knocking aside a part-filled metal goblet whose contents spattered across the table, Eurymachus turned to glare at Antinous. The goblet rolled from the table to clatter ominously on the stone floor. Telemachus whispered to Penelope, 'Our friend Antinous can afford to sound accommodating. He'll arrange to do away with whoever wins.'

'I can believe that,' she responded, eyeing the subject of their comments who, raising his cup, appeared perfectly at ease.

Eurymachus stared at Penelope whilst Amphinomus, the one contender who all along had avoided giving offence to her or her son stood to address them. 'As our friend Antinous says, the lady can marry only one of us so surely we can listen with respect to what she has to say.'

Eurymachus regarded Amphinomus with open contempt. Antinous lowered his goblet, smiled to himself, rubbed his chin casually then called across to Telemachus, 'And you, dear prince, when this is over, what might your intentions be?'

'Quitting Ithaca if he's any sense!' scoffed one. Shallow laughter arose but quickly subsided.

'That is for me to decide,' responded Telemachus. 'Now let my mother speak.'

'All of you hear me!' began Penelope as Telemachus stepped back a pace. Her confidence, drained by years of anxiety, returned in a tide of words. 'The absence of my husband has caused me long and unremitting grief but now - now I no longer think he is to return. You have waited long for my decision and guided by the gods I am at last ready to give it.' She raised an arm and pointed to the far end of the hall. 'There hangs Odysseus' great bow and his quiver of arrows. With them he hunted wild game and with them he fought the enemies of

313

his kingdom. Through all these years they have served to remind me of his strength and his courage. Now let them decide who is to take the throne of Ithaca.'

Penelope hesitated to assess their response but hearing no more than subdued murmuring she continued, 'The head of a goat will be set where the bow now hangs and any among you who accepts the challenge must shoot from where I now speak. The first man able to draw that bow and pierce the target will win the mantle and throne of Odysseus.'

'Really – a goat's head!' laughed Antinous. His was a laugh devoid of humour. 'And when is this formidable contest to take place?'

Eurymachus' expression darkened. A swell of babble arose throughout the hall as they turned to stare at the bow and arrows as if seeing them for the first time.

'It will be tomorrow evening,' Penelope replied. 'And as most of you carry items of value on your persons I ask in return for my decision and for all you have gained in the past from being here, that you each offer some gift in advance to the House of Odysseus.'

'A small price to pay after all these years,' remarked Antinous, drawing a jewelled ring from his finger. This he held up for all to see, adding, 'I'm sure every man here will agree to that.'

'Most of them will have to agree now he's done it,' breathed Telemachus. 'And no doubt he'll be expecting to get it back.'

'And,' continued Penelope, 'to celebrate in advance, regardless of the outcome, my son, Telemachus, will begin the evening of the contest by dispensing in generous quantity the finest wines from our private supplies!'

'The very finest we have to offer!' confirmed Telemachus, adding with a broad smile, 'And we'll begrudge you not a single drop.'

***

They relaxed alone in Telemachus' chamber unattended by slave or courtesan, their cups brimming, the room lit by the swaying flames of two lamps that cast their shadows large on frescoed walls. The yap and howl of faraway dogs drifted through the window on cool night air. The hoot of an owl sounded from somewhere closer.

'I hear you're to be liberal with my best wines,' remarked Odysseus regarding the goblet that he turned slowly in his hand.

'*Your* best wines!' responded Telemachus. 'Well, let me tell you, none of those wines are anything like twenty years old. The grapes themselves didn't exist on the day you left Ithaca. But you must agree it's in a good cause. Yours in particular, that is.'

'Aye, it's in a good cause for all of us,' agreed Odysseus, 'and the time we've set will for our contest not give Antinous or any of them opportunity to summon their kinsmen or allies from beyond our island.' He glanced into the darkness of the ceiling beams then added, 'At least we're dealing with real men and not the creatures of some other godforsaken world.'

'Maybe so but Antinous and a few of the others do have a number of men on Ithaca and they're as real as he is.'

'D'you know how many?'

'Can't say for sure,' replied Telemachus, 'but with the help of Euryclea I've sounded out members of our palace guard. She and I are confident that enough of them have stayed loyal, or have decided they are now, and will deal with any outsiders should they try to interfere. But the contest we've planned - what makes you think none of the suitors will be able to draw that old bow of yours?'

'Because it's no ordinary bow,' Odysseus assured him. 'It came by trade from lands far to our east where it's said such weapons were first used and as far as I know still are. It's a matter of technique as well as muscle power and the way it has to be strung – and that's no easy task. It took me a long time to master it and I much doubt any of them have ever seen its like, let alone handled one. When out hunting, that bow was as staunch a companion as any man could wish for.'

'So why didn't you take this staunch companion to Troy?'

'Ah, mainly because the bow is considered less of a warrior's weapon than is the sword or spear. Hand-to-hand combat's what is most regarded as true courage among men. That was certainly expected at Troy though the archer's skills were favoured by Paris. Yes, it was Paris who brought down Achilles, the greatest of our warriors, and it was an arrow shot by one of our men that in turn put an end to him. Maybe the archer's skills deserve more credit than most fighting men acknowledge.'

'They certainly do,' said Telemachus. 'If it wasn't for Noemon's Cretan archers I doubt I'd be here to discuss the subject with you. The skill of those men in rough waters was something to behold.'

Odysseus drank a little more wine before adding. 'You probably know my other reason for leaving the bow: it was a reminder, yes – something visible to assure people, your mother especially, that I would one day return.'

'Its presence did give her strength,' said Telemachus, 'that I do know.'

'Now there's something I would have informed you of earlier if I'd had the chance,' said Odysseus. 'I made my way into the dining hall long before sunrise a few days ago. Some of the firebrands were still alight but the suitors had departed and there was no one else in there. I dragged a bench over, jumped onto it and took the bow down. As I expected the bowstring was no good but I'd taken along a new one Euryclea had fetched from our armoury. I strung the bow, I tested it well then I unstrung and placed it back on the wall. Composite bows don't always retain their strength over a long period and woodworm can render them useless, but this one, I tell you, is as good as the day I last used it. I would never have suggested the contest otherwise.'

'That's most reassuring,' smiled Telemachus, raising his goblet.

'And there's something else I have to say before it takes place. There's a man you surely know, one called Amphinomus; he was considerate to me when I went in there begging for food. Your mother assures me he's the only serious contender among them who treated her with respect. Had it not been for him they might have forced matters sooner. I would have warned him to stay away from the dining hall tomorrow night but I think he'd take little notice of a beggar. He might listen to you if you find an opportunity to speak alone with him.'

'Of course - I know the man,' said Telemachus. 'Do I sense pangs of compassion, father? Not at all like you I would have thought.'

'Perhaps not, but I've witnessed so many men die these past years, no few by my own hand at Troy and so many others through the spite of the gods on my journey back here. If there is one worth saving out of that rabble, then – then why not, and my guess is he'll support us later on.'

'Very well - he has to my knowledge never insulted or caused offence other than by consuming what is ours like the rest of them. I'll warn him if I get the chance but we cannot arouse suspicion.'

'Then there's no more to be said. I'll make myself scarce until the contest begins.'

'Until the contest begins,' repeated Telemachus, raising his cup once more. 'And may Athena be with us.'

***

Midnight was well past when they began to leave. Their slaves, as always, walked ahead with firebrand, or assisted their drunken masters in negotiating their way to their lodgings in the town. Amidst the shadows of the colonnade Telemachus waited. When Amphinomus did appear, he was escorted by only a single slave. Two more of the suitors, each supported by a pair of slaves, tottered some distance behind. As Amphinomus passed by, Telemachus called his name.

Both man and slave hesitated. 'Who calls me?' Amphinomus asked, peering into the shadows. His slave raised the firebrand to dispel the shadows behind the columns.

Telemachus stepped forward, saying, 'I wish to speak with you.'

The man appeared less inebriated than most of the others. As he peered between the columns the pair who were behind him stumbled by, showing no interest in Amphinomus as he moved closer to face the shadowed figure. 'Oh, it's you – Telemachus. What d'you want with me tonight?'

'I must know if you hold any serious intentions toward my mother and if you intend to try your hand in the contest tomorrow?'

Amphinomus gestured his slave to step back then after some thought answered, 'I - I harboured every intention of taking part as I have courted her favour these last two years and more, but as of this day I've wondered if it's such a good idea. Whoever wins her hand will need to have loyal guards standing by day and night. He will need to sleep with one eye open and his sword at the ready if he's to preserve his own life and I fear the House of Odysseus could end up like that of Atreus and Agamemnon. I've no desire to see that and it's an outcome you above all must fear. Should certain of those men acquire your father's throne, your only chance of remaining alive will be to flee Ithaca. But why d'you choose this moment to ask me?'

'Because, my friend, unlike the rest of them you always treated my mother with a measure of respect and consideration and never did I hear you voice contempt for the memory of my father as others among them very often have. So – if you doubt the wisdom of acquiring the throne of Ithaca I ask why you need be present tomorrow. There will most likely be trouble whoever wins the contest. It could mean violence – probably bloodshed. In fact I'm rather certain it will.'

'I'm not afraid of any of them,' Amphinomus smiled, 'but I'll not get involved in violence if that's the way things are looking.'

'I don't suggest you're afraid; not at all. It seems a pity, though, that you risk becoming embroiled when you need not. That's why I suggest you reconsider. That is why I ask you to stay clear of the dining hall tomorrow.'

'Prince Telemachus, I say again I may not, no I *will* not take part in the contest for Lady Penelope's hand, but I nevertheless cannot miss what will be a most interesting spectacle.' Amphinomus pressed a fist to his mouth and glanced aside. 'I thank you for your concern but I - I have to go now. I feel rather unwell.'

Telemachus backed into the shadows as others approached and from there he watched Amphinomus walk unsteadily behind his slave until both had vanished through the courtyard gate and into the night. 'So be it,' he whispered.

Chapter 10 - The Great Bow

They began to gather in the dining hall, the suitors and their followers. There would be no latecomers that momentous, that long awaited evening. They saw the bow and quiver of arrows were gone from their accustomed place high on the wall. There instead was mounted the gristly, pale head of a freshly sacrificed goat. Above its grinning mouth dead eyes gleamed baleful in the dancing light of the firebrands. Fresh blood streaked the wall and patterned the flagstones beneath.

'A damned goat's head,' muttered one, eyeing the object on the wall. 'Why that?'

'What the fuck's it matter?' commented Eurymachus standing close by. 'Whole things a sham if you ask me.'

'Maybe there's more to this than you think,' responded the first man.

Nobly robed, Antinous stood by the passageway door through which he had just entered. He looked about before stepping across to sit in his accustomed place where a slave waited to charge his goblet and fill his plate.

Conversation throughout the hall was subdued, the mood tense. They looked from one to the other with unspoken questions. There was no Phemios, no harp, no song of the bard to entertain the assemblage. There was no Iros the ill-used clown, nor did the painted girls of the court flutter on the gallery above to peer down with seduction in their eyes and tokens of gold or silver illuminating their thoughts. As always meat sizzled on tripod braziers. As always smoke swirled while those in attendance scurried back and forth, eyes fixed ahead, mouths tightly closed. No matter how much the suitors cared to drink there would be more than enough good wine to help them celebrate. It was, after all, to be the end of one era and the beginning of another. And so the feasting began. After a time the intake of wine elevated their conversation to a babble yet they continued to strain their necks in anticipation of what was next to happen.

'Where's the bow? Where's the woman who's to be prize in all this?' some began asking.

They were still speculating when a smiling Telemachus trod casually down the steps from the megaron corridor and began to stroll around the periphery of the tables. 'It'll be soon enough,' he assured them on being questioned. 'Enjoy the good wine – it will relax you when it comes to the shoot.'

He passed by glowering Eurymachus who, like a handful of others, eyed him ominously. He observed the foppish Amphion attempting discreetly to waft away with jewelled hand the fetid breath of porcine Eudorus as the latter, whispering close to his ear, affected a flaccid grin. Further along and Amphinomus, seated with brimming goblet, glanced up to acknowledge him with a polite nod and gesture of his hand. Telemachus hesitated but unable to give voice to his thoughts he carried on to the further end of the hall where sat Antinous, joined now by two of his surly, lizard-eyed retainers. Telemachus sensed their hostility as he might the onset of a threatening storm and while resisting the temptation to let his hand drift closer to the hilt of his sword he maintained the aspect of a benign host. The two men glared aside at him from lowered faces while Antinous continued to eat, relaxed and seemingly indifferent to Telemachus' presence. Should another man win the throne of Ithaca he would soon find not a seat of power but an altar of death with Antinous brandishing the sacrificial knife. Telemachus' thoughts turned briefly to the vanished Leiocritius though the question of what had happened to Antinous' one-time crony was by now seldom on anyone's lips.

'The wine'll bugger our aim!' called a stocky man with scarred and ruddy face from the centre of the hall as Telemachus, having passed by the main doors and red-streaked wall from where the gristly target gazed down on them, veered right to continue past the side door and back toward the short staircase down which he had entered. 'Is that what you're 'opin' for?' the man pressed. 'Too pissed to 'it the thing – is that it?'

'What!' exclaimed Telemachus, 'am I hearing excuses already, my friend? Have you decided you're not up to the challenge?'

'He couldn't 'it the fucking wall!' mocked Eurymachus loudly. 'Not even from where he's sittin'!' Laughter erupted. The subject of his abuse sprang scowling from his seat, sword half drawn. Eurymachus did likewise, violently elbowing aside the youth who was attempting to pour his wine from a flagon, causing its contents to spray across floor and table as the boy staggered back. It looked for a moment as if blood was also to be spilled but following a colourful exchange of insults both were prevailed upon by their respective companions to sit down again.

Antinous hard-eyed the much-amused Telemachus. Under his breath he murmured, 'You're walking ever closer to the edge, boy. Make the most of things while you can.'

The smoke-laden atmosphere livened further as wine was dispensed in abundance. Telemachus strolled casually on, turning at the base of the steps to observe Amphion leave the munching Eudorus and make his way across the hall to engage in conversation elsewhere. Wine flagons coursed back and forth and the suitors' alcohol-fuelled impatience was expressed by increasingly raucous behaviour, in shouted abuse, hurled scraps of food and table thumping. Telemachus was joined by Medon and the noise hardly diminished as the latter proceeded about the dining hall to discreetly order palace servants and slaves to exit via the main doors. This task completed, Medon re-joined Telemachus and both ascended the steps. With a nod from Telemachus, Medon continued on to his mistress's chamber. On announcing his presence he entered to find Penelope looking from her window to moonlit hills beyond the town wall.

'Is all going as we wished?' she asked, turning to face him.

'All is going as we wished, My Lady' Medon replied.

'And my husband?'

'He waits outside the passage by the dining hall.'

'Very well,' she breathed, tightening the belt of her white gown, 'then it's time for me to go.'

Telemachus stood gazing across the hall when something caught his attention. A shadow danced amidst the smoke-blackened beams above as if a bat or a large bird had entered through one of the high windows. It flickered back and forth but its form remained vague and illusive, a shadow within shadows. Moments later it was gone. Telemachus waited to satisfy himself that everyone except for the suitors and their personal attendants had left the hall. The solid main doors opposite were still part open and despite the smoke haze he was able to make out in the darkened courtyard beyond some of the suitors' slaves gathered with firebrands held aloft. Euryclea's trusted slave, Leucon, appeared in the gap between the main doors and from there nodded across the hall to Telemachus. Telemachus nodded back. The doors slowly closed.

'When's the great event to get started, dear prince?' called a food-muffled voice. Telemachus peered over to see Eudorus gaping at him, lips mobile, cheeks bulging.

'Very soon, my friend,' answered Telemachus. 'Will you try your hand?'

'Oh, er, not at all, no I won't,' spluttered Eudorus, trying to swallow and reaching for his goblet whilst evidently having missed the irony of the question. 'When it comes to shooting at things, I'm no archer; my men do all that!'

Telemachus stepped back down into the hall, ignored the inevitable, demanding questions and was making his way to the side door opposite the deserted gallery when Penelope appeared at the top of the steps vacated by her son moments earlier. In her hands she cradled the magnificent bow, iconic symbol of Odysseus. Close by her stood Medon clutching not the gnarled stick, the imposed token of humiliation, but the quiver replete with newly feathered arrows. Noise diminished throughout the dining hall. Faces turned. Several men clambered to their feet, some visibly intoxicated and needing to steady themselves against table or companion.

'What have we got here?' shouted one man gesturing at Penelope as she held the bow aloft, 'The new fucking Artemis?'

Laughter rippled throughout the hall then silence asserted.

'I offer my husband's bow to whoever will enter the contest,' she announced coldly as she propped the weapon against the wall by the door. Medon placed the quiver by the other side of the door as Penelope continued, 'My husband's bow and his arrows await you. I will not return until the matter is resolved.'

Benches grated against flagstones. A number of the suitors were on their feet – mainly the younger men. Antinous rose from his seat but remained, arms folded, at the far end of the hall. Most of those standing looked to see who would step forward first, each wanting to ascertain how the great bow of Odysseus might best be handled. At last one man did. To everyone's surprise it was soft-spoken Amphion who stepped forward and turned to address them, encouraged by a grinning, hand clapping Eudorus. Smiling broadly, flexing jewelled fingers for all to see he declared, 'Well I wasn't going to bother, of course, but someone has to get things started. Does it have to be me?'

Anticipating a response, Amphion had backed only a few hesitant paces toward the steps when a drunken Eurymachus blundered forward, grasped him by the shoulder and pushed him roughly aside, exclaiming, 'You go back to your fucking slave boys! Let a real man get his hands on that bow!'

Amphion shrugged, grinned satisfaction, turned again and almost collided with the scar-faced man who a short time before had risen in response to Eurymachus' insult. He, too, had intended seizing the bow but Eurymachus, striding further ahead, scrambled up the steps to reach for the weapon. Penelope stepped well back, Medon not so far. The scar-faced man hesitated, muttered obscenities, spat then dropped heavily onto the nearest bench from where he glared vengeful anger at Eurymachus. All eyes were upon Eurymachus who, attempting to focus, was crouched, leaning awkwardly against the doorpost in an attempt to string the bow. Not only was this fine weapon of wood and horn stronger but its curvature was unfamiliar and quite unlike Eurymachus' hunting bow or any other he had encountered.

'Get a move on, man,' someone shouted as the irate Eurymachus fumbled and cursed.

'He can't tell the front from the back!' shouted someone - and it seemed the increasingly frustrated Eurymachus could not.

The suitors grew more impatient. Goblets thumped ever harder. Insults and discarded bones flew back and forth between each man's supporters. Eurymachus' face darkened with anger but at last, with teeth-gritting determination, he bent and strung the bow then arose muttering to his feet with an expression of defiance. He wrenched a bronze-tipped arrow from the quiver, bent forward to fit it with clumsy impatience, then as silence returned he stepped away from the wall and raised the bow. Eurymachus, finding the bow a tougher prospect than anticipated, tested the string back and forth then drew it as far back as he considered it ought to be drawn. He took aim, hesitated to reassess both angle and distance, paused again, then released the arrow. It sped through smoke-laden air to strike the wall over an arm's length to the left and somewhat below the target - then it clattered to the floor. Cursing aloud, he stooped to reach for a second arrow but the scar-faced man and two companions strode forward with raised fists to demand that Eurymachus step down and allow another to try his skill. Eurymachus hesitated. 'Trying to string the damned bow made my arm shake!' he declared. 'That first shot ought not to count!'

Fists and goblets pounded aggressively. More men rose to their feet, jeering loudly. They demanded Eurymachus give way as the big man and his companions advanced closer, each with sword drawn. Mouthing obscenities, Eurymachus threw the bow to the floor, blundered down the steps and with a dismissive growl, swayed along, looking at no one until he reached the gallery colonnade where he remained to seethe indignation amidst the shadows.

The scar-faced man was already at the top of the steps and, showing no more aptitude than had his predecessor, fumbled to fit the arrow before raising the bow. His aim was no better. Not having drawn the bow to its full extent his arrow also struck wide of the mark, closer to the main doors though not as low as the previous shot and again clattering to the floor.

'I'd like to see any man hit the target with this!' he declared, flinging the bow aside to where Medon caught it. 'It's not been used in twenty years and the woman knows it! It's set hard with age! This damned charade is another one of her tricks!' With that he strode back across the hall, head down, ignoring the taunts of others until reaching his seat and taking up his wine once more with his companions.

The failed efforts of the first two did not deter others from stepping forward. Eurymachus, having paused to urinate against the column, stood with scornful expression as a third and a fourth man tried unsuccessfully to draw the bow correctly and strike the target.

Amphinomus, having earlier affirmed to Telemachus that the contest was not for him, got slowly up, hesitated, then stepped forward. Other more belligerent, more determined men had failed in their attempt to master the bow of Odysseus so he considered it would be no great shame if he also failed, but perhaps greater shame if he did not try. Seeing him ascend the few steps to where the bow lay prompted a lull in conversation rather than the verbal mockery that resulted from the efforts of others. He collected up and tested the strength of the bow without gesture or comment, fitting the arrow almost as if this was a routine act. The gold ring on his finger glinted as, with one eye closed, he drew back the cord as far as he was able and took aim. To everyone's surprise, including that of Amphinomus himself, his arrow struck the wall less than an arm's length to the right and a little above the intended target, again with insufficient strength behind the shot so that it, too, clattered to the flagstones. Seeing his effort prove better than the others, Amphinomus smiled broadly, shrugged, handed the bow carefully to Medon then returned with modest satisfaction to his seat.

After this latest attempt several close by turned to Antinous. 'Are you not going to try?' one man asked.

'Think you could do better than Eurymachus?' queried another, adding, 'No, maybe not.'

'I'll decide what to do when I'm good and ready,' he responded, staring across at the steps where the bow and quiver rested as he lifted his goblet. It was by now clear to those close by that Antinous had no intention of becoming involved in the contest but was rather more concerned to observe the performance of those who did. The wine flowed in abundance once more and sporadic conversation resumed.

Others stepped forward to attempt the shot, each man thinking he might show how it ought to be done even though success had proved unattainable to even the strongest and most determined among them. Some expressed the opinion that the bow could never be drawn properly at all. Speculation simmered. During a brief interlude one man took it upon himself to collect fallen arrows and wrench away another still embedded in the plasterwork of the wall. These he dutifully returned stepping up to place them into Medon's care.

A tenth man was approaching the steps when Eumaeus entered from the side passage. Behind him followed the beggar, his tattered robe secured at his waist by a knotted cord, his eyes bright beneath the cowl. There they waited until the latest contestant also confirmed his inability to master the bow. Another man called for Antinous to attempt the shot but Antinous ignored him. His attention was fixed upon the vagrant. The newcomers' presence had attracted little notice until Eumaeus raised his arms to exclaim, 'Hear me! I have with me a man who would try his hand with Odysseus' bow!'

Heads turned to regard the gowned figure. Silence fell until one man exclaimed, 'By the gods, d'you mean that foul old tramp standing behind you? We'd be better off with Iros!'

'Boot 'im out!' called another. 'And where *is* Iros?'

There was moderate consensus over the proposed eviction until - 'Wait – hold it!' someone bellowed, 'Didn't he beat the shit out of Iros? Let him try! This has to be worth seeing!'

'Yes, let him try,' agreed another. 'If he hits the goat's head he can stick around in place of Iros! No, wait – we can make her ladyship take him in marriage!'

The suitors laughed and goblet-thumped. They no longer expected anyone would succeed in hitting the target but saw the beggar as offering ample opportunity for ridicule.

Eumaeus smiled. Odysseus remained impassive.

Antinous' expression set grimly. 'Enough!' he cried, standing with one foot on a wooden stool, one hand on his sword hilt. No longer the cool, detached Antinous this was a man whose simmering ambition charged his every nerve, whose once restrained beast of anger was freed by a surfeit of alcohol. 'What is really going on? Why are these oafs here? We've held on these past years through countless delays and now we're close to a time of decision we have this! Why - why have a clod-hopping swineherd and a damned vagrant entered now to disrupt the affairs of these islands and the determination of their kingship?' There was no response other than a collective, silent gaze. 'Their presence is no pointless diversion!' he declared, levelling a finger of accusation at Eumaeus and his cowled companion. 'You're being made to look fools by that woman and by her gutless son! This affair will never be resolved within these walls! Never! It has to be determined in the field with real weapons – yes, by blade and blood the way real men sort their problems out!'

'Shut up and sit down!' called Eurymachus, striding clear of the gallery but Antinous ignored him. Staring hard at Eumaeus and the beggar, he stepped back, reached down to grasp one leg of a stool then pointing at the two by the door, cried, 'Get that pair out of here or by Zeus I'll see they end up as corpses for burning!'

With no one willing to act on his words and neither of the intruders about to retreat he raised the stool above his head then hurled it at them with enraged force. Both stepped promptly apart as the stool spun across to strike the wall and there shattered with a resounding crack.

'Let 'em be!' someone called out. 'What've we got to lose?'

'Sure, what's it matter!' added another. 'Maybe we should draw lots for the woman!'

Antinous glared angrily but the majority made it clear by further dismissive comments that the mood was against him. Cursing under his breath he sat then took up and grasped his goblet in both hands. Eumaeus and the anonymous vagrant walked casually to the end of the hall where they ascended the steps. Eumaeus moved out of sight into the corridor, along which Penelope and Medon had already retreated, while his unlikely looking charge turned to peer across a sea of faces. They stared back at him as one, some appearing puzzled, the majority amused. The beggar appeared indifferent, as if the challenge no longer mattered. The suitors continued to watch with a number voicing impatience or abuse. In tight-lipped silence Antinous continued to appraise the figure on the steps and suspicion stirred within him as a serpent in a dark pit. He set down his goblet, one fist hard clenched, the other hand slipping to his sword hilt.

The beggar took up the bow. Derisory comments were followed by sporadic laughter as he examined it, as anyone might, on seeing such a weapon for the first time. He curled one hand firmly about the horn grip while with the other he tested the cord of animal sinew, drawing it slowly back and forth as if testing its strength. Several times he did this until Eurymachus called aloud, 'Get the fuck on with it or get out of 'ere!'

Someone threw a bone that passed close to the beggar before hitting the wall. This he ignored and reaching down to the quiver, he extracted an arrow. The arrow he held out and proceeded to examine by rolling it in his fingers before peering along its length. At last, with great care and concentration, he fitted the arrow to the bow then, no longer appearing quite the novice, he adjusted his stance and raised the weapon.

Murmuring spread through the hall as they watched him draw the string part way, then back to its full extent – something none of the suitors had been able to do with such ease. The murmuring ceased as he took steady aim, only to stand for several heartbeats in silent, statuesque poise while the onlookers held their breath and cooking fires spat. A sharp thwack and the arrow was released – a whistling hiss as it flew above their heads, a thud as it struck the goat's head to penetrate deep between the eyes. The head rocked from side to side with the force of impact. The protruding arrow swayed as a wind-blown branch in mockery of the suitors who stared in confusion at the target, at one another then at the man who had demonstrated with such ease a skill not possessed by any of their own.

'It's a fluke – that's what!' Eurymachus declared, moving toward the steps.

'Luck of the gods and nothing more,' agreed someone as Odysseus placed the bow aside and stood to observe their reactions.

'You damned fools!' cried Antinous, clambering noisily onto a table with sword raised high. 'That shot was no accident!' He levelled the blade toward the figure on the steps. 'The man is no stranger to that damned bow and by Zeus I know why!'

As Antinous spoke, the beggar pushed away his cowl and tugged open the cord holding his gown in place. He wrenched the gown open, letting it fall to reveal a cuirass of ornately decorated, burnished bronze that glinted firebrand light, a finely tooled leather kilt and stout belt from which hung scabbard and sword; all of which the suitors were quick to recognise only a man of wealth and power would possess. And in his eyes they saw burning the light of retribution.

'Don't you see who that is?' cried Antinous, bounding forward one table closer, kicking aside dishes and goblets before their startled owners who in turn scrambled from their seats. 'Don't you understand? Go for him! Cut him down! Cut him down now!'

Odysseus had taken up the bow once more as Antinous attempted a leap to the next table. But driven to precarious, wine-fuelled abandon, the latter missed his footing and nearly pitched to the floor. All of the suitors had clambered noisily to their feet, the greater number with swords drawn as Odysseus fitted a second arrow and calmly raised the bow. Seats clattered and overturned. Men were shouting, swearing, lurching in confusion. Antinous regained his balance and jumped onto the next table where, sword ready to strike, he would continue on. Two, perhaps three more leaps would have him within striking distance of his adversary.

Amid such commotion the enraged Antinous did not hear the thwack of the bow. He did not see the arrow that sped at him as he raised his sword high for that final reckless dash - an arrow that carried with it the vengeance of years, the retribution of a sorely affronted house. He hardly felt it pierce his throat as he pressed his attack, though the feathered shaft quivered before his eyes and the point protruded red at the back of his neck.

Antinous staggered to a halt. The sword fell from his grasp. Men stared up at him, their voices a meaningless drumming, their faces gaping masks. The hall tilted dreamlike before his eyes. Blood choked copiously from a mouth wide in stifled scream. Antinous swayed then plunged from the table to strike the floor. There he quivered amid fragments of broken pottery and spilled wine as death claimed him.

In the ensuing uproar few had noticed the arrival on the gallery above of Noemon and six of his archers. As the suitors pressed toward the steps bawling murderous intent, a number of them fell to the deadly strike of the Cretans' arrows. Eumaeus re-joined Odysseus and with blades flashing they leaped down to set upon those closest, to cleave flesh and split bone whilst directly behind them, armed with sword and small, round shield, appeared Telemachus with six members of the palace guard, likewise equipped. In crowding too close about the steps the suitors and their retainers found they could not weald their swords so began pushing back to gain more space while those at their rear attempted to press forward. Advancing upon them Odysseus' company was well outnumbered but better armed and driven by a fierce determination to conclude matters with keenly sharpened bronze.

For Odysseus this was a remission of guilt, a fitting conclusion for so many years of absence blighted by deception, misfortune and tribulation, for Telemachus it was a justifiable action to redeem his house after years of abuse, for Eumaeus it was little more than a necessary slaughtering of beasts.

From amidst frenzied disorder emerged bejewelled Amphion, scrambling for the main exit at the far end of the hall with tottering behind him a bug-eyed, arm-wagging, panic-stricken Eudorus. Both heaved against the stout, copper-banded wooden doors only to find them immovably locked. Eudorus fell to his knees, fists hammering frantically against the timbers but Amphion, seeing there was to be no escape, drew his sword and turned in desperation to defend himself. Three of the palace guard had fought their way around the hall toward the main doors. One came upon the crouching Eudorus and raising his sword, struck hard enough to all but sever the man's head from his body. The other two closed upon Amphion who seeing the fate of Eudorus, let fall his sword and stood impassively, eyes closed tight as the two guards in unison pierced him through. His death, too, was instant.

Some men jostled and pushed to attain the side door, others to the door beneath the gallery used by Penelope in her appearances before them. Both were locked. Several of the suitors upended tables to shield themselves against Noemon's arrows only to be pierced through where they cowered by the merciless thrust of sword or dagger. A number dashed to shelter with Eurymachus amidst the columns supporting the gallery. One man seized a firebrand from the wall opposite then leapt up onto a table, intending to hurl the flaming torch at the archers. Two arrows pierced him simultaneously, one in the chest, one through the cheek. He fell screaming between tables, overturning flagon and goblet, flinging the brand into the air with a shower of sparks. Blazing brightly it fell to ignite a discarded cloak and within moments dark smoke welled up, adding to the chaos of conflict.

Amphinomus, the one man who might have been spared, fought gallantly to defend himself but was pierced through his spine by the hard driven blade of a palace guard. The shouting and violence continued with the suitors and their followers, increasingly desperate, not knowing from which direction death might strike but well aware as their number diminished what their fate would be. A scream arose above the clash of swords as another of them, impaled by an arrow through his shoulder, staggered against a glowing brazier, knocking it over then collapsing onto the spilled and glowing embers. A bronze blade through the heart, dealt by Eumaeus, ended his shrieking agony.

Braving the peril of Cretan arrows, Eurymachus stepped out from beneath the gallery with hands spread and called aloud to Odysseus, 'Wait! There are enough men dead! The man who schemed to take your throne is dead! I and the rest took what we could! That's our only guilt!'

Hearing him speak the clamour subdued. The archers held back their shots. Others hesitated to see what would happen as Odysseus, levelling his sword at Eurymachus, delivered his uncompromising reply. 'You claim living off my house as your only guilt! No - you contrived to murder my son and you planned the same fate for me! Look to your sword or I'll cut you down where you stand!'

'Murder you?' he snarled, savage fury darkening his face. 'Yes - that I would and by the

338

gods I soon will!' Blade hissing from his scabbard he determined to make for Odysseus who was promptly confronted by two other men equally intent on making an end of him. He struck one man, cutting deep into his left arm, while his own cuirass deflected the thrusting blade of the second. Despite a profusely bleeding wound the injured man continued to parry but the other was more determined and would keep Odysseus occupied until fate prevailed.

Judging this a fine opportunity to gain advantage, Eurymachus struck the first man to face him, a palace guard, with a blow that pierced the man's helmet, shattering his skull above the ear with enough force to expose bone and brain. A second guard swung at Eurymachus, his blade was parried but not before it bit into Eurymachus' cheekbone, causing blood to flow copiously. Now this man fell, pierced through the middle by Eurymachus' deadly blade, his screams shivering the air as his assailant, determined to fall on Odysseus with bloody violence, trod hard upon his still writhing victim to close on his goal.

Telemachus, seeing what might happen beat one man aside with his shield and pushed vigorously through the mêlée to confront the gore-streaked Eurymachus, a man who feared nothing, a man who knew his own life must soon end unless the coming moments proved the gods were with him. Aware of his approach Eurymachus swung at him with a cry of, 'Die, you cur!'

The blow was deflected by Telemachus' shield but this was split and dashed from his hand. Dodging to avoid a second swing, Telemachus thrust his blade upward into Eurymachus' ribs. Fatal such a blow must eventually prove but Eurymachus was not yet ready to die. He staggered back as the blade wrenched clear then lunged like a raging bear at Telemachus, his sword descending as a thunderbolt. But Telemachus sprang aside to avoid the blow and Eurymachus' blade bit hard into a tabletop. As he heaved the sword free Telemachus struck again, his own blade flashing through the air to cleave the man's head down to his ear. Eurymachus, mouth agape, eyes fixed upward, let fall his sword then with a final gasp, toppled backwards to hit the bloodied floor. Telemachus, showing neither fear nor anger, took up the discarded shield of a dead guard and continued with brutal efficiency to end further the lives of his mother's tormentors.

With the help of a palace guard, Odysseus' assailants had met their fate and the scar-faced man who had earlier challenged Eurymachus was now his goal. Sword raised to meet the challenge the snarling assailant was struck by simultaneous blows of a Cretan arrow in the shoulder and a deeply penetrating sword thrust to the side by Odysseus. The man staggered, wild-eyed, yelling defiance, sword lashing thin air as those nearby backed away. Two, three steps forward then he reeled, lips quivering as he crashed to the floor. Joined by Odysseus and Eumaeus the palace guard, their number reduced now to four, made pitiless end to those still cowering in shadow amidst the gallery columns. They were no more troubled by appeals to the gods or cries for mercy than men might be when felling oxen. Eumaeus in particular, his hands and tunic liberally spattered with the blood of others, savoured this final butchery.

The fighting had ended but the groans of the wounded and the dying remained, punctuated by the crack and splutter of braziers. Their job finished, Noemon and his archers withdrew from the gallery while the remaining guardsmen trod amidst the stricken, plunging blade into those who might still be alive and peering beneath table and bench to ensure none of the suitors had taken refuge there.

Odysseus stooped to wipe gore from his blade with the fallen Eurymachus' gown then stood to survey the scene. The four guards departed via the way they had entered, their part in the grim task concluded. Eumaeus, muttering, 'All in a day's work,' was conscious of his own sullied appearance and desired little more than to make his exit and feel the cleansing touch of water. On gaining the acquiescence of Odysseus he, too, left the hall.

The dining hall lay in eerie silence – a gruesome vault of death illuminated by torches that, fluttering fire-wings in the once turbulent air, now burned calmly. The unwelcome company of so many years lay sprawled in grotesque and gory disarray over table and floor beneath a settling shroud of smoke. The walls were spattered red, the flagstones pooled with blood that spread to mingle with food and wine from overturned tables and shattered vessels.

The silence remained unbroken until Odysseus turned to his son. 'We have shed much blood. The very walls and timbers of this room will retain the memory of it. Now I ask myself how proud should we be of what we've accomplished this night.'

'Proud?' queried Telemachus, gazing across the hall 'No, I'm not proud but it had to be done and it will be seen as just in the eyes of the gods.'

'But not in the eyes of their kin on the islands,' breathed Odysseus.

'No, I expect they will -.' Telemachus hesitated then gripped his father's arm, saying, 'Look! Look up there!'

Odysseus glanced upward. A white owl had flown in through a high window. It circled a while before landing where it pranced back and forth on a wooden beam, wings outstretched as it peered down upon the carnage.

'I know her well,' said Telemachus.

'I also know her,' breathed Odysseus, 'though for too long she was absent when I needed her.'

As he spoke the owl took once more to the air and departed the way it had entered.

Medon appeared at the head of the steps. Odysseus turned to him, saying, 'Unlock the main doors. I'll have our men go out there and round up their slaves. They can come in here and remove the bodies of their masters.'

'What d'you suggest we have done with them?' Telemachus asked. 'Burning?'

'Yes, our people will build pyres outside the city wall. They must begin as soon as there's enough light. It must be done quickly – before news of this gets out and their kinsmen discover what's happened. As for now, we take their weapons and any valuables they possess, though they can never repay in death what they have taken from this house in life.'

Medon departed, stepping aside for three figures who approached slowly, in cautious silence, filing along the corridor from the megaron. The first was Euryclea in her dark gown, followed closely by Leucon with Penelope, clutching her robe, a few steps behind. Appalled on seeing horror within the dining hall, Euryclea stood for a time in silence. 'Need it have come to this?' she asked at last, eyeing Odysseus and Telemachus with reproach. 'I spoke just now with Noemon. He tells me every man of them lies dead in his own blood. Will the gods ever forgive us? Yes, they preyed upon us like jackals year after year but could you not have slain the worst of them and spared those few who came here out of weakness rather than ill-intent?'

'We'd have spared one if only he'd listened,' responded Telemachus.

'As for the rest,' said Odysseus, 'they would have returned to their homes knowing they were forever under suspicion and knowing I would sooner or later reassert my authority over all our islands. They would have met in secret and conspired further mischief. They would have risen against us either as assassins or in organised strength.'

'As their kin doubtless will,' said Euryclea.

'Yes,' agreed Telemachus, 'they will have no choice but to seek revenge by force of arms. It is a matter of honour. We must be prepared.'

Penelope eased past Euryclea to stand by her husband and son. She turned aside, ashen faced, when confronted by the grim sight within the hall. 'This,' she lamented, 'this has happened because of me.' She steadied herself with one hand on

343

Odysseus' shoulder, the other pressed against her face. 'I – I cannot bear it.'

'No,' responded Odysseus, 'the fault is mine and mine alone.'

Penelope appeared on the verge of fainting. Odysseus held her arm and turned to Euryclea. 'Take my wife back to her chamber. I'll join her as soon as I can – but not before I've bathed and freed myself from the stench of death.'

***

Under the lurid glow of firebrands and the harsh gaze of a replenished palace guard, those men so subject to the suitors' yoke lugged away the bodies of their masters on lengths of sackcloth. Menials of the palace entered the dining hall soon after with pales of water to clear the evidence of carnage, to swill and mop away blood, food and wine from floor and walls before it congealed. By dawn, to the casual observer, there would be little or no sign of the slaughter that had taken place there.

***

The modest chamber was dark, intimate and closed against the rest of the palace by a heavy wooden door. In one corner an incense lamp feebly glowed. Penelope lay asleep close by his side, her arm flung across his chest. After succumbing to physical passions that expressed far more than lust, they had talked through much of the night, she resisting sleep as long as she was able through fear of waking to find him gone. When she finally slept, Odysseus reflected upon what had happened in the dining hall below, falling asleep not long before the eastern sky began to brighten beyond their oxhide-covered window.

Odysseus arose quietly to find Penelope still asleep. He pulled on his tunic, lifted aside the blind and saw the light of the newly risen sun flood in to bathe brightly frescoed walls opposite their window. And still she slept. He intended to leave her undisturbed because she appeared so contented but then he hesitated at the door, returned to the bed, looked down at her and whispered, 'If I leave you now you may awaken and think I never returned.' He roused Penelope to reassure her of his continuing presence. At first startled she sat up, then smiling she watched as he stepped aside to extinguish the lamp. He returned to the bed and kissed her, saying, 'I've had little enough sleep but I must ready myself then go into the hall. I need to present myself once more as king. By mid-morning members of our court and others will be sent for.'

'I dreamt last night,' she sighed, reaching out to touch him. 'I dreamt you returned all over again. When I awoke just now I thought for a moment a dream was all it ever had been. Must you leave me now? Can other people not wait a while longer?'

'I'm not leaving you,' he assured her, 'I'll be back here to make myself presentable then you must join me as soon as I send for you. In the meantime you should ready yourself. They'll expect to see you radiant and self-assured now we're together again. It's what I want as well.'

Odysseus made his way to a room below, adjacent to the palace kitchens and called for the two slaves then in attendance; both were young females. Hot water, usually on hand, waited in a copper receptacle set above a grate of burning logs. They drew off sufficient into a ceramic bowl for him to wash his long hair, then with the tunic resting on his lap he sat patiently in the silence of that room where much of his facial hair was removed with keen bronze razor, leaving only a modest beard from his ears to his chin. Laying the tunic aside, Odysseus stood naked while olive oil was applied and scraped from his limbs and torso by supple, sensuous hands. He showed no physical response, no arousal, no carnal interest in either of the girls, never looked either in the eye but remained unspeaking even when their task was completed.

As he left the chamber one whispered to the other, 'Not like his son, is he. He'd have been all over us.'

'All over us,' repeated the other, adding with a coy smile, 'Hmmm, yes.'

Odysseus returned to the chamber in his attire of kingship, gem studded headband, pale tunic and richly patterned gown; clothes sealed tight those twenty years in an old pine chest resting within a dark alcove but sullied hardly at all by the passage of time. Odysseus last of all fastened on a short, jewel-hilted sword nestled within the ornately hand-tooled leather scabbard inlaid with silver and lapis lazuli. It was the weapon given him by Alcinous, King of the Phaeacians, and had served him well that fateful evening in the dining hall. Kissing Penelope, he left her to her own preparations then strode down narrow stairs to the megaron where his one-time seat of power awaited his return. There he would resume his position as ruler of Ithaca and rightful claimant of those domains yet to be recovered.

When the courtiers began to arrive, Odysseus sat casually upon the alabaster throne as if only a few days had passed since he had last occupied it. In the large circular hearth at the centre of the hall a fire burned bright and lively while a contented Phemios played and sang the praises of their newly returned king. At the far end of the great hall a number of female courtesans hovered in gaudy gathering to whisper in agitation among themselves; many concerned over their association with the now deceased suitors. Slaves were sent to summon Penelope, Telemachus, Euryclea and Mentor to join him and gather close about the throne.

When his call arrived Telemachus was still asleep. At his side lay dark-eyed Niobe, already awake. At the sound of Medon's voice she nudged Telemachus, gesturing toward the door as he stirred and opened his eyes. 'Medon is outside,' she whispered. 'He says your father is calling for you.'

'I'll be down there shortly!' Telemachus informed the figure beyond the hide curtain.

As he sat upright Niobe brushed a hand across his shoulder and kissed him on the cheek. 'You were dreaming last might,' she sighed. 'You spoke the name of another woman – Polyxena. You spoke it often. Were you not pleased with my company? Did this - this other woman, this Polyxena - did she serve you better than I do?'

'Niobe, I –. It was someone I met far away on my travels. As for your company, I prefer it to that of any other woman on Ithaca. That you must know.' Telemachus gazed into her eyes. She was beautiful and passionate but the flame within for the girl now so far away had burned brighter. Then, he wondered, might that flame expire all the sooner for being so bright? Then, too, Polyxena was a courtesan in the service of many men whereas Niobe never was. He swung from the bed, reached for his tunic, belt and sword then added, 'Right now I must ready myself and go into the megaron.'

Those members of the court who had served Penelope well, or at least remained aloof from her suitors, were seated or standing before the king's throne, some twenty in all. Wine was being served when Penelope arrived but she accepted none and remained discreetly to one side of the throne. Each noble, each official of Odysseus' house expressed gratitude over his return – as, of course, they had to. There was also a bald and portly scribe, seated aside and ready with stylus and clay tablet.

It was not long before the question arose they suspected Odysseus sooner or later would ask: 'Who amongst the palace guard, the servants, the freemen and the women of this house sided with the suitors or conspired with them against my wife and son? I will have their names recorded.'

The scribe poised his stylus. Phemios stopped playing. It was a simple enough question but for a time no one seemed able to respond until the newly arrived Telemachus, having heard the question as he approached, positioned himself between the throne and hearth. 'And what d'you intend doing if and when those names are given?' he asked.

'Intend doing! Why I'll give you the job of hanging the worst of 'em from the city wall. Aye, we let 'em feed the birds.'

Telemachus considered his father's response then declared, 'No, I won't do that!'

Penelope's hand flew to her mouth. Odysseus' face darkened and others shuffled uneasily as he half rose from the throne. 'What d'you mean, you won't do it!' he demanded loudly. 'If I order it then it will be done! D'you, my own son, dare to defy me on the very day I resume my rightful throne?'

All in attendance stared in disbelief, several moving aside as Telemachus strode forward to level an accusing finger at his father. 'I say I will not do it! I will *not* preside over the execution of our own people. In fact,' he added, calmly, 'I will not allow it.'

'Not allow it!' Odysseus responded, rising fully to confront him, a hand falling instinctively to his sword hilt. 'It'll be done whether you allow it or not!'

'Exactly what are you hoping to achieve?' pressed Telemachus, fingers resting on the hilt of his own blade. 'D'you want this to become another House of Atreus with yet more bloodletting? D'you want to make Ithaca a new Troy – a rotten carcase eaten by worms of vengeance? You have returned from an absence of twenty years, ten of which you spent wandering who knows where and all the time we and our people were left not knowing what might become of their land or their lives.'

'Enough!' cried Odysseus, raising a hand to silence him.

'I will say what I have to say!' countered Telemachus, standing firm, challenging his father by his very stance. 'These latter years have seen this house plagued by men who were convinced, as I and as most other people were, that you would never be seen again. Once the suitors gained power

349

over your possessions people dared not defy them with words let alone confront them in arms. Yes - those men got what they deserved but for all any of us knew one of them could eventually have taken the throne you once more occupy. What d'you think would then have happened to those who'd remained in open in support of you? I'll tell you what would have happened; they'd be dead or condemned to work in the stone quarries!'

'You're making excuses for what's gone on here!' declared Odysseus, 'I'll not have that!' He nevertheless eased back into his throne whilst the onlookers breathed a collective sigh of relief.

'I *know* what's been going on here rather better than you,' asserted Telemachus. 'I've lived with it through all the years you were far away from Ithaca. Putting to death even a handful of our own citizens will do nothing to help your cause or mine.'

'Our people are not to be blamed,' asserted Penelope, stepping across to stand by her son. Joined now by Euryclea and Mentor she continued, 'It's true - most would have feared for their lives if any of those men had taken your place and their orders had been disobeyed.'

'The town already reeks of death with those fires burning outside the wall,' said Telemachus. 'It must not be further desecrated.'

'I prayed daily,' added Penelope. 'I sacrificed and I begged the gods for your return but never would I have wished for the punishment of our people you now propose. Never.'

Aged Euryclea lifted a hand and spoke calmly. 'I agree. If these executions are carried out the House of Odysseus will far exceed in bloodshed that of Agamemnon. Surely that is not how you wish to be remembered. Most free men of Ithaca will be more than ready to join you and your son in arms and they will be needed soon. Let people see the good judgement and compassion that were yours in those earlier days have returned here together with the strength of your sword.'

'I say likewise,' added Mentor, stick-tapping his way forward. 'Had our people known you were alive and well, matters would have been very different. But they did not know. How could they?'

Odysseus sighed aloud, relaxed then exclaimed, 'Bah – very well! It seems I'm outnumbered by those whose opinions I most value so - so I'll reconsider my suggestion. That in any case was all it was intended to be. But this will be the last time I'll give way on such matters.'

'There's a more pressing situation we have to consider,' said Telemachus. 'The immediate threat we have dealt with; soon we'll have one far greater arriving on our shores. Need I go on?'

'I'm well aware this will have to be dealt with,' replied Odysseus. Those of the suitors' slaves who escaped from Ithaca will report what they saw though I'm informed many of them have remained on our island and offered themselves in our service.' Addressing Telemachus directly, he added, 'I understand we no longer have a captain of the palace guard; will you take that responsibility on yourself and see to organising them?'

'I'll do that gladly,' he responded, 'and I'll see to it all our citizens are informed of your return though I expect our actions last night and the visible results this morning will have hinted at it strongly enough. Before I came down here I saw crowds gathering in the marketplace, some already armed. Our people must be readied first to defend the town then to take back what rightfully belongs to this house. Once you – once we show ourselves armed and ready there'll be no holding them back!'

'I trust there will not,' said Odysseus, 'but there's one precaution we have to take: all fighting men must wear the badge of Ithaca. When we meet the enemy it must be clear to all who is who.'

'Quite so,' agreed Telemachus, 'I'll see to that.'

'Then I will next call for our elders, our priests and those who represent our trades and our artisans. There is much to be discussed.'

***

Beyond the city wall throughout that day flames clawed at a sunlit sky. Spectre tentacles of smoke writhed into warm air, carrying memories of carnage into the peaceful heavens. The pyres still burned at sunset, their timbers settling to shower angry sparks and spill glowing ash while acrid vapours sullied a warm evening breeze. Amid the ashes and charred wood lay fragments of white bone. From one smouldering heap a grinning skull with blade-shattered cheekbone rolled clear. A young boy kicked it playfully back into the ashes. Guards and slaves stood by to ensure all human remains were consumed.

Chapter 11 - The Final Challenge

The people had seen their king; he had walked through the marketplace with Telemachus at his side, both in body armour of gleaming scales but with their heads remaining uncovered. Following close behind were six men of the palace guard. The press of cheering citizens, craftsmen, farmers and traders offered barely enough space to allow them passage. They proceeded out from beneath the main gate and into the lower town then beyond the city wall so no one could doubt that Odysseus had returned. The message of Odysseus and Telemachus to all men was, 'See to your arms! Ready yourselves to confront our enemy!'

Two days passed but no rumour of hostile activity carried on the breezes. Orders had been issued to bring livestock inside the city wall at short notice or taken to less accessible parts of the island should the need arise. Noemon had moved his vessels and his supplies away from the harbour in anticipation of their enemy's arrival there but soon he and his men would join others within the city.

'This is a greater danger than our ancestors, than Ithaca herself ever faced,' announced Odysseus, seated on his throne with Telemachus and a number of courtiers and slaves in attendance, 'The enemy will most likely gather on Kephallinia but we cannot be certain, otherwise I would have taken the battle to them.'

Close by, Phemios strummed and flames shimmered at the centre of the hearth. Beyond it amid shadowed columns sat Penelope in conversation with her women and servants.

'We'll know soon enough,' said Telemachus. 'Our fishermen will report where their ships are gathering so we'll be well prepared.'

'Aye,' mused Odysseus, 'it will be like Troy but with our roles reversed. This time, however, we must bring matters to conclusion within weeks if not days. We do not have the resources of Troy nor have we enough time to call upon our old mainland allies. We must sacrifice again to Athena and to Zeus but before anything happens I will go to see my father. Do we have any news of him yet?'

'Not since you returned,' answered Telemachus. 'His farm and lands are away from others and he's not been into the town or palace in person these seven or more years.'

'Are we sure he still lives?' queried Odysseus.

One of the courtiers spoke up. 'Lord Odysseus, had any ill befallen your father we would have been informed. Livestock and produce from his estate were brought into the market for sale by his men not a month ago. Euryclea and I dealt with them and they informed us all was well.'

'That may be so,' added Telemachus, 'but he likely knows nothing of your return.'

'Then tomorrow at first light I'll take a party of armed men and set out to see him.'

'I'll go with you,' said Telemachus. 'There seems to be no danger here at present and we have men posted on the city wall and by the harbour. They'll ride out to warn us if unwelcome visitors are sighted.'

***

The eastern horizon glowed with promise of a fine day as they proceeded into open country to the

354

thump of hooves. The land appeared at peace with labourers tending their livestock, their orchards and their vines. Behind Odysseus and Telemachus rode twelve men, including Eumaeus and members of Ithaca's newly reconstituted palace guard. Their leaders, Odysseus and Telemachus, were attired in pale tunic and elaborately engraved and embossed bronze corselet. Odysseus' helmet of finely tooled bronze boasted cheek guards and a fringe of short, multi-coloured plumes. That worn by Telemachus was similar but less ornate and bore a single prominent red plume that swayed boldly as he rode on. Armed with sword and dagger, each also carried a spear.

Their followers were attired as best suited each man, with helmet of interlocking boar's tusks and body armour of bronze-scaled hide being favoured. Each man carried a sword and spear and each had a small circular shield slung over his back. Eumaeus wore a conical bronze helmet from which protruded a pair of boar's tusks, the result of his own hunting prowess. The upper part of his leather tunic gleamed with metal scales. He also carried a spear but his great sword, unused for many years and sharpened for this special occasion, was hoisted high across his back. It was fit to decapitate a hog or a man with ease at a single blow. The sword was hoisted high across his back.

Ascending to traverse a rugged, undulating land of sparse vegetation they now were able to see both sides of the island with the narrow isthmus connecting both halves. Fishing boats were visible where such were to be expected but nothing untoward could be seen. Well within view also was the much larger island of Kephallinia where their enemies must already be laying plans against them. They encountered no one until later in the morning when, cresting a final rise, Laertes' farm came into view: a rambling stone structure with outhouses basking in the green valley below amidst vines and olive trees. Smoke arose peacefully from scattered buildings and people could be seen going about their work with livestock or cart.

'I last stood looking across from here twenty years ago,' declared Odysseus as they halted. 'Aye, twenty years and I swear it's exactly as I remember it. Little or nothing has changed as far as I can make out.'

'Then let's continue on,' said Telemachus. 'I want to see his face when you arrive at his door.'

They approached to observe black-gowned Laertes standing in conversation with one of his workers outside the main building. Grey-bearded, balding and stooping under the weight of years, he nevertheless appeared a rugged man of powerful build. Telemachus pointed him out in case Odysseus failed at first to recognise his own father.

'Of course I remember him,' muttered Odysseus, though he squinted hard to make sure.

Laertes turned to face the newcomers and as Odysseus, Telemachus and their party dismounted his bushy face and pale eyes broke into a wide, sparsely toothed grin. Odysseus stepped over to him with hand outstretched as Laertes, eying him from head to toe, exclaimed, 'Well I-! By the gods it's you isn't it! Back on Ithaca and about time, too! There were rumours something was going on in the town so now we know what it was. What kept you away for so long, eh? Out with it – tell me now!'

Wringing his father's hand, Odysseus replied, 'Kept me away - you mean apart from the Trojan war?'

Laertes stepped back and, head tilted to one side, looked him up and down again as if to be certain this man really was his son then exclaimed, 'Yes of course, there was Troy! And – and what else? Did you kill many men? And why are you armed to the teeth now? No, wait - I'll have food and wine prepared for you and your men, then you can tell me everything. We can set aside the afternoon. No – all of tonight and all day tomorrow if you like. I'll see to it your horses are taken care of. My, what a day this has turned out to be. What a day!'

'I did encounter a few problems on my journey home,' said Odysseus, 'but now is not the time to go over it. As for your offer of food and wine, we'll drink to your good health but bread only will any of us eat at present. I'm told you no longer visit the town or palace but you were kept informed over what was going on there until recently.'

'Oh, I was well aware of the situation regarding Lady Penelope,' answered Laertes. 'I was visited by one of the men who were pestering the poor girl. He tried to bribe me, you know; he demanded I assist them by sending her back to her father in Sparta but I'd have none of it and sent him on his way. Doing what they wanted would have made matters worse. But she never called for my help, you know, and there was little point in my getting involved since there was nothing I could do. Most of the men still working here are as old as I am – and it's as much as we can manage to keep this place going. Telemachus is looking fit I must say – yes, a fine young man. And how *is* our dear Penelope now you're back home? I trust she was glad to see you again.'

'She is in good spirit and she was glad to see me though I'm not sure I deserved it.'

Telemachus, leaning against the doorframe, was unable to suppress a smile and remarked, 'No, you didn't deserve it.'

'And those men who were annoying her,' Laertes asked with a broad smile, 'did you get around to killing any of 'em?'

'Aye, all of them since you ask,' replied Odysseus.

'That's my boy,' responded Laertes, 'now people can get on with whatever they were doing.'

'I think not,' countered Odysseus. 'We're expecting trouble from the relatives and supporters of those men. It may be quite soon or it may be several days away but it *will* happen. As my father you may be in danger. You must return with us to the town. Your people can manage here until the threat is resolved. We can talk on the way.'

'Me – in danger? Bah! I'm too old to care. You'll see what I mean in a few years. It happens to all of us and sooner than you might expect. Why, it seems hardly any time at all since you set out to -.'

'You should come with us all the same,' interrupted Telemachus.

'Yes - until this is over with,' Odysseus added.

'Oh - oh, very well,' sighed Laertes, gazing at his house 'Just for a few days if you feel it's that important. I dare say it'll be a welcome break from drudgery.'

'D'you have a horse?' asked Odysseus. 'We should leave sooner rather than later in case anything unexpected happens.'

'Do I have a horse!' Laertes fluffed. 'This is a farm! Of course I have a horse. I have several – well, they're around here somewhere. I'll have one prepared and I'll fetch my spear.'

As Laertes stepped away Odysseus glanced aside at Telemachus, muttering, 'Did you hear that? He's going to fetch his spear.'

Telemachus watched him go, smiled and shrugged.

***

The sun was at its zenith, the heat of day oppressive when Laertes' farm was lost from sight and they retraced their journey across the island. Riding close to his father, Odysseus spoke of the events leading up to that bloody, final contest in the dining hall. He would not be drawn over his ten-year absence after Troy other than to relate the brief account of a vagrant wanderer he had offered Eumaeus on the occasion of their first meeting.

They were traversing another ridge when one of the guards riding a short way ahead called, 'There are riders across the valley to our left!'

Odysseus' party halted to peer across the broad valley, hands raised to shield their eyes from the afternoon sun.

'They'll be Antinous' men,' announced Telemachus. 'They'll have been concealed somewhere on the island waiting to back him up if the contest went against him. By now they'll have learned what happened. We must look to our arms!'

'Hmm – I should have anticipated this,' said Odysseus. 'They number fewer than ourselves but they're most likely a foraging party. Ah, but I see two of them riding away to the other side of the ridge. They'll be off to inform the rest of their rabble. We must send for more of our own men before heading into that valley.'

'We could use Noemon's archers if any are around,' added Telemachus.

Odysseus issued orders to one of his men, adding, '- and tell them to secure the city gates!'

The man galloped in the direction of the town whose surrounding wall was visible through an afternoon haze. Odysseus' men proceeded on, following the ridge a short distance, occasionally halting only to observe the other side do likewise. The opposing men continued along the parallel ridge, all the time watching Odysseus and his companions but making no attempt to approach. A little more time passed before a larger group of men appeared over the rise, on foot, to join the enemy party.

'They well outnumber us now,' observed Odysseus. 'They total forty or more. The rest are dismounted and they're all moving down the hill toward us.'

'Ah - I believe I can identify their leader!' declared Telemachus. 'I've heard traders describe him and I think that's a lion skin draped over his armour. It's Antinous' father is it not; the man they call Ox-eater?'

'That it is,' grinned Odysseus. 'His real name is Eupeithes - I recall him well and yes, he's wearing his old lion skin! The man still imagines himself as from the same mould as Heracles and now Antinous is dead I dare say he'll be hoping to make another from among his brood King of Ithaca. And unless my eyes deceive me he's grown a good deal fatter since I last had dealings with him. Aye, and that makes him a much better target for my spear.'

Overhearing their conversation, Laertes peered hard from his saddle to study the enemy leader as best his aged vision would allow and muttered under his breath, 'Or maybe for mine.'

'I see our own men approaching!' announced one of the guards. 'They number over twenty!'

'They'll be with us in good time,' said Telemachus.

'A more even match, I'd say,' growled Eumaeus, reaching over his shoulder to pat his sword hilt. 'There's keen bronze soon to head their way.'

'Our Ox-eater's men are stopping well above level ground,' said Telemachus. 'It looks as if they're waiting for us. Could be they've more men hidden over the ridge.'

'Waiting - aye that they are,' his father replied. 'The sun may be against us but if they decide to cross the valley we'll then have the advantage of higher ground.

'My guess is they'll approach no further,' said Telemachus.

'Then we'll leave the horses and go down to challenge them,' said Odysseus. 'They cannot be left free to roam our island and now they know we're here a challenge is what they'll expect and a challenge is what they'll get.'

A rumble of hooves signalled the arrival of their own reinforcements – twenty of the palace guard, each bearing spear and sword, four Cretan archers and the returning messenger.

'Over there, lads!' called Telemachus, pointing at the enemy. 'They're waiting to greet us.'

'Then we'll not disappoint 'em,' responded one of the guards as they dismounted and readied themselves for combat with heartening enthusiasm. 'And we've more men set out on foot to join us.'

'Wait!' called Telemachus peering along the valley. 'There are also more of Eupeithes' men coming our way – see, over there.'

'By the gods so there are,' growled Odysseus, raising a hand above his eyes. 'I can make out maybe twenty – no, it must be more - well armed and all on foot though still a good way off and with rough ground to cover. That'll slow 'em down.'

'They must all have landed at night,' said Telemachus. 'They outnumber us again.'

'That they do,' responded Odysseus. 'Eupeithes must have gathered all the men he could at short notice hoping to surprise us; and so he might have if we'd not set out across the island today.'

'We should go for their leader now!' declared Telemachus. 'We'd reach him before the rest of his men arrive and when they do the rest of ours will be here as well.'

Odysseus' party made their way in purposeful silence down the slope from the ridge, a slope not as steep or as rock-strewn as that negotiated by their opponents. Those on the other side, too, remained mute. It seemed to both parties that trading insults would achieve nothing other than hoarse voices though heads turned to assess the time it might take the enemy's footmen, still a good way off, to reach Eupeithes. All that mattered was who would be left holding the field before Eupeithes' reinforcements could join him. In a vividly cloudless sky the sun already hovered above the ridge opposite Odysseus' men. At his command they halted beyond spear shot. In between the opposing sides lay a dried up, rubble-strewn watercourse. It served as an appropriate division with each now able to confront the other on more or less level ground should they choose to advance further.

The four Cretans dropped to their knees to string their powerful bows. Telemachus and four other men moved to gather in front of them and conceal what was happening from enemy eyes.

'Wish I'd brought my old bow along,' muttered Odysseus as the Cretans fitted their arrows.

The Cretans arose as one, raised their bows and prepared to shoot. The men shielding them stepped aside and with a resounding thwack four arrows sped in hissing vengeance above the valley floor. Some of the enemy, including Eupeithes, saw what was happening but others, looking aside, concerned by the slow approach of their companions, did not. One arrow struck Eupeithes' raised shield, another was likewise deflected by one of his men. Two found their mark – one striking a man full in the face, the fourth penetrating deep into another's too lightly protected chest.

'Well that's two of 'em accounted for!' declared Odysseus, waving his men on as the Cretans prepared to shoot again.

Showing little concern for what had happened Eupeithes strode with swaying gate further down the slope until he reached level ground, followed closely by two of his armed men. Both were impressive figures, bushy-bearded, tall and broad with black horsetail plumes swaying defiantly above boar's tusk helmets. Eupeithes stood a while to gaze across at Odysseus then raising his spear bellowed out, 'Who among you will meet us now we aren't penned in as sheep for the slaughter the way my son and the rest of 'em were? It won't be so easy this time you sorry crowd of bastards!' The men arrayed behind him jeered and shook their spears. 'Come on, King Odysseus! he bawled. 'Let's settle matters now! Step over 'ere with two of your best men – real men I say - not that sheep-fucking son of yours! Meet me with these two men of mine!'

'He's playing for time,' said Telemachus as Odysseus prepared to move forward. 'He's delaying until more of his men arrive. He'll retreat if you step out to confront him.'

Followed by his two warriors Eupeithes approached until within spear shot, then stopped to lower his circular shield to the ground.

Odysseus turned to Telemachus. 'Look at the man; it's over twenty years since I had the pleasure of his company and what do I see now. He's not only fat as an ox but it looks as if most of his teeth are gone.'

'And seeing the way he walks,' added Telemachus, 'I'd say he's taken too much wine.'

'Aye, that he has,' agreed Odysseus. 'And I'd say he and the rest of 'em never planned on meeting up with us today.'

Eupeithes balanced and raised his lance ready to cast. The Cretans were ready to shoot directly at him but Odysseus stayed their actions, saying, 'No, it's what he wants - he's well protected with armour and shield. Aim at his men; they'll think we're going to do as he wishes.'

'So you'd prefer to take the Ox-eater yourself,' observed Telemachus as Eupeithes hurled his spear at the Cretan archers. They and others jumped aside as the weapon hissed by to embed itself in the ground where, denied human flesh, it quivered fitfully.

'That I would!' declared Odysseus. 'But you're right it would delay us too long. The sooner we get among 'em the better!'

Four Cretan arrows sped across the diminishing space but this time Eupeithes and the men to his rear crouched with shields raised and nothing was achieved.

Eumaeus, with grim enthusiasm, unslung his great sword and announced boldly, 'As you say, Lord Odysseus – the sooner the better!'

They started forward. Telemachus lifted and balanced his spear but before he could cast the weapon a figure lurched past him with spear raised high. On he went, his black gown fluttering like a sail in the breeze, his feet raising dust as a startled Odysseus called aloud, 'No – come back!' Turning to Telemachus he cried, 'We'd better get in there before they kill him!'

'He's already too close,' responded Telemachus as they and their companions strode briskly on.

Whoops of laughter erupted from Eupeithes' followers as Laertes scuttled across the arid watercourse. Eupeithes, amused at the antics of a foolish old man with even more years to count than his own, a man who wore no armour in the face of mortal danger, turned, grinning widely to witness the reaction of his own men – but his lapse in concentration lasted a heartbeat too long. Laertes drew back and hurled the spear with all his strength just as Eupeithes, alerted by a warning shout, switched back his attention. Reaching to raise his shield while attempting to lurch aside he collided with the man at his right. Laertes' spear struck deep before the confused Eupeithes could avoid the blow, piercing him close below his rib cage where his elaborate cuirass might have protected him from a shot moderated by greater distance. Eupeithes staggered back then crashed to the ground, his cry rising to the heavens while his men gaped in disbelief at the spectacle. Disbelieving, too, were Odysseus' men. They halted their advance as Laertes, having tottered to a halt, turned, crouched low and weaved from side to side as he stumbled back to safety. He was hardly aware of two spears hurled at him from amidst those few of the enemy who had advanced far enough, one striking hard earth close behind, the other flashing within an arm's length of his head to land skidding along dry earth.

'By Zeus,' breathed Odysseus as the raucous cheers of his own men broke the silence. They clashed their swords against their shields as dishevelled, red faced and gasping hard, Laertes trudged the last few paces doggedly to re-join them.

Odysseus hurried clear of his companions to meet his father, shield raised to cover him. 'By the gods you –!'

'I – hah, I s-skewered the bugger!' choked Laertes, clutching his chest with one hand and gripping Odysseus' shoulder with the other for support. 'Oh – it's years since I killed a man! Hah - by Zeus, years! Who said I -,' he bent forward, heaving and coughing hard before able to continue, 'who said I was no longer any use in this world! '

And though Eupeithes could be seen clutching the spear as he writhed in the dust between his dismayed supporters it was obvious that his life would soon be gone.

'A son slain by a son now a father by a father!' exclaimed Telemachus.

'Never did like the man,' declared Laertes, attempting to regain his breath. 'No - never did! I remember him all too well from the old days.'

Lost for words Odysseus stood shaking his head as Telemachus called aloud, 'Let's move! We've the rest of 'em to deal with!'

Eupeithes' two men kept their ground by the quivering body as more of their company surged forward onto the riverbed. Shouts arose. Spears were hurled at closer range from both directions. Telemachus' shield was struck a glancing blow, causing him to falter. Behind him a man screamed in agony as the deflected blade pierced his unprotected thigh to the bone. One of the enemy, impaled through the shoulder, fell writhing with the weapon lodged deep. Another deflected a spear with his shield only to have it lay open the neck of a companion whose blood sprayed as windblown chaff across those close by. No one offered the stricken men cover in the throes of death for on witnessing the fate of Eupeithes they were concerned more with the prospect of countering their immediate foe than they were with conquering Ithaca. And still their trudging reinforcements were too far away to engage.

Shouts of defiance rang aloud from both sides. Odysseus, and his warriors crashed fiercely into the enemy, shields thrust forward, blades flashing. At their head, voicing no cry, his jaw set in grim determination, the tall plume above his helmet swaying to proclaim a message of death, Telemachus dispatched a man at once, dodging the thrust of his adversary's blade to drive his own hard through boiled leather and deep between his adversary's ribs. For Telemachus this was work to be done, an exercise in agility and skill upon which his life and the future of his house depended. Anger did not possess him the way it possessed his father and others who, fired by demons of vengeance, threw themselves into the enemy's midst. Odysseus, with no thought for his own safety, spurred those with him to greater effort. The men close to Telemachus saw him as one sent by the gods with no purpose other than to slay any foolish enough to confront him.

Eumaeus, with a hefty swing, brought down one of the two men who had stood guard over the now motionless Eupeithes, splitting the boar's tusk helmet and skull of his adversary with a hissing sweep of his great sword. The second man was engaged and struck down choking on his own gore by Odysseus. Eumaeus took down another, slicing with an unstoppable stroke through shoulder blade and neck. He turned next to the sprawling body of Eupeithes where, heaving aside with his foot the fallen man's shield he kicked away the dislodged helmet, at the same time thrusting back another attacker with his shield. He raised his sword and cleaved through Eupeithes' neck. Protected by two companions who witnessed the act, Eumaeus impaled the head on his long blade and with a mighty bellow that rose above the discordant clash of combat, lifted the blood-drizzling, eye-staring trophy high for all to see – especially the enemy's reinforcements who now, almost within spear-shot had hesitated, unable, until they spotted the badges of Ithaca, to determine amid the mêlée who was friend and who was foe. The sight of Eupeithes' severed head instilled yet more confusion among the newcomers, a confusion that intensified as the first quartet of Cretan arrows sped into their less well-protected right flank to inflict injury and death. Worse was their situation becoming when they observed the armed footmen, summoned earlier from Ithaca town, descending intent upon bloody contest from the ridge. Those of the enemy engaged in combat were giving ground. Some, having broken or lost sword or spear and having no other within reach, stooped in desperation to seize one of the scattered rocks from the riverbed and employ this as a weapon that could split a man's head or dash aside his shield and break his ribs.

Laertes himself was far from idle though his earlier rash act was not to be repeated. Ill-suited through advanced years to engage closely with sword and shield he took up any wasted spear he could find to hurl back at the enemy, accounting as he saw for at least one of them though, because of the effort, his heart beat hard, his breath came short and his limbs sorely ached. As for the enemy's new contingent, the sight of Odysseus' fresh warriors and the lethal sting of Cretan arrows shook their resolve as much as had the death of their leader. The newly arrived Ithacans, seeing Odysseus and Telemachus gaining the upper hand over Eupeithes' men, strode with fierce intent toward the enemy reinforcements, clashing spear or sword against shield. Their opponents, diverted by the archers' shots, cast their spears too hastily and with meagre success.

The sun had set behind the ridge over which the enemy had with such confidence advanced that afternoon. Now they were giving way over shadowed, blood-soaked ground, stumbling over their own dead and injured with no hope of assistance now their second party was being assaulted. Telemachus, seeing how well the fight was progressing with his father and his companions, strode to join the Ithacan reinforcements, calling aloud, 'Athena is with us!' and there charged as a bull into the enemy with flashing bronze and grimly swaying plume. Among the cries and din of close conflict he once again was silent, his expression one of ruthless determination as he struck down or drove back any who dared confront him, wielding his bloodied sword and thrusting violently with his shield. One man raised a jagged rock high to strike him down but Telemachus sprang aside to sever the man's left arm causing the rock to fall and smash the assailant's own skull.

The enemy, their original purpose denied, were concerned only to head back to their vessels and depart the island they had so boldly invaded. So perilous did they see their situation becoming that none dared hesitate to recover the arms or armour from their fallen. They continued to retreat some way up the boulder-strewn rise where they hoped to gain sufficient advantage in height to hold back their pursuers. As Odysseus' company prepared to make after them his Cretans loosed further arrows, bringing down two more of the enemy. Those of their reinforcements able to do so were breaking away from Telemachus' in a desperate attempt to join their fleeing comrades.

'Keep 'em running!' Telemachus ordered his archers as the four Cretans prepared to loose another volley. Telemachus joined his father treading rubble-strewn ground close to the lower slope where they saw the enemy now possessed a ready source of rocky missiles. Telemachus, thinking that to hesitate would offer them opportunity to regain their confidence and rally, raised his sword and called aloud, 'Let's finish our work!'

But something occurred to stem his zeal and halt the onward surge of his company.

'What's happening?' cried one of his men.

Odysseus, ready to charge on, stopped to look around.

'The ground is moving!' called another, tottering as if drunk.

'Poseidon is awakening,' cried Laertes, falling awkwardly to his knees. 'The Earth Shaker stirs!'

A subterranean booming passed through their very bones and the land was alive. The ground quivered violently while sparse bushes trembled as if striving to free themselves from Earth's grasp. The tremors and drumming increased. Men on both sides stumbled in dismay as rocks were detached from rising land either side of the valley to dance along as though charged with a life of their own. Higher up the rise where the enemy had gathered, larger rocks were dislodged, plummeting down to the riverbed. A skull-sized stone struck one of Eupeithes' men violently in the back, shattering his spine. Two more of their number were killed or injured by the same cause as, dropping whatever encumbered them, some were thrown to the ground while others stumbled back and forth in blind confusion. Men on both sides called to the same gods for salvation but Odysseus' and Telemachus' company, most of whom were on the watercourse, were better situated to retreat and though in some disorder only one of them suffered serious harm from the avalanche. With the ground continuing to heave the spear embedded in Eupeithes' headless body was shaken free. Now unencumbered, the corpse bounced along as a discarded rag doll amid a clattering shower of stones then came to rest with limbs splayed. Having lain where Eumaeus had earlier dropped it, the severed head followed as though not wishing to be left behind by its one-time owner. Bloodied mouth agape it rolled to rest not a spear's length from Odysseus who had plunged his own shaft into the earth and crouched grasping it to steady himself. Telemachus, holding onto Laertes with one arm, held tightly to the branch of a dead bush with the other. But the tremors were passing and with a final shudder the ground stilled. Odysseus raised up then paused to regard the gristly head with dark amusement.

As a last wayward boulder rolled leisurely to a standstill in settling dust, Odysseus and Telemachus, blood-spattered and dust-stained, stood to assess the situation. They turned their attention to Eupeithes' men, their number much depleted as they stared down into the gully at the many fallen, at the twisted corpse of their leader and at a victorious adversary whose losses appeared not a quarter of their own. Visibly agitated they gathered and began to confer among themselves until one man, clambering onto a rock that protruded from the slope, called for their attention. On his command any who had managed to collect up shield or spear lowered it to the ground. Both sides looked on in silence as the one who had addressed them at some length stepped from the rock and weaved his way down to the watercourse. He held apart his arms to indicate he carried no weapon, lifted off his helmet then strode across the riverbed, stepping over the dead, glancing at the injured but heading directly toward Odysseus and Telemachus. He was a tall, well-built man of early years, stubble-faced, wearing the bronze armour and carrying the plumed helmet of a wealthy house. Telemachus had seen him account for two of his own men but in the chaos of battle had not managed to confront him directly.

'Let him speak,' ordered Odysseus as the man hesitated to gaze upon the grotesquely contorted body of Eupeithes. He stepped around the corpse to halt an arm's length before Odysseus. Telemachus stood close by prepared to draw his sword at the slightest provocation but noticed something familiar about the man's eyes and other aspects of his features as he addressed them.

'Those who determine our fates have today spoken; Zeus, Athena and Poseidon, and we hear what they tell us. I speak for all our men and say we will accept you as rightful King of Ithaca and her possessions. We pledge the allegiance of our people as it was in the days before Troy.'

'Who are you?' asked Odysseus. 'And on whose authority d'you speak for your men and others of their clan beyond this island?'

His answer, firm yet sincere, came as no surprise to Telemachus.

'I am Glaucus, elder son of Leiocritius who I suspect was slain by Antinous, son of Eupeithes. I speak also for men on the islands who await our return. The Houses of Eupeithes and Antinous will submit to the rule of the House of Odysseus. The majority of my people had no love for Antinous nor had they for my father, that I readily confess - but it was my duty and that of our followers to take up arms in their honour. Now both are gone that duty is fulfilled in the eyes of those gods who have demonstrated their judgement here today.' He hesitated and looked back across the watercourse.

'But whatever your decision, Lord Odysseus, I ask that we be allowed to make sacrifice in this place, to attend to those injured and dying and to deal with our dead as you must your own.'

Odysseus appraised him at length, glanced aside at Telemachus, who nodded in approval, then answered, 'We grant your request and we accept your submission but there may be others who hold lands belonging to us who will not abide by your words. These must also be brought to account.'

'Most of those you speak of are leaderless and have no idea what is happening. On Kephallinia there was insurrection against the House of Eurymachus and their men refused to join us because of it. You will meet with no resistance there.'

'Then the gods have indeed ruled in our favour,' responded Odysseus, 'and we accept your offer of reconciliation - provided *all* comply.'

'Go and attend to your dead,' affirmed Telemachus, 'and we will see to ours. Perhaps earth or flames should consume them together, united in death as I trust our people will be once more in life.'

Chapter 12 - The Fate of Ithaca

They sat face to face in her upstairs chamber. A shaft of morning sunlight illuminated the idle loom and the unfinished shroud draped carelessly over it.

'I thank the gods now I'm free of it: that throne and the sight and sounds of the megaron. After so many years in there, sitting day after day after day praying your father would return, worrying about you, and each night hearing the braying of those dreadful men. I'm happier now than I imagined I ever could be. And, Telemachus, I can laugh again when I'd almost forgotten how.'

'Yes, you always believed he'd come back when I did not. But then I never knew him.'

'Did I believe it deep down?' sighed Penelope. 'Yes I - I did insist; all along I did. Yet when he really did return, I could not at first believe it. For a time I dared not. For a time I thought it must be a cruel trick. But throughout those ten years after Troy I had to hold onto something even if it was an illusion placed there by Athena herself to prevent my descending into utter despair. Then there was my concern for you. Yet now, when I hear what you have done, how you fought as a true hero, I feel so proud and thankful.' She closed her eyes and grasped his arm, adding, 'I don't care to set foot in the megaron again and I will never again go near the dining hall – no, not after the appalling scene I witnessed there. The sight of it will haunt me for the rest of my life. Tomorrow morning I will conceal my face like a common woman and walk out into the marketplace. I will go through the city gate as I never could until now. I know there are people who beg there so I will take food. Then perhaps I'll go down to the sea. Yes, I will do that. We live on an island but I've not once looked out to the sea these past twenty years except from my window.'

'You cannot exclude yourself altogether from the great hall,' said Telemachus. 'You have to be there next to your husband at times and help preside over gatherings. He will need you also when visitors arrive. And you'll miss the company of the other women if you exclude yourself completely.'

Penelope stared at him for many heartbeats before replying. 'Yes, you're right,' she sighed, 'I can't ignore our affairs and I wouldn't care to be alone for too long.' She glanced aside at the unfinished winding sheet, adding, 'And I intend to finish that – if for no other reason than to see the last of the thing. There are too many memories woven into it.'

'As you wish,' agreed Telemachus, 'but when I recall how old Laertes performed on the battlefield I doubt he'll be needing it for quite some time despite all those rumours over the years about his health. I must leave you now; our visitors will be on their way up from the harbour but you need not become involved on this occasion.'

Telemachus arose, pushed through the curtain and walked in semi-darkness toward the stairs. From deeper shadows amidst the columns a figure emerged. Telemachus' hand dropped to his sword but as the figure stepped over to him he let the half-drawn blade slip back into its scabbard. 'Niobe, why are you here? I wasn't aware my mother had called for you.'

'She didn't,' the girl replied. 'I - I needed to see you. I'm sorry, I -.'

'You're upset,' he said, noting the cloud of anxiety that sullied her lovely face. Her wide, dark eyes glistened with tears. 'What is troubling you?'

She moved closer and gazed into his eyes. 'I am – I am worried now that your father, our king, is back because - I'm worried because he – because he -.'

'I think I understand,' smiled Telemachus, slipping an arm around her waist, feeling her sensual warmth and her perfumed breath on his cheek. 'You feel the old man might have taken a fancy to you and you'd rather he didn't – is that it? Well it wouldn't surprise me if he had.'

The girl stepped back, lowered her head and pressed a hand over her eyes.

'Niobe,' he assured her, 'you'll be for me only if you so wish and I'll make that very clear to him. I promise.'

The girl smiled weakly but Telemachus felt he could not simply leave her standing there without another word. 'You were the child of a slave,' he said, 'and you have served here as a slave.' He reached to brush hair from her cheek. 'Niobe, I declare you free as of today. Mother will agree and I'll have Euryclea record my decision so there can be no question over it.' Niobe raised her head and smiled again through her tears as he continued. 'I'll offer you an important role, and I do mean important. You can assist Euryclea in her duties and learn what has to be done. She needs someone to help now she's grown old, someone who will eventually accept her duties. There is much she and

378

Mentor could teach you. You would learn to read and understand the tablets, and other languages, and that in itself would bring the respect you deserve. Would that please you?'

'Please me,' the girl smiled. 'Oh yes, that would indeed please me. It would be good for me and – and if you wish it I will please you more than that other woman; the one you spoke of in your dreams: Aphrodite will be my guide.'

'Niobe,' he whispered, kissing her forehead, 'you have no need to call upon Aphrodite. You have always pleased me and I hope nothing will change.' Telemachus placed a hand on her shoulder, adding, 'As from now you are free to make your own decisions. So here's your first test: I have to ask you, and I ask now as I would ask a friend – will you come to me this evening? You are free to choose otherwise and I'll not be offended – though I may well be disappointed.'

Her face lit up and her smile broadened, 'Oh yes, Telemachus, of course I'll be with you.'

'Good, then if the night is warm we'll take a flask or two of wine and make our way down to the small cove where I sat alone before leaving Ithaca. But right now I must go downstairs before they send Medon to find me; there are visitors expected quite soon.'

Her smile remained though tears still shone in her eyes as Niobe whispered, 'Oh, yes,' and seared his cheek with fire-moth lips.

***

'Our kingdom is almost secure,' declared Odysseus. 'Soon it will be as it was before Troy and before long it will be yours alone.'

379

Telemachus sat by his father's side and considered his words. The air was graced by the gentle strumming of Phemios' lyre as Odysseus added in a lowered voice. 'I've had my fill of conflict and death. I want no more of it though it gladdens me to know you are ready to meet any challenge life or the gods themselves may throw at you.'

'Quite so,' mused Telemachus. 'Oh, and there's one small matter of which I should inform you: I've given the girl, Niobe, her freedom. She is to assist Euryclea and I alone will take her to my bed unless she chooses otherwise.'

'Hmm, you might have asked me,' grumbled his father. 'Well, I won't argue if it's her you want, but you didn't need to free her just for that, did you?'

'No I didn't need to – I wanted to. Nor did I need to ask you.'

Odysseus glanced sharply at him but said nothing. Wood blazed brightly in the big circular hearth. Sparks swirled up with the smoke into dark obscurity. Apart from Odysseus, Telemachus and Phemios only the palace guards were in evidence, standing at a discreet distance amidst the shadows of the colonnade. Light from torches reflected sinister glow from the arms and armour hanging there.

Then footsteps. Medon entered, minus the gnarled stick, to announce, 'Lord Odysseus, representatives of your kingdom have arrived and await your summons.'

Odysseus stepped across to settle into his throne. Telemachus moved to stand by his side.

Glaucus, son of the murdered Leiocritius, entered with a slave trailing close behind. Glaucus confirmed his loyalty as he had on the field of battle and now stood in respectful silence. His slave lowered to the floor a gilded bronze breastplate on which were placed gifts of ornate silver, gold cups and other precious objects.

Odysseus nodded his approval. 'Have the others escorted in,' he ordered. Glaucus stepped back to observe the proceedings.

'Do you expect treachery?' Telemachus asked quietly as Medon retraced his steps.

'Don't you?' breathed Odysseus. 'After all, we slew their sons and brothers.'

'I did have them checked for arms,' said Telemachus, 'though I doubt they'd have any fight left in them. What they need is the peace and stability we offer. Their people now have fewer working hands. They'll need to tend their farms and look to their trades without further strife.'

'Aye, so they will,' agreed his father.

Medon reappeared, followed by the ten and more dignitaries who were conducted in their fine robes to assemble before Odysseus and Telemachus. All were men who represented Odysseus' newly recovered lands though not all had confronted his forces in battle. Had it not been for the moderating influence of Telemachus these lately reinstated persons would have been executed and their heads displayed on poles by the main gate of the city. None other than Glaucus had been permitted to have a slave in attendance so the new arrivals were obliged to carry their own burdens, to kneel and present their weighty gifts. Here were objects of gold, silver and ivory, many inlaid with precious stones. And not one of these nobles could be seen offering much less than any other. Breaking a tense silence, each man arose in turn to pledge his allegiance and none requested favour or exemption.

The preliminaries were done and headed by Glaucus they filed from the megaron along the corridor to the dining hall where their own attendants and those of the palace waited. The palace guard followed. Odysseus regarded the offerings arrayed on the flagstones in a broad crescent between throne and hearth. 'This compensates us little for all that was taken by the suitors though I expect more will be paid back in time.'

'We should join them now,' said Telemachus. 'Without our presence some will surely brood over what happened in there.'

'Aye, so they might,' replied his father, 'and that may be no bad thing. And my bow is hanging back up where it used to be as a reminder. But we'll delay no longer and soon they will have food, wine and our women to offer entertainment. I'll ensure they leave Ithaca or return to their lodgings before the day is over and before too much wine passes their lips. I've seen to it the taverns will be closed until they're all gone.'

'I'll be away from here also after sunset,' said Telemachus. 'There are other matters needing my attention.'

**

The days passed with Odysseus, Telemachus and their guard conducted by Noemon and his crew to visit the islands and those mainland territories newly returned to the rule of Ithaca. Trade was once more free to pass throughout their kingdom but unwelcome news began to arrive from more distant seas. They sat that afternoon in the great hall, each with goblet in hand, Phemios and all the slaves dismissed, their only company the spitting fire in the great hearth and black beetles that wandered close to its realms of warmth.

'You were away on the hunt most of today,' said Telemachus, 'so you'll be unaware of what has been reported from the Peloponnese.'

'I heard old Nestor died in his bed three months ago,' said Odysseus. 'What else d'you have to tell me? I sense it is not good news.'

'It is not good news,' responded Telemachus. 'At first light today I was in the marketplace when Noemon brought before me captains from three separate vessels - all with tales to tell. One of their crews took goods ashore at the bay of Pylos not ten days ago but had to flee. He reported the city under attack and he took on board several refugees who'd escaped in fear of their lives. One of these men I myself met. They claim Pylos was assaulted by land and sea by hordes of armed men from the east with horses, wagons and vessels carrying more men and supplies but could tell me little more. There was an injured man, a palace official who was among the last to get away and was rescued from the water swimming for his life. He swore the city had fallen and parts of it were in flames. The others confirmed they had seen much smoke rising when they were out at sea.'

'That is truly bad news,' sighed Odysseus. 'Yes, truly bad. All evils come from those lands far to our east and always will; I'm convinced of that.'

'I made good friends at Pylos,' sighed Telemachus, his gaze lowered. 'You know of the brave and true friend who escorted me safely to Sparta. We fought together and I was accepted as his brother. And - and there was a girl. I never mentioned her. I never spoke of Polyxena. She begged to return with me to Ithaca and I refused. Who knows what might have happened had I -.'

Both fell into deep thought then Telemachus added, 'The other two vessels had sailed further south and their men claim Corinth is taken though they say Athens stood against the invaders. Mentor long ago told me the great hero Theseus built her walls because he knew the city would one day have to stand alone against great odds. We can only hope that at least is true.'

'I was once in Attica and I visited Athens,' confirmed Odysseus, draining his goblet. 'The walls of that city are the mightiest I ever saw,' equal at least to the high walls and fortified gates of Troy. Yet Troy fell in the end to trickery and not to force of arms.'

'There's no news so far of Sparta or Mycenae,' said Telemachus. 'Surely Mycenae will stand against them. I hear her walls are strong and well defended.'

'Aye, and so they are – the strongest in all the Peloponnese. But our soothsayers tell of warnings in the winds and signs in the heavens. They say there are many troubles to come. I sense it myself with each passing day. The men of our islands must join together and fight as one if and when danger threatens. But for now, I think more wine is in order.'

***

When several vessels from more distant lands sailed into the harbour later that month Noemon had one of their captains accompany him to report in person at the palace of Ithaca. He was a stranger to the islands, a wiry, sun and salt-spray roughened old man of the sea with few remaining teeth. The news he related was not welcomed. 'Mycenae is sacked and burned,' he declared in gruff accent. 'Mycenae as well as other towns thereabout.'

'Am I to understand you witnessed this for yourself?' Odysseus queried.

'I was not so close to Mycenae as some, My Lord, or I might not be here to tell of it. I took on board others, many others, until my boat was so overloaded as to be hardly seaworthy. There were men of Egypt who abandoned goods of great value close to the city gate so as to escape with their lives. It was they who witnessed first-hand what happened so in their distress they related it to me.'

'Then it must have happened without warning,' said Telemachus.

'They told me it did,' the man continued. 'They said the invaders came with the newly risen sun to enter the city disguised as traders. They had wagons drawn by oxen but the wagons contained armed men who poured out and held the Lion Gate until the rest arrived. The Egyptians told of burning and much destruction. They told of many ships crossing the Aegean Sea in countless numbers, island by island they said - more than anyone ever witnessed.'

'Mycenae,' breathed Odysseus. 'If Mycenae has fallen, who will be next?'

With the captain rewarded and dismissed, Odysseus turned to Telemachus. 'If they have command of the sea then they'll sooner or later arrive in our own waters. The perils I encountered after Troy are nothing compared to this. Ha! Those ten years – I no longer know for certain if I still believe all that I related to you. But – but then where does that leave me?'

'In much the same situation as the rest of us, father, but we cannot ignore what is happening.'

Deep in thought they drank wine, then Odysseus said, 'I'll have Noemon send out boats to keep watch to our south though I suspect he already has. We must look to our defences though they hardly compare with those of Mycenae.'

'There may be another way,' said Telemachus. 'In fact there has to be.'

'Another way?' Odysseus turned to him, puzzled. 'What other way?'

'It's something I've given much thought to of late because of the rumours we hear. Even if you add them all together our island towns and their populations are smaller than some of those on the mainland. If kingdoms with stronger defences and greater forces than we're able to muster have fallen so easily then we could never withstand such an onslaught. While there's still time I suggest we and our allies throughout the islands gather timbers from wherever there's enough to be had. We should build enough boats to carry all our citizens plus their goods and livestock – we have the men to do that and Noemon would oversee their construction.'

Odysseus stirred uneasily as Telemachus continued. 'We should sail west to Italy and there I believe we'll find ourselves beyond danger. I've learned much from those traders who visit us from the west. From what they tell me of Italy there is plenty of good land in the south.'

'Run from the enemy!' exclaimed Odysseus, rising from his throne. 'That isn't what I expected to hear from a son of mine! We stand against them no matter what!'

Telemachus also rose to his feet and declared, 'I've thought very hard over this! I have faced my share of dangers in this world if not in some – some other fanciful realm! I say we confront the truth, I say we accept reality and not cling to blind stubbornness!'

The one slave in attendance retreated to cower amidst the columns.

'Blind stubbornness!' bellowed Odysseus. 'Do you accuse me of – of -?'

Both stepped apart, each with a hand falling to his sword, each glaring defiance at the other. Both froze in statuesque pose, blades half drawn, then, very slowly, each relaxed. They began to laugh. Then laughing louder still they returned to their seats and Telemachus called for more wine. The slave, visibly shaken, scurried off, duly returning with a replenished flagon.

With the slave dismissed it was Odysseus who, eyes fixed upon the newly deposited flagon, broke an uneasy silence. 'Aye, you have a point and I don't mean just that of your sword. We could never stand against such powerful forces and I don't feel inclined to risk my life and that of our people for what is after all a poorer land than many others. Italy you say: hmm, it would be a fair voyage and the soothsayers many years ago predicted my death would come from the sea, though in spite of everything it hasn't turned out that way yet.'

'Sailing to Italy with everything we value would be a great challenge,' said Telemachus, 'but it would unite us as nothing else could and offer ourselves and our people a new beginning. Why, those new lands could become a new Greece, a greater Greece.'

'Invaders, sea voyages, a new beginning,' Odysseus sighed. 'Hmm, just when I was looking forward to a quiet life. Circe's island – now there's a temptation.' He smiled broadly, adding, 'Maybe she'd offer us all immortality.'

'Oh, really,' smiled Telemachus. 'I think Italy would be a safer bet since it undoubtedly exists, and there are mother's feelings to consider.'

***

Ten days had passed when, in the warm air of a clear night they met together in the palace courtyard. 'It seems all but a few are willing to join us,' confirmed Odysseus. 'I've had Noemon send three vessels ahead with armed men to see what is good and what is not so good about this land in which we propose to settle. They will wait to inform us on the furthest point south when we arrive.'

'What will happen to Laertes and his people? 'Telemachus asked. 'He prefers to remain where he is. I doubt if forcing him to sail with us will do much good. He says the barbarians will be after loot and women, not a few old men and a farm.'

'Your grandfather was always stubborn, aye, he'll think to do as he pleases and at his age maybe we've no right to deny him that, but they must be persuaded to join us. Mentor and Euryclea will not be left behind in spite of their advanced years and nor would I have it so. As for Eumaeus; he assures me he, his men and all his pigs welcome the idea.' Odysseus looked up at the sky then added, 'I suppose the stars will appear much the same wherever we are. Let's go inside where we can discuss this further and call for wine. I'll have your mother join us.'

***

Life had returned to the shadowed great hall. Courtiers stood or sat beneath the light of burning torches to consider their future. A robed and kingly Odysseus relaxed on his throne with Telemachus and Penelope seated close by. The hearth glowed and sparked while Phemios strummed languid notes.

'When the ships are ready,' declared Odysseus, taking up his goblet, I'll have our ancestors' remains disinterred together with their grave goods. Our priests will be first to depart with these together with the vessels and images from Athena's temple. All we cannot take aboard our ships or have no use for will be destroyed. The palace will be burned – the town also if we have enough time though some have already destroyed what was theirs. We will leave nothing here or on the other islands, nothing other than blackened stones laid open to the sky.'

'I never left the island after our marriage,' sighed Penelope. 'This has been my home in spite of everything that has happened.'

'I'm convinced now there is no other way,' responded Odysseus. 'One day soon the boats will be ready and that day will mark the last time we look upon these walls. A last time here to enjoy the company of those closest to us. Yes, and one day, one day for me, a last time to lay down my head and sleep.'

'You really are morose,' commented Telemachus. 'It isn't at all like you. I for one won't miss strolling the foul alleyways of Ithaca town. During the time I spent at Pylos and Sparta I began to appreciate the blessings of unsullied air and clean streets.'

'I'll not regret leaving that rattling old loom behind,' said Penelope. 'It can stay up there and burn - but before it does I will have the shroud presented to Laertes.'

'Ah yes, the shroud,' grinned Telemachus. '*That* I cannot wait to see the end of!'

Odysseus gazed at the untroubled Phemios who continued to strum gently and he asked himself had the old man's appearance ever altered? Did anyone know his age? In Odysseus' mind the seas rose and fell and the breeze carried his thoughts to distant lands, to the last days of Troy, to the bizarre and bloody adventures that the gods had called down.

'Our bard and his like must relate in song and poetry all that has happened,' he announced. 'We must pass on to others an account of our affairs and the troubles of our times or those memories may be lost forever. They must be recited through generations and though they may suffer transformation over the passage of years they will preserve our names and the essence of what we were.'

***

'You were dreaming, Telemachus.'

He heard her voice and was aware of her hand resting on his shoulder. He eased upright against the pillow, saying, 'Yes, I saw, I saw -.'

'You were restless; you were whispering but I did not understand your words.' Then pulling away Niobe asked him, 'Did you dream of that other girl you spoke of once before in your sleep?'

'No, I saw in my dream –. No, it really doesn't matter.' Morning light already spilled past the leather blind as Telemachus pushed away the bed cover. 'Niobe, we should have been up before daybreak. We must collect whatever we need and leave without undue delay. The ships will soon be loaded and their crews eager to sail. Yesterday there were two vessels reported to the south by Noemon's men. He was certain they did not belong in these waters.'

'I will be with you when we sail, won't I?' Niobe asked. She sat upright beside him, midnight hair cascading about her naked breasts.

'No, you must go aboard one of the larger vessels with the other women. You'll be safer there. I will leave later with armed men in a swifter ship in case unwelcome vessels try to follow you.'

Once dressed and ready, water flasks in hand, they hurried down to the empty megaron, Niobe in plain blue gown, Telemachus in white tunic with precious sword at his side. The walls of the megaron had been stripped of weapons three days earlier. The heavy alabaster throne was also gone,

391

though the seats that had stood close by it remained abandoned. The firebrands were dead so the gangling, painted soldiers adorning the walls below where the arms once hung were condemned to obscurity within the shadows. Four guardsmen stood outside the great wooden doors next to heaped kindling and olive oil soaked cloth, firebrands ready to begin the task of destruction.

Beneath a cloudless sky they crossed the marketplace, deserted except for stray dogs that darted to and fro in confusion. Both continued to the main gateway where the dispossessed once occupied the shadows only to find they also were gone but Telemachus cared not think what their fate had been. Members of the palace guard waited outside the gate ready to escort Telemachus and Niobe to the harbour where several boats had already slipped their moorings and were being rowed clear of a much congested quay. One of the larger vessels remained moored and it was to this Telemachus escorted Niobe. Before helping her over the side he reached to pull her close and kissed her, saying, 'Be brave, a new and better world awaits us.'

'And I will await you, dearest Telemachus.' Her wide eyes and loving smile filled his vision but served only to heighten the guilt within; a guilt neither she nor anyone else would understand. Telemachus and one of the crew assisted Niobe onto the deck then he raised a hand to her before turning to walk along the quay where Noemon's vessel, his good ship *Amphitrite*, waited. By the vessel, ready to board, stood Odysseus and her captain.

'You took your time,' grinned Odysseus. 'I suppose that girl kept you awake most of the night.'

'No, I was concerned over the orders we gave to burn the palace. It needs final supervision so I'll return to ensure it's properly done. I'll be with our men on the last boat.'

'It's too risky,' declared Odysseus. 'There's nothing of value left there.'

'Your father is right, young sir,' Noemon added, 'you should leave with us now.'

'No,' responded Telemachus, 'It has to be done.' With that he turned and left them.

'Shall we wait, sir?' Noemon asked as they watched Telemachus stride purposefully up the pathway to Ithaca town.

'No, he'll do just as he wishes. He's proved well able to look after himself.'

'That he has, sir,' agreed Noemon as both clambered aboard *Amphitrite* and the mooring ropes were slipped. 'He is truly a slayer of men.'

Under a warm sun he strode on but well before coming into sight of the town he observed rising smoke; thick, heavy smoke that drifted on a moderate breeze. There he stood and listened. Voices were approaching so he left the path and concealed himself behind a rock. The last remaining guardsmen lumbered chattering from the direction of the town burdened by all the possessions they were able to carry. Telemachus, crouching unseen, watched them continue toward the harbour until they were out of sight. Certain there was no one else to pass by he walked slowly back the way he had come until the harbour was once again in view. There he stopped and, finding a level rock, sat down to watch assembled boats large and small, sails raised and filling with the breeze, slowly make their way into open sea with pennants flying. There were more ships than he once could ever have anticipated seeing in the harbour. There was *Amphitrite* with, some distance behind, the last vessel that had waited to take on board the guardsmen. This was a proud fleet. A glorious sight. Once clear of Ithaca, others from the islands would join with them to sail west. He would wait until the last vessel had disappeared around the headland.

The last ship had vanished. Now utterly alone, he leaned forward, pressed hands across his closed eyes and recalled the dream, a most vivid dream, the dream about which Niobe had questioned him. Athena had appeared in ethereal majesty, spear raised heavenward in her hand as she had that night when he slept beneath the stars on the road to Sparta. Once more her words formed in his mind: 'Telemachus, do not join the ships when they depart these islands.'

'Why not?' he had asked, 'I cannot remain on Ithaca.'

'You will not remain on Ithaca; another course awaits you. The gods have decided. Let your people sail away to their new land. That land will serve them well and will always be there should you wish to follow later. For now you must sail alone as once did your father. You must go with the winds as the gods decree.'

'Sail alone! But why have you asked me to do this, and to where shall I sail if not to Italy?'

'All will become clear. You will understand.'

He recalled how her image wavered, defused then drifted slowly as a mist into the night with his questions unanswered. The breeze sighed and, leaving the rock, he stood to gaze down at the harbour, deserted as never before except for sea birds swooping for scraps of food. 'What have I done?' he breathed, setting off down the path. 'I'm trading my life for a dream. There may still be small boats abandoned down there. I've enough experience of the sea and I know which way is west even if our ships are out of sight. I'll set off after them. A small boat should sail quicker than some of those larger vessels.'

Telemachus ran, part leapt down the path and was out of breath by the time he regained the quay to find it eerily silent. Ox carts stood abandoned together with those goods considered at the final moment as unsuited for transportation. A few smaller boats remained there; two, moored close by Noemon's boathouse, rocked gently in the water. On reaching these he found the larger one had been made ready to sail then left behind as if no longer needed. It could have held five or six men but there was just the one simple sail and one pair of oars. He knew as he pushed clear of the quay and grasped the oars that this craft was never intended for long voyages or rough seas but the weather was fair and all that now concerned him was to be out in open water with a fair wind and the sail raised.

Once clear of the harbour and into livelier waters the confidence that had taken him this far began to waver. He struggled with the sail, unsure of how to position it and how best it might be secured as the spar swung to and fro. But eventually it was done; the spar was steadied, the sail filled and his hand was firmly on the tiller. Telemachus had to continue south past the larger island of Kephallinia until able to steer west. Glancing up at the sky he realised that although the sun had yet to reach its zenith he might find himself alone at sea when darkness fell. 'I've no option, have I,' he muttered, 'I reach our ships, I reach land or maybe I drown.'

It was early afternoon when he rounded the south of Kephallinia. Passing between it and the lesser island of Zakynthos he hoped to catch sight of the fleet but there was only empty, open sea. In spite of this the wind appeared to be with him and his confidence strengthened. By late afternoon he was thirsty and, reaching for the leather flask, became aware that though well filled at present, it would only last him for another day, perhaps longer if he was frugal. It was then the wind began to bluster. The sail thudded, the mast and spar shook. The sky darkened as ragged clouds blotted out a lowering sun. The boat swayed this way and that until Telemachus became uncertain over which direction he was headed. 'So - I go as the winds and the gods decree!' he called aloud against what had become far more than a breeze.

He struggled to his feet, grasping the spar, attempting to pull in the sail but this was wrenched from him to fly wildly. The small vessel shook violently and was taking on water. With a leather bucket recovered from the bow he attempted to bail out. He well recalled the storm that had struck on his way back from Pylos but here he was alone and far less experienced in the ways of the sea than he had imagined when setting out. The boat, in danger of becoming awash, recoiled with the impact of each wave and her mast, seized by a howling gust, gave with a crack and swung overboard taking spar and sail with it. Even in this moment of despair, drenched and clinging to a directionless hull, Telemachus did not give up hope. The storm was not as severe as the one he had experienced with Noemon and he hoped it would abate before sunset. But then what? He had no idea where the wind and currents were taking him nor where he might be the following day.

Darkness was falling when the wind died to a steady breeze. Telemachus continued to bail until it seemed the small craft would remain safely afloat. The sky cleared and although sleep would prove impossible he hoped that, by morning, an island or coastline would be in sight. 'I should have brought an offering for Poseidon,' he said, looking into the night. 'At least I still have the oars.'

Morning arrived to welcome him with warm sunlight but still there was the disappointment of an empty sea with no land in sight. A warm breeze continued throughout that day and by the afternoon Telemachus' clothing was dry, although he was running short of fresh water. He looked to the oars but saw no point in using them until land was sighted. With a second nightfall closing in, the wind freshened but not enough to offer further cause for concern. He tried to sleep but there was no comfort to be gained and he had the impression there was a rapid current carrying his boat along beneath the night sky. Through his mind passed his father's account of Scylla and Charybdis, seeming at present more authentic, but these, he told himself, must be very far away. He sat in the stern, arms folded, eyes shut tight, hearing the sigh of the waves and recalling his travels over land and sea, his visits to Pylos and Sparta, the people he met and that first encounter with his father. Then there were the events leading up to the slaughter of his mother's suitors and beyond. He hoped a reappraisal of these memories would hasten the passage of time.

With the sky yet to lighten he was wondering how the vessels from Ithaca had fared when his boat grounded. The shock caused him to struggle up, grasp the tiller and stare into near darkness. The boat rocked gently and, vaguely illuminated by the stars and a half moon low in the sky, he perceived land rising ahead. 'Where am I?' he asked the night as he eased over the side to feel sand squeeze through his toes. He attempted to haul the boat further up onto the sand but could shift it only so far.

Treading clear of the water Telemachus became aware of familiar odours - a scent of pinewoods and orchards. The air was pleasantly warm and walking further up the beach he came upon a grassy bank. Here he sat, finding it dry and comfortable. For a time he listened to gently lapping water then, overwhelmed by tiredness, he lay back and closed his eyes.

The morning heat was gentle when Telemachus became aware of bird songs and the buzz of insects. He raised himself, aching, ran fingers across a stubbled cheek then clambered to his feet. His small boat had refloated and drifted along a shore edged with pine trees. He set out along the beach, toward a rocky headland, passing the boat, thinking there

398

might be a stream with fresh water to ease his thirst when two things caught his attention. He noticed, half buried at the landward edge of the sand, a small bronze vessel. It was similar to those made locally on Ithaca and used in the palace kitchens. Had men from Ithaca been here? Telemachus pondered over this for less time than he otherwise might have because a path he spotted leading inland through the trees was of greater interest. It was frequently used; that much was obvious.

'I hope this isn't where father's man eating savages live,' he breathed, striding warily along the path, a hand resting on his sword hilt. The path meandered through trees and over a ridge but at length he came upon a clearing surrounded by alder bushes. At the far end was clustered a group of substantial stone buildings, rustic in style and part overgrown by climbing plants. He vaguely recalled his father had spoken of such buildings.

Part concealed by bushes he waited to see if any of the occupants would appear. A wooden door set into the largest of the buildings swung inward and three young women stepped into the sunlight. All were slim with hair spilling well below their shoulders. Each wore a long white gown with ornate belt at her waist. One, fair-haired, was adorned with pectoral, armbands and rings that appeared to be inset with flashing gemstones. 'By Zeus,' breathed Telemachus, 'what have we here?'

The three stood in conversation, each with a jewelled goblet in her hand, their voices golden trinkets of sound drifting tantalisingly on scented air. They turned as one to look directly at him. Concealed or not, they knew he was there.

Telemachus stepped from amidst the bushes and walked toward them, hesitating several paces away to ask, 'Do you understand Greek?'

The question was simple enough but it belied the turmoil of his thoughts because the three were seductively beautiful. The one wearing precious adornments stepped toward him and with a smile, replied, 'Now you are here, of course we do.'

'I - I was sailing west,' he stammered, deeply impressed by her appearance and her manner. 'I was, er, lost at sea. What land is this?'

Not caring to express further comment he appraised her from head to toe. Her gown was diaphanous, hardly concealing her sensual form and firm breasts. He gazed into alluring green eyes and saw in her dimpled smile more than a hint of amusement. 'By the gods,' he breathed, 'am I now confronted by one of father's fantasies?'

'Yes, you are,' she said. 'Confronted, I mean.'

'What! You know my words but I –.'

'I read your lips, Telemachus.'

He stepped back, exclaiming, 'And you know my name! How is this? Who are you and I ask again where is this place?'

Offering out her goblet she replied, 'This island is Aeaea and I am Circe. Your father was once with us and, yes, you have his eyes. Take this and drink. I know you are thirsty after your voyage.'

Telemachus reached out a hand then promptly let it fall to the sword which he drew with a swish of bronze and levelled at her. 'Don't touch me!' he exclaimed. 'You deceive people. I remember now what my father said. I'll find fresh water then see to my boat and that is *all* I want!'

'Just like daddy,' chimed one of the others. 'Just like daddy,' repeated the third.

'And pointing his nasty sword at us,' pouted her companion.

'We knew little of affairs beyond this island,' insisted the richly-adorned Circe, lowering the goblet. 'All was done for our amusement. Those silly games with the animals – that was wrong, I realised so when Odysseus came here. But you must understand the eternity of years we have to endure. We never change, you see. We need to find diversions. We must shed memories of our past or our minds will become cluttered and burst asunder. Your father stayed with us through a full cycle of the stars but the gods made him depart when I did not wish it.'

'Nor did we,' agreed the pair, peering intently at Telemachus.

'A handsome boy,' remarked one. 'More our age in looks as well.'

'He told me what you did,' said Telemachus. 'What eventually happened to those other men?'

'Once they were again themselves they built a boat and sailed away,' answered Circe, lowering her gaze. 'There were many before them. We were once visited by Jason with his heroes, his Golden Fleece and his wife, Medea. Yes, Medea. 'Now there *was* a bitch.'

'Oh, a *real* bitch,' agreed one of her companions. 'I'll gladly expel her from my head when the time comes.'

'Only my girls and I live here now,' said Circe. 'Telemachus, you will come to no harm with us, I promise in the name of Athena who watches over you. Let us offer the refreshment and rest you need, then tomorrow you may repair your boat and depart - if that is your wish.'

'If you *really* want to,' added one of Circe's companions.

'We certainly won't force you to stay,' agreed her friend.

'Though *I* wouldn't mind if you did,' cooed the other.

Telemachus returned the sword to its scabbard then followed her, accompanied by the other women. They entered the house that was much more than a house. It displayed all the comforts of a palace yet no trophy or weapon was visible. Telemachus drank enough water to slake his thirst, then honeyed wine, after which he was left alone to bathe in the courtyard's ornate, glittering fountain with his sword close at hand. Finding olive oil, a bronze razor and mirror had been placed close by he was able to soothe his salt-roughened flesh and remove the stubble from his face, all the time wondering if he was being watched. He re-joined Circe and her companions and was ushered by her to a small, darkened room where, left alone to rest, he lay upon the bed to ponder over the events that had befallen him. Soon he fell into a deep, untroubled sleep.

He awoke not knowing how much time had passed, his first thoughts being of his boat and possible escape from the island. He quickly dressed then pulled aside the blind to reveal the rays of a lowering sun that illuminated the brightly frescoed walls of his room where were depicted a wooded countryside populated with mythical beasts. For a while he sat wondering what next to do, then - 'Telemachus.' Her voice drifted softly from beyond the doorway as did her perfume, enticingly sensual. He stepped over and drew the curtain aside to find her attired as before but with her hair rearranged and held by ivory clasps to flow over her left shoulder in a gold-tinted cascade. Her full lips were subtly reddened and her long eyelashes darkened. 'You slept through much of the day,' she informed him. 'When you have bathed again will you join me at the table? The sun will soon be gone.'

'Sounds like a good idea,' he replied, 'I'm hungry and I guess it's not a good time to sail away.'

'No it is not a good time to sail,' she smiled. 'The sea will not welcome you.'

Was there now any point in anticipating trickery or had deception already taken hold of him? On leaving the chamber his belt and his precious sword were left by the bed.

He returned from the fountain to find Circe waiting then followed her alluring form along the dim passage to a colourfully curtained room of modest size where incense suffused the air to complement her beguiling perfume. There was one small window, covered by a blind, and another curtained doorway set into an adjacent wall. Illumination was provided by shell-like oil lamps positioned about the room and on the table an ornate wine flagon and golden plates containing fish and vegetable delicacies had been laid. Cushioned seats faced each other across the table and upon one of these she invited Telemachus to sit. He gazed at her, saying little as Circe described to him details of the island, saying at one point, 'When you go out in the morning you must explore our gardens and there you will have time to think over what you wish to do.' At first he was tempted to ask if, from anywhere on her island, a more seaworthy boat than his own could be found but the subject seemed of less importance as he listened, captivated by her voice and her gaze. Soon he no longer felt compelled to be on his way. 'Perhaps in a day or two,' he thought.

From time to time two girls would enter the room, refill precious goblets with warming wine and remove empty dishes. They were not the two he had seen with Circe on his arrival and although of similar appearance they were somehow more distant, detached and seemed all but unaware of his presence.

'How many of you are there on Aeaea?' he asked as the girls left them.

'How many? You know, I'm never quite sure, but my company and that of my other girls will be yours whenever and for whatever you desire.'

Shadows cast by the lamps closed in spectral intimacy about Circe and Telemachus. His father had described her as an enchantress, one who offered to share immortality with any man who would remain with her. No longer was he inclined to disbelieve it. Her presence, her beauty he found overwhelming, his desire for her fired beyond all reason. It hardly mattered what either spoke about or if they conversed at all until she glanced aside at the second door, whispering in a voice that caressed his senses with promise, 'Perhaps you will keep us company through this evening, Telemachus. Perhaps through tomorrow. Perhaps beyond.'

Telemachus cared less about the next day or any that might follow. From his mind had receded thoughts of Polyxena, of Niobe, of all women he had known. Of all his travels. Of his mother. Of his newly discovered father. Of all he had lived through on Ithaca and what had happened during those last eventful months. All that mattered for now was Circe, her girls and her beguiling realm, a timeless bubble drifting in space. It would be a while before that bubble burst and his memories reasserted.

Epilogue

The fleet had sailed for many days in lively waters, keeping good order without incident other than a moderate storm of short duration early in the voyage that had caused few problems. *Amphitrite* had pulled ahead of the other vessels and Odysseus was standing in the bow with Noemon when land was sighted ahead on the horizon. They had with them a trader from Ithaca, a man who had previously travelled these waters. He confirmed their destination as the mainland of Italy, adding, 'We must follow the coast southwards and when the land itself turns west, there we should find our people waiting.'

'Then all will be well,' said Odysseus. 'And once we're all ashore I'll see what that unruly son of mine has been up to.'

THE END

CREDITS

My thanks to Matt Poitras at MP Filmcraft, **www.mpfilmcraft.com** for permission to use his superb Mycenaean warrior image and to Lynda Buxton for her invaluable assistance in reading through and pointing out the numerous textural and other deficiencies in my work.

Also by The Author

SHADOW OF THE BEAST
THE MAN WHO SOUGHT ETERNITY
THE DEVIL IN EDEN
THE SINGING STONES

Further works by Jeff Clarke may be found on
www.jeffreypeterclarke.co.uk

And on his author page at:
https://fiction4all.com/ebooks/a1549.htm